THE
GRIEF HOUSE

THE
GRIEF
HOUSE

REBECCA THORNE

R A V E N 🐦 B O O K S
LONDON • OXFORD • NEW YORK • NEW DELHI • SYDNEY

RAVEN BOOKS
Bloomsbury Publishing Plc
50 Bedford Square, London, WC1B 3DP, UK
29 Earlsfort Terrace, Dublin 2, Ireland

BLOOMSBURY, RAVEN BOOKS and the Raven Books logo are
trademarks of Bloomsbury Publishing Plc

First published in Great Britain 2024

Extract from *The Sundial* by Shirley Jackson published by Penguin Classics. Copyright © The
Estate of Shirley Jackson. Reprinted by permission of Penguin Books Limited.

A catalogue record for this book is available from the British Library

ISBN: HB: 978-1-5266-5623-0; TPB: 978-1-5266-5628-5;
EBOOK: 978-1-5266-5627-8; EPDF: 978-1-5266-5624-7

2 4 6 8 10 9 7 5 3 1

Typeset by Integra Software Services Pvt. Ltd.
Printed and bound in Great Britain by CPI Group (UK) Ltd, Croydon CR0 4YY

For my friends, who picked me up and kept me going:

Kevin Wignall
Chris Whitaker
Tom Wood
Simon Kernick

The question of belief is a curious one, partaking of the wonders of childhood and the blind hopefulness of the very old; in all the world there is not someone who does not believe something … anything, no matter how exotic, can be believed by someone.

– Shirley Jackson, The Sundial

PART I

The Fool

Grief brought Blue to Hope Marsh House. Mother had been gone three years, but still, it was difficult to let go of her deep-rooted habits, and so, like her, Blue tapped her chest twice if she passed a ring of trees, saluted every magpie and avoided motorways.

Crocuses floated in the roadside fields, the ground saturated with the light, ceaseless rain. She didn't stop, other than to piss that one time behind a wide oak stump, and drove until the land flattened and the north country was far behind her.

Blue had never been so far south. The furthest she'd travelled from Blackpool was the Midlands when she was twenty-odd, a demonstration she'd done in an old-fashioned theatre in a mining town. Mother had organised it, organised most of them until Blue gave it up.

Mother didn't get over it, dubbed it *the calling*. Blue had turned her back on the calling, denied her purpose, shunned the blessed spirits, and how could she do that? Think of the people who need you, Mother had said. They rely on your guidance.

But Blue had no more guidance to give.

Today was Friday. Monday would be three years exactly since Mother died, and Blue still felt its pressure in her chest. Grief filled her as water might fill the lungs of a drowned man. For months she'd obsessed over Mother's life: the life she led with Blue and that other life, unfathomable and unknowable, which her death had forced into focus. Blue was consumed with grief, with guilt, with loneliness that gnawed at the guts of her. Nothing quenched it. So, as the anniversary loomed, she clicked on a Google ad for *bereavement retreat* and discovered Hope Marsh House.

The website proclaimed it a haven to work through loss – woodland walks, gentle activities, daily therapy: a place of safety.

A far-off shape rose from the bog and teased with the promise of a house. The landscape tricked the eye and reduced the distance between her and it; the road meandered and dipped and cared nothing for Blue's time. Fields flashed by: a trailer abandoned in that one, an old tin bath used as a trough in this. There was no livestock. The bath overflowed.

Hope Marsh House glowed, its pale stone a beacon in the grey mizzle. It looked more like a stately home than a retreat; two storeys high with painted white sash windows, a dark grey, slate-tiled roof, and two smoking chimneys. Back home, she still lived in the two-bed ex-council house she'd inherited from Devlin. Still slept in the box room at the front. The double bedroom had been Mother's.

Blue drove through the gates and on to the gravelled drive flanked by alders and silver birch. The breaks between trees revealed the estate's forty acres; a burst-bank stream wound along the left perimeter. Last week, the owner had emailed Blue and reminded her to bring wellingtons.

Mr and Mrs Park were the facilitators. Blue called them owners. It made it feel more like a jolly, a trip away to recoup. Thinking of them as facilitators reminded Blue that this wasn't a holiday, that she had something to work through, and she didn't want to think about that. If she did, she would likely turn around.

There were reasons Mother's death was so brutal.

Blue slowed the car to a crawl. Squeezed her eyes shut, reminded herself that this was necessary, that she couldn't go on without help, but her heart buzzed like a bee in her chest and her dry tongue stuck to her palate. Entwined in her grief was something else, the roots stubborn as knotweed.

But this was a safe place, she told herself, a sanctuary where no harm was done.

Hope Marsh House was in front of her.

A light shone in an upstairs bedroom, and two figures stood at the glass: a white woman, a black woman. The latter dabbed the skin beneath her eye with the sleeve of her orange jumper. Is she a guest, too? Blue thought.

Another window offered a view of the stairs and a slice of the corridor. Someone stood at the top, back to Blue, and all she could see was a vague shape, a smudge of pale hair, the head angled as though trying to listen through the wall.

Out front, a newish Prius in mud-splattered silver sat before the rusted spikes of a vast boot rack. A black Range Rover dominated the space to the right of the entrance. Blue parked her car, older and more dented, beneath an alder tree, cut the engine and stepped out. The change in soundscape caught the women's attention; they looked down, saw her, shrank back from the window and a minute later the front door opened and one of them stood on the threshold. Blue recognised Mrs Park from the website: fifty-odd and soft-featured, with wide-set green eyes and a bob of blonde hair streaked with white. The woman exuded calm – her expression, her posture, the way she stood and watched Blue lift the rucksack from the boot with pedagogic patience, as though Blue were a favourite student and not a stranger. The antithesis of Mother.

'You must be Ms Ford?' A measured smile warmed her face, and drizzle jewelled her hair with pinprick diamonds.

Blue felt untidy; the comfortable tracksuit she'd donned for the trip looked dirty and cheap next to Mrs Park's clean linen tunic. She brushed away the crisp crumbs from the front of her joggers, tucked a strand of dark hair behind her ear.

'Call me Blue,' she said and gave a nod, a smile, tried to look friendly and hoped the host wouldn't press for a handshake. Though it had been years since she'd given a reading, Blue still wouldn't touch people's hands.

Mrs Park didn't press for one. Instead, she held Blue's upper arms, and Blue felt the heat of her palms through the hoody.

'Welcome,' Mrs Park said. 'My goodness, what extraordinary—'

Blue looked down, so her eyelids covered her irises. Her sunglasses were in the glove compartment; she wished she had them to hand. The usual explanations were on the tip of her tongue, but unlike most who saw the strange helix colours of Blue's eyes for the first time, Mrs Park pulled back and looked embarrassed, as though she were the oddball and not Blue.

'I'm sorry, I've made you uncomfortable; how dreadful of me, I forget myself.'

'No, it's fine, it's OK,' Blue said, but she kept her eyes lowered.

'Please, come inside; it's warmer and drier in here.' And Mrs Park ushered her in, cheerful and kind, and Blue thought she might be able to relax after all.

They stepped into a boot room lined with pegs, coats, gaiters and hats, wellies in neat rows on one bench. A black fabric suitcase sat in the corner, big enough to hold a grown man. It must belong to the woman in the orange top, Blue thought, or the person standing on the stairs.

Mrs Park led the way into the house.

The main room was huge, open plan, and a staircase rose from its centre. It was indeed dry, but Mrs Park had been wrong about the warmth. Though decorated to give the impression of it – throws on the sofas, velvet curtains, lit fires – the room was cold.

'You have a lovely home,' Blue said, recalling polite things people said on TV.

Mrs Park's cheeks bulged as she returned the smile, the skin around her eyes creased. 'Thank you, it's Georgian. We kept the original features wherever we could.'

Blue tried to find comfort in the glowing light and the smell of woodsmoke, but a chill had set up camp in her bones.

'Let me show you your room,' Mrs Park said, 'then I'll introduce you to my husband and the other guests. This way.'

She followed Mrs Park up the green-carpeted stairs. The floor on the landing was the same shade, the walls painted a paler sage, the lamp-shade green, too.

'A calming colour,' Blue said as she reached the top, 'or so I've heard.'

'Yours is the room at the end,' said Mrs Park.

Blue followed Mrs Park to the bedroom. It looked out over the front corner of the house; a second window showed the stream with the burst banks and, beyond it, thick forest.

'It'll be a relaxed day today; the first and last of the retreat always are.' She watched Blue lift her rucksack on to the bed; the bag with the wellingtons she put on the floor. 'It's just you and three others so far: Sabina, Jago and Milton. One more guest is due tonight, and the last two will be with us bright and early; we'll not start the activities until everyone's here.' She stood at the window, her expression expectant, as if waiting to hear how lovely the room was.

Although the pervading colour of the hall was green, the bedroom was all pure white. The colour of new beginnings, the Fool's colour, Blue thought, though she had never been one for reading her own cards. She'd lost all conviction, but Mother's faith had been fervent, and she had been made happy by her daughter's talent. So, too, were the people Blue had read for; they'd hear the story of their tarot with comfort, and in turn, they'd left her comforted: she thought she was doing a bit of good in the world, thought she was making folk feel better.

No, white didn't bring comfort. The Fool's colour indeed.

Mrs Park cocked her head to the side. 'Do you like it?' she said, as Blue knew she would.

'It's lovely,' Blue said. What did it matter, she thought, if she liked the room? It was Mrs Park's house; surely what she thought mattered more? Blue felt the old, familiar question needle her: *what would the cards say about you?*

But she had stopped that.

Mother had called her a little god. Blue's last boyfriend (back when she still tried to maintain relationships) had suggested she was neurodiverse, and it was like a gift, this label that summed it all up, before she'd been dumped because of it and felt a wretched misfit again.

It was a phrase she'd since read online – neurodiverse: an umbrella term that encompassed all the things she thought were not quite right in her head.

'Anything wrong?' Mrs Park said, and Blue pulled herself out of her thoughts. 'I know it's daunting, coming to a place like this,' the host went on, mistaking the lapse for grief or fear, 'but we'll take good care of you. I promise. It's my speciality, looking after people, helping them iron out all their crinkles. There's a guestbook downstairs, and you can read their testimonies for yourself. It might help you feel calmer.' She squeezed Blue's shoulders as a favoured aunt might, or a teacher, or a friend, but Blue wasn't sure which role best suited Mrs Park. Blue had no aunts, hadn't gone to school, lacked friends.

Mrs Park said, 'Now, I've left a folder of information on the dresser for you. As you know, there are no computers here, no televisions, no electronics of any kind.'

'Aye, I know. I left it all at home, save for my phone.'

7

'Bring it when you next come downstairs; I'll show you the safe, and we'll hide it away. It makes a world of difference, believe me.'

She knew she'd have to give up her phone. Leaving the laptop at home had felt odd enough; only the knowledge that Hope Marsh had no Wi-Fi made it bearable.

'OK,' she said. Mrs Park nodded, said she would meet Blue downstairs and left her to it.

Alone, she reassessed the bedroom. It was uncomfortably upmarket, far removed from what she was used to. She waited to feel the comfort the furnishings promised, but the room refused to give in. Above, bare beams drew lines of dark shadow on the high, pared-back ceiling, and there wasn't a cobweb, not a speck of dust. The mirror didn't have a single smear. She could see the alder tree through the window; catkins hung limp like dead fingers.

Beyond, a man strode across the field. He carried a wide black hold-all beneath his arm and a thinner, longer bag slung across his back. He exceeded six feet and was broad with it, and his shaggy hair poked out from his hat, steel grey. Must be Mr Park, Blue assumed, and as though he could hear her thoughts, he stopped dead. He looked at the house, at each window, landed his gaze on the one above the front door, and his expression shifted. It seemed a pained look to Blue, but she was far off and couldn't be sure. Perhaps it was relief, she told herself. Perhaps it was straight-up exhaustion. He lifted a hand, pinched the bridge of his nose as if trying to rid himself of migraine or of a vision that was unwelcome, unpleasant.

Downstairs, an old-fashioned telephone rang.

3 1/2

A telephone sat on the kitchen worktop; a spiral-corded Bakelite with a rotary dial. It rarely rang, and Blue used it as a toy; she had no others. She didn't find her lack of toys strange or that, when the rest of the world ran on electronics, her mother should still have a thirty-year-old phone. She knew no other families to compare to her own.

'Saucepan and spoon or two pan lids?' her mother asked, smiling down at her. Mother and daughter were quite different. Bridget Ford's eyes were amber whereas Blue's were turquoise, ringed with orange; Bridget's skin was milk whilst Blue's was maple syrup; Bridget's accent was American Deep South and Blue was Preston through and through – but both wore clothes like Quality Street wrappers, bright and creased and dirty.

Bridget turned away and bent down to stare into the cupboard that housed the cooking things. A smear of rank oil ran a line beneath the oven door, a spillage that was older than Blue.

'May the circle be o-open, bu-u-ut unbroken,' Bridget sang. 'May the peace of the go-o-ddess be ever in your heart.' Her foot tapped to the rhythm, and Blue began to nod her head along.

Blue was three-and-a-half. A late developer, she had only just started to talk, surprising her mother the week before with a string of words, almost a sentence, as if she wanted to make sure she could talk before giving it a try. It was as though, even at three years old, she didn't want to crash her mother's mood with potential failures.

Dark moods were terrible things.

'Merry meet and merry part, and merry meet again,' Bridget sang, a little louder now that she was upright.

Blue looked nearly the same age as her brother Bodhi, though her brother was a little older. He leant against the kitchen door frame, a look of disdain on his face that was impressive for such a young thing. Their baby sister, Alondra, Arlo for short, sat behind their Mother's feet, and Blue worried she might trip over her.

She didn't.

'Well, what's it to be?' Blue's mother asked, still tapping her toe to the tune she had started. Around her neck, she wore strings of crystal beads and one large turquoise pendant, and both her thin arms clanged with bangles. Today she wore a summer dress that reached mid-calf and was made of layers of orange and bright yellow cotton. If she spun around, it floated. Her face was thin, the skin fragile and wrinkled around the eyes and throat, and grey streaked through her waist-length hair. Blue thought she was lovely.

She compared Mother to other women whenever they collected the giro cheque from the jobcentre. They would stand in the queue, Blue in her one clean dress, Bridget Ford in her layers and beads. She was the most colourful, the prettiest, the kindest. Blue didn't understand what made Mother take her on these trips; she didn't take either of her siblings.

Bodhi's face was always dirty and formed into a permanent scowl. Arlo had ringlet curls that stuck to her head with what Blue used to think was water but was probably grease. She presumed one of the tenement neighbours babysat whilst they were out because, if the queue stretched long, sometimes they would be gone for hours. Whereas Arlo wasn't any trouble, and could be left a whole day in the makeshift playpen of the dry bathtub, Bodhi was different. He was capable of devilry.

'Executive decision,' Bridget Ford said now. The bare electric bulb glowed behind her head and cast her face in shadow. 'I'll take the pan lids; you can have the saucepan and spoon. Now, with me. May the circle be o-open bu-ut unbroken.'

The saucepan was laid on the table, the wooden spoon placed in Blue's palm. Bridget's warm fingers curled Blue's little ones around the handle.

'May the peace of the goddess be ever in your heart,' she whispered in her little shell ear. 'Merry meet and merry part, and merry meet again.' She kissed Blue's cheek; Blue smelt the soap on her mother's skin, the mint toothpaste from her mouth and the pungency of her unwashed hair.

'May the circle be open but unbroken, may the peace of the goddess be ever in your heart.' Bridget began to clap her pan lids together, and Blue hit the saucepan with the spoon as they played her mother's favourite game: the Ford Family Band.

Bridget stamped her feet on the sticky lino in rhythm to the cooking pan tune. Her skirt fanned out as she danced in circles; the many layers of coloured fabric brushed Bodhi's face. He had no instrument to play and didn't tap his foot.

'Aren't you going to dance, drummer girl?' Bridget laughed and spun and clashed the lids together above her head. Her bangles slid to her elbows; her arms were so thin. Mother and daughter repeated the refrain, faster each time, until Blue's arms ached and dizziness made Bridget laugh.

'Merry meet and merry part, and merry meet again. May the circle be open but unbroken.'

Blue tapped her feet against the legs of her chair and nodded her head, mesmerised by her mother. The light played on the streaks of grey hair as she danced. Arlo sat by the oven and, when their mother began to laugh louder and picked up speed to match Blue's beat, Arlo began to shed silent tears as though fun was a thing to fear.

The laughter and song stopped.

Mother quit spinning, though Blue carried on hitting spoon to pan until Bridget stilled her hand. She didn't pick Arlo up. Bridget never picked Arlo up. Instead, she sat on the spare kitchen chair, sighed the life from her lungs and rested her head on the foldaway table. The baby's upset drained her.

Disappointment chewed up the last of Blue's giddy joy, and the sweat that had built on her chest turned clammy.

'Drink? Juice?' Blue said, trying to rouse her dear mother. Bridget turned her face away, so her cheek was on the table, and aimed her gaze at the yellow paper that peeled from the damp kitchen wall.

The fun was over. Blue's mother might get up in a few minutes, or she might stay that way until nightfall. Had she slumped on to the futon bed they shared, Blue would have curled her body against Bridget's and waited for her mother to come back from wherever it was she disappeared to. But she had slumped at the table. Blue might have to put herself to bed, get herself up in the morning, and her mother might still be there. Times like this were easier now Blue could open the under-counter fridge unaided and reach the cheese slices.

Bodhi had left the room, but Arlo still sat by the oven.

The development of Blue's speech had led to an increased awareness of the world. She was more conscious of the two other children and how their needs were the same as hers, though dealt with differently. Her mother kept their mealtimes separate, though Blue didn't know why; Blue would eat cereal alone every other morning at the kitchen table, and on the days she wasn't given breakfast, she presumed they were, though she was never there to watch and was glad of it. Days without breakfast were bad enough, to watch others eat what you weren't allowed would be torture.

Did hunger drive Arlo to tears? Blue eyed her mother's nonresponsive form. Should she feed her sister if their mother could not? Could babies eat cheese slices?

She got down from the chair and opened the fridge, looked behind her to see if the noise would stir her mother. It didn't. A sickly scent wafted from an open packet of green-tinged ham. Blue picked out three slices of plastic-wrapped orange cheese and peeled away the cellophane. She got three in case Bodhi came back; she knew her mother wouldn't eat.

'See Mummy dance?' she said, getting down on her knees, so her face was closer to her sister's. She didn't know how old Arlo was; she had looked the same ever since Blue could remember, a baby younger than her. She could smell her sister's sweet, milky breath and the fainter, cloying scent of her nappy.

Her tears had stopped; that was good.

'Cheese?' She held out a slice, but Arlo didn't take it, so Blue folded it into her own mouth and chewed. She had intended to hug Arlo, but now she had stopped crying, Blue thought better of it. She didn't like to touch anyone other than her mother; didn't like the feeling it inspired in her stomach and heart. It was confusing, unpleasant, frightening; a jolt of auras that weren't entirely her own.

An idea occurred to her: babies liked milk. She got up from her knees and returned to the fridge.

A glass bottle with a flattened-out red foil lid was in the door, two inches of lumpy liquid at the bottom. She took it out. Her mother had turned her head and watched with glassy eyes.

'Don't drink that,' she whispered, cheek still on the table.

'Not for me.'

'Then why'd you get it out the fridge?'

Blue was about to speak when, miraculously, her mother sat up, her eyes soft, and said, 'Oh my love, my sweet love, were you getting a drink for me? But that's no good; the milk's sour. Oh, my sweet, sweet love, I'm so sorry, I'm sorry.' She drawled with tear-filled eyes, and Blue said no, had to repeat it before her mother stopped.

'Well, then, who's it for?' Bridget looked dazed and younger for it.

Blue glanced at Arlo on the dusty floor, kicking her heels into the patch where the lino had gone spongy.

'For baby,' Blue said.

The Queen of Cups

Blue would soon be called downstairs and asked to lock her mobile away, and with that forefront in her mind, she got out her phone, intent on making the most of her last moments with technology. No use: reception was nil, the Wi-Fi was unknown.

The figure in the field had resumed his walk and gained on the house in broad strides. Something shifted in the woods behind him, a movement in the trees that rippled their shadows like smoke. Somewhere nearby, a dog barked three times, gruff and deep, then was quiet. The sound combed through the hairs on Blue's arms, lifted each strand and chilled the skin. She didn't know there would be dogs. If she had known—

She turned from the window, sure that any second now, the salivary animals would break out of the house and charge towards their master. She dropped her mobile in her pocket and left the room. She would ask one of the Parks about them. If there were dogs, big dogs, then Blue could … do what? Leave? Run away? She was sick of running away.

A murmur floated up the stairs and down the pale green hallway; Mrs Park on the phone in some distant corner. A good owner makes a good dog, Blue reminded herself, just as a good mother makes a good child.

Mine died almost three years ago. The thought had been a refrain these last few months, and she wondered, hoped, if she would soon stop keeping track of the days.

The door beside her swung open; she startled.

A woman stepped out from the room next to Blue's. 'Sorry, I didn't mean to make you jump.'

It was the guest in the bright orange jumper, so vivid that Blue couldn't help but draw her conclusions: determined, joyful, curious. She had a subtle German accent, softened by time and practice, Blue thought. Her dark eyes were deer-in-headlights large, her neck slim and her black hair cropped tight to her skull. 'Are you going downstairs or coming up?'

'Down,' Blue said, disarmed by her looks and the nearness of their bodies in the narrow corridor.

'Me also. I'm Sabina,' she said, and Blue thought (feared) she might lean in and kiss cheeks as Blue had seen Europeans do on TV, but she didn't.

'I'm Blue.' She could smell the vanilla of Sabina's perfume, honey, too. 'I think Mr Park's back; I was going down to say hello.'

'You've just arrived?'

'Yes, you?'

'I've been here maybe one hour.' Her hand gripped something.

'They told you to bring down your phone?' Blue said and showed Sabina her own, and Sabina nodded, said how odd she would feel without it. It was a fair ice-breaker, Blue thought; a way to connect without having to explain why you're here, who you've lost.

'I've had to give out the landline number in case anyone needs me,' Sabina said.

'Wise move,' said Blue, who had no one to give it to. It was hard to keep relationships alive; the quirks of Blue's capacities soon wore thin. It was creepy, her last boyfriend had said. Couldn't she stop it? Couldn't she try and be normal? She'd spent a lifetime trying to be that.

'It's only for a week; we'll get through it,' she said, and Sabina said yes, she supposed so, and Blue saw that her eyes were still puffy, her jumper stretched at the sleeve where she'd pulled the ends over her fists. Mascara smudged the cuff.

'At least we're all in the same boat,' Sabina said. Blue didn't know if she meant the mobile phones or their grief.

Mrs Park's voice grew louder, and Blue and Sabina looked to the sound. 'Oh, I understand,' the host said, 'really, and I'm so sorry for it; I wish there was more we could do. You'd have thought the government would have dealt with it after the last time.'

Sabina raised her eyebrows in question. Blue shrugged and held out her arm in a gesture that said *after you*.

'You think someone cancelled?' Sabina asked over her shoulder, and Blue saw the sharp profile of her cheekbones, nose, strong chin.

'What, because of the weather?'

'Maybe they chickened out.' Sabina gave a nervous half laugh, and Blue realised that she wasn't the only one tempted to bolt.

The clouds broke apart and let the sun briefly shine. A ray came through the stairwell window and picked out motes in the air. It was the first dust Blue had seen at Hope Marsh House. Would it settle on some piece of furniture? How long would it be before one of the Parks swept it up?

'It's a fine house, don't you think?' Sabina said. 'Like a country hotel.'

The only hotels Blue had stayed in were the cheapest bed and brekkies, where four rooms shared a bathroom, and breakfast was a solitary slice of white toast with a scrape of jam so thin the flavour was indiscernible.

'Yeah, it's nice.' Blue wondered how many fine hotels Sabina had been to, if she ate in restaurants rather than fried chicken shops, if she bought wine and actually liked it.

'As soon as you're ready, just call,' Mrs Park said on the phone. Her voice came from the end of the open-plan room, behind a door held ajar. 'We'll welcome you back whenever you're ready; I'm just so sorry for you. Such a thing to happen.'

'Someone definitely cancelled,' Sabina whispered to Blue as they reached the last step.

Two men sat by the fire. One was tanned, dark-haired, with broad shoulders and muscular forearms, and he sat with his left ankle balanced on his right knee. He didn't seem to notice the two women, or the older man who sat near him, or the fire. Hands and eyes were glued to his phone.

The second man was older; his back curved and his chin rested on his chest. White hair grew in thick locks to his earlobes; his wizened face was as pale as his hair, and Blue wondered if he was the figure she'd seen through the hallway window when she'd first arrived.

He glanced at them but made no effort to stand or speak, and just as Blue was about to introduce herself, the door to the boot room opened, and the man from the field stepped in, the musk of rain close at his heels. He had removed his sopping raincoat and hat, and slippers had replaced his boots.

17

Both women stepped back. He was a head taller than Blue and Sabina and his dishevelled, damp hair added to the air of wild animal.

'You must be Blue and Sabina.' His voice was an unhurried growl that came from the base of his throat and held the vaguest notes of a Somerset twang. 'I'm Joshua Park. Welcome to Hope Marsh House. I apologise for the state of me; one can't help the rain.' His swarthy face was weather-beaten, his eyes a serious grey, and the skin beneath them sagged with exhaustion.

'Dreadful, dreadful,' came Mrs Park's voice.

'Sounds like Molly's held up,' Mr Park said. 'Why not make yourselves comfortable in front of the fire; I'll get myself dried out and then give you the grand tour.' His eyes twinkled on the last line, and Sabina exhaled, ostensibly needing proof of the giant's humour before she could let herself breathe.

'Have you met Milton and Jago?' Mr Park said and led the way to the fireplace. The older man looked disinterested, and even when Mr Park introduced the women, he hardly moved, only lifted his white caterpillar eyebrows at Blue's name.

Jago looked up from his screen. He was handsome. He knew it. 'Hi, hi there,' he said in public-school drawl. 'Excuse the rudeness, just need to fling a couple things out into the ether before these guys lock my phone away.'

'There's no reception,' said Sabina, and checked her phone for bars.

'Preparation, yeah?' Jago said. 'So as soon as there is reception, these updates will load. It's automated, I have an app for it.'

'Updates on what?'

'Oh, like Instagram, Twitter.' He leant towards Sabina, raked one hand through his thick chestnut hair. 'I was going to do a TikTok, right? But I can't think what to do. No inspiration.'

'Are you an influencer?'

'Businessman. Well, an entrepreneur, really. Social media is vital, the lifeblood of the whole enterprise.'

'What's the enterprise?' Sabina said and Blue wondered if Jago had caught the humour in her voice, felt sorry for him when she realised he hadn't.

'It combines nutrition, allergy awareness and inclusivity ... it's the current star market, you know?'

Sabina sat in the armchair furthest away from Jago.

'Nice to meet you,' Blue said to Milton. Mr Park made his excuses and left to tidy himself up. He stepped into the passage beyond, where Mrs Park sat by the telephone, the receiver cradled to her ear. The husband rested his hand on her shoulder, the wife raised her hand and squeezed his in response, and the door swung closed.

'That your real name?' Milton said. His breath was a wheeze, more pronounced after the effort of speaking. A navy Stetson hat lay in his lap, and he absent-mindedly stroked its headband.

'Yes—' Blue began.

'– Milton is an interesting name, too,' Sabina said and nodded to the chair beside her. Blue took it.

The pleasure of being defended was tarnished by worry that the old man would take offence, but he just said, 'Hmm,' and no more.

'What do you think of Mr Park?' Sabina whispered loudly.

'He's very ...' Blue couldn't pin down what the man was and settled simply on, 'big.'

'Big. Yes.' Sabina nodded as though the words had been wise. 'He didn't ask for our phones.'

'He was all wet, probably didn't want to damage them.'

'Maybe they'll forget to take them.' Her hope was palpable.

'Do you think?' Jago said, animated.

'Maybe.' Blue couldn't hide her smile.

'Don't laugh,' Sabina said but laughed along too. 'It's unnatural, in this day, to be without one. Where have you come from?'

'Blackpool,' Blue said and felt herself a stranger among strangers. There was comfort in the anonymity. 'You?'

'London, for the last six months. And you, Milton?'

'He'll take them,' the man said. His watery eyes stared from beneath those bushy white brows, irises so pale as to be almost colourless. 'They always take them.'

'You mean our phones?' Blue said, just as Sabina asked, 'You've been here before?'

'If you need a phone, bring two,' Milton said. 'That way, you can give them a spare to lock away and still keep your own.'

Jago clicked his fingers, leant towards Milton, said, 'Now that's clever, that's what I should have done.'

'Is that what you do?' Sabina said.

'I'm too old for that nonsense. It's just some advice, for if you come again.'

Mrs Park came into the hall. A crease ran the length of her cream tunic. 'We've had a cancellation,' she said without fuss. 'The lady who was due tonight comes from Cornwall, and the weather's a nightmare; her house has half a foot of water in it. Poor thing, can you imagine the stress?' She gave a mournful shake of the head and explained that it would just be the six of them tonight until the other guests arrived in the morning. 'I just hope they can make it,' she said.

'Who else is coming?' asked Sabina.

'A lady and her grown-up son, from Shropshire,' Mrs Park said as her husband appeared behind her, holding a chintzy tea tray with a pot, cups and plate of plain biscuits.

The Parks perched on the sofa and drank tea, made small talk. No one took biscuits from the china plate, and Milton didn't lift his cup once. Sabina, Blue learnt, worked for a German AI company and was subcontracted to Google. The Parks had been running the grief retreat for eight years, and before that, Mrs Park had been a nurse, Mr Park, a retired mill owner. Jago was a fitness instructor trying to build an allergy-friendly nutrition brand through Instagram. Milton was taciturn.

'You worked for the civil service, didn't you, Milton? In Coventry?' Mr Park urged, and the older man nodded, said yes and coughed into a handkerchief. Every so often, his nubbly fingers would feel around the headband of his hat.

Blue had the strange sense it was a lie.

'And you, Blue? What is it you do?' Mrs Park asked. Blue had the grim fear the woman recognised her, that Blue had read Mrs Park's cards years ago, and Blue had the impulse to touch her own hair, face, upper arm to reassure herself that her black hair was still chin-length, her pierced nose had healed over, her tattoo removed.

'I worked in a hospice—'

'You're a nurse? That's cool,' Jago said.

'An orderly,' said Blue and felt like even that was a stretch. She emptied bins, cleaned floors, removed furniture and apparatus from one room only to put it in another. 'But I've taken a break for a few weeks.' Mrs Park gave her a sympathetic look; she felt the weight of it like a blanket

20

around her shoulders, intended to give comfort but too heavy, too close. 'It got a bit much recently, working with so many sick people, seeing them passing. Some of them were still very young and I just, well, I—'

She trailed off, felt hot for the first time since her arrival, and was aware of all she had left out.

The wind hollered, caught her attention and drew her gaze to the front of the house. A shadow crossed the stairwell. Thick clouds passing the window, Blue thought. Or a wide-winged bird.

What if she told the truth and, in doing so, jogged a memory, made Mrs Park realise that she did know of her, had read about Bluebell Devine in some true-life magazine? She didn't look the sort to read weeklies featuring out-of-body experiences and resident psychics, but who could tell? And the stories were still online, free to anyone who searched Blue by her old stage name. Her pulse quickened.

The fire cracked, sparks burst.

Sabina jumped, so too did Jago, as half a fiery log tumbled from the grate and on to the hearth. Cinders spat on to the carpet. Milton batted the smoke away with his hat; Sabina stamped out the embers with her small white trainers, then grabbed the coal glove, jammed the ashy log back among the flames and received a hearty well done from Mr Park.

Only Mrs Park didn't move.

'It must be a difficult job, looking after the dying,' she said, her gaze still on Blue, oblivious to the rain clouds, the shadows, the spitting fire. 'So important, too, to help them pass peacefully.'

Jago looked at his phone, Sabina stared uneasily at her toes, Milton gave another chesty cough. Blue wondered if talk about death on a grief retreat was taboo? Or perhaps it was the idea of peaceful death that upset them.

Either way, Blue felt herself blush at the uncalled-for praise. 'It's just as important as what you do here,' she said.

Milton shifted in his seat and watched the hosts as if they shared some intimate, uncomfortable knowledge.

The Empress

Molly is most comfortable when that house is full of guests. As she stands in the kitchen, her anxiety begins to soften like the edges of room-warm butter. Thursday is her least favourite night of the week, when the driveway fills with sob-stifled thank yous from departing guests. She accepts their kisses, hugs, gratitude, all that gratitude, when what she really wants is to hold on to them, pull them back in, tell them they can stay, she is happy for them to stay, to offload more of their heartache into her safe hands where she will nurse it and keep it secure, unforgotten. But they leave, partially mended, and she is left behind with her husband.

Though it's not Joshua with whom she dreads being alone.

She can hear him now. Molly has excused herself to prep dinner, but her other half (how she loves the truth of that phrase) has stayed in the hall. His deep voice carries through the wall as he tells stories to Milton, Jago and the girls.

Girls. They're women, of course, she knows this, but grief brings out vulnerability; it can reduce even the most mature to mere children. How many adults have sat in her sessions and wept? Too many to recall, though some she remembers with startling clarity.

Adrian Buckley, for example, whose neighbour had died and he couldn't get over it. He had visited Hope Marsh eighteen months afterwards and admitted to Molly what he had failed to disclose to anyone else: his grief had not been for her death but the life they could have shared had he been brave enough to respond to her small, shy advances. Adrian Buckley had been too afraid of humiliation, of risking their

23

friendship, of rejection, and now he was bereft. He had knelt in a torrent of tears at Molly's chair and hugged her, pressed his cheek to her breast and wept, and she had rubbed his back, smoothed his hair, soothed him as she would have done a baby if she'd ever had a baby. She remembers the shock of his head on her chest, the pull of his desperate need for her maternity, the chasm of yearning it had reopened.

Molly had learnt that what people need most is not a one-size-fits-all counsellor but a mirror, an echo. Those who felt their knees weaken beneath the weight of their pain needed someone to help them stand firm. Those who were lost needed to be reminded how to read their own map. And those, like Adrian Buckley, who felt exposed and broken and hopeless, needed a parent to guide them back to their capable, adult selves. Molly is those things in turn; she is whatever her guests need her to be. And, oh, how she loves it.

And on Thursday nights, alone with the man she has loved for over twenty years, she is herself down to her very bare bones.

But today is Friday, and four guests out of five have made it, and dinner needs attention; a tour shall be given, and Jago, Sabina and that strange-eyed Blue will be surreptitiously assessed so Molly can establish who they need her to be. Milton, too. He has suffered a lot; she fears this latest crisis may be his last and how poignant that will be. He is their most frequent repeat guest; this is his fourth stay in three years. She feels a need to sit down and ponder this, reflect on how she'd feel if Milton never returned, but now is not the time for self-indulgence.

Right now, what her guests need is to be fed, so Molly will become their feeder. She lifts an apron from the hook by the fridge, pushes her hair out of her face with a band, collects the bowls of chopped onions, carrots and celery that Joshua prepared earlier and begins.

Laughter travels through the wall as though it smells fried onions and wants a taste. Joshua has a talent for making people laugh; it helps loosen their nerves and relax them. Molly knows they make a good couple, the perfect couple. Joshua has a favourite joke for their team-work, one that appeals to his black sense of humour. He'd coined it after he put his back out carrying a dead-weighted suitcase – he and Molly were diazepam and tramadol: one to loosen the tension, the other to ease the pain.

Molly smiles whenever she thinks of it.

The sofrito has cooked, so she adds the meat, browns it on all sides, then fills the casserole dish with ale, chopped tomatoes and herbs. Leaves out the mustard (Jago's request). The kitchen steams and the windows mist, hiding the rain. Damn the rain.

At least they're not like that poor woman in Cornwall, flooded with no way out. Molly will give a full refund. Joshua will quibble about the deposit, but Molly will give it to her anyway, and the Cornish woman will evangelise Molly Park.

Well, Molly thinks to herself, at least four have made it, and more will arrive tomorrow. The more people inside that house, the better.

She pauses, a packet of dumpling suet in her hand. When had she started calling it that house and not hers? She doesn't know, tries not to think about it. She has a meal to prepare.

The Four of Swords

Blue gave up her phone.

Milton kept his seat by the fire, and Mr Park steered Blue, Jago and Sabina through the passageway that led to the kitchen, where he opened a small door to reveal a safe built into the brick wall.

'At least it looks secure,' said Blue.

'Fort bloody Knox,' Sabina said.

'We'll hand them back on the last day,' said Mr Park.

'And if there's some disaster?' Sabina asked.

'There'll not be,' he said.

'But if there is?'

Amusement lit his grey eyes. 'There's this old-fashioned device called a landline in the hall, and a laptop and Wi-Fi in our apartment, through there.' He nodded at a green varnished door at the far side of the kitchen.

Mrs Park startled, and added, 'Strictly for emergencies – they're our private living quarters, after all,' as though embarrassed by her own need for boundaries.

'Any chance I could connect to the Wi-Fi first?' Jago said. His tan looked jaundiced in the low kitchen light, his face made of sharp contours and shadows. Beneath the taut muscle, the styled hair, he looked unwell. 'I have this automated app, it loads updates and—'

'Phones need to be turned off,' Mr Park said, not unkindly, and held his palm out for the mobile.

'You'll be fine without it,' Mrs Park said. A red chequered apron covered her tunic. 'Plenty to keep you occupied this week. You'll feel so well looked after that you'll hardly miss your phone. Most guests enjoy the break.'

Jago nodded and said, 'Yeah, I can imagine that, yeah,' but his shoulders became hunched, his hands sequestered in his pockets.

The kitchen was large and low-ceilinged, done up in the cottage style – wooden work surfaces, a butler's sink, pine table with chairs and the heat-shedding Aga.

An uncanny change had occurred in Mrs Park; she'd sloughed the therapist's persona like snakeskin. With the flour-smeared apron on, she looked the picture of a farmer's wife, her chin-length hair held back in an Alice band cut from the same red cloth. The colour was reflected in her cheeks, so they looked rosy, plump, unnaturally wholesome. A rich scent of roasted meat filled the room.

'Dinner smells wonderful,' Sabina said. 'A casserole?'

'Beef and ale.' Mrs Park looked bashful. The dinner, she said, wouldn't be ready for another hour, leaving time for a tour of the retreat. Mr Park made his excuses and left via the dark green door. Blue looked wistfully at the fresh bread on the tabletop, thought of the plate of biscuits she'd not touched in the lounge. Hunger hit her and hard. It would, she decided, be easier to be out of the kitchen whilst the food cooked than trapped inside it, tormented by the smell in the air.

'I take it Milton won't be joining the tour?' Sabina said.

'I will,' he wheezed from the passageway door. No one had heard him arrive, his approach muted by the soft soles of his shoes and the rubber feet of his walking frame. The brimmed navy hat was on his head.

'You look like Rick Grimes,' Blue said, 'from *The Walking—*'

'Don't know who that is,' he said, then turned and walked out, the door left open for them to follow.

The passageway divided the house: the kitchen on the right, two spacious rooms to the left, and at the end, a door with a disabled logo.

'This is where the holistic activities take place,' Mrs Park said as they entered the first of the two rooms. It was as bare and clean as a surgical theatre. The far wall, a canvas of glass, showed the rain-clogged fields and the small wood beyond.

'Beautiful view,' said Sabina.

The river flowed along the edge of the land, crossed by an ornate stone bridge whose path disappeared into the close-grown bosk.

'We'll do yoga, art classes …' said Mrs Park.

The trees leant over the river, over the field, stretched stout branches towards the house and beckoned to the people inside it.

'… therapeutic dance and crystal healing …'

Their twigs, like fingers, picked out Blue.

And the room was too big, too light, too much a contrast to the world outside. For months, all Blue had wanted to do was get here, get the week over with and go. It would help her move on and become a normal person and have normal friends and a normal job and live a normal life, but she hadn't stopped to think about the intricacies. She couldn't do yoga, for Christ's sake, couldn't dance, wouldn't touch another crystal for as long as she lived, and definitely couldn't sleep in a house where trees and water pressed in from all angles when all she'd ever known was the town.

And the dogs – she'd forgotten to ask how many they had, if they'd be allowed near her, how big they were, and her skin prickled; she could hear them pant in her ear, could feel the slick of their drool on her leg—

'A heron! Look, by the bridge.' Sabina ran to the window, pointed to the grey bird by the water. It balanced rock-still on tall yellow legs; its feathers blended into the stone and shade of the bridge.

Jago joined her at the glass. 'Oh wow,' he said, 'she's right, look, over on the bank.'

Crows circled, ready to roost. The setting sun stretched the shadows of the trees into long, sharp limbs that pointed across the field and straight at the house. *In there,* they said, *let us in there.*

'Ever so many birds live here. In winter, the starlings come down on their way to the heath. Have you ever seen the murmuration?' said Mrs Park, and Sabina said she had always wanted to, Jago said he'd seen them all the time growing up and Blue wanted to disappear.

'You catch them around Blackpool pier, sometimes.' Blue tried to distract herself and join in, but the words were sawdust.

Milton stood next to her, inscrutable, and whispered, 'You don't have to do any of it if it's not your thing. I tell her to bugger off at the mere mention of therapeutic sodding dance.'

Panic loosened and she exhaled, embarrassed that her fear had been so obvious. 'Thank you,' she whispered back, and Milton hawed a response.

29

'There's a buzzard, look, on the telegraph pole.' Mrs Park pointed – tawny feathers near matched the wood. Sabina stared in wonder; Mrs Park looked from her delighted guest to the bird and back.

'If you'd rather, you can sit with me by the fire when they do all that bollocks,' Milton said and coughed into his elbow. 'Only if you'd rather.'

She tried to whisper another thank you but found there was a lump in her throat. The small kindness reminded her so much of her stepfather that she couldn't finish. Such memories rarely surfaced, and she found that she had to bundle them up and shut them away before they had the chance to overwhelm.

'I'll show you the therapy room next,' Mrs Park said.

The room was like the last, but with tinted windows, so outside was less of a distraction. Eight armchairs sat in a circle.

'We hold a mixture of group therapy and one-on-one sessions,' Mrs Park said, and though a yellow-crested bird alighted near the window, Sabina didn't look.

'I'd rather the dancing,' she said.

Sabina excused herself before dinner; she wanted to wash her face and change her clothes. Blue suspected it was the prospect of therapy she wanted to wash off, the fear of honesty among strangers.

Due to the small party, Mrs Park decided that they'd all cosy up in the kitchen to eat; it was the warmest room in the house.

'On account of the Aga,' Mrs Park explained, as Blue peeled off her jumper and draped it on the back of her chair. A glass jug of water sat in the centre of the round table, alongside the fresh-baked loaf that permeated the air with its subtle, sweet yeast.

Milton shuffled across the flagstone floor, rested his walking frame against the wall and sat in the nearest chair. Cross-stitch mottos hung from the picture rail: *a friend is for a reason, a season or for life* and *weep freely; not all tears are evil*. On the windowsill were framed photographs; two were of young black Labradors, and nerves vice-gripped her stomach. At least they weren't Alsatians. Mother feared Alsatians.

'So,' Blue said, 'these are your dogs?' She looked around for water bowls, food bowls, leads, and felt a little calmer when she didn't find any. Perhaps they weren't allowed in the kitchen. Maybe, she thought, they keep them away from the guests.

'Black Labs,' Jago said with boyish delight. 'I love black Labs. We always had Labradors when I was a kid.'

'Milo and Jupiter,' Mrs Park said with poignant fondness. 'Yes, we had two pups.' She bent to the Aga, lifted out the casserole and took off the lid.

The smell made Blue's mouth water, the meat and the ale and the dumplings. The dogs looked out from the photo as if they, too, were desperate for food. Their dense, dark fur made their teeth all the whiter, and their tongues lolled blood red, their eyes unnaturally bright as though ready to pounce from the frame, lunge at Blue, fight her for every scrap of promised food, and Blue had to look away.

'They passed, sadly,' Mrs Park said. 'Years ago now.'

'I'm sorry,' Blue said and felt a pang of guilt at the rush of relief. 'I thought I'd heard … never mind.'

'Losing a dog is the worst,' Jago said.

'There are worse things to lose,' said Milton. 'Far worse.'

'What do you think you heard?' Mrs Park, motionless at the Aga, waited for Blue to answer.

'A dog, earlier. I thought it was—'

'– It must have come from outside. Someone going for a walk nearby; sound carries out here on the flats. So it must have been some-one else's dog.'

'Yes, of course,' Blue said. 'I'm sorry that they … you know.'

Mrs Park removed her oven gloves, held them to her belly, leant back on the worktop, and sighed. 'These things happen,' she said and looked towards the window. At first, Blue thought she would look at the dogs' photographs, but Mrs Park's gaze moved beyond them; out the window, across the wet field to the woods' boundary. A small grey slab rose from the ground. Blue wondered if the dogs were buried there.

'Did they bite someone?' she said.

Milton choked out a laugh. Mrs Park's cheeks lost their rose; she looked at Blue as though she'd stepped out of line, and Blue reran the question in her head, wondered if it had been inappropriate, too famil-iar. Before she could apologise – did she need to apologise? Had the question crossed a line? – Sabina came in.

'Has anyone been into my room?' Sabina said, and it was so unex-pected that no one answered. They looked at each other, bewildered, and Sabina said, 'Upstairs? Have you? To change towels or sheets or something?'

'We've been down here; you've only been gone a few minutes.' Blue poured Sabina a glass of water from the jug. 'Sit down a minute; you're shaken.'

'What's wrong?' said Mrs Park, but she didn't step forward, and the oven gloves stayed clutched to her belly.

Sabina shook her head. 'The strangest thing; my bedroom door was open.'

'Open? Didn't I give you the key to lock it?' said Mrs Park.

'Yes, I locked it, but it was—'

'Wide open or just unlocked?' Jago asked.

'Wide open.'

'It might have been the wind; a draught pulled it. It could have happened when Joshua came home.' Mrs Park adopted a no-nonsense manner to keep her guests calm, no doubt, but the colour in her cheeks didn't return.

'Was anything taken?' Blue asked.

Mrs Park said, 'There's been no one here to take anything; we've all been downstairs.' She sounded hurt.

'Could Mr Park have opened it?' Blue said.

'It must have blown open,' said Mrs Park.

'You definitely locked it?' Jago said.

Only the old man stayed silent.

Sabina looked to Blue, said, 'I thought so, but maybe … I can't remember; did I lock it when we came downstairs?'

Blue could remember the shock of seeing her, the smell of vanilla, the way the light caught her cheekbones, but she couldn't remember what she had done, what she'd said.

'I'm sorry,' Blue said, 'I can't—'

And Mrs Park said, 'It must have been the draught.'

Sabina shrugged and sat opposite Blue at the table. 'Maybe it was a ghost,' she laughed. 'One that opens doors, like in *The Haunting of Hill House*.'

'That ghost closed doors,' Blue said, pleased they had some common ground.

'You've read it, too?'

'Saw it on Netflix,' she said.

'Hope Marsh is many things but haunted isn't one of them.' Mrs Park sat the casserole dish on a trivet beside the fresh bread. She hung the apron on a hook and slipped the Alice band into a drawer. Her bobbed hair fell back around her face, and she looked once more like a therapist in her white cotton smock. 'You've never seen anything, have you?' she said to Milton.

'Not yet,' he said.

'Ever had complaints about doors with a life of their own?' Sabina said and shot Blue a sidelong look.

Mrs Park caught the tease, tossed it back. 'Only when there's a draught,' she said.

The bowls were filled with casserole, their noses with the steam and the rich hoppy smell of it, and just as Mrs Park lifted the knife to break through the crust of the bread, Mr Park joined them.

'No butter?' he said.

'Here.' Mrs Park slid a blue paisley butter dish to her husband. 'Did you go upstairs? Sabina found her door standing open.'

His mouth was full, so he shook his head and frowned at each person in turn.

'Blue thinks it's a ghost,' said Sabina and nudged Blue's foot under the table and laughed at the shock on her face.

'I never—'

'A joke,' said Sabina. 'But something must have opened it; I left it closed.'

'Well, it's a very old house,' Mr Park said. 'Who knows what's lurking in the—'

'Joshua!' said Mrs Park. 'Ignore him; he's provocative.'

'Problem with old houses is the insulation.' Mr Park pointed at the ceiling with his fork. 'No matter how well insulated the roof or wall cavities or windows, the wind always gets through. More cunning than a mouse, that draught.'

On cue, a flurry of wind beat the house, and rain rushed at the windows, upsetting a frame that leant on the glass. The black dog trapped inside looked unimpressed.

'Weather's picking up,' Milton said, more to his casserole spoon than anyone else. 'It's only going to get colder.'

'If you do feel chilly tonight, you'll find extra blankets in the drawers of the divan,' said Mrs Park.

'Don't mother them,' Mr Park said, though he had meat in his mouth and could have said smother.

'And if we see ghosts in the night?' Sabina said with a grin.

Blue said, 'You won't see ghosts.'

'How do you know?'

'They don't exist.'

'That's what I like to hear,' Mrs Park said. 'A woman with a bit of reason.'

'Millions of people claim to have seen them; do you think them all mad?' said Sabina and crossed her cutlery over her plate.

'No, not mad,' said Blue, 'their brains are very efficient.' She paused and double-checked her audience, made sure she hadn't upset them; people got a bit funny when it came to the supernatural. 'Your brain translates your surroundings into things you can understand. For example, light bounces from an object into your eye; the optic nerves transfer that information to your brain, which translates it into an image. It does this quickly, but not always perfectly.'

'You're saying that sometimes the translation's imperfect, and we see things that aren't there?' Jago said. He ate twice as quickly as anyone else and had already finished his plate. Mrs Park served him seconds.

'Aye, kind of,' Blue said. 'You see a shadow in the corner of your eye, but you're not facing it full-on; you just get a slice of it. Your brain forms that hazy image into something you can understand. The most easily understood image, and the most comforting, is the human form, so your brain is more likely to mistranslate the shadow as a face or a person. It's not until you turn to it fully that you realise it's something else, or that it was never there in the first place.' She stopped, self-conscious and painfully aware of what Mother would have thought.

'I agree,' said Mrs Park as she stacked the bowls in the middle of the table. 'The brain is remarkable but causes mischief. Take trauma, for instance: your mind struggles to place a traumatic event in your long-term memory. So, it tries to lodge it elsewhere – usually, the short-term memory. The downside is that the traumatic event comes to the surface at the slightest trigger, and you relive your initial reaction to the trauma.

The only way out of the loop is to train your brain to address the event, process it and store it appropriately.'

Blue thought of the difficult memories locked inside her head, those that were hers and those she had inadvertently inherited from others.

'Until that happens,' Mrs Park continued, 'it can cause flashbacks, both visual and sensory and, in awful cases, it can fool you into thinking that something or someone is there when they're not.'

The sky darkened, and the rain on the window looked black.

'Blue, are you all right?' She put a hand on Blue's shoulder. 'You're pale.'

5

Bridget Ford burned bundles of sage to cleanse the aura of their squalid Preston flat. She spent a whole giro cheque on crystals blessed by a shaman from Nepal. She carved symbols into candles and lit them at certain stages of the moon's cycle – a triangle with a smaller triangle inside it for protection; three circles in pyramid formation for peace; a clockwise spiral for spiritual rebirth.

And she was convinced that Blue was special.

When Blue turned five, Bridget took her to visit a mystic healer on the outskirts of Blackpool, the only one she could find who agreed to see children. A late birthday treat for her daughter – the visit cost half the weekly benefits, and so she had eaten only leftovers (of which there were few) for nearly a month to save up. Blue could count her mother's ribs through her yellow T-shirt.

Little Arlo was left behind in the dry bathtub, her romper suit damp and grease-stained. Bodhi followed Bridget and Blue to the bus stop, kicked his toe into the pavement, dragged his feet. This was no treat for him.

On the bus, Mother stroked Blue's hair with her fingers. It made her feel sleepy and safe, and she curled her tiny body into her mum's. Bodhi stood in the aisle and practised his balance when the bus rounded corners.

His eyes, so dark they were almost black, followed Blue like a south magnet on the hunt for its north. He dragged his feet and slouched when he moved, never smiled, and Blue felt he was always angry with her, as though she had taken his spot on the only bed, as though this trip to the healer was her idea.

She wished he had stayed behind in the bathtub, too.

They hopped off the bus two miles from the place to save enough money for the fare home. They trudged in quiet conversation; Blue's mother hummed and said hello to anyone that passed her, though they never returned the address. Blue held her hand, and Bridget would count to three and swing her daughter up in the air. When Blue's legs got tired, Bridget gave her a piggyback, and Blue clung to Bridget's ribs with her thighs. Bodhi slumped behind and stared at her so hard that Blue buried her face in Mother's shoulder.

It took nearly an hour to find it; all Bridget had was the address, which she checked against every bus stop map they passed.

The house was plain enough, a red-brick two-up two-down in a street full of similar homes. It was already lunchtime, but the curtains were drawn. A notice taped to the letter box said cold-callers weren't welcome. The front wall was a gallery of turquoise Buddhas, Chinese symbols made from twisted metal and animal heads carved in wood. Where the other houses had window boxes, this one had rusted wind chimes.

'It's definitely the place.' Her mother looked for a bell or a knocker but couldn't see one. She was about to rap the glass with her fist when Blue spotted it.

'I think it's the tongue,' she said.

Mounted on the wall was a brass monkey's head, mouth agape. Its eyes bore into Blue's, and she didn't like it. She turned her head, but Bodhi was right there behind her.

Blue held tight to her mother's hand and closed her eyes.

She heard the ring of the bell as her mother pressed the creature's tongue.

'You must be Miss Ford,' said a falsetto voice, and Blue opened her eyes to see a fat, bald, brown-skinned man dressed in a long purple tunic. Full-moon glasses perched on his nose, and his double chin was wax smooth.

'Come in, come in,' he sing-songed, 'I'm Devlin Devine, at your service. You, my little lady, must be Bluebell Gaia Ford.' He gave an odd little bow and stood back to let them through. He was so fat there was hardly room, and both Bridget and Blue had to press against him to pass.

Devlin offered them drinks and biscuits. Bodhi stood by the garden door with his arms crossed and didn't take a single thing. He stared so hard, so horribly, at Blue she worried her biscuits would absorb his hate and spoil. He had a way of making her food taste bad.

The kitchen was cleaner than Bridget's and smelt of toast and coffee instead of rancid grease. Devlin watched them, patted his stomach, and said he wouldn't have a biscuit, but they must help themselves; he chatted to Bridget about their journey and the weather and blushed whenever she looked him in the eye. Blue took a fourth biscuit and put it in her pocket for later.

Devlin took them through to a room at the back of the house, the air suffused with spices and wax.

'Oh, my goodness, it's beautiful! Look at the crystals, Bluebell, look at the— Oh, my, is that an altar? Are those runes? Why, they're stunning!' Bridget flitted from table to small table, looked at the pendulums laid out on velvet cloths, at the bowls carved like folded wings that held dozens of smooth, coloured tumblestones. Burgundy velvet lined the walls, and tiny crystals surrounded the ceiling bulb and diffused the low light into rainbows.

'But we mustn't touch,' Bridget warned, though there was no fear of that as Blue was too scared to touch anything. This room was dark, cluttered; the musky, herbal incense strong. Blue wanted to go home.

Devlin stood with his hands on his round belly; a third chin bloomed against his chest whenever he nodded.

'Shall we sit?' He indicated the round table in the centre of the room. A five-pointed star was etched into its surface, a deck of well-thumbed tarot cards at the centre.

Bridget explained what had been happening. Devlin listened, watched Blue, nodded and hummed and blushed as Bridget spoke. He leant forward and looked at Blue so intently she had to duck her gaze.

'I see now what you meant on the phone; they're quite extraordinary – amber into turquoise, like the Helix Nebula in reverse. And they're set, are they? The colour? I hear that children's eye colour can change over time—'

'Colour's fixed by the time they're a year old, usually,' Bridget said, her Deep South accent strengthening as her excitement grew. 'Bluebell was born with the turquoise, and the amber just grew over time.'

'And what do you make of your lovely eyes, Miss Bluebell?' Devlin said, dropping his face low to the table so their gazes met.

Blue shrugged and tried to think of something polite to say but couldn't. She pressed the pocket of her skirt to make sure the biscuit was still there. It was. She wondered if it would still taste good when she got home.

'And how long have you had your … talents?' he said. Blue didn't know what to say. Was hitting a saucepan with a wooden spoon a talent? Was babysitting a toddler in a dry bath whilst her mother cried herself to sleep a talent? She could wash her own clothes in the steel kitchen sink, she could heat soup and tins of beans, she could sing all the words to 'May the Circle Be Open'. Is this what the strange man meant? She was five years old. She didn't know.

But her mother looked on, expectant.

'Always,' Blue said because she couldn't remember a time when she hadn't done these things.

'And do they speak to you?'

'Who?'

Devlin shrugged. 'You tell me,' he said. 'Spirits, helpers, guides, masters … we all have a name for the voices we hear that no one else can.' He lowered his voice to a whisper. 'I call mine the angel.'

Bridget simpered, but Blue shook her head.

'They don't tell you things? How about inside your head? Can you hear them speak to you in your thoughts?'

Blue shook her head, and her mother's shoulders sagged.

'Do they make you feel anything? Happy, sad, or excited?'

Blue started to shake her head again, but the sight of her mother's shoulders made her stop, and she thought about the dinners Bridget hadn't eaten and the fact they had to get off the bus so soon and how it had all been because she'd wanted to bring Blue here, to this man, for reasons that Blue didn't know. Something was expected of her.

'Sometimes,' she tested the water, and her mother's back straightened, and Devlin looked excited, and so Blue said, 'Yes, sometimes folk make me feel things.' And she thought, it ain't a lie; Bodhi frightens me, Arlo makes me sorry. And Mum … even then Blue couldn't put a finger on what it was her mother made her feel.

'Can you describe it to me? These feelings?'

'It's like if someone's sad or something …' And she didn't know what to say, because the only feelings she felt were her mother's, and their life was so closed and private it felt a betrayal talking about it to this fat man with his round glasses and his crystals.

'It's OK,' her mother said, 'you can tell him.' And she nodded at Blue to go on.

'Like, if Mother's upset, they'll show me how she's feeling, like they'll make me feel it the same. Sometimes.' She picked at her fingers underneath the table.

In the shadowed corner of the room, away from the crystal-filtered rainbows and the cool turquoise Buddha, Bodhi stood. Blue was a little taller than him now. His chin was down, his pale hands clasped at his belly, his dark eyes holes that Blue couldn't fathom.

Devlin talked on, and Blue looked at him so as not to see her brother. For half an hour, Devlin questioned her; could she sense emotions in other people, did she ever have dreams that came true or visions that told her things? Blue was asked to touch different crystals and say if they made her feel happy or sad, tingly or numb. The smell of incense in the air got thicker.

'And can you say anything about me?' Devlin asked, and his chair creaked a little under the weight. He had picked up the tarot cards and shuffled them, smoothed his palm over the top between each cut of the deck. He pushed the cards towards Blue. 'Have a go; touch them and see if you can pick up my energy.'

Blue reached for the cards. They were warm.

The chairs were uncomfortable, too big for Blue, and the table too high, so Blue sat up on her knees. It was to be more comfortable, but her mother sat bolt upright, said, 'Are they telling you something now?' as if her movements were a symptom of divination.

'Are they?' Devlin said; his eyes dashed to Bridget and back. Bridget, in her zeal, had put her hand on Devlin's arm and a bead of sweat caught on his brow.

Blue rubbed her head; the strange smell made her queasy. She scratched her neck, and again her mother startled, each movement of Blue's absurdly important.

'What are they telling you, sweetheart?'

'Nothing,' she said, a little petulant, wishing to go home.

41

'She's young, still; only five, did you say? It can take many years for these things to take shape; I don't know of anyone who got a real good handle on the sight before puberty.' Devlin patted Bridget's hand, and Bridget looked so sad and Blue couldn't do a thing to help.

'Is there anything I can do to make her understand this, to hone it? I've always had my own abilities, of course, just small talents – basic capacities, really – but I just have a feeling about her, I just know she has it, the real thing, you know?' And she held Devlin's hand, clutched it an inch from her chest and Devlin licked his lips and stared at his hand, at her, and next to the table stood Bodhi.

Head bowed, fists at his sides, eyes as black as hell. Those eyes had a grown man's rage.

Blue didn't know where to look, couldn't suffer it.

'She's so young,' said Devlin. 'Leave it a few years, come back when she's ten or so, and we'll try again then.'

The incense was unbearable, the pressure in her head too much.

'There must be something I can do before then?'

Even with her eyes closed, Blue could still picture little Arlo, left behind in the cold, dry bath. She could still see the wrath in Bodhi's eyes and knew he was there, right there beside her. She worried that he'd already spoiled her saved biscuit.

'We've come all this way,' Bridget said, and Blue thought about the long trip home they'd have to take, how her legs were tired, how her mother touched Devlin's arm when Blue wanted her to hold her hand and carry her away.

Blue opened her eyes, and Bodhi stared straight at her.

The rage that filled Bodhi filled Blue.

The abandoned sadness inside Arlo filled her too.

'You're lonely and unloved,' Blue shouted at Devlin, the rage hot wasps in her head.

She thought of her mother's blank face on her bad days, of her crying in bed when she thought Blue was asleep, of the fears she heard her whisper to her pillow, and Blue said them now, to Devlin, wanted him to feel these things instead of her mother.

'No one likes you, you have no friends, you're all alone, and you're scared you're a horrible person. You pretend you don't care, but you do care. You hate it, you hate it, you—' Blue had her hands over her ears and her fingers over her eyes; she felt someone touch her shoulder. She jumped, couldn't bear that feeling, and only when she heard her mother's voice in her ear did she relax. She buried her head in her mother's shoulder and was comforted by her thin arms and the familiar scent of her long grey hair.

'It's OK,' her mother whispered. 'It's OK, my sweet child, my clever thing.'

'My goodness, I think there's something there; you're quite right, Miss Ford, you were right all along. With a little guidance—'

'My clever girl,' she crooned.

Blue could tell from the lilt in her voice that her mother smiled. Blue rested her weight against Bridget.

She didn't understand a thing of what had happened; why Bodhi had looked at her like he did, or how those words had found themselves in Blue's mouth.

But at least she had made her mother happy.

The Magician

The motto *food is medicine* hangs above the stove. The plates are empty; they've eaten every bite – the casserole, a dumpling each, a slice of buttered bread. Molly's chest swells with pride and relief at the sight of the gravy-smeared dishes. Even Milton ate the ready meal his health-care team had packed for him, which Molly warmed through. He didn't complain once about his heart, chest or joints. Jago had extras; he didn't skimp on the bread or dumplings, though his blog condemned carbs to hot hell. And Sabina, who Molly thinks is far too thin, has had her fill.

Molly suspects Sabina is more a drinker than an eater. First, she'd asked if wine would be served with dinner. Now, she asks for a digestif and looks crestfallen when Molly says no.

Instead of booze, Molly tells them they will get a hot chocolate. Sweetened with coconut and vanilla, instead of white sugar, she tells Jago, who'd looked terrified when she said the C-word. She doesn't miss the sardonic look Sabina shoots Blue, nor the brief flash of childish delight that crosses Blue's face and makes those peculiar eyes sparkle. Such strange eyes, like the Eye of God, fitting for a strange woman.

Blue is aware of her strangeness, that's obvious to Molly. She will be comfortable with it by the end of the week; Molly will make that her mission. But first, the hot chocolate.

Milton refuses the drink. He taps his chest, says he's had enough. He doesn't say goodnight, or thank you for the meal, or sleep well. Instead, he collects the walking frame, hobbles out and closes the door. They hear him cough along the passage to his room. Molly doesn't take offence;

they're used to his strange ways now, and he's been through a lot. Each visit to Hope Marsh has been down to a separate grief: his wife, his daughter, his mother, and his sister. The women in his family seemed to drop like flies. Not for the first time, Molly wonders if he doesn't just make them up for the sake of a familiar holiday. He wouldn't be the first man to crave such attention, and Molly does not judge; he's just a harmless old man who needs love. She does wish, though, that he'd take cocoa; it would help him sleep.

Jago is another matter. His pain has a deeper, more intricate root, and Molly wonders how the others will respond to it when therapy begins. Will they accept him, as she does, or will they turn?

Joshua stays at the table with Jago and their girls (Molly thinks of them as being theirs). She goes to the stove, pours whole Jersey milk into a pan, and adds organic, raw cacao powder, coconut sugar and vanilla extract. She stirs, smells the steam, takes a small spoon from the drawer and has a taste. Sweet but not too; the cacao provides a savoury edge. She pours her husband's cup first and sets it aside. She tells the guests that he doesn't like it hot, only lukewarm, and Sabina says how good it smells, and Jago agrees. Blue stays quiet, but Molly can see her look over, her top lip caught between her teeth in expectation. One might think she had never been given hot chocolate as a child.

If that's so, then this will be extra special, and Blue will hold Molly in her heart forever. Molly imagines the note Blue will write in the guest-book come Thursday morning – how effusive Blue will be, how grateful, how the hot chocolate was the best she had ever tasted and made her feel so well looked after, and everyone who reads it will know what a good job Molly has done.

There's more to do, yet. Molly asks Joshua to explain what to do if the fire alarm sounds – he stops her sweetly and says yes, he knows the drill, and laughs at his own pun. He is a remarkable man, she tells herself as she stirs the final ingredient into the mugs. She married a remarkable man.

A good night's sleep is essential, Molly says as she sets the mugs on the table. Blue looks to the window, expression wary as though the glass may break just by her looking at it. Or is it the photos she's looking at? Milo and Jupiter stare out of their frames. The dogs, the poor dogs. Molly would have put her plate on the floor and let them feast on her leftovers if they were alive. Joshua would have told her off, but he would have patted Jupiter's rump all the same and given the dog more attention even than his wife. They'll never have dogs like that again. They'll never have dogs at all.

Jago downs his in one and tells Molly it was terrific, my God, so delicious, a real treat. Sabina says that she hasn't had hot chocolate since she was last in Mönchengladbach and Molly does well to hide her smile and tell her calmly that she hopes Sabina enjoys it. Blue looks at Sabina as though she's never been to Germany and can only imagine what it's like, and sips her hot chocolate. She grins. It's not quite the response of overwhelming delight that Molly had hoped for, but a grin is a grin nonetheless.

And tomorrow? Tomorrow they will tell her how well they slept, how comfortably and deeply, and Molly will smile and tell them that's what all the guests say.

The Eight of Pentacles (Reversed)

It was still early, but Blue was tired and welcomed Mrs Park's announcement that it was bedtime. The entrance hall was freezing after the Aga-warm kitchen, though flames still capered in the grate; Mr Park locked a guard around the hearth, wished Blue, Jago and Sabina a peaceful sleep. The windows showed a black, rainy night, and Mrs Park drew the curtains, told them not to worry about the weather.

Sabina lost pace as they neared the top of the stairs, rubbed the tops of her arms. Blue saw goosebumps rise on the nape of her neck and knew they weren't from the cold.

'You're worried your door will be open again?' she whispered, aware that the Parks were in earshot. Jago had bounded ahead, waited at the top with his muscular arms folded, and the low light caught the shadows under his eyes and made his muscles seem more sinewy than strong. His room was on the opposite side of the corridor to the women.

'Silly, isn't it?' Sabina gave a mocking half-smile. 'I'm perfectly rational, don't worry. Even if it is open, I'll bat it away with logic.'

'Just remind yourself that it's your brain playing tricks,' Blue said. 'That's what I do, now.'

'There was a time when you didn't?'

Blue shrugged. 'When I was a kid. But what kid doesn't believe that stuff?'

They reached the top, and the corridor stretched out either side. In the semi-darkness, the pale green walls looked morbid grey, the bedroom doors like marble headstones.

They were all closed.

'We can rest easy in our beds tonight,' Sabina said.

Blue wondered which room was Milton's.

'I'm knackered,' Jago said, 'like, weirdly knackered. Do you think it's the fresh air? I mean, I've barely been outside, but I guess it infiltrates, doesn't it? No pollution, no cars … They say fresh air makes you—' He yawned and covered his mouth. 'My God,' he said. 'See you in the morning, yeah?'

They said goodnight and the women watched him walk to his room, then Sabina lowered her voice. 'Hey, do you fancy a drink before bed? I have whisky in my room. I was scared earlier that they were going to go through our bags and confiscate it. God knows how I'll fall asleep so early without it – I mean, ten o'clock! Can you believe it? Do you want some?'

Downstairs, Mrs Park reminded her husband to lock the front door. Mr Park sighed.

'Maybe tomorrow?' Blue said, not wanting to refuse outright or admit that she rarely drank and wasn't keen on straight-up spirits.

'All right,' said Sabina, 'I'll hold you to that.' And she disappeared into her room.

Blue went to her own, closed the door and imagined Sabina on the other side of the party wall. Should Blue have accepted the drink, had she messed up the opportunity to gain a friend? Would Sabina drink alone— Blue stopped, told herself firmly to not overthink.

She undressed, washed her face, brushed her teeth, and then tiredness hit her in earnest. It had been a long journey, she told herself, a long day.

The light from her lamp caught the trees outside, and she saw nothing else through the window; clouds masked the stars and made the night absolute, and the weather could be heard but not seen. She listened to the wind brush treetops as it ran amok in the woods, could hear it, too, in the rush of the river as it egged on its flow.

The sounds followed her to bed, infected her thoughts. The noise was nothing like water and more like a landslide, as though mud, silt and rock charged through the riverbed, carved a path through the trees and into Blue's head, and the noise formed the soundtrack to her sleep, the imagery of her dreams.

The stones dug into the soil of the woodland, worked the roots, set them free and now the rocks were carrying the trees. They lifted them off the ground by a foot or more, carried birch, alder, hazel and beech in formation along the riverbed, broke the banks of the stream and carted their live load towards the house. The trees' branches stretched forward, their denticulated new-sprung leaves and thin twigs curled into fingers; some beckoned to Blue, some grabbed for her, some lifted rocks from the stone river and hurled them through the air at her window.

They would break the glass; they would invade her bed; they would lift her with their many arms and push her back against the tide of the stone river, feed her to the many mouths of the many trees.

No, not the trees.

From behind the trees came the wet gnash of jaws and the sound of barking. The tree trunks were packed, a mesh of prison bars that shielded the animal, but Blue knew the hackled fur would be black, and the eyes would be black, and the maw would show black gums full of teeth.

Another bark and Blue woke, bolted upright in the unfamiliar bed, in the too-white room. Her head was woozy and dull, her mouth desert dry. She used the white sheet to smear the sweat from her head and neck, grabbed for her phone to check the time before she remembered it was in the safe. She rearranged the bed sheet, thought that the scratches she could hear were made by starched cotton on cotton, thought her heavy head was due to the nightmare.

The sound came again, not from outside but from in; the sound of nails on wood.

Claws at a bedroom door, but not hers.

Sabina's?

Blue jumped from the bed, adrenaline-fuelled, made for the hallway.

Nothing.

The corridor was a tomb of cold air, disturbed by the rush of the door, by her panting and trembling.

It was nothing, she thought and ignored the distant sound of a bark. It was a fox or some other nocturnal creature. This is the countryside, what did she expect?

She stepped back into her room, was about to close her door when she heard it again. It was the grind of a handle and creak of a hinge.

Blue craned her neck far enough to see around the frame and along the corridor.

Milton. He stepped out from a room at the far end, then locked the door behind him. The key scraped the mechanism. He didn't have his walking frame, he had one hand pressed to the wall to keep upright. Blue heard his rasping breath.

She ducked her head back into her room, listened to his feet tread carefully towards the stairs. If that was his bedroom, why was he leaving it? The rooms were all en suite; each had bottled water. She heard each painstaking step as he descended to the hall, strained her ears to listen.

Did he forget something earlier? Was he looking for it now?

She followed the sound of his footsteps and heard the rustling of papers or possibly books. There was a franticness to the movements, to the noise. After some minutes, the door to the passageway opened and closed.

Perhaps he couldn't sleep.

Blue felt woozy with tiredness, her thoughts restless and fretful. Back in bed, she lay still, determined not to overthink it or draw unwarranted conclusions. She hauled on another blanket until she was so warm that her muscles gave in and relaxed; she prepared herself for a long night of wakefulness, but she fell asleep almost immediately.

It was dreamless and so deep that the dogs and the trees and the old man were forgotten, and the fogginess of sleep didn't lift until after she'd showered the next morning.

Saturday, she thought as she rubbed moisturiser into her skin. On Monday, it would be three years since Blue had last seen Mother. Years, too, since she'd seen Bodhi and Arlo.

She drew the curtains back, and the rain clouds were still there, as were the alder trees and birch. The wind had severed the catkins, and they drowned in the puddles on the driveway. The stream was indistinguishable from the field; the persistent rain had burst the banks further and made a nebulous wetland. The bridge poked its arch above the surface, but the path to it had gone.

Two herons stood in the water.

The woodland waited, watched, leant in.

No time to feel fear; if the weather got worse, then the roads would be impassable. No more guests would be able to arrive; no guests could— She didn't let herself finish that thought.

Something had changed; the view altered. What was it? Her car sat in the drive, decorated with the alder's detritus. Sabina's Prius was still in front of the ancient, sharp-speared boot rack.

Jago's Range Rover was gone.

Blue scanned the driveway on either side; perhaps he had moved it. The car wasn't there. She hadn't heard its engine start or the noise of heavy tyres on gravel, but then she'd slept solidly.

The entrance hall was empty. A fire burned in the grate; the balls of ashy-edged newspaper visible at the edges told Blue it was recently laid. Journals lay stacked on the coffee table, ready for a guest to ink out their pain. Blue walked past them.

There was no sign of Jago.

Mrs Park was on the phone in the passageway with a drawn face and worried voice. The burst bank, Blue thought, the errant guest and the flooded field. Mrs Park raised her hand, forced a cheerful smile and mouthed *good morning*.

Mr Park was in the kitchen refilling coffee pods for the espresso machine. 'Porridge is cooking,' he said by way of hello, 'and there's fruit on the table. Can I get you a coffee or tea? Or any toast?'

'You sound like Mrs Park,' said Blue.

'Who did you think made me ask you?' he said with good nature.

'The stream's flooded,' Blue said, 'and the drive—'

'I know.' Joshua Park washed a hand over his face, sighed and rolled his shoulders. 'I'll wait until Sabina and Milton come through and then I'll talk to you all about it. I don't fancy going through it all three times.' He had combed his grey hair, and he looked neater this morning, but the stress scored his face. 'What can I get you to drink?'

'Tea, please,' Blue said. 'Where's Jago?'

The kettle rumbled in the corner of the room and Mr Park licked his lips before speaking, put a tea bag in Blue's cup, got the milk. He didn't look at her and she wondered if he'd heard.

'Mr Park?' Blue said. 'Did something happen? Is Jago all right?'

'He'll not be with us for the rest of the retreat. He had to go, some urgent family business to take care of.'

'Poor Jago, what was it?' Blue said.

'As I said, family business. I can't divulge – guest confidentiality, you understand.' Mr Park stirred the mug with a careful hand. A scratch ran the length of his right thumb, the knuckle bruised.

'Are you OK? Your hand—'

A patch of tiny glass shards glistened on the stone floor, and Blue thought he must have smashed a glass, grazed himself, but Mr Park said, 'Yesterday – I knocked it when I tried to sort the damn stream. Here's your tea, look.'

Blue had finished it by the time Milton shuffled in, complete with walking frame and wheeze. Sabina appeared shortly afterwards and asked Mr Park for a double espresso, no sugar, no cream.

Mr Park went straight to the point. 'Jago's gone. He had some urgent family business to take care of.'

'Urgent family business?' Milton said.

'What happened? When did he leave?' said Sabina.

'Crack of dawn. It was all very sudden.'

'How did he find out about it?' Milton said. 'His phone was in the safe.'

'We had a call on the landline,' Mr Park said. 'What's more, the last two people set to join us this week can't make it.'

'Because of the rain?' Sabina asked.

'Because of the flood, more's the point. We got gentle weather, by all accounts. The rest of the region's underwater.' Mr Park sat heavily on the chair next to Blue and drank his black tea. Mrs Park's voice drifted through from the passageway.

'You've seen the stream, no doubt, and the state of the drive,' he said, 'and the road's flooded; I wouldn't recommend driving through it.'

'How did the boy get away?' Milton had declined tea and sipped at bottled water.

Mr Park said, 'Just a minute, I forgot to put your breakfast in,' and put Milton's pre-made porridge in the microwave, then reached for a bowl and a spoon for the old man. The guests were silent. Milton's question hung in the air like midges above a millpond.

'It's hot, watch yourself.' Mr Park put the bowl on the table and then sat back down. He kept his scratched right hand beneath the table.

Milton didn't touch his spoon. He looked pale and unwell, and it reminded Blue of Jago's vague jaundice. Maybe Jago was seriously ill, she thought. Maybe that's why Mr Park is hesitant to answer; patient rather than guest confidentiality.

'Well?' Milton said. 'How'd he escape?'

'You make it sound like a prison,' Mr Park said and he looked gratefully at Sabina when she scoffed. 'Jago had a Range Rover,' Mr Park said. 'And he was so keen to get away no weather would have stopped him. But unless you're in a four-by-four, I wouldn't recommend it.'

'So we're stuck?' Sabina looked from Mr Park to Milton to Blue, waited for a contradiction.

'Doesn't make much difference, does it?' Blue said. 'Considering we're booked in until Thursday, we wouldn't be leaving—'

'– That was by choice.' Sabina's voice was tinged with panic. 'It's different if we're trapped. Sounds like Jago got out just in time.'

'I wouldn't be so sure.' Milton peeled away the cellophane from his porridge bowl and ate. His hand shook, and his spoonfuls were careful and small.

'You're not trapped,' reassured Mr Park. 'The rain's due to ease off by lunchtime; by this evening, the road will be clear enough to drive through should you choose to. As it is, I'm going to have to excuse myself this morning and clear the culverts. Something's blocked the passage beneath the bridge – most likely branches and debris from the woods – hence why the stream's overflowed. If I can clear that, then some of the water will flow.

'Molly and I realise that this isn't the experience you've signed up for. We would understand if you would rather head home – once the road is cleared, that is – and rebook for another time. We'd give you a full refund—'

'What would happen if we stayed?' said Blue.

'Well, Molly will continue with the therapy and therapeutics as normal, but I may not be on hand to do the other things we advertise – the photography, the walks and so on – until the flood's dealt with.'

'I can help you with that,' Blue said. She didn't want to spend the anniversary of Mother's death on her own.

'I will too,' said Sabina, resigned. 'I brought my wellington boots, after all, and I'd rather do something then sit trapped inside.'

'The taxi's collecting me Thursday. I'm not leaving before then,' Milton said.

'Right, that's that, then,' said Joshua Park, clearly relieved. 'We'll sort out some kind of discount for you, to make—' But Sabina waved her hand and said there was no need, and Blue wished she hadn't because she wouldn't have minded a bit of money back. It was more expensive than a holiday abroad, this retreat. Not that Blue had ever made it out of the country.

'I'm not helping with the river,' Milton said.

Mrs Park walked in as her husband served the porridge, her anxiety plain. 'You heard about Jago?'

'I've explained,' Mr Park said.

'It's his poor m—'

'Molly,' Joshua snapped, red-faced and tense, 'it's confidential, we can't say anything.'

'Of course, I'm sorry, it's the shock of it. I forgot myself.' She moved and stood near her husband, and Joshua reached his arm around her waist and told her that they'd agreed to stay and the women would lend him a hand with the stream.

'That's good of you and probably for the best.' She rested a hand on Sabina's shoulder and grimaced. 'I don't think the roads will be cleared today after all. Our nearest neighbour was on the phone; their house is a couple of miles away, but their farmland stretches to our border. A fire engine's coming to pump some water out of the road, but not until later. There are a few places near here struggling with the weather.'

'As long as it stops raining, we'll be fine,' Mr Park said, and they all turned in silent agreement to the window, where the rain gently rattled the glass.

'It'll stop in the end; it always does,' Milton said.

'So, three of you this week rather than seven,' said Mrs Park. 'A little different from the usual course, but you'll get more one-on-one time. Silver linings, and so on.' Mrs Park cleared the table, carried the bowls to the sink with a light step, looked out at the rain as though it were the sun.

'Well, no time like the present.' Joshua Park finished his tea and wiped a napkin over his lips, said to Blue and Sabina, 'I've some waterproof over-trousers and macs you can borrow; bring your boots down, and I'll meet you at the front in ten minutes.'

They followed him along the passageway to the main hall, the warmth lessening with each tread.

The fire was out.

'Damn draught,' said Mr Park. 'Still, no need for a fire if we're outdoors.'

The weather outside was a squall, and Sabina looked at Blue, one eyebrow raised, and whispered, 'Wish I'd got a lift with Jago.'

Mr Park went to gather the spare waterproofs; Blue followed Sabina up the stairs. At the top, she stopped dead. Blue knocked into the back of her.

She followed Sabina's gaze.

The bedroom door stood wide open.

The Hermit (Reversed)

'It were the wind,' Blue said, and Sabina shook her head. 'It'll just be a fault with the door, you'll see. Mr Park just went outside; the draught will have pulled it open.'

'I don't think it's the wind,' she whispered, so quietly Blue wasn't sure if she was meant to hear it or not.

Meagre rays from the overcast sun streamed through the skylight, and they were white and cold, highlighting the tops of Sabina's ears, her forehead, the tips of her eyelashes. Sabina had been the last to enter the kitchen this morning; Blue knew she had either left her room open, or the weather had pulled it. There was no other rational explanation.

'Course it's the draught,' Blue said and gave a short, hollow laugh because Sabina was an analyst; intelligent and well read, nothing like Mother and not the sort to believe in ghosts. That conviction must have shown in Blue's face because Sabina laughed too; a laugh as short and hollow as Blue's.

'Sorry, what a fool I'm being. Of course it's the wind; what else could it be? I'll meet you downstairs. Thank you.' She reached sideways and gave Blue's hand a brief squeeze.

Caught unaware, the heat of Sabina's palm was nothing compared to the confused, tortuous, incessant root sadness that tangled through her touch. Blue flinched, jerked her arm away so vigorously she almost fell backwards downstairs.

Sabina lunged to help her; Blue grabbed the banister, batted the offer away.

'Jesus, are you OK? You nearly fe—'

'Just slipped is all; I'm fine.'

Blue felt her colour rise and couldn't meet the other woman's eye. Something more substantial than grief had anchored inside her, but Blue couldn't see. She didn't want to see it. It's all in my mind, she told herself.

'You slipped because I touched you?' Sabina looked at her cautiously. Her dark brown hand still reached out. 'I'm sorry, I just did it to … I don't know, a thank you, I guess? For being nice … Why did you react like that?' Sabina stared at her hand, at Blue, and Blue felt the weight of presumption.

'It's nowt bad, and nothing to do with you.' She righted herself, walked ahead so she didn't have to see Sabina's expression as she explained. 'I've sensory processing disorder,' she said. It was an explanation she'd found online two years before, and fit like a glove. 'It sends my brain haywire if someone touches me, especially if I don't know it's coming.'

'I'm sorry.' Sabina sounded sympathetic, but there was fascination in there, too, and Blue dreaded it.

'It's OK.'

'I've heard of SPD. Do you struggle with anything else? Sound or colour?'

Where would I even begin? Blue thought, but aloud she said, 'Touch is worst.'

Nausea curled through Blue, as though Sabina's emotions were being forced hard down her throat. Sadness, grief, turmoil, guilt.

Why guilt?

Nobody's perfect, Blue told herself, and the door was pulled open by the draught.

Mr Park led them across the field. The bridge had two culverts beneath it, he told them, and in miserable weather, branches often got stuck and debris gathered, until the passage was blocked and the banks overflowed. It usually happened once a year, but this winter, it had happened three times; they couldn't do a thing to stop it because the bridge was historic and protected, had a higher listing than the house itself.

The ground sucked at their feet, and water bubbled up through the grass with each tread. Trees stood sentry on the opposite side of the bank. Leafless and newly budding, they looked as they had in Blue's dream. The taller wore crowns of crows' nests, and tangles of mistletoe sat suspended in their tops. Twisted-twig fingers stretched and beckoned.

From the other side, she heard a dog bark, loud against the rush of the wind, but Blue would not think of that dream, or the claws at the door, or Milton's midnight excursion. She hadn't told anyone what she had seen; Jago's departure and the bad weather had vied for centre stage.

'Who'd walk a dog in weather like this?' Blue said, and Sabina gave her an odd look. Mr Park mustn't have heard.

The sky was grey, and the rain fell thinly, but the air was fresh and made crisp by the breeze. It made the task of lugging pitchforks and spades less arduous, made Blue not mind the rain, because who could mind rain that was so clean? Made her not mind the trees, even, because surely that's all they were?

Harmless trees.

They walked the rest of the way in silence. Mr Park kept his eyes on the stream, navigated the best route to the bridge so they could avoid the deeper water. A few times, Blue looked back over her shoulder. She saw Mrs Park at the window, watching them. Only the oldest part of the house was visible; its windows were slick-dark like a spider's eight eyes.

It took five minutes to reach the edge of the water. A gap in the boundary hedge on the field's far side gave them a fresh view of the flood beyond it.

'My God, look at the road,' Sabina said. 'It's completely gone.'

'It dips,' Mr Park said, his attention fixed on the broken banks of the stream, 'so it's the first thing to flood. I wouldn't worry – the water won't reach the house because it's half a metre higher than the road and the field.'

Instinctively both Sabina and Blue looked behind them. The field glistened, puddles dotted the driveway, and it was clear that the land sloped gradually up to the house. Blue hoped Mr Park was right and the water wouldn't reach them.

They set to work and followed Mr Park's instructions. He dealt with the culvert on the far side and Blue and Sabina with the nearest. It was hard work, the weight of the water more than either Blue or Sabina had anticipated. But the sound of rain on the water was gentle, and Mr Park's deep timbre matched the tone of the wind, the combination like a lullaby.

'Good for the soul,' Sabina said, 'physical labour.'

'As good as any therapy, that's what I always tell Molly,' Mr Park said.

'And she agrees?'

'No, she usually gives me a whack.' He laughed, stood to stretch and assessed the work done so far. 'We came to realise long ago that you need both to heal properly – stimulation to your body and your mind. Though it's not always easy convincing people; some prefer to physically work through things rather than talk them through, though Molly has a way of bringing them to touch.'

Not Milton, Blue thought, remembering his words the day before. Why did he keep coming back, she wondered, if he didn't participate? And what was he doing whilst they were away from the house?

Sabina said, 'She hugged me when I first arrived, and it was like the hug of a grandparent.'

'Maybe leave the "grand" out if you tell her that yourself. But yes, she has that way, naturally maternal. Full of love she is, so much that it bursts out of her. She was put on this planet to care.' He attacked the culvert with fresh vigour, lanced a mess of twigs with his pitchfork and pulled it free. 'You'll not find a better woman.'

'That's sweet,' Sabina said, and Mr Park grunted, said he wasn't usually one for such nonsense; the weather had turned his soul to mushy peas.

'The truth is, she could have done a lot better, chosen any man she set her eyes on, but she kept me,' he said to the water, to his pitchfork. 'We've been through it all over the years. It was her idea to turn this place into a retreat; I mocked the plan at first, but she was right. I'm glad she was right.'

Sabina stared at her spade, inscrutable. 'I lost my sister,' she said.

Mr Park nodded as though he'd expected it and was ready to listen, as though his comments about his wife, his personal life, were the bait in the trap for confession. He worked on, and his fork cut the blockage in a steady rhythm.

'Last summer,' Blue said.

'How did you know it was last summer?' Sabina shielded her eyes from the cloud-filtered sun, covered her expression from Blue, and Mr Park looked at her warily.

Blue cursed herself, worried that they would think her odd, a weirdo, a freak when she had just wanted them to think her ordinary. For once, she had just wanted to be accepted as that.

'I don't know, I just did. Maybe you mentioned it last night or ...' She could tell Sabina didn't believe her, and Mr Park had stopped his work.

'I didn't talk of my sister last night or of ... I don't speak about it. How did you know?'

'It were just a guess, I'm sorry, I didn't mean to—'

'It wasn't a guess. You said it as though you knew it.' She put down her spade, squared her shoulders. 'I have a right to—'

'I don't think she meant anything by it,' Mr Park interjected. 'I presumed she was just moving the conversation along.'

'How did you know? Did you google me? Did you find something—'

'I don't know how I knew.' Blue could have reminded them that, without her phone, there was no access to search engines, but felt it was pointless. The hole she had dug herself was deep enough. 'I get feelings sometimes ... people will say something, and I'll hear what they say but also a bit more, like their words are a stone in smooth water: I can hear the stone fall, but I can also hear the ripples. Does that make sense? I'm sorry, it probably doesn't, I know it sounds weird—'

'Like a sixth sense?' Sabina's tone had lost its spikiness; she seemed calmer. And though Blue was glad Sabina had cooled down, it was the last thing she wanted them to think.

'No, not really,' Blue said. 'I can just read people's body language and tone of voice a bit, that's all. Only a bit, only sometimes. Nothing special.'

'Like NLP? Derren Brown and that kind of thing?'

'Not like that, no.' Blue picked up the fork, stabbed it into the water and felt the tines break through more mulch. 'Neurolinguistic programming makes people believe things you tell them, or can help you manipulate their actions. This is more the other way around: I can read more into people than their words alone, as though I'm reading between their lines.' It was something else Blue had found online, a rationalisation for what Mother had called the 'third eye'. It could all be scientifically explained – she was sensitive to others' emotions, and the figures and faces she saw were hallucinations. They were not ghosts.

She had taught herself not to believe in ghosts.

'Do you get it with everyone?' Mr Park asked. His voice was sceptical, and Blue thought it was an attempt to diffuse the tension.

'No. Some people are closed off; others have their hearts on their sleeves.'

'You've not tried to make work as a psychic, then?' Mr Park said. 'With eyes like that, you'd be—'

'– I work in a hospice,' Blue said.

'That's what my mother says about me, that my heart is there for all to see.' Sabina grabbed the upper end of a branch. She pulled it up and out of the culvert; the water rushed in after it. The bridge was almost clear.

Blue watched her throw the branch to the side of the stream and thought, you're not like that anymore.

Sabina took a deep breath. 'You know about my sister, then?' A trickle of muddy water ran down her outer thigh. Blue could tell that Sabina wanted her to say no.

'Only that you miss her.'

'I'm sorry I snapped,' she said, and Blue nodded, told her not to worry.

'I think I have it!' Mr Park struggled with his pitchfork; he had dug it right into the culvert, twisted the handle to try and set it free. 'I don't think it's a branch, though.'

An image of dead dogs spun through Blue's head. She watched Mr Park lug the fork, knew there would be bone and black and teeth and a lolling blood-red tongue. Something barked in the trees.

Mr Park freed the culvert with a final pull. In the tines of his fork was the twisted, pierced body of a pale brown rabbit, huge and swollen with water. The air filled with the rotten gases from its pierced insides. Sabina gagged and buried her nose in her elbow.

Blue looked away. 'How did it end up under the bridge?'

'God knows, maybe dropped by a fox. I'll let the trees have it.' Mr Park flung the dead thing into the woods. A pink line of blood smeared his pitchfork. Its stench lingered in the air. 'These things happen,' he said.

The open culvert sucked at the stream like a parched throat; the water level around their legs dropped a couple of inches. They cleared the last of the debris and piled it on the far side of the bank, another gift to the woodland. Blue tried to see where the rabbit had landed, wanted to prove to herself that it wasn't a dog and wasn't a vision, that it was real and Mr Park had dealt with it. The smaller trees hid behind the larger like medieval, bent-backed gossips, creaked the news to the breeze as it meandered through their branches.

Chop its feet off, Blue, and hang them around Mother's neck for good luck.

The trees grew louder as the humans turned their backs.

Sabina walked beside Mr Park, made polite conversation about the retreat.

A conviction implanted itself that the trees would be closer somehow, following them, would be at Blue's back. She told herself not to be foolish.

The rain was lighter but still fell, and the seams on Blue's coat leaked. The work had exhausted her; it took an effort to drag her feet through the mud, and she had to use all her concentration to keep upright. Yet she kept her ears pricked for the bark of a dog, heard instead other strange sounds – the rain on wet ground, the sound of heavy feet treading water, a bovine exhale and a whinny that sliced through the silence.

In front, they were oblivious; they talked about the yoga and therapeutic dance that Mrs Park led, and Blue felt her ears ring and muscles ache. Then she thought of the therapy room with the soft armchairs and tinted windows, the seats in a circle. The fact that in a few hours she might have to speak about it – Mother and Bodhi and Arlo – sapped her courage like the ground sucked her feet.

That's why I'm here, her thoughts scolded, to face it. The dream of the trees, the noise of the dogs, was all a distraction from the present. The mind's clever games; they don't mean anything.

A fat drop of rain hit her cheek, and she wiped her hand across it, felt river mud mar her skin with damp and grit. The smell of it stuck beneath her nails; swampish water, rotten mulch. She wanted to take off her wet clothes, have a hot shower and lie down on that clean, white bed.

It wasn't too late; she could leave if she wanted, go back to her small life, her shit job, the ex-council house she'd inherited and lived in alone.

The puddles had deepened nearer the house, and they had to detour around them. They reached the driveway and approached Hope Marsh House from the front. The road was still flooded. Had the water dropped enough to drive through?

Mr Park and Sabina walked on. Blue looked to the road. Looked back to the house.

Stopped dead.

'Sabina,' Blue said, 'someone's in your room.'

5 to 9

Her mother got a call on the Bakelite phone a week after the session with Devlin Devine.

It was the Blackpool psychic himself.

Arlo reached for the cord and curled her fingers around the spiral.

Bridget's face lit up when she heard the man's voice, and throughout the conversation, her expression alternated from delight to bashfulness in the same way it had done when Devlin had told her that Blue might have a gift after all.

Two things were asked. First, would she be happy for Devlin to give Blue guidance in the tarot? Second, would she have dinner with him that Saturday? She said yes to the first and no to the second: dinner was impossible as babysitters couldn't be trusted, but lunch would be wonderful, fantastic, delightful, provided that Blue could come too.

Scarcely a month later, they moved into Devlin's house, and by the end of that year, Devlin and Bridget were married. Devlin asked for Bridget's hand in Blue's presence, made a show of wanting the child as much as the mother and Bridget said, in a voice thick with emotion, 'I've been alone for such a long time.'

You had us, Blue thought.

Blue's beautiful mother now shared a bed with the fat, balding man with the full-moon glasses, and Blue had to sleep away from her for the first time in her life – on her own, but not alone.

(*I've been alone for such a long time,* how could she?)

67

Blue was rarely frightened by Arlo and only sometimes by Bodhi; the constancy of their presence desensitised her to the strangeness of their existence. Still, she'd hoped they would stay in Preston. Arlo could stay in the dry bathtub. Bodhi could be left in the hall. But, alas, they came to the new house too, and shared the shadows of her box room at night, whilst her mother and the new stepfather got comfortable in the bedroom next door.

Arlo gurned and reached and crawled about, and was easy to ignore. Bodhi was dissatisfied, always, or so it seemed. He slumped his shoulders and stared at Blue's mother as though she had no right to this new happiness, didn't deserve it, as though he were jealous of it, and it twisted so firmly in Blue's gut that she found it hard to tell which feelings were hers, which were Bodhi's and which, if any, were her mother's.

There were few other children in her life. Bluebell Gaia Ford was not sent to school and so had no school friends. Bridget said they'd home-school, that parents did it all the time, that they'd free themselves from the mind-stagnating conventions of government-funded institutions. Blue watched *Sesame Street* and *Playdays*. The house had books on crystal healing, candle carving, palmistry and suchlike, and it was from these that Bridget taught Blue to read; rune stones and gems were enlisted for basic maths at the round kitchen table. Devlin taught her the tarot cards in the room swagged with velvet, and Blue began to associate the smells of coffee, toast and warm milk with the alphabet, and the heady scents of sandalwood and jasmine with trickery.

At first, Blue scrutinised Devlin the same way she used to keep vigil over her mother's mood, but she didn't watch for shifts in the mystic's mental state. Instead, she tried to find horrible secrets about the man who had stolen her mother. She tried to find holes in the new relationship, mean streaks in his character, reasons why Bridget should leave at once and return with Blue to the dirty, run-down flat in central Preston.

She found none. Even when Blue touched the tarot deck after her stepfather, all she would pick up was a warm, cinnamon-spiked sense of contentment and, once or twice, when Blue had remembered a meaning or a card's correct placing in the arcana, pride. Blue didn't know what to do with such feelings.

Worse than the shared ownership of her mother was the fact that Devlin made Bridget happy in a way that Blue had never been able to, no matter how desperately she tried, not even with her gifts and abilities. She felt her mother's happiness in each touch and goodnight kiss, felt the joy tethered to someone else.

Devlin wasn't an evil man, but Blue wished he was, and the guilt of that want gnawed and made her miserable. Bodhi's scowl deepened whenever Devlin kissed Bridget, and the times when Devlin played with Blue in the front room, Arlo would sit in the corner, uncomforted, and cry.

Blue tried to play with the kids that lived on the road, encouraged more by Devlin than Bridget. In good weather, when Blue had finished her lessons, and the children nearby had come back from school, she was shooed outside, and Blue would stand alongside their games of hopscotch or follow their race through the gullies that cut between the rows of terraced houses. Bodhi and Arlo couldn't keep up, which was nearly the best thing about it. Blue was never invited for tea, and the children her mother asked were never allowed to come into the house (warned by their mothers not to go past the front gate), but at least she could watch them play in good weather.

In bad, when rain kept everyone indoors or black ice made races unsafe, Blue would sit at her window and shuffle her tarot and try to imagine which card each child would pick. The manipulative Page of Wands, reversed, for Levi, who pinched his sister when he thought no one was close and blamed her tears on their dog. The innocent, unrealistic hopefulness of the Six of Cups, reversed, for Rosanne. When she was bored of this game, she would talk to Devlin's customers.

An older man came when Blue was nine; odd because most of Devlin's clients were women. This man was narrow and tall, with a mass of grey curly hair and black skin pockmarked with light patches. He walked with a stick and spoke with an accent and smelt of cloves and leather and tobacco.

'I'm Jacob,' he said and took a paper bag from his pocket and held it open for Blue to peer into. 'Mr Devine told me on the telephone he had a daughter.'

Sweets nestled inside the bag, white and black striped, each wrapped in clear plastic and scented sharply with mint and when Jacob said, 'Take a few,' Blue did.

Bodhi watched from the doorway; his four-year-old face screwed up with the injustice.

'Thank you,' said Blue and turned her back on her brother as she popped the sweet in her mouth. Her tongue caught the sugar, the back of her nose the peppermint and then her throat caught a rotten meat tang. Caught between revulsion and the urge to be polite, Blue stalled, trapped the sweet between her teeth, tried to keep it away from her tongue and fought the urge to retch. Bodhi grinned.

Jacob put his hand on Blue's head and ruffled her hair, fingertips touching Blue's scalp. The horror of Bodhi's trick, the disappointment of the spoiled sweet, and the touch, the bare-skinned touch, were too much.

Blue jumped, hit her head on the worktop behind. The sweet fell out her mouth, and she didn't pick it up. Instead, she rubbed the sore spot, and her mother rushed forward.

The poor old man apologised and asked if Blue was OK, and Blue had to say to him, 'It's fine, just made me jump, is all.'

Her mother thought she'd hit her head hard, but Blue rubbed it not because of the bump but because of the touch.

It didn't happen with everyone. Blue got it from her mother all the time, but she always had done, her emotions so strong that Blue couldn't see past them to the root cause. The children outside could tag Blue, and all she would get was a rush of their excitement, as though the game's adrenaline was contagious.

Only once did it shock her, and that came from Rosanne, the chubby blonde girl who lived over the street. Her mum worked overnight in the supermarket in town, and her dad wore a vest and had a can of drink glued to his hand and rarely left the house.

'What are the scabs on your face?' Blue had asked her one afternoon. Rosanne had been off school for two days, and a bloom of golden crust with a redraw centre marked her cheek.

'Impetigo,' Rosanne said. 'Contagious, so you'd best not touch.'

Emboldened by her honesty, Blue said, 'And what are the marks on your legs?'

'Dad's belt,' she said. 'For cheek.'

'That contagious too?' said Blue.

'I caught it from Mum, Dad says.'

Blue didn't need to touch Rosanne to feel it. Side by side on the low brick wall, the girl's watchfulness leaked into her, infected her with the need to be careful, to be quiet, with the conviction that if she could just be a good kid, then everything would be all right. The reversed Six of Cups through and through. And when Rosanne slapped Blue's arm and yelled, 'You're it!', it took her a while to shake off the horror and give chase.

But Jacob's touch was nothing she'd felt before.

It sank her stomach and dragged at her heart. The corners of her mouth pulled southwards, her spine curled with defeat. But it wasn't sadness, wasn't loneliness; there were so many layers she didn't know what it was.

The old man followed Devlin through the kitchen and into the velvet-swagged room. Times like this Blue would generally spend with her mother, but today she sat by the door of that room and listened.

The cards made a soft swish as they were shuffled, and Blue smelt the rich amber incense as it leaked beneath the plywood door.

'Clear your mind,' Devlin said, his voice slow and the intonations more pronounced than in everyday life. 'Let go of all your fears, your hopes, your anxieties; clear your heart and allow all of these emotions to flow into the cards.'

Blue sat with her hands on her knees, ear angled to the door, and her mother watched from the worktop, smiling because she thought Blue was learning and was glad of it.

'Ah, the Five of Swords,' Devlin hummed, and Blue leant forward, could picture Jacob lean forward too.

'You're ready to confront your past and move towards a period of self-healing ... Ah yes, look at that: the Three of Cups; your heart is open. For a long time, it was closed, but you've opened like a flower to the light, and the past is the nectar of your soul, ready to nourish your present.' And Blue thought, no, that's not right at all. He's run from his past, wants to escape and deny it, not confront it.

'Oh, a five-five!' Devlin gasped and oohed in his high pitch. 'A divine connection, indeed. The Hierophant, the fifth card in the arcana major, combined with the Five of Swords. There is wisdom and great spiritual-ity. You've dealt with your past life and can move forward with clarity and wisdom; you are free to move forward and, yes, that's right ... excuse me, sir, you're divorced, I believe?'

'No, not divorced—'

'But you were married?'

'Yes, I—'

'She died?' Devlin's voice softened, and Blue pictured his double chins wobble as he nodded his head in sympathy. 'She was very spiritual, also. She went to church, I believe, but also … Yes, she went to readings too, didn't she? You didn't know? She went in secret, then. Look at that, the High Priestess. Yes, she was spiritual indeed, and you feel lost without her guidance; your soul feels adrift. Ah-ha! Yes, that's it, I see now … There is another woman and tension and conflict surrounds the love for your wife, and your attraction to this new person is both the obstacle and the desire. Look, the Star card …'

The door stayed shut for twenty more minutes, and when it opened again and Jacob stepped out, he had tears on his cheeks and he trembled. He shook Devlin's hand at the front door, thanked him profusely and Blue, moved by the man and troubled by the lies he'd swallowed, rushed forward.

'Mr Jacob, please,' Blue said and tried something she'd never done before. 'Thank you for the humbugs.' She held out her hand and shook Jacob's.

'You've recovered from your bump?' The older man clapped his hand to Blue's.

It was instant: miserable, wretched guilt flowed from Jacob into the child. The light bent around the older man's form, the air became still, and Jacob's hand was clammy with heat, but Blue didn't let go. The guilt planted roots that invaded Blue's veins and blocked them, made her light-headed.

'You haven't confronted your past.' Blue felt the truth of it but knew there was more. 'There's something else; it's like a sickness, and it's killing you from the inside out.'

Arlo sat by the man's feet, Bodhi stood close by his elbow, and whether it was because she had made this bold move, or whether he was still riled up from his prank with the sweet, Blue didn't know. But it all changed then. Her brother looked at her, parted his teeth, readied his tongue. Bodhi mouthed silently, and Blue read his lips and repeated the words aloud. Or was it Bodhi who copied Blue? It was so subtle, so intertwined, that she couldn't tell.

'Your wife was dying, and you couldn't take it and found someone else, even though you loved your wife and were pained by her passing.

You found someone else to comfort you, but you told nobody, not even your kids, and it's eating you up. You think you're terrible because of it, but you're not; you're just human, is all.'

The man looked afraid.

He pulled his hand away, shook his head, wiped the last of the tears from his face, fumbled for his hat and his stick, and hurried out the door without a goodbye.

'I'm sorry,' Blue shouted, confused because she'd spoken the truth and wasn't that better than lies? 'I didn't mean to upset you; I didn't … Mother, I didn't mean it; I'm sorry.' Bridget Ford ran to her and pulled Blue's body into hers, but it made the girl feel no better, and behind her, Bodhi smiled as if he'd just won a prize.

Devlin closed the front door, and Blue grew cold and afraid.

Devlin let out a low sigh.

Blue thought of the red welts on Rosanne's thighs, of the belt her father wore, of the fact that a paying customer had just run away.

Blue had always tried hard to be a good girl, balanced the weight of her mother's mood upon her behaviour, and so she'd never been beaten, rarely told off; she was a good girl. Still, now she could feel Devlin's body behind her, surrounded by the weight of Jacob's revulsion, could taste the stale rot from the humbug, and she braced herself for a smack to her legs, for a cuff of her ear, a pull of her hair, a snap at the nape of her neck.

The hand came down on her back.

A gentle touch to the base of her spine. A kiss to the top of her head.

'Don't ever apologise for that, my girl.' Devlin choked and kissed Blue again on her crown. 'I'm proud of you, lass, very proud. We just need to hone that gift of yours, is all.'

The Devil

Molly is on her knees in front of the hearth and prods the embers with a poker; she will make the hall as warm as she can for her guests. Her remaining guests. She will not think about Jago.

Joshua and the girls will be back by lunch; she wants Hope Marsh House to be cosy, to feel like home. Milton, behind her in the armchair with the Stetson in his lap, has not complained of the cold. Yet. But he doesn't complain about anything, barely makes conversation. Joshua finds him hard work, but not Molly. Molly doesn't ponder why he comes to the retreat if he's not participating in the activities or attending therapy sessions, or talking to the other guests; she knows why he comes. Loneliness, like cancer, corrodes from the inside.

She tells Milton the room will soon be warmer, and he nods to his hat. She offers to fetch him a blanket for his knees, and he looks at her with one white eyebrow raised, and she knows not to ask him again.

The hall is a little warmer. The fire cracks through the kindling, and outside, rain taps the windows, the wind rustles leaves and the longer clumps of grass. Molly breathes in, breathes out, feels her pulse slow. It is as though the early morning never happened, as though she did not have to clean anything unholy, or witness any impious act in the cold, dawn light, or watch her poor husband leave through the oak front door.

He was gone for forty minutes. Molly had felt calmer the minute she saw him return. She feels calm now, knowing he is close, just there at the stream with their two girls, whilst Molly looks after Milton at home. All is as it should be; all is well.

Then the front door opens.

Sabina is first. Her coat and wellingtons drip muddy water across the wooden floor and on to the green stairwell carpet. She thunders upstairs. Molly asks what's wrong, calls after her to see what's the matter and just as she's about to follow the woman upstairs, Blue and Joshua scurry in.

Milton doesn't get up. Instead, he turns his head to see the entrance, tilts his ear their way.

Blue pales when she sees the man by the fire. She says there is someone in Sabina's room, and Molly laughs because it feels like a poorly executed joke, says there isn't anyone else in the house. Jago has left us, she says. Blue swallows; she quivers like a lost rabbit, and Molly wants to hug her better, but there's an anguished wail upstairs, and both women follow the noise.

Sabina stands in the hallway, back to her open bedroom door, forehead pressed against the sage wallpaper. It was open, again, it was open, she says, and her breathing is laboured, her pupils dilated.

Molly knows full well the door was locked but doesn't let on. She tells Sabina that it must have blown open again, must have been unlocked, and Sabina stamps her foot hard and points at the door, says she locked it, she locked it, she did.

She says Blue saw someone standing at the window.

When was this? Molly asks. Her pulse thumps in her fingertips.

Just now. Sabina almost shouts it, stamps her foot again, as though the answer were obvious, but Molly had to check. Just now, it can't have been Molly Blue saw.

Blue looks at Sabina, looks at Molly, looks at the open bedroom door but doesn't move closer, and her colour is so wan that Molly fears the girl's about to be sick. Was Milton upstairs, Blue asks, there was someone with pale hair—

Of course not, Molly tells her, and she walks to the room, looks inside, beckons both women in to see for themselves. There's no one here, she tells them.

Sabina follows her in. But the door was open, she says, and Blue saw someone inside. So if it wasn't you, then it must have been him; Blue saw someone.

Is anything missing? says Molly.

The bed is unmade. Sabina's clothes from yesterday are piled in the chair by the window, and her suitcase is open on the floor. A purple washbag spills small bottles and pots across the dresser. Molly smells the sharp tang of stale spirits. She found a half-empty half-bottle of whisky in Sabina's suitcase when she poked around this morning, hidden beneath the grey T-shirt Sabina slept in, but that was an hour ago, and they were all at the culvert by then. So they couldn't have seen her.

Molly tells Sabina that it must have been a trick of the light or a cloud reflected on the glass. Molly is pleased to see Sabina frown, contemplate what she has said. In the hallway, Blue says no. I saw someone, she says.

See for yourself, says Sabina to Blue, there's no one here now. They must have fled and left the door open.

It must have been Milton, says Blue, who still has not come into the room. Molly stands in the doorway and tells her how impossible that is; he's been downstairs the whole time, and besides, he's in no fit state and can't even make it up the first three steps, let alone up and down a whole flight.

Blue's latte skin has turned grey. How does he get up to his own room then, she asks.

Molly explains that his room is downstairs, at the end of the passage-way. The accessible room, she calls it.

Blue shakes her head.

There's no one here, and nothing's been disturbed, Sabina says from the middle of her room. Molly watches Blue carefully, warily, as she edges along the corridor and at last looks inside. The girl's gaze locks on something in the middle of the room.

Molly looks behind her; there is nothing there.

Blue shakes her head, steps backwards away from the door.

Sabina looks to the middle of her room, to the fixed point of Blue's scrutiny. What is it, she says, what's wrong?

Nothing, whispers Blue, and she darts her gaze away, looks at the floor, at the wall – anywhere, it seems, but that mid space in the bedroom. Her hands tremble.

The Five of Wands

She would not go through this again.

Blue sidestepped until she couldn't see into Sabina's room anymore, fumbled in her back pocket for her room key.

'What's wrong?' Sabina said and stared at Blue as though Blue were unstable.

'What is it?' Mrs Park stared too, shrewd eyes assessing her, trying to work out what was wrong with this woman, what cure was needed, what intervention.

'It's nothing.' Blue whispered it, the words designed to calm herself more than the two other women. 'It's nothing. It's nothing.'

She wanted to say there is nothing there, that thing doesn't exist, what I can see is not real. She locked these words in her head.

'Blue, my dear, why don't you—'

'I need to shower,' Blue said and undid the lock, slipped in her room and bolted the door behind her. Eyes closed, she tried to force out the feeling that the world lay crumbled around her, that it was too much, too heavy a burden to live with, but with her eyes closed, her mind showed her that image again. That thing. That g—

'They don't exist.' She said it aloud.

She heard the women talk in the corridor. Sabina would check on Blue in a bit, she said. Mrs Park would ready lunch; a bit of home-cooked food would do everyone good. Then she would check on her husband, check on Milton.

The older man who was too unwell to walk up the stairs and yet Blue saw him, was sure she had seen him … She would not think about that.

The shower went some way to clear Blue's thoughts. She stood beneath the water, forehead pressed to the tiled wall, and concentrated on the prickling sensation as the water pummelled her back.

She must have seen that face before, and like a fly in amber, it stuck in her memory and had risen to the surface today, a subconscious distraction from Mother's anniversary. A justification to run from this retreat full of strangers, of unfamiliar sights and sounds, of odd dreams and strange sights. Run – run away. There's an excuse now; this house is not safe.

She wouldn't run. She would conquer. Blue would stay and make herself join in the dancing and art lessons and the therapy. She would talk to Milton and see that he's nothing but an old man with poor health and that whatever she saw last night was just a dream.

And what she saw in Sabina's room wasn't real.

She finished in the shower and went to get dressed. She'd neglected to turn on the extractor fan; the windows and mirrors were fogged grey with steam. Her things were still neatly packed in her rucksack; she hadn't put clothes in drawers, hadn't arranged bottles and pots on the dresser as Sabina had. It would be so easy to pick up her bag and go.

The instinct was hard to quash; a sense of dread told her she shouldn't have come. The mist began to fade from the mirror, and Blue thought about how hard she'd worked over the last three years to try and make sense of her life, how this trip had been part of that plan and had given her a short-term purpose.

She closed her eyes, breathed in and out. The fear, she told herself, was useless. Fear was a block to progress.

The fear held firm.

Blue was afraid to open her eyes.

Convinced that, if she did, the face looking back wouldn't be hers. The hair would not be black but very pale. The eyes would not be her turquoise helix eyes, but— It was unbearable, she couldn't look. Blue turned her back on the vanity table, faced the wardrobe.

She forgot there was a mirror there, too.

The mist on that glass had cleared.

Terror seized her chest and rang like an unholy bell in her ears.

Her face stared back, haggard, black hair a damp mess, her body naked. Her hands trembled as she pressed them to her mouth to stifle a cry.

She sat heavily on the bed, grabbed the pillow and squeezed it in her fists, bit down on its edge to stop her cries from being heard. She cursed the vision in Sabina's bedroom, cursed every vision she had ever seen, damned them to hell for their misery. She damned Mother, damned Devlin, damned herself for lacking the courage to stand up to them sooner.

Sabina was next door, and Blue wished she could go to her, confess how lost she felt, be hugged and feel comforted.

Impossible.

The moment they touched, Blue would be overwhelmed. The glimpse of it on the stairs had been too much; she couldn't even graze Sabina's hand without falling apart.

'Blue?' Sabina rapped on her door as though Blue's thoughts had moved her hand. 'Are you OK?'

Blue pressed the heels of her palms to her eye sockets and told herself to get a grip.

'Just out the shower,' she said with forced composure. 'Give me a sec to get dressed.'

'Let me know when you're ready, we can go down together.'

Blue wiped her nose, dried her eyes, made herself look in every mirror. She dressed in clean clothes, neatened her hair. Hunger ate at her stomach; she'd feel better after food and a mug of strong tea.

It would all be OK, she told herself. She knew what she would do.

11 to 12

Devlin taught Blue tact, but it didn't come naturally.

It was Bridget's idea to use brutal honesty as a selling point and, when Blue turned eleven, she began reading alongside Devlin. She did this twice a week, and Bridget charged clients double when Blue read. They only accepted cash, relied on word of mouth instead of advertising, and when a Japanese woman with short pink hair asked if Blue got any of the money, Bridget looked shocked and said of course, she saved it for the girl's future. Yet the house gathered more crystals, more pendants, and the incense became more expensive.

Truth rarely comforted, and Blue discovered that the sort of people who had their cards read by Devlin and were used to the soul-calming kindness of his blithe mistruths were drawn even more to candour's flagellation. Whereas Devlin would tell a young woman on the rebound from a bad relationship – one who had few friends and couldn't keep a job – that she had a beautiful soul just waiting to spread its wings and soar like a butterfly reaching for a sunflower, Blue would say,

'You're poisoned by blame; you keep pointing at other people because you're too scared to look at your own actions and too lazy to fix your own problems. You expect a prince to come and solve them, but you're the one who's got to do it.'

Customers who cried at Devlin's readings would listen open-mouthed to Blue, too shocked to cry and too humbled by her accuracy to argue. Yet they always rebooked. She didn't understand it; if someone spoke to her like that, she'd give them a wide berth, not come back for more.

Sometimes Blue just needed to touch someone to feel their story. Sometimes they needed to handle each of her well-thumbed cards. Arlo stayed well clear of the room with the velvet drapes but, if it were a nasty tale or if there was a deep sense of self-hatred, Bodhi would watch, hidden behind the folds of velvet, and Blue started to wonder whether he was there to listen to the story or revel in Blue's discomfort.

It was never pleasant. Each reading left Blue exhausted, tainted, unhappy, but also gave her a sense of achievement. She didn't like the way it made her feel, but she did like the thank yous from the customers. She liked the way they smiled at her when it was all over, and when they said she was special, she thought it a good thing.

Until she turned twelve and she changed her mind about that.

Bridget Ford ushered Blue into the room at the back of the house; Devlin was already at the round rosewood table with the pentacle etched in its centre. Bridget had made Devlin a larger black kaftan with a pearl-beaded collar, and the linen was taut across his belly. A smile, as genuine as it was broad, spread across his face as he watched his wife and step-daughter walk in. He was there to supervise; Blue would be reading the cards alone, and Devlin was proud enough to burst.

Two other people were in the room. Typically, if folk came together, they would take it in turns – one took tea in the kitchen with Bridget whilst the other sat with Blue and Devlin. Tarot was a private thing, Devlin said.

Not in this case.

A man and a woman stood at the display of healing stones. She was in middle age, her wispy hair grey, and though she had washed it freshly for the occasion, Blue knew that she usually didn't bother. Didn't wash her clothes, either, unless circumstance demanded. She turned and smiled at Blue. Her make-up, inexpertly applied with a nervous hand, told Blue she looked better plain-faced. The change in the woman's expression prompted the man to look, too.

He was weary and wrinkled as an ancient tortoise, with a hump in his back in place of a shell. The waddle of skin at his neck was loose and yellowed; his rheumy eyes bulged. Blue could smell the sickness come off him, the air sour with it. He was the woman's father.

The girl looked to Devlin for guidance; she had only taken charge of a handful of readings so far. Her stepfather beckoned for her to sit down without indicating which person was to go first. It was a new test, Blue realised, to see how far off she was from doing these wholly unguided; Devlin wanted Blue to use her intuition.

Or rather, he wanted the clients to *think* Blue used her intuition.

Blue cleared her throat and tried to sound grown-up. 'If you would like to take a seat, we will begin.' Then, with a nervous look towards Devlin, she followed her gut and added, 'Madam.'

The woman took a seat, and Blue was relieved to have guessed right. 'I've heard a lot about you.' Her accent was a local one, Blackpool or Preston undoubtedly, and she blushed as she met Blue's eye. 'A few people have recommended you. They all said you were spot on.'

'That's very kind.' Devlin accepted the compliment on Blue's behalf. He knew such things made Blue uncomfortable. He also knew it added mystery to have a girl who was simultaneously adept at reading tarot but unnerved by attention. Bridget had feared Blue's shyness would put people off, but Devlin had said, 'No, not at all; reluctance gives her gift authenticity, proves she's not attention-seeking.'

Blue shuffled the cards as Devlin explained to the woman why two packs would be used – one for the reading and one to cleanse – and then he looked to Blue, which was her cue.

'If you'd please shuffle them now, so as they can get your energy a bit,' Blue stuttered, and then added another 'please' as an afterthought. She pushed the cards across the pentacle and brushed her fingertips against the woman's hand to get the touch.

Whilst the woman looked at the cards, and the old man looked over her shoulder, Blue caught Devlin's eye. She mouthed the word *outside*, then indicated the old man with a flick of her gaze. It would be better if he were out, is what Blue wanted Devlin to intuit, because Blue didn't want to say it aloud, worried she would come across as rude and get told off.

The old man had no teeth. He stared at the cards in his daughter's hands as she shuffled. Devlin opened his mouth to speak, but the woman said, 'Do I need to cut them or anything? I always see people cutting them and the like on telly.'

'Yes, please,' Blue said, 'and I'd like you to think of a question as you cut them, something you want the cards to focus on.'

The woman cut them twice and pushed the deck back across the table.

Was Devlin going to say anything?

No, it didn't look like it. Was it another test to see how capable Blue could be? She was twelve now, thirteen in a few months, and her mother liked to tell her that she'd soon be a woman. She didn't feel like a grown woman, not at all.

Blue looked again to Devlin, then to the lady and her father behind her.

'Do you want the other chair, or would you rather—' Blue nodded behind her head to the kitchen door, hoped the old man would slope out, but the woman butted in, said it was all fine and Blue could go ahead and begin.

Her cheeks were pink with excitement. 'I'm wanting a reading on me love life, you see. That was my question. Nothing scandalous,' she added with an awkward, girlish laugh. 'Just a hint, you know, to see if there's anything there for me.' She nodded like a dog and looked at Blue. Loneliness smogged the air.

Blue turned the first card. By the time she was nine, she had memo-rised all seventy-eight in the tarot deck and could recite both the major and minor arcana. At ten, she knew what each meant on their own. By eleven, she understood their subtle differences and how one card could represent many different things depending on when it was dealt in the reading, what cards were before and after it and whether it was the right side up or upside down. There was such a spectrum of possible interpretations that you could never be wrong, Devlin said. The critical thing was conviction in your reading, not accuracy ('But ain't that just lying?' Blue had asked him. 'An interpretation is never really a lie,' was Devlin's reply).

At twelve, Blue realised that Devlin had no special gift for reading the future. What he had was a talent for storytelling and intuition for knowing what people wanted to hear. He had a kind, fat face and a high-pitched voice and a vague aura of show business. What he lacked was any business sense or ability to manage money.

Blue looked at the first card, the Wheel of Fortune, reversed. It was like the first tab of a flow chart in her head, the direction of the reading dependent on the next card dealt and how the woman would react to it.

The next was the Hanged Man.

86

Then the Tower.

Three major arcana in a row was rare, but rarer still was the woman's reaction. The colour drained from her face; her blusher looked like daubs of red on a dirty white canvas.

'Do you know what they mean?' Blue asked.

Something stirred in her, so when the woman replied and said, 'That looks just like him,' and pointed at the hanged figure, Blue turned to Devlin. 'I need you to wait outside.'

Blue must have looked severe, as Devlin immediately stood to leave and said, 'Are you sure, lass?' even though he never called Blue lass in the velvet room.

The remaining cards were beneath Blue's palm, and she could feel every one of them, knew what they would be, knew she couldn't turn them over whilst anyone else watched.

'Aye, please,' said Blue, and she looked at the old man hunched over his daughter.

The door closed. There were tears in the woman's eyes – she looked terrified, and Blue was terrified in turn, could feel tears burn behind her lids, could feel everything coming off this woman and the old man that stood behind her.

'Your father's with you,' Blue said, and the woman looked wide-eyed but stayed quiet.

The old man startled, stared at Blue with shock, joy, despair, confusion, relief and great, great sadness, and the young girl understood it all. It came as a cold horror, and Blue had to concentrate not to tremble, stutter, or call for Mother.

'You can see me,' the old man mouthed, the sound quiet as the breeze. 'You can see me.'

Blue felt each word as though they were spoken aloud. Yet only Blue heard him. He said he hadn't been seen in so long. Since his death, he had followed his daughter, watched as she mourned for him and dragged herself through life, never happy, peace out of reach.

'He's here?' she said, and then her shock evaporated, and her face hardened, and she drew her hands into her lap, squeezed her arms into her body and tried to make herself small. 'What's he said?' Her voice quivered, and the old man looked wretched to hear it.

Blue didn't know why she alone could see this old man.

'He says he's always with you,' Blue said as the silent words fell from the dead man's mouth, 'that he'll be with you till you pass on.'

The woman sniffed and wiped her eyes, stood from the table and picked up her handbag. 'I think I'll be going,' she said. 'I didn't come for this … this mumbo jumbo.' She waved her arm at the crystal balls, pendants, talismans, tumblestones, and the twelve-year-old girl with the tarot cards.

Blue stayed in her seat, didn't look at the woman at all but at her father. 'He says he's glad you did it.'

The woman stood still.

'He was miserable and ill and longed for it to end, and he wanted to release you from the burden of care.'

A cry burst from her lips, and she held fast to the back of the chair as though she were in danger of falling. 'You're making this up,' she said. 'You're just lying, you're just a naughty kid, a lying—'

'– And afterwards, you felt the guilt of it; it were like a stain that wouldn't wash out. But more than that, he says you felt relieved that you'd done it, relieved that you'd set him free and yourself. He says your relief that he was dead made you feel guiltier than … than how he died. Do you know what I mean by that?' And Blue hoped the woman did know because she couldn't bear to say it aloud.

The woman collapsed into the seat. The tears that had welled in her eyes had gone, dried by shock and by horror.

'How do you know all that?' she said, but what could Blue tell her?

'He wants you to look after yourself, to care for yourself as well as you cared for him, show yourself the same kindness and patience and love.'

The woman nodded as though she understood, but her face crumpled, and confusion took over. 'How can I,' she said, 'when I did that to him?' and she asked it to Blue, expected her to know the answer, but she was just a kid and didn't know. All she could do was give voice to the old man.

They sat in the room until the exhaustion overtook Blue and her head ached, and the old man said it was enough. Blue called for her parents; they came through tentatively, and she knew they'd listened at the door, as Blue used to do when she was younger.

Devlin's eyes were puffy from tears.

Bridget's were wild with excitement and possibility.

That night Bridget put Blue up to bed. She told Blue she was a marvel, that she was proud of her and loved her, and she would do great things.

'But he was dead, Mother. How comes I could see him?' Blue waited for Bridget to tell her that she couldn't really, that such things didn't exist, and she had seen the old man as a vision, not a ghost.

Bridget stroked her daughter's long black hair away from her forehead and her touch reminded Blue of being little, when it was just Blue and her mother in the small, dirty flat in town. She longed to be soothed by her lullabies.

'He chose you, sweetheart. You've an amazing gift.' Bridget's long grey hair was in a plait that hung over her shoulder. Blue reached for it, brushed the end against the back of her hand and tried her very best not to cry.

'Why me?' was all she could say.

'Because you've a heart so big and so pure that it attracts love and feeling from all kinds of places, places normal people can't access. You're rare, my love.'

Blue said, 'But I want to be normal, like the kids on the road. You know, just ride bikes and play music and—' Mother's face had gone hard, her lips a tight line.

'Think of all the people you could help.' She stopped stroking Blue's forehead. 'And of how many people would love to be able to do the things you do but cannot. Think about how much dear Devlin has given up to help you learn—' She forced a smile and took a deep breath, but her eyes betrayed disappointment. 'Those normal children will grow up to achieve nothing.'

'Am I not normal, Mother?' she asked, and Bridget smiled warmly this time, returned her soft hand to Blue's hair.

'No, sweetheart, you're not normal. You're special. Doesn't it feel good to be special?'

Blue wanted to say no, it did not feel good, not at all, but 'aye' was all she could muster.

Her mother was happy, her stepfather proud, and Blue knew she should be grateful and glad. The kids she used to run around with had grown distant of late; Blue's inability to talk about teachers and football and music made her odd. Home-schooled and friendless, she had no one to turn to.

When she slept that night, and for months afterwards, she would see those rheumy eyes stare out of that toothless head; she would feel the same horror that had filled her when she realised what that woman had done to her dad.

She would remember her mother tell her that no, she was not normal.

The King of Swords (Reversed)

Rain thrummed on the skylight as Blue made her way downstairs. In the kitchen, Mrs Park stirred a soup-filled pan on the Aga whilst Mr Park poured cups of dark tea from a pot and beckoned for Blue and Sabina to sit down. He thanked them both for their help at the stream as though that was the last thing to have happened, and the episode upstairs had been a daydream. Milton sat with a bottle of water cradled in his hands, his walking frame beside him. He had nodded when the women entered the room but offered nothing more, and Blue wondered if they had all come to some agreement not to mention it.

The Labrador pups looked out from their frames, growls caught in both their throats, no birthday-card sweetness about them. She thought of Jago. 'I love black Labs,' he'd said. Where was he?

Blue cradled her mug, took a small sip so as not to burn her tongue. The tea was stone cold.

It doesn't mean anything, she told herself. The room was cold, and the cups were cold, and the tea wasn't freshly made. Cold tea doesn't mean there are—

But steam steadily rose from Sabina's mug, from the Parks' too. Blue touched the pot, felt the burn and drew back her fingers. Something had turned her cup cold. She tried hard, very hard, to forget what she had seen in Sabina's bedroom.

'Here we are.' Mrs Park placed the soup pan in the centre of the table. Mr Park handed out bowls and ladled home-cooked vegetable soup into each, the sauce made thick with yellow split peas and pearl barley, crisped lardons giving it salt. Freshly baked rolls sat ready to be shared, golden and with a pale split down their middles. Blue took two, and they warmed her palms, and she reminded herself that she hadn't seen Bodhi in three years, and that hallucinations can't spoil solid food. She sliced a thick wodge of butter on to her side plate and tried to shake off the sensation that the dogs were watching.

'Under normal circumstances, the first of our counselling sessions would be this afternoon: an hour each of individual therapy whilst the other guests write in their journals or read …' Mrs Park paused to butter her bread, and Sabina gave Blue a sidelong look. Blue could smell the thyme and the bacon from the soup, could almost taste the soft, yeasty bread from its steam. Mrs Park carried on. 'But these are hardly normal circumstances. I thought you might want some restorative yoga instead, to help ease your muscles after the labour you did this morning?'

'Jesus Christ,' Milton murmured.

Sabina eagerly spoke from behind her hand. 'Yes, that would be' – tried to swallow her mouthful of food – 'sorry, that would be perfect, I would like that a lot.' And Blue almost laughed at her desperation to keep out of the counselling room, felt a pang of regret that she'd not see her again. Blue understood now; this was not the right place for her. It was too immersive, too intense. A traditional form of therapy would probably be better, one that didn't put her so far outside her comfort zone, one where she could address Mother's death, Mother's life, Mother, safely and at her own pace. Hope Marsh House had been a mistake. That's why she saw things, imagined things, sensed things that were not there.

'I think I'll head off after all,' Blue said politely. 'What with the weather, it's best if I go while it's still light. I'd have loved to have stayed, but—'

'Is this because of what happened up—' Mrs Park began, but her husband put his hand on her arm.

'I understand,' he said. 'It's wise. I checked the road; the water is fairly deep, but you'll be fine if you go slow, and it's only the dip that's flooded. I'd like to say that it'll soon clear, but this bloody rain won't let up, and it would be impassable if it got deeper.'

'Do you think it will get deeper?' Sabina asked with the same claustrophobic nervousness she'd shown earlier.

'The rain's not heavy, but nor is it letting up,' Mr Park said.

'Well.' Sabina sighed. 'I guess I should go too.'

'I think,' said Mrs Park and shrugged off her husband's hand, 'it's foolhardy; you can't drive off in a flood, for heaven's sake, it's not safe. The government advice is to avoid travel.'

'Molly,' Mr Park warned.

'We'll be fine,' said Sabina.

'I'm not going anywhere,' Milton said.

In silence, they returned to their food.

The weight of the spoon in Blue's hand was enough to make her stomach growl. She dug out a scoop of bacon, barley, soft onion, her lips and tongue ready for it, desperate for it, taunted by its scent and promise.

'Please, reconsider,' Mrs Park said.

It was cold.

Congealed.

Blue's mouth filled with the foetid sweetness of long-dead flesh.

She dropped her spoon.

'Everything all right? It's not too hot for you?' Mrs Park said, and Blue forced a smile as though nothing was wrong, said it was lovely and that she couldn't wait to taste the bread.

The first roll was hard, the yellow butter rancid. Blue watched with envy as Sabina pried her roll open. Steam rose as the fat melted into its fluffy centre. Blue's mouth felt dry, her tongue like leather; she knew this had nothing to do with Mrs Park's cooking, that it was most likely a physical manifestation of stress. The food was perfectly edible, fresh and hot like everyone else's, it was only her mind that told her otherwise. Even so, whether she imagined these things or not, if she stayed, things would only get worse.

There were five of them in the kitchen, no visions of the dead, and she told herself again it was an illusion – a symptom and not a reality. All Blue had to do was keep her head clear for a bit longer and she could escape.

She was still ravenous, and so determined to prove her theory that she plunged her spoon back into the soup. Mother's overcooked microwave meals had given her an iron stomach; she could get through this. Soon she would be away, and the visions and the dogs and the trees would be left behind.

'Is your lunch OK? You look queasy.' Mrs Park put her hand to Blue's arm, and Blue realised she was trembling. 'Are you sure you're not too tired to drive?'

'Don't pressure them, Molly,' Mr Park said. 'It's safer if they head off before the weather worsens. They don't want to get stranded here.'

'I'll be stranded here,' Milton said.

'It wouldn't be so bad if they were.' Mrs Park smiled a sad smile at her husband, then turned it towards Blue and Sabina. She'd hardly eaten. 'It's strange enough only having three guests, having fewer still will be … ah well. As soon as the weather's cleared, you must come back; I'm sorry it was such a wasted trip.'

Spoon by cold, congealed spoon, Blue ate; it would be quicker to force it down than it would be to have Mrs Park coo over her empty stomach.

Sabina offered the woman a few words of comfort, a reassurance that she would certainly be back, that Mrs Park shouldn't feel guilty; the weather wasn't her fault. Blue nodded along, eager to finish the food and leave.

She left the last inch in the bowl, said she'd take the uneaten bread roll for the journey and wrapped it in a piece of kitchen paper. Mrs Park made espressos to help keep them awake whilst her husband went to get their mobile phones.

The coffee turned cold as soon as Blue touched it and tasted of stale cigarette butts. She forced it down.

Blue flinched again as Mr Park reached for the pantry door that hid the safe, hit by a sudden certainty that the thing would be behind it, that Blue would see the pale hair, pale face again.

There was nothing.

Mr Park took out their phones and handed them back.

'That's Jago's phone,' Sabina said, craning her neck. 'Why didn't he take his phone?'

'We must have forgotten it,' Mrs Park said. She gathered the bowls, stood and turned her back to the table. 'We'll get a courier to send it back to him when the weather clears.'

'He wouldn't have left his phone—' Sabina said.

'You're right.' Mr Park stared into the safe and his hand worried at his chin. 'It was a rush; it all happened so quickly that I didn't think of giving him his phone. Strange that he didn't ask for it, it was practically glued to his hand before.'

'Satnav,' Milton said. 'Didn't he need it, to drive away? Most people have it on their phones.' He watched Mr Park with an unblinking gaze, his watery eyes steely and cold. Blue had the impression he was either waiting for Mr Park to slip up, or was communicating some silent reminder.

'He must have had it in his car,' Mr Park said. He shut the pantry door on the safe. 'As I said before, it was a rush. Don't you worry, we'll send it back to him as soon as we can. Knowing Jago, he'll have everything backed up on the cloud.'

'Such a rush,' Milton said, 'and none of us heard a thing.'

'We were considerate.' Mrs Park was measured. 'Kept things nice and quiet.'

Sabina stared at her screen. 'Still no reception,' she said.

Blue didn't waste time turning hers on. She excused herself and went to her room. It didn't take long to collect her things; she had never fully unpacked.

Outside, the sound of the car boot unlocking was a balm, the weight of keys in her hand reassuring. Joshua Park helped load the bags into their cars, then stood beneath the portico with his wife and Milton, ready to wave them off. Sabina hugged Mrs Park and shook Mr Park's hand, stood awkwardly in front of Milton until he tipped his hat and wheezed goodbye. Blue waved from her car.

'It was nice to meet you, Blue,' Sabina said, and instead of a hug or handshake, she mirrored Blue's goodbye and lifted her hand to her shoulder, palm out.

Blue slid into her seat and shut the car door. Severed catkins and falling rain obscured the windscreen, and through the blur, Blue could see Mr Park wind his arm around his wife's shoulders. Milton stood with his hat held to his chest like a graveside mourner.

The need to get away, to be on familiar ground, was so desperate that Blue was suddenly terrified she'd never see her lonely house again, never escape this flat, vast wilderness. It was a fear so visceral, so strange and solid that it could not be unfounded.

Something was wrong.

She felt it in her guts, in her cold, numb fingers, in the sweat that bloomed on her brow. Even before the key turned, she knew that the car wouldn't start. Still, she went through the rigmarole, turned the key over and again. The engine didn't cough. She looked over at Sabina's car; she could tell hers wouldn't start either.

The windscreen wipers were immovable, and the headlights didn't turn on.

Blue raked her fingers through her hair, clutched a handful at the back of her skull. Sabina's door opened, and she heard her call out the trouble to the Parks, heard her say Blue's name. Blue had to get out, had to face the problem.

It wasn't a run-down battery.

It wasn't water damage to the electrics or engine trouble.

Mrs Park tried and failed to hide her pleasure that the vehicles wouldn't go. So relieved was her expression that Blue was tempted to think it was her, that in her desperation to make them stay, Mrs Park had tampered with their cars. It was easier to believe her unhinged, deranged, dangerous, than to face the other possibility.

She had the dreadful sensation of being spied on.

Something pale shifted in the periphery of Blue's vision, movement in an upstairs window.

And she knew, then, that there was no way out.

The Wheel of Fortune

Molly scratches her cheek; her hand hides her smile. She doesn't know what's happened to the cars, laughs to herself as her husband lifts Blue's bonnet and hums and haws; he knows as much about mechanics as Molly.

This was not Molly's doing, but it doesn't mean she isn't glad. Three guests, after all. Thank God for that. Sabina confidently tinkers with her engine, and soon her fingers are black with grease. She says it's not the radiator, not the electrics, not the something or other. Molly doesn't catch it; she isn't paying attention to Sabina. It's Blue that's drawn her.

The girl stands with her back to the house; one hand grips the hair at the nape of her neck. From the rise and fall of Blue's ribcage, Molly sees that she's deep breathing, so as not to cry or panic or both.

Molly asks Joshua to go inside and call the AA. He shrugs, agrees that it's the best thing, and Blue asks how long Molly thinks they will be. Her voice shudders. She looks to the ground instead of the house, just as she did upstairs, and Molly senses that she has missed something. She searched for Blue Ford online as soon as the booking request came in, just as she did with Sabina and Jago (no need with Milton – by his admittance, he had no online footprint. Even his mobile was a big-buttoned brick). She had found a private Facebook page, a private Instagram account – no Twitter – and at the time, Molly thought that Blue valued her privacy. Now she wonders if this strange girl with turquoise and amber eyes, who shakes like a leaf and sees things where there is nothing to see, is perhaps more complicated than Molly first thought.

Strange, Molly says, that both cars should— but she doesn't finish the sentence because Sabina cuts her off, says it's just a coincidence, that coincidences do happen, and Milton chuckles and puts his Stetson back on his head just as the clouds unleash a fresh burst of rain.

Molly suggests they wait inside where it's dry and watches closely as Blue hesitates, then nods. Sabina rolls her shoulders as she stands upright by her car. Milton shuffles towards the front door, throws an odd look at Blue as though he too sees an eccentricity in her. But before any of them get inside, Joshua appears; the keys to the covered barn are in his hand.

The AA won't be able to reach them today, he says. There's a backlog of people in dire straits up and down the county – folk stuck in ditches, stranded in flooded roads. Blue and Sabina are safe, with a place to stay, and are therefore the bottom of the list; no one will be free to come out until tomorrow at least.

At least? Sabina says and looks fit to panic but swallows it back, and Molly wonders how much more pain Sabina has swallowed, digested, refused to confront. Sabina asks if Joshua could call the RAC instead, or any of the other roadside assistance companies, or if there's a local mechanic who could— Joshua holds up his hand and says again that no one can come out until tomorrow.

It's like someone wants to keep you here, Milton says, and Sabina shudders, Blue turns pale, and Molly tries her best not to take offence and tells Milton not to be silly. Still, it feels like a slight. First Jago, ranting and hurling those words at her, and now this. Has she not made a home away from home for them? Has she not fed them, made sure they slept soundly, checked in on them in the dead of night to ensure they were well covered with warm blankets?

Blue asks what they will do, and Joshua holds up the key, says they'll push the cars into the barn to keep them dry and call the AA again in the morning. In a moment of petulance, Molly feels like telling them to do what they damn well please if they're going to be so ungrateful, but she holds her tongue. This is a second chance to win the women round, and second chances are rare. She opens the hangar doors and says she will help push the vehicles inside. Another car hides at the back, covered in a tarpaulin.

Milton, too old and frail and broken in body and soul, cannot help push the cars. Rather than look defeated, Molly catches a brief glint in his washed-out eyes, and he fakes despondency, says it's a shame he's no use to them; he'll have to wait inside. He turns, shuffles towards the front door and is it Molly's imagination or is he moving more easily, breathing more freely?

It was a mistake to tie herself to a task because now that house is unguarded. Milton is no threat, Molly knows this, but didn't his invalid brother live in Birmingham, close to the rehab clinic where Molly worked, close to Eleanor? … No, she will not think of that.

It will take another ten minutes to get both cars into the barn, possibly more. Joshua meets her eye over the bonnet of Blue's car, flicks his gaze to that house and back again. A silent agreement passes between man and wife. So much of their communication is nonverbal; more than twenty years of marriage has solidified into a collective consciousness. Love, risks, joy, loss, grief – Molly knows what each eyebrow raise, each frown, each smile on her husband's face signifies.

Molly excuses herself, says her knees aren't what they were, that she'll leave the stronger folk to push the cars, and she'll check on Milton, alone inside that house.

Relief washes over Joshua's face, and he says that's a good idea; he can manage the cars with the women and Molly can go inside, sit with Milton. Understanding passes between them, silent, profound.

Guests should never be left alone in Hope Marsh House.

The Sixties

'Tell me about yourself,' Mr Hope said. He was bald and flabby-necked, and his belly pressed tightly against his shirt. He sat behind a desk that was covered in ledgers. His secretary's desk was in the corner, paper ready-spooled in the typewriter. 'What do you like to do on the weekend?'

What could James say? He didn't listen to the Beatles or the Temptations. He couldn't play football or cricket. Couldn't dance. He did not hold placards and protest Vietnam.

Perspiration gathered at the nape of James' neck.

'I like to paint and play cards, but not at the same time,' he laughed. Then, worried that he might sound like a gambler, James added, 'Just casual games of whist and a bit of gin rummy. And I don't drink, so there'd be no chance of me—'

Mr Hope looked disappointed. 'I don't mind a drink myself. Everyone needs to let off steam.'

'Oh yes, I agree. Very important,' James said. His father had given him a suit to wear, and his mother had taken it up at the cuff. James had kissed her, thanked his dad, hoped he wouldn't disappoint. He had sat on the bus for over an hour and gone over everything his older brother had told him about interviews, but he was a proper civil servant, not a dogsbody, and his advice was kindly meant but redundant.

'It's quite a gap,' said Mr Hope and shook the single piece of paper that was James' résumé.

'Yes,' he said, 'well, I was in a sana—'

'You stayed in the forces after national service, that it? Usual reason,' Mr Hope said, and James opened his mouth to say no, to say that he had only completed half his national service, but the man had moved on and turned the résumé over to see if there was anything written on the back. There wasn't.

'Pretty light for a man of twenty-six,' the man said, 'pretty light, I'd say. You type it yourself?'

'My mother did,' James said and felt the shame of it spread like a wet patch at his groin. A clock ticked on the wall, and James wondered if it was broken, or slow, or if he had died and this was purgatory.

'Somewhere else to be?' Mr Hope said.

James' instinct was to apologise, but as his gaze fell from the clock, he looked out of the window.

Outside, a woman leant against the open canteen door, cigarette between her lips, weight on one hip. She wore a plain white tabard over a navy dress. A hairnet covered her black hair, and he imagined it would be thick and shiny and soft to touch. Her neck was short, her shoulders narrow, breasts large, and her hips were wide and solid, and he thought of working here every other day. Seeing that woman every other day. A lump thickened his throat.

'Hmm?' Mr Hope said again and stared hard at James.

James pictured going home and telling his mother, *No, didn't get it.* He imagined his brother patting his back (very gently), telling him, *Next time you'll get it, Jim, next time.* He glanced at the woman with the cigarette at her mouth. He thought how bleak life would be if he never saw her again.

'No, nowhere else to be,' James said, and he thought, what would his brother do? He thought, if there's a man lucky enough to hold that woman, then what would he do? And James let the words tumble from his mouth before he lost his nerve: 'I have another job offer, and I promised I'd let them know today. I kept this appointment as I've wanted to work here for so long. I really admire your company, Mr Hope.'

And Mr Hope baulked and looked at the résumé and turned it over again. He looked at James with narrowed eyes. 'An offer?'

'Three days a week at British Leyland,' he said. It was the biggest factory he knew, so big that he hoped his lie could not be easily caught.

'That so?' Mr Hope said, and in the yard, the woman stubbed out her cigarette on the red-brick wall.

'They were impressed by my references,' James said, and he sat straighter. He recalled his dad's advice and stopped fiddling with his hands, kept eye contact. 'You're welcome to check if you need reassurance.'

The woman went back into the canteen, and her gait made her wide hips sway, and something inside James pulled that way, longed to follow.

Mr Hope rubbed his chin and read the names of the references, all family friends. One of them was a doctor from the sanatorium.

The stress was doing him no good. James' left lung began to ache. He breathed deep into his belly, told his lung firmly to behave. Don't make me look weak, lung, he thought, don't ruin this for me now.

Mr Hope rubbed his chin again, sat back in his chair and frowned at the CV in his hand. His shirt was thin, and James could see the curly, dark shadows of belly hair.

'I don't believe a word of it,' the man said. 'They'd never take on a man of your age who has next to no experience. But,' he dropped the paper and put his hands behind his head, elbows splayed like wings, 'I admire your bloody gumption, I'll give you that. Never in a rain of pig's pudding have I seen someone so keen to get a job filing paperwork. And we do need someone. I tell you what, we'll give you a trial. Three weeks, half pay, and if you get through that, then you're in.'

'Yes, thank you, yes.' James jumped up and shook Mr Hope's hand, as firm as he could. The other man laughed and clapped him on the back and the ache became an itch, and James thought, no, not now, not now, no.

'Go see Morris on the way out, and you can fill out the necessaries,' Mr Hope said, and James turned and ran from the room and Mr Hope laughed, as though tickled by the young man's eagerness.

James raced down the corridor, turned a corner out of earshot, shrugged off his father's suit jacket and coughed and hacked and coughed. He jammed the jacket sleeve in his mouth to dampen the sound, that horrible sound, and he coughed until his ribcage was sore.

Sweat clung to his brow, to his hairline, to his upper lip. His shirt stuck to his back. His stomach ached. His thighs screamed at him for crouching in this hunchbacked, bent-kneed, broken-bodied stance.

The coughing stopped. He took the sleeve from his mouth and was scared to look at it. It was damp, that was obvious, but damp with what he didn't know and did not want to look. It had been years since he'd hawked up mouthfuls of blood, so thick it clotted against his teeth. But several years isn't enough to erase the fear of it. James doubted he would ever cough again without feeling the testicle-clenching dread that comes from seeing your blood splatter a handkerchief, the crook of your arm, the downy cheek of a nurse.

He sat for several minutes in the corridor, hopeful that no one would walk by. Hopeful too that he would have enough breath in him to walk with his chin up to Morris' office, fill out the paperwork that would give him a job, and finally relieve his parents. They said he was no burden, that they loved him and would care for him, and James had discovered what it was to not be a burden but to feel a burden. To know that none of this is your doing, but to feel the shame as though it were. To walk in the thin grey space between people's compassion and hostility, kindness and pity, awareness and ignorance. The last six years had been difficult.

'You're welcome to stay for a bit of lunch if you like,' Morris said when James had filled out the various forms. 'It'll be the dregs at this stage, whatever the workers have left, but you're welcome to it. Quite a journey back you've got.' Morris gave him directions to the canteen, said he was to tell Marie or Barb that Morris had sent him. *Marie* rang in James' ear because that was her name, he didn't know how but he knew it. That was her name.

He entered the yard as the other men left it, his crumpled suit jacket flung over one shoulder. The factory workers moved as a unit, broad chests beneath blue overalls, breath heavy and voices loud. James was small among them and slower to move, a minnow swimming against the migration of blue marlin. But the new work card warmed James' shirt pocket, and he smiled at the men, even said hello if they caught his eye, and they smiled at him in return and said, 'How d'ya do,' in Birmingham accents. They didn't look at him with pity or shy away as though James were a leper, or patronise him in the way some people did, as though spending two years in a tuberculosis sanatorium had robbed him of intelligence. He felt like one of these men. He was going to be one of them. His head was held quite high now. A worker, a wage earner, a gainfully employed young man, even if he could only manage half hours.

The canteen was dead ahead. Through the glass, he saw two women wipe tables. He only had eyes for one.

A mop had been propped against the wall, and when he pushed the door open, the mop toppled.

'Ah, no, I'm sorry,' he said, and stooped to pick it up, rested it against the wall, and it fell again, and he picked it up and held on to it and didn't know what to do. 'Sorry,' he repeated, and a blonde woman came forward and helped him.

'S'alright,' she said, 'stupid place to have put it anyway, my own fault.'

'Are you Barb?' James said, not looking at where the black-haired woman stood, for fear that he might topple over himself. She stood way back at the end of the room. She felt very close.

'That's me,' the blonde woman said. She was taller than James, slim with wavy hair pushed away from her face, clear-skinned and pretty enough for a cinema poster. She smiled, gave a laugh, said, 'Morris must have sent you. Everyone else calls me Babs. Are you after a bit of lunch?'

And James said yes, please, and still couldn't bring himself to look at Marie. He wished that he'd gone straight home; he wasn't sure he could cope with this. Why'd he come? He was a semi-recovered invalid who lived with his mother, would probably always live with his mother, because what other choice was there when he could only work short stints before he had to rest up?

His face reddened; he felt it. 'Only if it's not too much bother.' He added, 'I can help clear up afterwards if that would help.' And his new confidence was an eggshell, fractured by the knock of a broom, the fear of embarrassment, the proximity of this black-haired woman.

Babs waved a hand, told him to take a seat and she'd bring some stew over. 'It's just the leftovers, mind, but at least they're hot.'

'Thank you.' He folded his suit jacket and placed it on the bench next to him, the still-damp coughed-on sleeve bottom-most and out of sight.

From the back of the room, in a purposeful, accented voice, Marie said, 'I'll see to him, Babs, you head on home.' And then she was standing right there, and he smelt the kitchen grease on her tabard and saw the dry skin on her fingers, and she was right there, next to him, and his heart was in his throat, in his mouth.

'I'm Marie,' she said. 'Hello.'

The High Priestess

It was mid-afternoon by the time they had sorted the cars and crept back inside. The ache had set in Blue's muscles, along with the crush of defeat that she couldn't drive away, was trapped in that house with … with whatever it was she could see.

'Well, it would be silly to waste the rest of the day,' Mrs Park said as Blue and Sabina collapsed into the armchairs beside the fire. The chair was soft and Blue lolled her head back and Sabina said, 'I'm exhausted. I slept so well last night, but now I'm just—'

'Me too,' said Blue.

'You'll sleep soundly tonight,' Milton said from his chair.

'Everyone sleeps well at Hope Marsh,' Mr Park said and fed a log to the fire. 'It's quiet.'

'What about the peace?' said Milton.

'Yes,' Mrs Park said, 'that too, of course, along with all our activities, which help settle mind and body. As I said at lunch, we could start with light yoga and move on from there.' Mrs Park suffused her voice with saccharine cheer and smoothed the creases from her linen tunic. Blue straightened her head to look at her, felt sorry to see that Mrs Park's smile was forced and realised she must feel awkward; her guests wanted to leave, and the schedule she had planned was superfluous. 'We may as well try to carry on as normal, seeing as you can't … Who would like to join me?' She spoke with purpose, broadened her smile, but her eyes looked desperate. 'Sabina? Earlier, you seemed quite keen.'

'Earlier, I was, but now I'd like to sit here in front of the fire and sleep.' Sabina arched her back and stretched her arms above her head. 'I'm sorry; the stress with the cars has had its effect. But, to be honest, what I'd like to do is drink an enormous glass of wine and eat my weight in crisps.'

'It's not even three o'clock.' Mrs Park's smile faded and the fire spat cinders into the cast-iron guard. 'A bit early for … and we don't drink alcohol; it's one of the rules. It clouds the mind, you see, makes it harder to work through your—'

'I'd happily cloud my mind,' said Sabina and Milton rattled a laugh.

'Molly, we can safely say that today has been far from normal. Best to leave the retreat business at the front door, eh?' Mr Park said. He opened a wooden chest and retrieved a blanket. 'Make yourself comfortable, love, and I'll make us some tea.'

Mrs Park sat on the edge of the sofa, the blanket over her knees, hands clasped in her lap and she looked at once older, vulnerable, delicate. 'I'm sorry it's turned out like this,' she said. 'We go to such efforts with the retreat – all we want is to make it comfortable and peaceful, a safe space, you know?'

'Stop; it's not your fault,' Sabina said. 'We'll relax here for a day or two, and then a mechanic can come and fix the cars and we'll be on our way. We'll come back again, maybe in the summer when there's less rain.'

'By the time the cars are fixed, you might decide to stay for the week after all,' said Mrs Park.

Darkness leeched from the corners of the room, and they saw thick clouds gather through the windows. Joshua Park came in with a tray of tea things, only to disappear again, saying he had an idea what they could do.

He returned with two board games and a box of Jenga bricks. Sabina laughed and clapped her hands on her thighs, said she really wished they had some wine now, and Blue felt the tension ease a little. She could get through another night, another two even, if they stuck together, kept cheerful and occupied, if she kept her gaze on the German woman with the giddy laugh, on the old man with the weak heart, and away from dark corners.

They started with Jenga, built the tower up, and egged each other on as the blocks were removed and restacked. Despite his grumpiness, Milton proved best at it and said he was years ahead of them all in practice. Only Molly Park struggled. On her third go, the tower tumbled; a slight twitch of her hand sent it down and Blue suspected she'd done it on purpose. She thought Mrs Park wasn't enjoying herself.

When they rebuilt the tower (the best of three method would decide an overall winner), Mrs Park sat on her hands and looked prickly. Sabina and Mr Park rebuilt the tower. Milton divided the fallen blocks into threes and passed the sets in turn to the others. The structure was sound, they played again and took it in turns to remove and replace – Milton, Mrs Park, Mr Park, Sabina. And then Blue.

Middle row, outermost left brick. She touched it with the tip of her index finger, jolted as if she'd been burned.

'Once you've touched it, you have to play it,' Milton said. 'Rules is rules.'

It was nothing, Blue told herself. A flash of nothing, four meaningless words, it won't happen again.

She stretched forward, pincered the brick between thumb and fore-finger and fire burned through both. It was not nothing. They were not four meaningless words. They were names: *Eleanor, Lauren, Jessica Pike.*

The sensation's familiarity was an odd comfort, but the experience was incomplete. No images accompanied the names, no emotion; Blue couldn't untangle one from another. The tower seesawed, Sabina gasped and Blue wavered, too scared to let go, too scared not to. The girls' names washed colours across her vision: the grey-green of hopelessness, the dark, dark red of red pain.

Eleanor.

The tower collapsed, rained bricks on the table and floor.

Lauren.

Sabina laughed and Mr Park whooped.

Jessica Pike.

'That makes me the winner,' Milton said.

'You can put the block down now.' Sabina nudged Blue in the side so that her hand dropped, the brick fell and the names melted in the ether.

'You did very well, though. I think the blocks aren't quite even in places. You did very well,' said Mrs Park, and her husband put a hand on her knee to stop her.

'It's just a game,' Blue said.

Mr Park asked which they would like to play next.

'Since I've been crowned Jenga King,' said Milton.

Mr Park passed the two boxes across the table to Sabina, but Mrs Park snatched them away.

Her forced smile faded. 'Let's do something else.' She poured the Jenga blocks back into their box so haphazardly that the lid wouldn't close, and she held it down with her thumb. 'I'll find something else.' The blanket fell to the floor, and she walked out with the board games clutched to her chest.

'Oh dear,' Milton said, and Sabina grimaced. Mr Park pinched the bridge of his nose and sighed, and as he sighed, the air became still.

The light from the fire grew stronger, the shadows cast by the flames more defined.

Tendrils of scent wove through the room, curled through Blue's nostrils.

The rank, cloying smell of long-unwashed bedding, of sweat and sourness and meat. Blue gagged, hand to mouth, and closed her eyes tight, wouldn't look.

Eleanor, Lauren, Jessica Pike.

'Jesus, Blue, are you OK?' Sabina leant towards her, put a hand on her sleeve. Blue's arm trembled.

Blue nodded, opened her mouth to speak, but the smell swam over her tongue, hit her at the back of her throat, and it was worse than any spoiled humbug of Bodhi's, any soured milk or stale biscuit.

Milton dropped his hat, pressed himself up, moved to help her.

My God, she thought, can't they smell it?

Mr Park was up, too, his face wild with concern.

'Are you sick? You're pale as a—' Sabina started, and the weight of her hand on Blue's arm, the warmth of her skin through Blue's sleeve, made her feel human again – 'and you're shaking.'

The fire hushed, the stink faded.

'Here we are.' Mrs Park lumbered back in, a boxed jigsaw held like a prize to her chest. She stopped dead when she saw Blue. 'What's happened?'

Milton stood in front of her, Mr Park at one side, and Sabina still held her arm. Blue shook herself clear, apologised and felt her colour rise. They all looked at her.

'It's nothing,' she said and found the taste and nausea had left her. Humiliation surpassed terror. 'I'm sorry. Probably just low blood sugar or something.'

'Right, well, that we can solve.' Mr Park marched out to the kitchen, returned with a large tin of wrapped chocolates. 'Don't look at me like that, Molly; we can relax the rules on healthy eating just this once.'

'You'll ruin your dinner,' she said fondly, and Mr Park handed the tin to Blue.

She took one, concentrated on the sweetness of the chocolate-covered toffee, the caramel flavour and buttery scent, tried to keep the shock of that smell from her mind. It was impossible.

Mrs Park stacked the journals and pens neatly on the floor to make a space on the coffee table. She asked if Blue felt better, if she suffered from hypoglycaemia, if anything else would help her, and Sabina saw Blue's discomfort at the interrogation and changed the subject.

'You're not a fan of board games, Molly?' Sabina asked.

'They were meant for—' Mrs Park began, but her husband put a hand on her hand, and she said, 'Not really, no.'

The wind sucked at the chimney with a howl and a groan.

Sabina helped herself to a chocolate.

Mr Park rubbed his wife's back.

Milton picked up his hat and smoothed its beige headband.

Flurries of rain tapped the window.

'Right; let's talk tactics.' Mr Park's face came alive as he divided the puzzle between the base of the box and the upturned lid. 'Corner pieces and edges – dig them out and put them on the table. Then we can start to put the frame together.' He showed more relish in the task than Blue had seen him show all weekend, and his enthusiasm eased the tension. Even Milton held out his hat and accepted a handful of pieces to sort through.

'You don't like Jenga, but you're happy to play at jigsaws. Why one and not the other?' Sabina leant over the coffee table with her elbows on her knees and Blue marvelled again at the woman's directness.

Mrs Park blushed and focused on the puzzle, its pieces spread out in the upturned lid.

'Everyone has their own preferences,' Mr Park began. 'We have all sorts of games on hand for guests to play, and I just forgot that Molly—'

'It's all right, Josh,' Mrs Park said. She put the puzzle lid down. 'Truth is, I always associate those sorts of games with children. We weren't blessed with our own. I made a sort of peace with that, years ago, but sometimes it upsets me still, and silly things can set it off, I suppose.'

'I understand,' said Sabina, with her cocktail of sympathy and interest, 'and I'm sorry.'

'We've all had our trials,' Mrs Park said. 'It's easier, sometimes, doing things that I don't associate with children. I doubt an eleven-year-old would want to help find the corner pieces.' She fished out a corner and, with a flourish, placed it on the table. Blue wondered why, of all the ages she could have chosen for a fictitious child, she had settled on eleven.

'I find ice-cream parlours hard to walk past.' Sabina stared hard at the jigsaw. 'I'd take her to as many as possible whenever she visited me, and we would rank them; we had an Excel spreadsheet and would give marks on flavours, toppings, size of the scoops, and at the end of the trip, we'd revisit the place that scored highest.'

'With your sister?' Blue asked.

'And my niece.'

'I'm sorry,' Blue said. 'Did they both—'

'I lost them both when my brother-in-law died. My sister hasn't spoken to me since.' Sabina fondled the pale blue edges of her puzzle piece.

'What happened to the brother-in-law?' Milton asked and Blue was glad he had spoken because her words wouldn't come. Though relieved Sabina's sister was alive, Blue found it hard to swallow the shock of it. She had been sure, so sure.

'I was driving him to the airport and lost control of the car,' Sabina said, and Blue realised why she had badly needed to come to a place like Hope Marsh House.

'That must have been very difficult,' Mrs Park said, in a tone that screamed *therapist*. Sabina deflected the attention.

'Did you ever try to adopt?'

Blue winced, thought it acutely personal, but the Parks didn't bat an eyelid. Maybe Sabina wasn't the first guest to ask.

'We looked into it,' Mr Park said, and Mrs Park looked intently at the jigsaw pieces with her lips pressed.

'But you didn't apply?'

'We did, but these things don't always turn out how you'd hope,' he said.

'They turned you down?' Sabina said, incredulous. 'I can't think of a better couple to adopt a child.'

There were tears in Mrs Park's eyes and she dabbed them away, thanked Sabina for her kindness. Milton held his hat, watched the Parks, didn't say a word and the three names rang loud in Blue's head.

'Do you have children?' Sabina asked Milton.

'We had one of each,' he said. The past tense carried louder than his voice and Molly reached for him, placed a hand on his knee and he swatted her off, said, 'Please, don't.'

'My parents adopted me.' Sabina cut through the tension and nudged Blue's foot with her own. 'I bet you didn't read that in my stars?'

'No, I didn't,' Blue said, and it was on the tip of her tongue to say that she never read stars, only tarot, but she stopped herself. 'Was it your adoptive parents who wanted you to come here?'

'They're my only parents.' She moved her foot away and Blue wondered why Sabina could ask direct questions without awkwardness, why Sabina's tone was deemed acceptable and hers not, wondered if she would ever learn to say the right thing, use the right tone, pick the right words.

'Was your sister adopted, too?' Blue asked and tried to soften her voice like Mrs Park.

'No. My parents had two daughters before they had me – both of them blue-eyed, blonde-haired *Venuses*,' she said with a wry smile. 'They adopted me from a family in Berlin and then my younger brother from Vietnam. They are very ... charitable, my parents.'

'They must have big hearts,' Mrs Park said.

'Yes, though I think my sisters' hearts were made smaller as a result. Do you have any nieces or nephews?'

'We're both only children,' Mr Park said, 'so it's ...'

'Just us,' finished Mrs Park.

Blue slotted a jigsaw piece into the border of the skyline, a mottle of blue and white. It hit her like a taser, and sent a live wire from fingers to brain. *Eleanor. Lauren. Jessica Pike.*

Her fingers jerked away.

The wall lamps dimmed, brightened, dimmed again, and Mrs Park said, 'The weather's affecting the electrics.' Milton grunted assent. No one noticed Blue's jolt.

Who had put the connecting pieces of the puzzle down? Who had touched what? To whom did these names belong?

Eleanor. Lauren. Jessica Pike.

Mr Park leant forward and rummaged through the jigsaw for more edges. Mrs Park spun a piece slowly between her index and thumb, her eyes glazed. She stifled a yawn.

With redoubled effort, Blue tried to block the names from her head and blink away the memory of the long pale hair, the white skin, the dark eyes. She told herself it didn't matter, that it could be explained, that the stress of the last few days and weeks and years had splintered her reason.

But the face had seared to her retina, the names repeated, and she couldn't pull one from the other, nor could she link them with anyone here.

Never had she experienced this outside the readings and demonstrations of old. But her adult life had been small, she saw now, her interaction with people purposefully limited.

'What are you doing?' Sabina said with some amusement.

Blue had leant forward, her fingertips pressed into the remaining pieces of the puzzle as she tried to fathom who she'd tapped into. She felt nothing but the bricks of closely built walls, sensed secrets and skeletons behind them, interlinked and indistinguishable. She heard nothing but those names – Eleanor, Lauren, Jessica Pike. Saw nothing but long hair and pale skin.

'Nothing.' She felt their gazes upon her, her neck hot with their bewilderment. 'Making sure they're tight together, that's all.'

'Is this one of your funny tricks?' asked Sabina and Blue laughed it off, said no, don't be silly.

'What tricks are they?' asked Mrs Park.

'Blue has some magic way of knowing things about people. What did you call it? Reverse NLP?'

'It's nothing really.'

'She used it to find out about my sister; I thought it was a ruse to get me to talk about her.' Sabina showed less of the outrage she had shown earlier.

'I didn't use it, not on purpose.' Blue braced herself for questions from Mrs Park, tried to think of a way she could fob it off, but Mrs Park zoned in on something quite different.

'Would you like to talk about your sister?' Mrs Park said, careful not to look at Sabina head-on, as though the other woman were a deer who would spring rather than admit vulnerability. Blue quietened her breath, listened to every word spoken, watched every gesture; more could be gleaned if she paid attention.

'Honestly? No, I wouldn't like to,' Sabina said. 'I know that's why I'm here, but ...' She shrugged her shoulders and let the end of her sentence hang in the air, a bomb she doubted anyone would want to catch, yet Mrs Park caught it with deft hands. Mr Park bowed his head, studied the puzzle as if he'd received an unspoken cue from his wife. Blue saw what a close-knit couple they were.

'You don't have to. Perhaps you'd like to talk about your niece instead?' Mrs Park passed Sabina the tin of chocolates, understood perhaps that it was easier to open up when your hands and eyes were occupied with another task, be it the piecing together of a puzzle or the touch of bright, sweet wrappers.

'It's impossible to think of one without the other,' Sabina said. 'My niece is the image of my sister.' She tried to smile but gave up and let her face fall. 'Blonde, dark eyes, thin as a twig, just as headstrong and deter-mined, but far funnier, much sweeter.'

The wall lamps dimmed again, didn't brighten so quickly this time. Sabina smiled, but her smile was a sad one. 'She's my sister's only child, my parents' only grandchild.'

Blue heard footsteps above, the light tread of small feet on old wooden floorboards. No one else noticed.

'I'm her godmother,' Sabina said.

A swell of wind fed the fire. Flames licked the room in dark orange.

If she climbed the stairs, Blue would see that Sabina's bedroom door stood open. She would see the girl. But Sabina's niece was alive in a German town, mourning her father's death. Blue waited for Sabina to carry on, but her words had dried up, and her body language offered Blue nothing.

Blue looked at Sabina in the armchair, ostensibly engrossed in the small coloured jigsaw pieces, but Blue knew she paid them no attention; she just didn't want to talk.

There wasn't a cut-throat side to this woman; Blue was sure of it. She was capable, good-humoured, so beautiful that Blue could barely look at her without feeling the rush of her looks. A woman like this couldn't be ...

Yet the dead old man had followed his daughter, and she hadn't been evil; she had tried to do the right thing by him but shouldered the guilt, nonetheless.

'What happened to your niece?' Blue said, and Sabina's fingers hovered above the jigsaw.

'What do you mean?'

'Sabina will tell us when she's ready,' Mrs Park said. She was calm but firm, and Blue keenly felt the admonishment.

'I used to do jigsaws with my gran when I was a kid,' Mr Park said with the skill of a man experienced at defusing friction. 'Always loved them. And card games. Whist was my speciality; ever played?' The conversation turned to safe ground, and Sabina visibly relaxed. She and the Parks reminisced about childhood games, childhood summers, what they would do this summer. Milton contributed little, but nodded at the mention of gin rummy. Blue listened. She skimmed each piece of the jigsaw, picked out blues to make the sky, tried to find more than that one mad glimmer of insight.

There were no holidays abroad when Blue was a child, none as an adult. Would they be interested in the day trips to psychic festivals her parents had taken her on, where they toured crystal-filled tents, and soothsayers read the lines of their palms? Mother had talked of going to Glastonbury, Devlin had promised it as a honeymoon, then a late honeymoon, then a second honeymoon, but the promise faded to ashes.

The Parks' gentle banter soothed the conviction that Blue was being watched, that something sinister lurked in this house, in these people.

These were good folk, she told herself. Ordinary people, the sort she'd wanted to be around all her life. The only abnormality in the company was her.

Mrs Park told Sabina about her career as a nurse, how she met Joshua Park in her late twenties.

'I'd never met anyone like him, someone who had left it all behind to follow their passion. You used to run a paper mill, didn't you, my love?

Worked his way to the top and then, well, the world was his oyster after that.' Mrs Park squeezed her husband's knee. He didn't take his eyes off the jigsaw but smiled, and to Blue's surprise, he blushed.

'I never fitted in in the business world; too many morally bankrupt intellectuals vying for attention, and they were all so soulless, so immoral, so uncreative. The mill I worked for was left to me by the owner; I met Molly shortly after I'd sold it and we set out together. Never looked back.' He nudged her fondly with his shoulder and added four yellow pieces to his corner of the puzzle; a bank of primroses took shape.

They were all assigned a colour to search for among the rubble. Mr Park's was yellow.

The colour of loyalty and happiness.

Of cowardice and deceit.

'I'm going to grab a jumper.' Sabina stood and stretched her arms high. 'And I may as well take my case back upstairs. Do you want me to take yours up, Blue?'

Their bags waited at the front door, brought back in from the cars and abandoned. Sabina waited for an answer, and though Blue told herself to get a grip, buck up and stop being ridiculous, stupid, scared, she knew that if she were to pick up her bag and follow Sabina upstairs, they would see that her door stood open, that something unholy lurked there.

'I'll take it up after dinner,' Blue said, and then to Mrs Park, 'if that's all right with you?'

'Of course,' Mrs Park said. 'You're a touch pale; a good dinner will sort you out.'

'Speaking of which, I better get cooking.' Mr Park rose from the sofa with a groan. 'Risotto OK for everyone?'

Blue had never tasted it, but Sabina's enthusiasm was proof enough that it was worth a try. Mrs Park offered to make coffee and followed her husband into the kitchen, whilst Sabina fetched jumper from her case. Blue saw her slip a slim metal flask into her back pocket.

'Not exactly the week I'd envisaged,' she pointed to the coffee table and the incomplete puzzle, 'but it's surprisingly relaxing; I'll never mock my friends for their jigsaws again.' Sabina pulled on yesterday's orange jumper and returned to her armchair by the fire.

'What do you make of this place?' Milton said. It was the longest sentence he'd uttered so far.

'The retreat? I don't think I can really judge it,' said Sabina. 'I doubt most guests spend their morning fishing dead rabbits out of rivers and then doing jigsaws in the afternoon. What's it normally like?'

'Busy.'

'Because there are more people here, or because Molly's schedule is so …'

'Full?' offered Blue.

'Oppressive,' said Milton, ever dour.

'You must find it useful, though, if you keep coming back?' Sabina said.

'Not yet,' he said, 'but eventually, I will. What do you make of those two?' He nodded his head to the passageway door. Sabina followed his gaze, but Blue kept hers on the old man, wondered which pieces of the Jenga tower he'd touched, which pieces of the puzzle. Which name belonged to him.

'They're a lovely couple,' Sabina said, and Blue agreed, said they seemed friendly, helpful.

Milton pondered their answer. Blue felt she was being put through some sort of trial. Was he testing the waters before he confided in them?

Did she see him last night wandering the corridor upstairs, or was it a dream?

'I've heard them tell the story of their lives four times now,' he said. 'Word for word, it's the same every time. Odd, no?'

'They're just well used to telling it, like a play they've rehearsed over and again,' said Sabina. Milton looked to Blue, who shrugged and smiled and couldn't think of anything to add.

If a test had been set, they had failed. He stood up and reached for the walking frame. 'I'm going to my room,' he said.

'Mrs Park's bringing coffee,' Blue said, 'won't you stay?'

'I've only just finished my tea, so no. I'll see you at dinner.' He walked off without another word. The tap of his frame on the flagstones echoed, even after the passageway door swung shut.

'Do you think he's all right?' Blue said.

'I doubt he'd come to a retreat specialising in grief therapy if he was all right,' Sabina said, reflective.

'Maybe his wife died?' Blue said and thought about Mother and Devlin. 'It can take a long time to recover from the loss of your spouse, far longer than most people appreciate.'

'I know,' Sabina said, and Blue felt foolish and insensitive.

'I'm sorry, I didn't mean anything about your brother-in—'

'I know, it's OK.' She reflexively touched her back pocket. The metal hip flask caught the firelight. 'Why did you come here anyway?'

Footsteps and a muffled clatter came from the kitchen and another, softer rush of wind through the chimney breast.

'My mother.' There was little else Blue could say. That Bridget Ford could be reduced to small talk was incomprehensible; the thought that she could spin out well-practised lines Park-style felt impossible. How could Blue trap Mother's life in a phrase or sum up the discombobulation of her death in a sentence, a paragraph, a single conversation?

'My turn to apologise,' Sabina said. 'Are you sick of it yet, people telling you they're sorry?'

'Not many people have, to be fair.' She'd had no one to turn to. Blue dealt with her death alone, so too the horrors she'd discovered after her mother had died.

'Is your dad still alive?' Sabina said.

'No.' Blue wanted to ask about Sabina's childhood, job, dead brother-in-law; discuss anything but Mother.

Yet this is why she had come to Hope Marsh.

'It must be hard, dealing with it alone,' Sabina said. 'I can understand why you'd need to come somewhere like this. It's a brave thing to do.'

'Well, the same applies to you,' Blue said.

'Not at all; this was booked for me, as you know.'

'I was right, then?'

'Yes, you were right. I'd have been happy not to come at all, but my parents decided something must be done and so—'

Blue felt it then, a flash but not enough to get a handle on. Sadness was at the core of it, orbited by guilt.

'Why did something have to be done?' Blue said, wanting to know, afraid to know. 'What happened after—'

'Can't you tell? I thought that was your party trick.'

'Not all of it, no.'

And what would happen if Blue did find out? What would be proven? That Sabina's niece and not her brother-in-law had died? Or that Blue had lost her grip on reality, again?

Which would be worse – to think that figure was a hallucination, or face up to the possibility that it could be something else, something more horrifying?

And then what would that make Sabina?

13 to 14

Blackpool Front was a hive in summer. Devlin booked space at a working men's club near the pier and advertised public demonstrations. When Blue was deemed old enough, she sat onstage, too. Her parents used the pretext of experience, of more money earned, of publicising her name so that she could start her own tarot business when she was sixteen.

There wasn't a chance she'd do anything else.

Devlin said that tarot was enough, but after Blue had seen the dead old man, years ago now, Bridget had hoped (and Blue feared) that it might become a trait, that soon she'd see ghosts everywhere and Blue could charge a fee to translate the words of the dead.

It wasn't the case. Few ghosts wandered Lancashire, it seemed. The only other spectre Blue had seen was a sad-eyed, pinch-faced woman who had shadowed a bearded man around the aisles of a covered market when Blue was thirteen. She'd asked Mother why it was that a woman would walk around a market in a torn minidress and one thigh-high shiny white boot.

She pointed the woman out.

'Where, Blue?' Bridget Ford said. 'All I see is a man with a beard and a peak cap.' And then her mother had paused, her eyes bright, almost feverish. 'Oh my goodness, is it another? Do you think you've finally seen another? Where are they? Where has that man gone? We've got to find them.'

They didn't. The crowded market hid them fast, and Blue would never see that man again, nor the woman who had walked so close behind that, had she lived, her breath would have dampened the bearded man's neck.

That night, after Mother had tucked her into bed and the house was still, Bodhi moved out of his shadow and came to her. Blue lay in bed, head on her pillow, almost eye to eye with the small boy.

'Another one,' Bodhi whispered and the words were his own, they did not leak into Blue's mind or coat her tongue. They hit her ear, cold and pure, as though real. And Blue did not question why he spoke to her now, or why his voice was so clear. She wondered instead if he would answer the questions Mother could not.

'How comes I see ghosts and no one else can?'

'You don't see ghosts,' he said, and for a moment he was light to her, he was joy, he was all she had wanted Mother to be. But his lips didn't smile. 'You see victims.'

And there was no joy in this child, no light.

Blue didn't understand. 'Why did she follow that man?'

'The taking of life binds them.'

'How come I don't see more of them?' It was a question she'd overheard Mother ask Devlin, who hadn't an answer to give.

'You see what there is.'

'What does that mean?'

'You can't see what's not there.'

'You mean there aren't very many?'

But Bodhi wouldn't say more, and when Blue said that's fine, if there weren't that many to see then maybe there wasn't any work in it, perhaps she could do something else, Bodhi laughed, and Blue had to close her eyes.

Ghosts were rare and couldn't be banked on, so it was decided that Blue should concentrate on the tarot alone. At fourteen, she held her own small audience in the clubs, a couple of hours before the limelight-loving Devlin Devine's. The tables were clothed in cheap red satin and the wall behind Blue's chair draped in glitter-starred gauze. The bar was open, though Blue's show started at three-thirty, and bowls of peanuts were sold with the beer.

The hall was dimly lit with side lamps, and she had to ask her mother to fetch one more so she could see the cards better. She waited onstage, two decks of cards on the little table. Her mouth was dry. In the quiet lull before the punters came in, she could hear the heavy knock of her heart.

Six people turned up that first day. She read them in turn, too shy to look at the audience, too aware of the empty tables and chairs, worried that her parents would be disheartened. It takes time to build a reputation, Devlin said.

The second show was less formidable, the third less again, and by the fourth, Blue held her chin up and didn't stammer, though she struggled to meet people's eyes.

A middle-aged woman with a couple Blue presumed were man and wife sat at a table in the middle row. A slick of fear coated their seats, rank as fish guts and so strong Blue tasted it. She beckoned them forward, and it was the man who stood first; greasy brown hair grew to his armpits and he had a thin goatee beard in need of a trim, narrow eyes, narrow shoulders, a narrow pigeon chest.

The young woman was a step behind him, fragile as a half-starved sparrow, hair like tawny feathers.

It wasn't right.

She looked to the wings for Devlin and Mother, tried to show her discomfort in her expression, hoped they'd stop the show, but they grinned; Devlin nodded her on, Bridget gave a thumbs up.

The young woman stood with the man onstage, so close that strands of his long, greasy black hair touched her cheek. Her shoulders hunched, her eyes never looked for Blue's. She was used to not being seen.

Yet it was the young woman, not the man, who sat at the table and spoke.

'Was a birthday present, this, from me mum,' she said. Blue glanced at the brandy-cheeked woman, whose hair had whitened prematurely. 'Never done this before. Don't really know what to do. I don't really—' She sighed and took the deck of cards listlessly from Blue when she asked her to, and shuffled them once, barely rearranged them at all. She cut the deck, pushed it back, and Blue touched her hand.

Held it.

Blue saw things no fourteen-year-old should see: bruises on her arms, back and belly, her phone broken, ribs broken, spirit broken, photos burned, her skin burned, her hair pulled out in clumps that bled, the baby that died inside her, the black eyes, swollen cheekbones, the second

123

baby inside her and the kicks that killed it. Blue saw her pulled upstairs by her ankle, saw that same ankle break, saw her locked in her room whilst it healed disjointed.

Blue saw her walk again, saw her walk to the kitchen, walk to the kitchen and open a drawer and get out a knife and plunge the knife into the cold man's heart.

There was a police cell, a jail cell, a courtroom, bail refused. The dead man's family called her names and spat at her. Blue saw that this happened several years ago but lived in her memory fresh as bread.

Blue didn't look at the ghost of the man, who cursed and laughed and picked at his crooked front teeth. Instead, she kept the woman's hand in hers and read the cards.

'The Eight of Pentacles: life will be challenging for a few months, but then it will get better – the Wheel of Fortune tells me this. It's upside down, so tells me your fortunes will soon reverse, and all the hardship you've received over the last few years will go away.'

'That's not what the Wheel means.' A woman in a pink velvet blouse shook her head from her seat near the front. 'It means—'

'It does when it comes after the Eight of Pentacles but before the King of Wands.' Blue dared to look the speaker in the eye, drew on all of Devlin's old tricks. She had never spoken back to an adult, but nor had she held so delicately someone's fate.

'You'll find happiness, you will; you just have to hang on for a little while longer.'

It was the first lie she'd told at a demonstration. The cards showed Blue the bedroom the woman found it so hard to leave, the food she found so hard to eat, the phone that never rang, the shower that was never used, the friends who had left her and the vodka and razor and pills and their promise of peace. Blue saw the woman's funeral, heard the wails of the woman's desolate mother echo through the near-empty church. Blue understood what the cards predicted, and the only way to change that, to help her, was to tell her different. If Blue spoke the truth, the woman would buckle. The dead man at her shoulder would win.

In the wings, Bridget clasped her hands, her mouth in a perfect 'o'. Devlin's kind, round face creased in concern, his weight held on his toes as though ready to pounce onstage and scoop Blue up.

'Happiness?' The young woman sounded unsure, but her shoulders straightened some.

Blue turned over the following two cards, knew what they would mean, knew that she would ignore them and tell the woman what she needed to hear. The gaze of the crowd bothered Blue less; the urgent need to rescue this woman eclipsed the usual nerves. She leant forward, touched the Knave of Swords.

'It'll take all your will to keep focused, but if you can look forward instead of back, keep your eye on the future, then you'll pass through this period of turmoil—'

The dead man's hand came down on the table.

If she looked up, Blue would stare into the dead man's face. A sulphurous smell stung Blue's nose and eyes, and it wasn't the man's dead body; it was the reek of the dead man's soul.

'Yes? Then what?' the woman's mother asked from the audience.

'You OK?' whispered Devlin from the wing.

Even bold Bodhi hid behind Bridget's skirts.

The dead man crouched. His chin rested at table height so Blue could see his dead eyes and his snarled dead lips. He knew that Blue could see him.

I'll wait for her, the dead man mouthed, strings of saliva suspended in his maw. *Tell that fucking bitch I'll wait for her. When I get her—*

Blue whimpered, clamped shut her eyes, but still she could see the dead man, feel what the dead man wanted her to feel, and it was everything terrible, everything bleak. Heat spread from Blue's groin down her thighs; her underpants and trousers stuck fast. She was too terrified to be ashamed.

'Then what?' the mother repeated, and Blue felt a touch to her shoulder, the warm, gentle hand of Devlin Devine.

'She just needs a moment,' came Bridget's reply. 'She'll be quite fine in a moment.'

'Are you OK, lass? Do you need to stop?' Devlin's voice was soft, and Blue grabbed his hand and held it tight, still too afraid to open her eyes. She had to go on.

'You can't do it; you can't give up,' Blue said, her voice quiet so no one else would hear, glad Devlin was there to shield her from the small crowd. 'You need to carry on living. If you give up now, he'll have won, do you understand?'

'Aye,' the woman said, and her voice caught. 'I know, but I can't do it, I just ... I have nothing. There's nothing. It's all nothing—'

'You have to hold on—'

'– I know my mum'll be—'

'– not because of your mum,' Blue said, 'because of him.'

The audience murmured. The woman's mother walked towards the stage, and Bridget asked her to sit back down, to wait a moment, just a moment.

The dead man's hatred was livid and hot. Even with her eyes shut, Blue could sense it.

'He's waiting for you.' Blue opened her eyes to a slit, enough to take in the woman angled forward to listen, to see the dead man behind her, his mouth close to her ear. His tongue flicked like a snake's in and out, in and out, and he watched Blue all the while.

'If you pass now, he'll be waiting for you.' Blue didn't know if this were true, had no idea what happened after you died, if the dead man really would be able to hurt her, but Blue had her attention, and she didn't stop. 'You have to keep on living, for years and years, so he can't get to you. The only way to be free of him is to keep on living.'

Blue willed her to understand, and the woman nodded, said OK, that she would, she promised she would, and Blue felt the relief rise in a flood of tears. She turned her face to Devlin, buried her head in her dad's soft shoulder. He was safety and warmth, and he promised Blue that the woman had heard her, had agreed, took Blue offstage and to the back where he filled her with sweet tea for the shock and helped her change into clean, dry clothes whilst Bridget explained to the audience that the show was over for the day. She handed out cards with their details and asked them to book for their next demonstration.

They did. It was sold out within a week, two more booked after that as word spread about the strange young girl who could sense things, really sense things.

'In some cultures, you'd be considered a shaman,' Bridget told Blue at bedtime one night, just the two of them up in her room. She still tucked Blue in, still kissed her forehead goodnight even though she was a teenager now. Bridget would carry on doing this until the day she could no longer get out of bed.

'What's a shaman?' Blue asked. Her curtains weren't drawn, and the windows across the street were lit up with flickers from TV screens.

'They're wise men and healers. They're more respected than the hunters, the makers, the chief, even. In some places, they're seen as gods.' Bridget kissed her, and Blue breathed in the slight musty dampness from her mother's hair and the herbal musk of her dress. 'You're a little god, my sweet girl.'

The ability to communicate with murdered souls did not feel godlike to Blue. That night, in her box bedroom decorated with tarot posters Mother had bought, she didn't feel omniscient but scared. In everyday life, she felt feeble.

In the morning, she asked her mother to explain what she meant. Devlin shot Bridget a look, told Blue not to worry; her mother had exaggerated. Bridget shot Devlin a look straight back.

'It's not healthy,' Devlin said to Bridget later. 'It's not the kind of thing you should say to a child,' and Bridget had cried, and Devlin had apologised, and Blue listened to it all from the top of the stairs.

Bridget sank into a slump. Didn't speak, eat, wash. Arlo sat in the room with her, pounded her tiny fists into the wall or floor whilst Bodhi followed Blue with a scowl and told Blue that this was all her fault.

When the email arrived towards the end of the week, Devlin read it aloud, and the words brought Bridget back. He had been to the library to check their inbox, paid ten pence to the librarian to print this one off.

'It's from the mother of the woman you read for, you know the one I mean? The one with the—'

'Aye, I know.' Blue inched towards the kitchen door and wanted to get out before Devlin could tell Blue that the woman had succumbed to the vodka and razor and pills, that her words had been useless. She pictured the dead man at her shoulder, remembered the promise of what he would do when death reunited them.

'She says her daughter's got herself a job. First she's ever had in her life, working at a bicycle shop!' Devlin took off his glasses to wipe dry his eyes. 'Isn't that wonderful? She says it was you who helped her. Ever since your reading she's had a new focus, seems more determined than her mum's seen her in years. Isn't that just … just …' Devlin leant back on the kitchen chair, unable to say just what it was. He rested his hands on his large round belly. 'You did a good thing, lass; you should be right proud. You helped that woman.'

From the hallway came Mother's voice, dreamy as though she was half awake.

'You're a little god,' she said.

The Five of Cups

'Here we are then.' Mrs Park opened the door. The moment was lost.

A tray with coffees and small almond biscuits was put on a side table by the stairs. 'So as not to disturb the puzzle,' Mrs Park said. 'Where's Milton?'

'He went to his room,' Sabina said. 'Molly, do you have any sugar?'

Mrs Park went back to fetch the sugar bowl, and Sabina reached for the flask in her pocket, shot Blue a devilish smile.

'Fancy making these Irish?' She poured a glug of whisky into her coffee and then some into Blue's before she could say that she didn't drink, didn't have the head for it.

'It's Saturday night.' Sabina winked and then gave a shush and suppressed a smile as Mrs Park came back with the sugar bowl.

Blue was tempted to leave the spiked coffee where it was and pick up the unadulterated cup, but that would mean the whisky would be left for Mrs Park.

'Demerara, that all right?' Molly Park said.

They were all adults, Blue told herself. The flood had put paid to the retreat; there was no reason Sabina couldn't enjoy a drink. Blue, too, for that matter.

The coffee filled her mouth with a sharp, sweet heat, and an antiseptic burn hit her throat. Sabina eyed her over the rim of her cup. They returned to the puzzle and pieced it together, and when Mrs Park excused herself to help with dinner, Sabina added another small glug to their mugs.

Blue volunteered to take Milton's jigsaw pieces in with her own and she touched each in turn but got nothing, only the numbness of whisky and the taint of despair. Hers, his; she couldn't tell.

The wooziness intensified when Joshua Park called them through for dinner, and Blue rose from her chair. She was relieved to be able to line her stomach with food. She forgot the strange visions, forgot the car cloistered in the barn, the open doors, the floodwater, the fear she would never get home.

Instead, she saw the shape of Sabina's body beneath her jumper and jeans. She saw the motherly kindness in Mrs Park's eyes, heard the humour in Mr Park's baritone, caught the struggle in each of Milton's chesty breaths and felt sad for him. Blue carried her coffee cup to the kitchen and drank the dregs as they sat at the table. She no longer worried about the rules, any of the rules.

A bottle of Sancerre stood proud on the counter, and Joshua Park poured a glass for his wife. 'You can take the night off,' he said and then poured a drink for everyone else, and even Milton seemed to cheer up.

The whisky and wine loosened Sabina's tongue. She revealed herself as a raconteur, made everyone laugh with anecdotes, and when the food was all eaten, and Mrs Park sat a bowl of bread-and-butter pudding at the table, Joshua Park used his hand as a gavel and stood up.

'It's Saturday night, we're flooded in, the retreat's on hold' – he opened the pantry door beside the safe to reveal a far deeper cupboard stacked with, among many other things, a wine rack – 'a dessert wine to go with pudding!'

'That's for special occasions—' Mrs Park said.

'What more of a special occasion than this?'

'It's for Ea—'

'Easter's a month away; we'll buy another before then.'

'Just one and small glasses—' said Mrs Park.

'Enormous glasses,' said Mr Park and emptied the bottle between the five.

Tension oozed from Blue's body like tree sap. The golden-amber wine was sweet and delicious and melted the last of her unease. Mrs Park looked unsettled, but even she had to smile when Sabina suggested they go and listen to music by the fire and that Molly Park, head of the retreat, host extraordinaire, should play maestro.

Another bottle of wine was brought out, and Blue was amazed at how easily the rule on alcohol had been abandoned.

In front of the fire, Mr Park told his own stories about working his way up the ranks, life as a chancer, a businessman, a determined anti-rogue, and Mrs Park turned on the sound system. She played soft, sweet jazz, the music at odds with Mr Park's tales of colleagues who spent a fortune every night in Birmingham strip clubs, who got so drunk on a Thursday they turned up drunk to work the following morning.

'Were you an angel then, Mr Park?' Sabina asked, one eyebrow lifted.

'I had no interest in that lifestyle,' he said. 'I was smart enough to know how to play the game and get out early.'

'You never joined your colleagues at the clubs?' Sabina said.

'I was happy to wave them off and let them dig their own early graves.' Mr Park drank the rest of his glass in one swig, unscrewed the lid off the next bottle. 'I learnt that it's not always wise to follow; sometimes it's best to forge your own path.'

'You clearly worked very hard,' Sabina said.

'I work hard to get what I want,' he replied, and Mrs Park surprised them when she took the bottle from her husband's hand and topped everyone up. All talk of the past was drowned.

Another log was thrown on to the fire.

The box of chocolates was brought out once more.

Only Milton stayed silent, his chin resting on his chest as though he had fallen asleep. Twice, Blue caught him blinking, muttering to himself, and she knew he paid full attention.

Sabina relaxed into her armchair, the long-stemmed glass at home in her hand. 'Have you always lived in Blackpool?' Her accent stretched the last word and made it exotic.

The glass of wine was Blue's fifth, and she was glad to be in a soft chair. Glad to be close to this woman, the first person in so long who seemed like someone Blue could befriend.

'I was born in Preston. When did you move to London?'

'In my twenties. What did you do before your job at the hospice?'

'Worked in a warehouse. What did you do before you became an analyst?'

'I've always been an analyst. I studied computer science for my degree. Did you go to university?'

'No. Where did you go?'

'Munich. Where did you go to school?'

'I didn't.' Blue spoke without thought, felt the wine and the whisky and the rich risotto churn. She wanted to reword her answer, but Sabina cocked her head, said,

'You were home-schooled?'

'Aye.'

'She must have been a huge part of your life,' Sabina said, and Blue had no idea how she could sum up how big a part of her life Bridget Ford had been. 'Do you have siblings?'

Blue shook her head. 'I don't see them anymore.'

'So it was just you and your mum?'

'After my dad died, yes.' And it had been, for years after Devlin's heart attack. Just the two of them, in that house. They travelled to shows together, stayed in cheap guest houses together, stood on stages hand in hand until the night a man caught Blue by the throat.

'Tell me about Germany,' Blue said. 'What do you miss about it?' And she leant her cheek on the headrest, and listened to Sabina's stories about growing up, rebellion, fights with her siblings, how she ran away from home, ran back home, left for university and felt home-sick for the first time in her life. She could see what a relief it was for Sabina to talk about something other than her losses, saw her face relax, the lines on her forehead smooth over, and the lines around her eyes deepen with each smile. Her accent got stronger when she spoke about her family, took on a faint twang of London when she mentioned her work.

Blue imagined Sabina's cards as she once imagined the kids' cards who lived on the street. Shuffle the deck and hand them to her, let the tips of their fingers brush, feel the rush of her. You would be the High Priestess, Blue thought. You would be the Queen of Cups.

Wooziness hit Blue with the last sip of wine, and she lolled back in her seat.

'You're a good listener.' Sabina mimicked the posture.

Mr Park yawned. 'My God, it's nearly midnight.'

'Anyone for cocoa?' Mrs Park said with a slur in her voice. Her cheeks were bright pink, her nose too, and her hair was slightly dishevelled.

'You and your cocoa.' Mr Park kissed the top of her head, and Blue saw it through the fug of alcohol, the haze of the fire. It made her melancholic for her mother and the grief Bridget felt when Devlin died.

'I would like one,' said Sabina, 'and so would Blue.'

'Would I?' she laughed.

'Yes, good for the soul.'

'That's fine, just fine,' Mrs Park said, flushed pleasure-pink at the chance to cosset. Her husband collected the wine glasses, refused help from the guests. Blue watched as he chased his wife, listened to Mrs Park giggle as they walked to the kitchen.

'They are adorable.' Sabina followed Blue's gaze.

It didn't take Mrs Park long to make up the drinks, and Blue thought of Bridget's evening chamomile teas and her bedtime kisses of old.

Languor curled its lazy cat tail around them, and their sips of hot chocolate were alternated with yawns. Goodnights were wished, and eventually, Sabina and Blue climbed the wooden hill together.

It was all Blue could do to keep steady on the stairs. She fell halfway up, hit her shin below the knee on the next tread. She cursed but was glad of the pain. It gave an excuse for the tension in her jaw, the sting behind her eyelids.

Wine made her maudlin. She missed Mother.

'You OK?' Sabina's hand was on Blue's lower back, the pressure light and self-aware as though she was afraid to touch her, and Blue felt the straightjacket tension of her own oddness.

'Aye, just slipped; I'm fine.' Her voice dragged. She heard Sabina's breath behind her, caught the scent of whisky and red wine.

Rain tapped on the skylight, tried to draw Blue's attention: *she's right there, behind you, so close.* Outside, the clouds shifted, hid the moonlight, the stars, the leaning trees, the flood.

A door slammed.

They stopped dead.

'It was downstairs,' Blue said but didn't believe it. 'It was the kitchen door or the one to the Parks' rooms.'

'It was my door,' Sabina said, 'my bloody ghost.'

'They don't exist,' she said. A reflex.

'My demon, then.'

'They don't, either.'

Sabina shook herself. 'Foolishness.'

The corridor stretched on either side of them. The banister slumped its prison-bar shadow on the floor.

'Do you think a mechanic will come tomorrow?' Sabina said. 'Fix the cars so we can go?'

'The rain's got heavier,' said Blue.

They walked the short hallway together. Though they had drunk the same, glass for glass, Sabina kept a steady step. Blue ambled, sometimes brushed the wall, sometimes touched Sabina's shoulder, couldn't keep a straight line.

Dreaded what she would find when she reached her room.

Feared, even more, its emptiness.

'Have some water before you go to sleep,' Sabina fumbled through her pocket for her room key, 'or you'll feel terrible tomorrow. Do you have something to drink?'

'I'm fine, honest; it was the slip on the step that made me lose my balance, not the wine.' Blue laughed to lighten the mood, but that, too, sounded slurred, and she hoped it was only her ear that caught it.

Clouds shifted and the moon offered a blue beam. Sabina's face was caught in the night's half-light.

'Will you be OK?' Sabina asked, and she lifted her hand and stroked a strand of black hair away from Blue's face, tucked it behind Blue's ear, and Blue forced herself not to flinch. Told herself it was a gesture of kindness and care.

But her skin burned where Sabina touched it.

Heartache hollowed out her chest.

There was more, much more, but Blue's gift ricocheted off the shell Sabina had built around her nut-kernel heart.

Blue's eyes shocked open. Sabina gave her a look she couldn't read, and it shook her further, because without Sabina to read, there was only herself, and she was sick to death of her own heart.

'You're lonely,' Sabina said, and Blue realised that the look was pity. Pride made her legs itch to run; anguish made her want to crumble, be comforted by her. By anyone. To say, *can't you see how alone I am? Can no one see how alone I am?*

'I'm sorry,' Sabina said, 'whisky makes me mawkish. Ignore me.' And before Blue could stop her, tell her that it was OK, that she could talk about it, needed to talk about it, please let her talk about it, Sabina had stepped out of reach and opened her bedroom door. 'Can I offer you a final top-up? The flask is empty, but the bottle's in my bag.' She stifled a yawn.

Blue swayed on her feet.

The boozy blood drained cold from her head.

The scent of rotten meat stung her airway.

Her throat became tight, dry, irritated.

A figure stood, semi-concealed by Sabina's door. Blue saw the slim shoulder, the lengths of pale hair, the tight fist of an angry child.

The constriction in her throat became stronger. Some invisible hand pressed her mouth and nose and she couldn't breathe out, couldn't draw fresh air in, could only stand there with the horror of the image blistering her eyes and the smell assaulting her senses.

'Well?' Sabina said.

The vision was horrible, the knowledge it was so close to Sabina even worse.

Repelled, Blue stumbled, squeezed shut her eyes, had to right herself before she fell, and still she could not breathe.

She couldn't go into that room. Couldn't go near Sabina if she was the reason for this … this thing.

'Your niece,' the words choked out of Blue's dry, tight throat, 'what was her name?'

The figure moved. First an ear visible, now the edge of a cheekbone.

'Can't you tell?' Sabina said.

'No,' said Blue. 'What was she called?' And held her breath, begged Sabina not to say it, to have a different name for the girl she had lost. Don't let it be Jessica Pike, Blue thought. Don't let it be Eleanor. Don't let it be—

'Lauren,' Sabina said.

'I'm sorry,' said Blue and hope drained like water from a plug-pulled bath. Behind Sabina, Blue saw the blonde hair, cheekbone and shoulder of someone, something, slightly older. Before those dead eyes could see her, she turned, fled to her room, slammed the door. Bent double, hands pressed to her knees, she breathed sweet air without constriction.

'Goodnight then!' Sabina called, and Blue could hear her door close, pictured her there in that clean, white room, blind to the girl who stood by her shoulder.

16 to 21

A routine developed; Bridget booked shows monthly: a slot for Blue in the late afternoon, as she was still just a kid, and Devlin in the evening to give the glamour certain audiences craved. Leaflets were handed out after each.

The private tarot slots filled up. At sixteen, Blue gave three readings a week, and in between, she studied for the five GCSEs the council said she had to take, home-schooled or not. Devlin gave one a day; any more than that, he said, would drain him. Bridget looked after the diary, the advertising, the money and, when Devlin suffered his first heart attack, the role of medicine woman. Meditation, Bridget assured them all, was the key to physical health; no amount of medication or healthy diet could match up to the power of one's mind.

Bridget bought a lot of crystals that year, carved a lot of candles, and they reminded Blue of the old flat in Preston, their life before. Her dreams became staccato bursts of long-buried memory: Bridget's cheek on the melamine tabletop, the smell of the old futon, the queue for the giro cheque, the absence of anyone telling Blue they were 'right proud', the lack of that warm hand on the base of her back.

Money was still always wanting. Blue watched from her window as the neighbours left for shops or factory floors, left dead early and returned at teatime. She saw them pack their cars for holidays, saw their computers light up their windows, heard their mobile phones ring, saw the shop-bought gifts they hauled into the house each Christmas. Bridget said they were trifles compared to the liberty their own lifestyle provided. Devlin said he was sorry he lacked the fitness to do more.

Ten hours of work a week and two monthly stage shows were insufficient to keep a family, but it wasn't until Devlin's second heart attack that Blue discovered how little they had. He fell at home, a fat starfish of a man laid out on the kitchen floor, and the paramedics had to use a special machine to haul him up and into the ambulance.

When they heard his fate in the hospital corridor, Bridget wailed so loudly, so keenly, that Blue felt she had exhausted all the sound-waves and the air couldn't cope with one more cry. Bridget clung on to Blue's arm, begged her seventeen-year-old daughter to tell her it wasn't true, asked her who would look after Bridget now, who would love her like that. Blue swallowed hard. 'I'll always look after you, Mother,' she said.

A doctor who witnessed the scene gave Blue a glossy green pamphlet from the psychiatry services that offered grief counselling. When Blue brought it out, showed her mother, Bridget screwed up the paper and burned it on the gas hob. 'They'll stuff your mouth with pills,' she explained, her eyes wide and her long grey hair unplaited and unbrushed, 'they'll turn your own head against you.'

There were no savings. Her mother had no pension. Devlin had left the house to Bridget and Blue, so there was little fear of returning to that small, old flat, but still the bills piled up. When Blue turned eighteen, the child benefit her mother relied on stopped.

'They say I should get a job, but you're my job,' Bridget said. A visit to the benefits office had left her catatonic for a week. 'They wanted to see my business records, to prove that we're gainfully self-employed, that if I can prove I work a certain number of hours, I may be entitled to something.'

And so Blue discovered that her mother hadn't kept a single record of their fees, bookings, expenses. If someone paid in cash, the money was spent on sundries. If someone paid a cheque, the money was spent on bills. Even the amount of money charged per session couldn't be determined for sure: Bridget decided how much to charge based on the direction her candle flames slanted.

The sense of imminent doom shook Bridget. Blue couldn't let it shake her too, or all would fall apart. She took to the library. Her exam results had been impressive for a girl who had never set foot in a class-room – a C in Maths and English. The librarian helped; found books on setting up a small business, showed Blue how to use the computer to register herself as a sole trader, didn't ask why Blue needed to know this so young, or why it was her and not Devlin who now checked the emails weekly, or why Blue hadn't just stayed at home and cried her small, broken heart out. The librarian let Blue get on with it, and stayed quiet.

This new determination brought legitimacy and organisation to their lives. It helped her focus on something other than the hole left by Devlin, which she did not think about. If she fell into that hole, if she let herself sit awhile in the velvet-swagged room, if she remembered the warm humour, the shows of patience, let herself miss the soft touch on her shoulder or the ruffling of her hair or the reassurance Devlin had given, she would never claw her way out. She did not think about it.

Blue standardised the fees and gave two readings a day and two shows a month, though she kept to the afternoon slot because, no matter how hard she tried, she just didn't have Devlin's pizzazz. She discovered she was entitled to some financial help and took it, told herself it was for the short term; the end goal would be to become self-sufficient.

Blue hoped Mother would be proud, but she doubted Bridget noticed. Bridget spent days on the sofa, her long grey plait curled around and around her fingers. She wore the bejewelled black kaftan Devlin had died in and her collarbones jutted like girders.

Arlo kept her company, and the company was not the kind Blue would want. The baby sat in her stained romper at Bridget's feet, cried and pulled at her wet curls. Bodhi lurked in the doorway with his bitter-lemon scowl, as though it was Bridget's fault Devlin was dead, and if she hadn't brought him into their lives in the first place, they wouldn't all be in so much pain now. At least, that's what Bodhi's scowl looked like to Blue.

Blue stepped over Arlo when she had to, dodged around Bodhi, didn't look at either. There was too much to do. On top of the readings and admin, she'd discovered that the house and clothes didn't clean them-selves. Mother had no clue as to how to work the washing machine and little inclination to learn. The mention of it brought back memories of Devlin, and the black dog pounced on her back.

Blue's readings changed, too; they were tainted by experience, the blithe innocence gone. She still felt people, felt their pain, shame, and delight, but she was also aware of Mother's. Less inclined to brutal honesty, Blue swayed towards repeat business, held on to snippets of information for 'next time'. Folk left reassured; their pleasure made Blue's mother smile, and Blue thought maybe that would be the key to her happiness. Keep this up – the business, the housekeeping, the bookkeeping, the cooking, the laundry, the advertising, the shopping, the readings, the shows, the studying, the bill-paying, the admin – and it would all be OK. She just had to keep it up.

The show at the working men's club between Thornton and Fleetwood was the third Blue had done in as many weeks, and because of this, perhaps, it hadn't sold out. Maybe weekly shows were too frequent; people lost their thirst for it if their thirst was readily quenched. Of the ten tables, only six were occupied. Blue barely noticed the couple at the back.

No ghostly forms haunted them, no victims at their side, only sadness. It smothered them, impenetrable and murky as pea soup and so distinct that Blue knew, in an instant, what caused it. The sorrow was hopeless, the grief sour and unjust, the mark of a lost child. Blue thought of the people she had consoled, right back to the woman and her dead father. She remembered how happy her mother had been when Blue had helped those people. How easier life would be if Bridget were well.

From the side, Bridget watched. Her hands worried at her waist, her bottom lip pinched between her teeth. Bodhi stood in the place Devlin should be, waved at Blue but didn't smile. Arlo was in the bathtub at home.

Blue warmed up her act on a thin black man in his fifties, spread the cards in the Mars Retrograde formation. The trials of his eldest daughter's poor choice in men, pride at a son's employment, uncertainty over his own job and fearing he was too old to start anew, all masked a more profound fear: that his wife no longer respected him. Nothing Blue hadn't seen before. She sent the man away with instructions to be patient with his children, to retrain in his current job rather than search for a new one (Blue saw in the cards what would happen if the man chose otherwise; a financial disaster that could so easily be avoided).

'I know I'm only young and not yet married,' Blue said, in her final quip, 'but I can see that your Tilda feels the same about you; she loves you fiercely but has changed in many ways over the years. She worries you've lost interest in her; you worry she's lost interest in you – one of you needs to reach out to the other, and all will be well. You must come back and let me know how you've got on.'

'Ha, how did you know her name?' the man said, and Blue smiled, kept schtum, was pleased to see Mother's eyes light up as the audience clapped.

Next, she chose the bereaved couple, invited them both up. A hush fell over the small audience as they climbed the few steps to the stage and sat opposite Blue. Loss had drawn lines across their faces: brow creases, crow's feet, wrinkles at the neck.

The woman held her husband's hand across the table, said, 'We're here—'

'I know why you're here.' Blue reached out to her, squeezed her other hand. 'I know.' Blue pushed the deck of cards to the man, asked him to shuffle whilst Blue purified the cleansing pile with a sprig of sage. All for the show of it; another trick of Devlin's.

To bring back a dead child was more than Blue could do, but also more than was required. The bereaved came for reassurance that their loved ones were safe, at peace, in a better place and, as her fingers touched the hands of the father, Blue knew they needed closure most of all.

It came in a flash that passed through Blue quick as a memory.

'You're here because of your son, John. No, sorry, not John, but Jean.' The subtle change in pronunciation made the mother's eyes widen, and the father blinked back tears.

'Aye, Jean-Paul, but we just called him Jean,' the mother said.

In the wings, Bridget pressed her palms and held them to her lips in prayer.

The mother turned over the first card at Blue's instruction and the Queen of Pentacles stared back, upside down.

'There were arguments, before he left you. You argued about money, about his role in the household now that he was older.'

'That's right, Mike wanted him to pay his way.' The woman turned slightly away from her husband, who winced at the mention of money.

'He'd left school.' The man leant towards Blue. 'He was old enough to get a job—'

Blue held her hand up for silence and turned the next card. 'The Seven of Swords. There was mistrust at the time of his … He took something from you, didn't he? You were angry with him—'

'He stole money. Took it right out of—'

'And there was no chance to make it up.' Blue's hand hovered over the third card – the Moon. 'It's this lack of resolution that's troubled you. Jean left under a cloud that couldn't be cleared before he died, and you're under this cloud even now. But there is light; the moon is lit by the sun—' Blue reached across for the mother's hand, but she pulled back, face pale.

'He's dead?' the man said.

'You didn't know?' Blue looked at the cards again to make sure she hadn't read them wrong. She knew what she'd felt – grief, loss, despair. 'He is at peace, though. He's rested and his soul is full of forgiveness and—'

'I knew it.' The woman's face was ashen. 'I knew he was gone, I felt it. We haven't seen him in nigh on two years – the police have given up; we've searched every street and corner of every town in the northwest. I knew he was gone.'

Her husband hugged her shoulder, and Blue put her hand on the man's other arm, tried to catch something, anything, that she might have missed, but there was only the same anger, the deep-rooted rage the man pointed at himself for an argument about money with his son.

The boy was so far gone that Blue couldn't discern what had happened to him, where or why.

'How do you know he's at peace? Was there any pain, did he … did he miss—' The woman couldn't say anymore. The red tablecloth scrunched under her grip.

'He missed you and loved you, and he would have come home if he could have.' Blue hoped to heaven that it was true.

'It was the drugs that got him in the end, wasn't it?' the man said and Blue couldn't answer him, didn't know, felt the hotness of shame flush her neck. She didn't know. This had not happened before. She couldn't backtrack, couldn't risk her reputation even if this audience were small.

The council tax was late, the water bill was due next week, and Mother had bought a new set of witching candles that cost nearly forty quid.

'The moon gets its light from the sun,' Blue touched the final card, determined not to falter, 'but never sees the sun head-on. You can't see or touch your child, but he sends you his light from beyond. And his forgiveness.' Blue squeezed the man's upper arm in what she hoped was a gesture of comfort.

Offstage, Bridget wiped her eyes. Bodhi smirked. A woman in the audience stifled a sob. Blue felt the absence of a hand on her lumbar spine. *You all right, lass?*

She pinched that thought from her mind, apologised to the couple for her lack of tact. They were calm, resigned to the news that they had feared for so long. Their son was dead.

For the first time Blue could remember, the cards hadn't told her the whole truth. Nor had her intuition. It knotted inside her, made her doubt her insight, readings, ability. Was she too complacent?

'You were marvellous,' Bridget said in the dressing room after the show. 'My little god.'

'Playing God isn't the same as being one,' Blue said to her image in the black-spotted mirror.

'I had a word with the owner; we'll come back in two weeks. The shows will go on.' Bridget laughed a hoarse little laugh, her throat not used to the sound.

Blue looked at the reflection of her mother's smile. She tried to believe that things would get better.

Justice

Joshua sleeps soundly. Molly does not. She rests little when guests are in that house.

There are few secrets between the couple. After an age together, there is no need. Insomnia, however, Molly keeps to herself. So, too, the sleeping pills she takes every Thursday when that house is empty and the thought of a long, sleepless night is too unbearable to fathom.

Sleeplessness is less of a problem when she has something to do, a way to exhaust herself sufficiently to rest. So she slips out from the covers of the bed, unconcerned about disturbing her husband, who sleeps like the dead. She pulls on socks, wraps a fleecy dressing gown around her shoulders. She hears the rain, knows that that house will be cold.

Old houses are wont to be cold. They are draughty. Old buildings creak, they groan at the rafters, have doors that don't stay closed. Their cavities are a mausoleum to dirt and dried insects. They harbour smells that take Molly by surprise and have no cause, no culprit, that make her nose sting and disperse as quickly as they arrive. Joshua has spent hours searching the attic for rotten mice, the chimney for decaying birds' nests, the cupboards and furniture for turned food. He has never found a thing.

Tonight it is just the cold that bothers Molly. So she will begin upstairs, where it's warmest. Where earlier Blue thought she saw something. Where that door won't stay closed. Never stays closed. Where the two poor girls sleep alone, when rooms that would ordinarily be filled stand empty, with no one to watch over them. If Jago hadn't ruined everything, Molly would feel better. If she could get the image of her husband cradling the boy's limp body out of her head, she would feel better. They had been so lucky; had it happened any earlier, the other guests may have seen. Any later, and the weather would have made it impossible to get the boy out.

The kitchen floor chills the soles of her feet. The broken glass has been swept up. She does not worry about being heard; her socks are silent, every door hinge is well oiled, the draw of her lungs soft and regular. There are no longer dogs to bark, to sniff at her, to skitter their claws across the flagstones and give her away. Poor Jupiter, poor Milo. Joshua was terribly sad when they died.

That house breathes around her. She feels every cursed brick of it; every window is an eye, every doorway a rude mouth, every space a reminder of past hope. Some fulfilled, some not. Here, the therapy room where her dreams of healing were realised, where she consoled Adrian Buckley, and her counselling gave him strength. There is the art room where she taught Eleanor to paint the stream and trees, tried to teach her to love through art.

She walks upstairs, the way lit gently by the clouded moonlight.

But it takes more than a week to teach someone to love. Much more. Some people can never be taught, however hard Molly may try. However much time, patience, adoration, guidance, mothering she pours into them. She suspects the German woman will be like this.

Molly is in the bedroom now and looks down at her. Sabina is asleep. Molly regrets letting them have wine; her rules on alcohol are there for a reason. Show Molly a person who can drink in moderation, limit themselves to one glass of wine when there are five tempting bottles on the table, and Molly will herald that soul as a rarity. Molly's alcohol fog wore off hours ago; it certainly didn't help her sleep. But then, Molly didn't drink the cocoa.

Alcohol makes the sleeping draught stronger.

She doubts Sabina will be up before ten. She looks peaceful, lying on her back in her cream satin pyjamas, one hand above her head, one on her belly. The exact position in which she slept last night. The duvet is crumpled on the floor, and Molly reaches for it, drapes it back over Sabina. She notices something on the dresser, a distraction that Sabina is better off without, so Molly picks it up and slips it into the cushioned pocket of her dressing gown. With nothing else amiss in the room, Molly takes out her phone, opens the camera and captures one close-up photo of Sabina's sleeping face.

The image is saved to the SD card, never the cloud. It joins hundreds of others, pictures she looks at and thinks, these are the people I have cared for, the people I have helped, the people who will remember me, exalt me as their comforter, their confidante and saviour. They will never forget me. These photographs and thoughts will console Molly on Thursday evening when that house is quiet, if not empty, and she needs something positive to focus on before the sleeping pills pull her under.

She has deleted Jago's image.

The key turns silently in Sabina's lock, turns silently again in Blue's, and Molly performs the same routine – neatens the duvet, removes the little distraction – but she does not take a photograph. Beads of sweat cling to Blue's brow; her forehead is furrowed, her mouth tense, her eyes flit left and right beneath her lids with such rapidity that Molly is unnerved. It must be a nightmare.

A pair of jeans lie on the floor. A pill packet pokes its nose from the pocket. Molly doesn't know how she could have missed this yesterday; she was so thorough. But there it is: a small prescription of anti-anxiety medication that Blue failed to mention on her form. Molly specifically asks all guests if they are taking any medicine, prescription or not; other drugs can interfere with Molly's cocktails. She is meticulous about it – she manages the dosages accordingly, relies on her guests' honesty, and now she discovers that Blue has not been honest at all. She has lied to Molly.

Molly returns the pack to the pocket. Tomorrow she will take the medication and carefully remove each pill and replace it with a placebo, as she has had to do before when guests have been naughty. She will make a small incision in the white, plastic casing around each pill, slide out and replace every one, then thinly glue over the cut. The foil will remain intact. Otherwise, all sorts of nastiness can occur: headaches, hallucinations, mood swings, heart palpitations, fevers, disorientation, paranoia, all sorts. Medications should never be mixed blindly. They should be controlled. No wonder Blue is having a nightmare.

A sound makes Molly flinch. It is subtle, from the depths of the house. A footstep, she thinks, though everyone else is asleep. Cold air creeps

147

around her neck, and Molly no longer wants to be in this part of that house. She wants to be in her bed beside her husband in the newer extension that has never had anyone else sleep in it – no guests, no previous owners or long-dead people from bygone times. No Eleanor.

Molly locks Blue's bedroom door, hurries down the stairs, through the passageway towards the kitchen.

She stops. She hears the measured scrape of a drawer creep open.

The passageway is cold, dark; the layout is known by heart in her muscles and mind, yet she feels she has been swallowed into another world, that if she reached out her fingers to the left, she would feel a void where the wall should be. The noise repeats.

There is something in the therapy room.

The feeling of being at sea sweeps through her. Molly could walk to that room, open the door, and confront what's there, but she knows she will lose her head if she does. She needs her husband. The urge to feel his weighty, sleeping body beside her is keener than anything else.

There is nothing there, she tells herself. There is nothing there.

Accustomed to the dark, Molly sees the outline of the door to that room. As if in response to her gaze, the door shifts, moves, soundlessly inches open until a gap appears, and she sees the shape in the gloom, sees the terrible sight of a pale figure, and from the depths of her belly, horror rises. Nightmares spin through her mind, draw on her fears, drain her hope.

A faint voice inside her head tells her to enter the room, flood it with light, raise her voice, stamp her feet, banish and berate. She can't. All she can do is repeat the thought: there is nothing there, there is nothing there.

Goosebumps climb from her ankles to her neck. She feels blindly, silently, for the kitchen door and escapes the passageway, the sound of the papers and drawer, the sight of that room, that figure. The feeling does not leave her. Dread has settled in her bones.

The Sixties

James' father stood on the doorstep of their little brick house, his weight in his toe-tips, his expression resolutely casual. Tension caught in his lips. 'And? Did Mr Hope like you, did he … Well, how did it go?'

'Hello to you, too, Dad. Come on, I've been on the bus for over an hour,' James said. 'Can't I have a cup of tea first, before the interrogation?'

And maybe it was his smile, or his straight back, or the laugh caught between words, because his father's eyes widened, his face turned whiter than a bed sheet, and he said, 'You got it? You bloody got it?' He didn't wait for James to answer, but jumped from the step and called over his shoulder to James' mother.

'Marge? Marge, Jim got it! He only bloody got it!' And he whooped, whooped right there in the street, and cried out, 'You got it! My boy, my boy, you only bloody got it!'

James had to step back or else he'd have fallen over. His dad ruffled his hair, and he laughed, really laughed, and when James looked at him, his dad's proud eyes were brimming, his dad, who James had only ever seen cry out of fear or sadness.

His mother stood in the hall. 'I was getting worried. I thought you'd be back hours ago.' She looked at her two men in the street. She smiled, but her hands wrung. 'Is it true, then? Did you get it?' she said.

'Yes, Mum,' James said. 'Three-week trial, and if I pass that, Mr Hope will take me on. A proper job, Mum.'

'And you think you'll be OK doing it? It's not too strenuous? The journey's not too far? You'll manage it all right?' Her hands still wrung, and her face was tight, and he could tell she wanted to shrug it all off, to join her husband in the street and cheer for her son and clap and dance, but she couldn't.

'I'll be fine, I promise,' James said.

'And you like it, this job?' she said. James nodded.

Behind him, his dad laughed and ran into the middle of the road.

'He's only gone and bloody got it!'

His mother dashed out and bought rump steak to celebrate, and they ate it with mash and cream sauce, and James told them about the factory. He reassured his mum that he'd be in an office and wouldn't go into the factory proper, where dust could clog his damaged left lung. His dad laid out a career path for him, told him that he should try and get promoted in a year or two, once he'd shown them all how clever he was.

'Maybe you'll meet a girl there,' James' mother said. 'A nice one, you know.'

'Heaven's sake, Marge, one step at a time,' said his dad and rolled his eyes at James, and James laughed, and his mum laughed too.

'That's how it's done now,' his mum said. 'Look at his brother, he met Florence at work.'

'Different in the civil service, they practically live at work,' his dad said.

'Still, you might meet a nice girl. A secretary or something. Isn't the hospital just round the corner? You might meet a nurse.' His mother pushed potato on to her fork, and James tried to hide his smile. 'Someone to look after you,' she said.

She did not add the words 'after I'm gone', which James had only ever heard her say when she thought he was out of earshot. All her significant worries, her great shames, he had heard eavesdropping. 'It's ruined him, my poor boy; it's ruined every chance for him,' was one. 'Why didn't I let him have the vaccine?' was another.

And he knew his mother almost as well as she knew him. She had visited him every day for two years whilst he was away, making the long bus ride to the sanatorium where, for the first six months, she was not allowed in his bedroom at all, and they could only look at each other through a plate glass window cut into the wall. He had been glad he was twenty years old and not a child, because how could a child stand that?

And she'd been there, for the eighteen months afterwards when James could do little more than walk from one room to the next before getting out of breath. She taught him to paint, played him at cards, rubbed his back when the coughing fits took over, had handed him handkerchief after kerchief and surreptitiously checked them for blood. She had stopped asking the doctors when James would get better. A few rare people, they said, never recover.

And she had watched over him tentatively, fearfully, charting the snail-pace progress as he learnt to live with one healthy lung and one lung that was little more than scar tissue. 'It'll kill him in the end,' he'd once heard her say.

After dinner, James' dad nipped to the pub to buy a small bottle of brandy. To toast with, he'd said.

James stacked the three plates, the cutlery, the sauce boat and carried them into the kitchen, where his mother filled the sink and snapped on her yellow rubber gloves.

'Phone your brother and tell him,' she said.

'I will,' James said, 'but there's something else I want to—'

'He'll be so pleased. And write a letter to Grandma. She's not so good on the telephone.'

'Something else happened today,' James said, and he thought of the pale bowl of stew, of the light that had bounced off the melamine table-tops, of Marie's smile.

His mother plunged the dishes into the soapy water, handed a tea towel to James and told him to sit on one of the chairs whilst he dried. He sat and felt very tired; his muscles ached, and his throat was sore from the coughing and all the talking. His mother passed him a plate; he dried it and put it on the table.

'There's something else, Mum,' he said again, and his mum said, 'Oh yes?' but he knew she wasn't listening. She was thinking of all the people she could tell the good news.

James thought of Marie. Marie, who had walked with him back to his bus stop and had drunk tea with him in one of the little tea rooms and had said she looked forward to seeing him again, looked forward to seeing him every other day at work.

'Not so much something,' he said, 'as someone.'

Now he had his mother's attention.

'Someone? Oh yes?' she said, and her eyes were wide. Her face was pale. Soap suds dripped from her gloves to the sink. 'Do you mean a—'

'A girl,' James said. 'I met a girl.'

'You met a girl?' she said. 'A girl?'

'Her name's Marie,' James said. 'She's Polish, works as a cook.'

'She's called Marie?' his mother said, and the front door opened, and James' father came in.

'Donald? Don! James has met a girl!' And she rushed to her husband and got soap suds on his jacket. 'He's met a girl called Marie!'

And his dad said, 'A girl? Bloody hell, what a day you've had!'

'She works at the same factory,' James said, and his mother laughed and pressed her gloves to her chest and looked at her husband again.

'Donald, did you hear that? She's called Marie and works at the same factory! In the kitchen, as a cook, and she's lovely!'

'You've not met her yet,' James laughed, and his dad laughed too, and his mother laughed and hugged them in turn.

'She's called Marie,' his mother said again, 'and I bet she's lovely.'

The Page of Wands (Reversed)

Sterile dawn light crested the trees. Blue's white sheets were clammy with sweat, her hair plastered to her forehead, and she woke not from the cold or the light or the sound of the rain, but from the hammering of heart against rib.

She dreamt of the dead man last night.

Before anything else came back (the events of the previous evening, the state of the weather, the long pale hair), she remembered the cruel twist of the man's cruel lips, the rotten smell of his rotten soul and the reaction of Mother.

'You're a little god.'

After the letter, she'd let Mother hold on to that idea; even Devlin had tactically ignored it. Though she never bought into Mother's fantasy, Blue had believed that perhaps there was something good in it, that maybe her strange talents helped people. It's all she had wanted to do; it made the terror worthwhile.

She should have left it well enough alone.

A flurry of rain drummed the window and Blue brushed the hair from her face, rubbed her temples free of the dream. The dull throb in her head reminded her of the alcohol. The ache in her back reminded her of the work at the stream – and the dead rabbit, the floodwater, the submerged fields, the cars that wouldn't start, the face at the window, the thing in Sabina's bedroom.

The feeling of suffocation.

She started upright and reached for her phone from the bedside table to check the time, check the signal, and see if she could contact someone, anyone, to get her out of here.

She had to get out.

Her phone wasn't there.

Nor was it in the pocket of her jeans, her hoody, her bag. She searched the room stark naked, looked in every drawer and under the furniture. Mr Park had returned the phones yesterday – Blue had looked at the blank reception bars, frustrated she couldn't use it but relieved that no one could google her and find out who she was, what she'd done. So where was it?

The headache was made worse by her hurry. She pulled on clothes, gave her teeth a harsh brush, didn't bother to wash her face and left the bedroom to search downstairs.

Sabina's door was shut; no sound came from within. Blue pictured her asleep beneath the white sheets. Pictured that face in the corner of the room.

At the top of the stairs, she slowed, aware of low voices in the hall. The Parks must be awake. How early was it?

The couple stood by the door that led through to the passageway. Mrs Park faced Blue but didn't notice her. Her arms were folded, her gaze downcast. Mr Park whispered, gesticulated, pointed to the door, then the ceiling, then out to the side, and Mrs Park's head hung lower. Her mouth kept its tension; regret and defiance held in its firm line.

'For Christ's sake, Molly,' Joshua said, loud enough for Blue to hear.

Mrs Park looked up, clocked Blue, touched her husband's arm in a warning and smiled too brightly at her guest.

Mr Park sighed and shook his head. He couldn't or wouldn't look Blue in the eye, said he'd put the kettle on and walked away to the kitchen.

'You're up earlier than I expected,' Mrs Park said. 'Did you sleep well?'

'Yeah, OK, but too much wine.' Blue tried to laugh off her awkwardness at the intrusion, but her stomach churned as well as her head, and she appreciated how true her words were. 'I can't find my—'

'– that's why I don't recommend alcohol at the retreat; I knew Joshua shouldn't have opened that first bottle last night. It only leads to trouble; I'm so sorry. Tonight will be different; you'll sleep far better as a result.

It's so important, a good night's rest. Guests always comment on it, how well they sleep here, how peacefully. They're always grateful for it.'

'Have you seen my phone?' Blue tried again.

'Isn't it in the safe?' She smiled an apple-cheeked smile, uncannily wholesome, and Blue wondered what the Parks had discussed.

'Your husband gave it back yesterday.'

'Of course, I forgot, what with the wine fog.' She brushed down the front of her smock and gave a small laugh. 'Silly me. They must have dropped out of your pockets last night; I found them on the armchairs earlier, so popped them away for safekeeping.'

'But I had it last night; I checked it before—' Blue said.

'They're such a distraction. It's easier to sleep without electronics.'

A creak came from the ceiling and a light thud of footsteps. A wave of cold air washed the room.

'Can I have it—' began Blue. Goosebumps ran the lengths of her arms, her neck.

'No point holding on to them until you're ready to leave. There's no reception here, and phones are such a distraction, don't you think?' She laid out the journals that Mr Park had put away the day before when they had all agreed the planned retreat wasn't feasible.

At least, Mr Park, Milton, Blue and Sabina had agreed.

'I'd like it back though if that's all right?'

'Let's have a cup of tea and some breakfast first. I put on a lovely Sunday breakfast, I promise you.' She gave Blue that same eerie smile, looked to the stairs and said, 'You're both early risers today!'

Sabina trod heavily down the stairs. She looked brighter, well-rested, unaffected by the smell of rotting meat that spread through the air like a swarm of locusts, oblivious to the pale-skinned, pale-haired, black-eyed figure close behind her.

It made Blue gag. Her knees almost buckled. She reached for the back of the nearest chair, was vaguely aware that Sabina and Mrs Park rushed towards her. She felt a hand on the small of her back, thought for a terrible moment that it was that thing, that it could touch her and she could feel it, until she realised with relief that the hand was too large, too warm. It was Mrs Park. Blue wished it had been Devlin.

Blue closed her eyes. She was overtired, overstimulated, had drunk too much.

'I'm fine, I'm sorry, I'm fine.' Blue forced herself to straighten, opened her eyes. She focused on the fact it wasn't real. The projection of someone else's fear or guilt would not undo three years of hard work.

Mrs Park fussed and Blue reassured her, blamed her sore head, said she could do with a coffee and a painkiller.

'I could do with coffee, too,' said Sabina, but she walked over to the chairs by the fire. 'I just want to check … I think I dropped my phone last—'

Blue took a deep breath through her mouth, and her tongue tasted foetid air.

'It's in the safe, right as rain,' Mrs Park said. 'Let's get you both through to the kitchen; I had a full English planned: sausages, bacon, eggs, mushrooms, all locally sourced—'

'Could you get it out of the safe, please?' Sabina said.

'You'll not need it; better to leave it where it's secure. How do you like your eggs? I can do—'

'No, I would like it now. Please.'

Mrs Park opened the door to the hallway, beckoned them both through, and Blue crept forward, kept her breath shallow, her gaze on the floor, stunned that no one else could smell it, see it.

'Maybe after breakfast,' Mrs Park said to Sabina. 'A good feed will do us all—'

'No, not maybe. And not after breakfast. Mrs Park, thank you for finding it and keeping it safe. I would now like my phone back.' Sabina stood still, hands clasped behind her straight back.

What had Sabina done? Why was it so impossible for Blue to accept she might have committed some crime?

Because it's not real. Because none of it is; my mind made a theatre.

The thought helped; the stench melted, the vision too.

Breakfast was served, drinks poured, the phones reluctantly returned. There was still no signal. Blue wondered if she could get the Wi-Fi password, thought it better to ask Mr Park. The man hadn't joined them yet. Nor had Milton, but Mrs Park didn't wait for either man before she served.

The food was hearty and good; the saltiness helped Blue's sore head, and the paracetamol cleared the last of the throb. Sabina asked for mustard, but there was none left and so she had to make do with brown sauce. The hunger was bottomless; Blue ate twice as much as Sabina. Mrs Park, she noticed, ate little. She looked exhausted.

'The elephant in the room.' Sabina pushed her empty plate away. 'Do you think a mechanic will make it out to us today? I would call the AA myself, but of course, I've no reception.' She smiled gently at Mrs Park, bore no resentment about their phones. She seemed to understand as well as Blue did that Mrs Park's want for them to stay was not malicious.

Mrs Park gave a resigned smile, said, 'I'll call now. Or you can, if you'd rather, from the phone in the passage?'

Blue looked back to her plate and the smear of egg and beans, took a final slice of fresh white bread and used it to mop up their remnants.

It'll all be OK, she thought.

The yolk was putrid, the bread stale.

It's gone cold, that's all, Blue thought, and remembered Bodhi, how milk would sour when she saw him, how biscuits would soften and treats would turn rank.

Gaminess rose from the last of the sausage, its fat turned solid and grey.

It's just bad meat, that's all. A small piece of bad meat.

'I'll let you phone; you know more about the access here than I do,' Sabina said, and Mrs Park nodded, brushed the crumbs from her smock and excused herself.

Blue picked up the slice of bread again. It was warm and light, the yolk soft.

Why is this happening now? After three years, why is my mind playing tricks on me now?

And another voice, one of logic and calm, answered and Blue thought about why she was here, the issues she might need to discuss.

'It'll be three years tomorrow,' she said, surprised at her candour, 'since Mother died.'

Sabina didn't speak. Chin down, she squeezed her hands around her empty coffee mug.

'I'm sorry,' Blue said. 'I didn't mean to make you feel awkward. I don't know why I said it, I'm—' Her voice cracked.

'No, please. I never know what to say in these situations, I'm not good at all with all ... all this.' Sabina gestured around, as though it were not Blue she struggled with, but life itself. 'I've never believed in

157

any of this stuff – this talking through things, and healing by dance and yoga and drawing pictures like I'm a child. I would have rather gone to a spa and got drunk on my own.' She lowered her voice and leant towards her. Blue could smell last night's whisky on her breath. 'I'm pleased the weather is shit and has cancelled the retreat. I only wish I could go home. Honestly, I'd rather be at work. It's therapy in itself; I think of nothing else when I'm in front of a computer other than the task in hand.'

In her mind, Blue saw a tall woman with a broad forehead and an aquiline nose, dark blonde hair pulled into a ponytail that reached her midback. Cracked lips pulled into a scream. She doubled over, clutched her middle, and Sabina reached out, touched the woman's shoulder. The tableau melted.

'When you're at work, you forget about your sister,' Blue said.

'Stop it, stop … that.' Sabina pushed her chair from the table, crossed her arms in the same way her sister had in Blue's vision. 'You know nothing about it.'

'They need to wait, to see—You all right?' Mrs Park stood at the kitchen door, eyeing her guests.

'Will they send someone?' Sabina regained her composure. Blue stared at her empty plate.

'They're checking the access and weather; there's still a backlog from yesterday, including us. They'll call back and let us know. Shall I get you both some tea? It's taken its toll on all of us, this uncertainty. Our brains aren't adapted to sudden change, generally speaking.'

Mrs Park turned the kettle on and cleared the table, came close to Blue and brought the chill with her.

'I need to lie down, just for a bit,' Blue said, gripped with terror that any second she would see something, smell something, taste something inhuman. Comfort came from the weight of her phone in her back pocket. She didn't wait for a response before she left, gaze down so she wouldn't see any dead things.

To run seemed dramatic, but still she ran, climbed the stairs two a pace, and locked her door.

She stood on her bed, searched for mobile signal, took the chair from place to place and stood on that, tried every corner of the window, prayed the extra height would give her a bar, but there was nothing.

Instead, she got a view of the field.

The driveway was one silver pool, the clouds and the alders reflected. The road away from the house was a river; the lane beyond the grounds was one too. The landscape's only point of familiarity was the bridge's head, two feet of its stonework above the water.

And the trees.

Stone upon stone of cold, hard dread formed a cairn in her gut. No escape.

How long would she be stuck here, hounded by an image of the dead, surrounded by people who didn't know her, couldn't understand or help her? How long before she lost her mind?

Her car was unusable, but her feet and her legs still worked.

She could borrow more waterproofs and put on her wellingtons, walk across the flooded land until she reached a house, any house other than this one.

If she knew which way to go. How far was it to the nearest farm?

Satnav was inaccessible. Blue had a compass app but no notion which way to go.

Another stone dropped on to the cairn.

The Wi-Fi code. Mr Park would give it to her, Blue thought; he was less uptight about his wife's usual rules.

Blue saw him through the window. The lone figure waded through the bog that, days ago, had been field. Dressed in gaiters, waterproof trousers, waterproof mac and hat, none of his features were visible; his sheer size betrayed him. He carried a bundle of long-handled tools across his shoulders: a spade, a fork, a hoe.

He was near the house, a few hundred yards to go. Blue made to leave but was stopped by a knock at the door.

'May I come in?' Sabina tried the handle before Blue reached it. Blue had an impulse not to answer, to keep it locked and hunker down, because if she opened it, what if that thing was there?

Sabina repeated Blue's name, knocked twice, sighed.

'I came to apologise,' she said, 'for snapping at you. It was cruel, and unnecessary and I ... I'm used to being able to hide. I've never met someone I can't hide from.'

'I've never met someone so difficult to read,' Blue said.

A door opened below; Joshua Park thudded into the boot room.

'Will you let me in?' Sabina said.

Blue wanted to go down and talk to the man, not stand in her room idle and impotent. Still, she let Sabina in, and Sabina apologised again, and Blue said there was nowt to forgive.

She edged closer to the hallway, but Sabina didn't move from the threshold.

Downstairs, Mr Park came into the house.

'Did you mean that, about me being hard to read? You were accurate, made it seem so simple. So obvious.'

The desire to get away made Blue antsy and itched in her fingertips, in her toes. Another door closed, the one to the passageway. Joshua Park had moved on through the hall, but there was a chance Blue could catch him in the kitchen.

'I can normally tell more, but I'm out of practice. It's been a long time since I've done it—'

'You used to do it a lot? Were you some kind of a fortune teller?'

'I did a bit of tarot – basic talents, nothing special.' Blue suppressed a sigh. She remembered her first meeting with Devlin, and Bridget's talk of her own small talents and basic capabilities, and the memory was raw and too close. 'I worked in a hospice, not a circus.' She tried to brush her discomfort away with a laugh, and suggested they go downstairs to see if they could help with the floodwater. 'They might need to sandbag the doors,' she said, 'and I really want to talk to Mr Park.'

'Before you worked at the hospice, what did you do?'

She sighed in earnest, said, 'Bits and bobs, you know. I worked in a factory for a while, then a warehouse.' She had worked anywhere she could get a contract, stayed until someone recognised her or came across an old true-life-story magazine in a waiting room. She stayed as long as she could, left as soon as she had to.

'You just do tarot as a hobby, then?' Sabina finally stepped out of the room so Blue could too and Blue wanted her to stop, to shut up, to leave her alone and quit asking.

'Not anymore,' Blue said. The desire to run built firm in her legs and the desire to scream filled her lungs and her head. She had one simple, immediate goal: find Mr Park. Why was that so out of reach?

'Why did you stop?' said Sabina.

'Because it's rubbish, all of it, all right? It does nothing but harm and I've left it behind me, so stop asking, stop going on and on at me. It's none of your business so don't pretend like you care when no one cares!'

'Jesus,' Sabina stepped back, 'what the hell happened to you?'

Blue felt the hurt fly off her like bats from a cave and the air filled with its quick feeling. 'I'm sorry,' said Blue and her own wave washed through her as a flood of otherness and isolation. 'I just had one too many rough experiences. I was too young for it,' she said, 'and it made me grow up too fast.'

21

After the demonstration where Blue revealed Jean-Paul's death, Bridget came out of herself. She planned more shows and gave the paperwork to Blue to file correctly in the new way. Blue saved enough money for a fifteen-year-old Toyota and casual driving lessons from a man down the road. Bridget began to look at clubs further afield, more frequently too, until Blue was on two performances a week, some as far off as Manchester proper.

'We'd get bigger audiences if you would do a stage show, if you would just try,' Bridget said. They had passed by posters for famous psychics on Blackpool Pier, showmen who pretended to talk to ghosts in front of crowds of three hundred or more.

'I'm happy with the small clubs, Mum.'

'Think of the ticket sales; so many more people would come to see you.'

'Exactly,' Blue said.

'More chance to find a boyfriend, too.' Bridget nudged Blue with her shoulder. Her shoulder was tense.

'Don't need one,' Blue said, though what she thought was, how the hell would she find one? Who would be interested? She remembered the boy from the street she had kissed when she was fifteen, Matthew. Plain-looking and plump, with soft lips and a wave to his thick, blond hair. Most important was that he was a boy, a flesh-and-blood boy. A boy who had wanted to kiss Blue.

She had puckered up in the gulley behind their house. Watched through half-closed lids as he leant towards her. She hadn't known what to do with her hands, had the urge to touch Matthew's cheek or stroke his hair, but what if he didn't like that? So she kept her hands by her sides, didn't lean in too far in case he changed his mind, didn't want to do anything that might stop him from wanting to kiss her, because good God did she want him to kiss her.

The truth hit when their lips met.

He'd done it for a dare.

Kiss the freak for a fiver.

Blue had pulled back. She wiped the taste of his lips off her mouth. He laughed and ran off, and Blue staggered through the back gate before tears came. When she cried, Blue hated herself for it, hid in the velvet-swagged room and made Devlin promise not to tell Bridget. Devlin told her that he was a wrong'un, that not all men were like that, that there was nothing amiss with her, and Matthew was the one with issues.

A god to Mother, Blue thought, a freak to everyone else.

'Good job you have me to look after you then, isn't it?' Bridget said and slid her hand through the crook of Blue's arm.

'Aye,' Blue said.

It was at the same club two years later that Blue met Jean-Paul's parents again. They hadn't bought tickets.

The small wooden stage was lit up with fairy lights, and Blue wore a purple linen kaftan that her mother had sewn with beads and sequins, a gold scarf around her neck. Her hair was loose to her waist in a conditioned mane of dark waves, which, her mother claimed, looked magnificent. It was a mask of sorts; when she got home, she could tie it up in a bun and pretend to be a normal twenty-one-year-old.

An elderly woman was at the table with her when it happened, a carpetbag at her feet, a handkerchief balled inside her cardigan sleeve. She wanted to know which of her seventeen dead birds waited for her on the other side.

Blue never got a chance to answer her. The door at the back of the room swung open. Jean-Paul's mother charged like a wild cat. She ran from the far end of the hall, jumped on to the stage. Her hands wrapped around Blue's throat before she had time to blink.

White, cruel anger osmosed from her fingers to Blue's neck, from Blue's neck to her whole body, until Blue's brain, heart, belly was spiced with it.

'You killed him!'

She squeezed, yelled in Blue's face, sprayed spittle on Blue's nose and chin. 'You left him to die!'

Two security guards in monochrome uniforms pulled her roughly off. Each held one of her arms whilst she bucked; their biceps flexed as they fought to restrain her.

'She left my son to die.' She arched and craned her neck, knocked a chair to the floor.

'She said he was dead.' They bullied her into the corridor, let the doors swing shut; the sounds of her struggle echoed behind them.

Bridget rushed onstage, stood in front of the table whilst Blue offered some comfort to the old woman.

'I'm terribly sorry, folks,' Bridget said in her milk-and-honey Southern drawl. 'Our guest had been unhappy with her last reading; she's yet to come to terms with it.' She waited for a few beats whilst the audience murmured, shook their heads in disapproval, waited until their eyes turned sympathetically back to Blue.

'We should all keep her in our thoughts,' Bridget said. 'She's going through a painful period. I shall light a candle for her tonight, at my altar.' She lit a thick branch of sage, held the leaves high and walked through the audience. Blue was afraid the fire alarm would go off, but it didn't.

'I invite you all to close your eyes,' said Bridget, 'and send her peaceful energy whilst I re-cleanse our collective aura.'

Blue gave two more demonstrations, but her heart wasn't in it, and they received only one enquiry about private readings.

There was no dressing room at the club, and Blue used a store cupboard to change in, the alternative being the women's bathroom. When she stepped out, Jean-Paul's father was there. The man had gained weight since Blue had last seen him, and the ghost of a suntan remained. Two white lines marked out where his sunglasses met his ears. A gold chain caught the light at his throat.

'He died last week,' the man said.

Blue apologised, on instinct reached out to comfort the man, but Jean-Paul's father sidestepped and wouldn't be soothed.

'Overdose, the pathologist said. He died in a squat. In Newcastle. We never checked Newcastle. We checked every town in the west but didn't go across to Newcastle, but we would have done. We would have checked every street in this whole damn country if it wasn't for—' He pointed at Blue with a shaking finger. The father's face contorted, stubborn in his grief. He would not cry.

'The police had stopped looking, his friends had stopped, he had no one but us. We would never have given up on him, never, if *you* hadn't told us … We would have found him. We would have saved him, our boy. Our son. I would have saved him. He was my son, I would have—' Sweat caught in the creases of his forehead. His chin puckered tight.

Blue tried again, felt her own eyes sting with the father's held-back tears. 'I'm sorry, if I had known—'

The man surged forward, gripped Blue by the collar, pulled her close until Blue could taste the sourness of his breath and feel the pressure of his knuckles on her throat.

'You said you did know. We trusted you, 'cause you was so sure. We stopped looking because you said he was—' The man pulled Blue closer, nose to nose, and Blue could feel the livid anger that masked the fear, rage easier to express than grief.

The man pushed her roughly backwards, and Blue's spine grated the coarse brick wall. He still held Blue's collar with one hand; the other pulled back, flat and back-hand-ready, and it was only Blue's quick fear that saved her; her chin flinched away as the back of the man's hand made like a paddle for Blue's face. The man's knuckles grazed Blue's jaw, and the wall took the brunt of the slap, the man's angry cry louder than bone crunching brick.

Blue's eyes scrunched shut. She felt the release of her collar, threw her hands up to her face, expected another hit, but all she heard was the grown man's sobs. It was like nothing Blue had heard before – not the gulping, hiccoughy tears Mother shed when she thought of Devlin or the duvet-muffled, drawn-out weeping when her mood had sunk through the floor. This was a throat-sore, gut-deep, spirit-crushed wail. It forced her eyes open, the noise tip-of-the-tongue familiar; the sound Blue would make if she ever dared.

She never dared. Not even now, with the man pulling his bloody, swollen hand back, and what was the pain of this hand compared to the pain he already felt? A parent's ravaged heart.

His son was—

'I'm sorry.' Blue squeezed the words through her teeth, her nose blocked with snot, her throat choked with saliva.

'Sorry! Sorry?'

The punch landed in Blue's guts, drove up and knocked the air from her lungs, threw bile up into her mouth, robbed her of any sensation outside pain.

The bouncer heard the noise. He rounded the corner, saw the father shove Blue against the wall, reached him before the fist met Blue's body for a second go. He pulled the man away, bundled him towards the fire exit.

'It's on you! All of this, it's on you!' Jean-Paul's father was flung outside.

A drop of blood had fallen from his hand, a black drop on the age-yellowed lino.

'You all right?' the bouncer came back, asked Blue.

A smudge of it was on Blue's kaftan, a damp, dark smear on dry purple linen.

No words came, so she nodded, and the bouncer patted her heavily on her back and asked if she wanted a cuppa. Blue shook her head, couldn't meet the man's eye.

The door to the store cupboard stood open. Blue crawled through and locked herself in, sat on the floor beneath a shelf of polish and rags, hugged her knees to her chest. She sat still and sat quietly. She thought of the blood on her clothes, tried to hate the man who had hurt her.

There was no hate.

She pictured Jean-Paul and felt the pain of his parents. What of the people she had read for tonight? How many other demonstrations had she got wrong? Shame and fear washed through her: shame at selling mistruths, fear that she would have to stop it all and how else would she earn any money? She thought of Matthew, his revulsion at her kiss years ago, felt the trickery-fuelled adrenaline course through him, his desperation to be liked by everyone other than Blue. Briefly felt what it was to have friends and care what they thought about you.

'Blue? Are you coming out?' Mother called, a dull edge to her voice that made Blue's stomach drop.

She opened the door and stepped out to her mother, waited for her concern but it didn't come. Blue guessed the bouncer hadn't said anything.

She slipped Bridget's small hand through her arm and turned towards the back door, stifled a wince as the movement tugged her bruised abdominal muscles.

'Shall we go home?' Bridget asked.

'Aye.'

'Will you book another show?'

'Not just now.'

Bridget drew in a soft breath, paused as though to say something, but didn't. They walked outside, let the door swing shut behind them, and Blue checked the street to make sure the man wasn't waiting. She should have taken her mother out of the other exit and asked the bouncer to walk them to the car.

'I'm sorry about tonight,' Bridget said at last.

'It wasn't—'

'Maybe I shouldn't have lit the sage; maybe it put people off. The second half was flat, didn't you think it flat? I think it's because I lit the sage. Sage doesn't normally have that effect, but it was the only thing I did—'

'It wasn't anything you did; it was the woman, the mother who—'

'I shouldn't have lit the sage.' She stopped and took her arm away, bit the edge of her thumb. 'I should have given you a hug. Now I think back to it, you were alone there on the stage and I should have gone to you, but I didn't, did I? I left you and lit the sage, and I shouldn't have done that. Do you think the audience noticed that, too? Judged me for it, do you think, for lighting the sage instead of going to you?'

The cold was close about them, the pavement lit orange on this side by the street light, blue on the other by a strip bar's neon sign. Blue's stomach ached.

'You didn't do wrong.' She held her mother by her avian-frail shoulders. 'You were just right.' Blue took Bridget's long grey plait and playfully wrapped it around her neck like a scarf, trying to make her smile. 'Nice and warm, now,' Blue said. Her shirt rubbed against the graze on her spine.

Bridget didn't smile. A man approached the strip bar and walked in; the road flooded briefly with loud light and bright music. Bodhi, small and dressed in plain clothes and a scowl, stood by a dustbin.

'Devlin would have gone straight to you, wouldn't he?' Bridget said. 'He always went straight to you. Why didn't I go straight to you? What sort of mother—'

168

'You're the best mother.' Blue kissed her forehead. The muscles in her shoulders and neck throbbed. 'The best.'

Bodhi kicked his toe against the curved black bin.

Blue took back Bridget's arm in hers and walked towards the car. The street was empty now, and she was glad of it. Bridget would be worse, she knew, if people watched. Blue would be worse if Bodhi stood there staring.

In the car, Bridget cried and tried to mask it with her hand. At home, Blue put her to bed, wrapped her up in Devlin's old kaftan and soothed her as best she could. Bridget wouldn't eat but took a sip of milk.

'Do you see him, ever?' she asked as Blue tucked the beaded linen around her.

'No.'

'That means he's at peace?'

It means we didn't kill him, Blue thought.

'Aye,' she said.

'How is it you can see them?'

In all their years together, she had never asked this.

'I don't know.' It was the truth.

The blood had dried hard and thin on the front of her clothes.

She let her mother sleep. Blue put away her tarot cards, folded the sequinned cloths they had used to decorate the stage, put away the candles, crystals, pendants. She hand-washed the stain out of the kaftan her mother had made for her and put it out to dry. She tried hard not to think about Jean-Paul's mother and father. She tried hard not to think about Jean-Paul.

Bridget didn't leave her room for two weeks, and Blue didn't try and cajole her. She did little other than go from bedroom to living room in the month after that, and Blue was glad of it. It meant that when Jean-Paul's mother told her story to the true-life magazines, Bridget wasn't in a fit state to read them. She was unaware of the phone calls Blue received from similar rags asking for comments. When the local paper called Blue out as a charlatan in a sparse, space-filling article, Blue was able to put it straight out for recycling before Mother could see. Then she cancelled their delivery.

She cancelled the remaining shows, cancelled the private readings.

Their money ran out.

Blue got a job in a factory, a zero-hour contract filling boxes with packets of biscuits that would be sent across to Ireland on a boat. Bridget didn't notice anything had changed until Blue replaced their old box television with a second-hand smart TV.

'Where did that come from?' she asked. Her reflection was savage in the smooth black screen; her long plait was frazzled, the skin of her cheeks hung in deflated jowls. Blue must make her eat more.

'I bought it.' Blue stood with her toes pointed inward, waited for her mother's reaction. Blue had started wearing plain, coloured T-shirts instead of linen robes, kept her hair up in a bun and considered cutting it short.

'With the money from the tarot?' Bridget asked.

'There's no money in tarot,' Blue said. Hurt lingered on Bridget's face then melted away to stupor.

She didn't press further. Blue suspected Bridget knew she worked somewhere but didn't want to address it. They watched a programme on the Cornish coast; a man in a windbreaker with long dark hair stood on the edge of a cliff. They each had a cup of chamomile before going to bed. It'll all be OK, Blue thought.

When Blue got home from work two days later, Mother was on the phone in the living room. She had brushed her hair. The phone was pressed to her ear. A pen was in her hand, a notebook open on her lap. Worry needled Blue's fingers and toes like the pincers of cold, hungry ants.

'She'll be delighted; it's been such a long time,' Bridget said. 'So much must have happened since we last saw you.'

Blue's stomach throbbed where the bruise had once been. She remembered the look on the bereaved father's face, felt the hand at her neck, and her skin grew clammy and cold.

'Next Wednesday at 4 p.m., that's right. Yes … yes … oh thank you, yes.' Her mother laughed her old laugh.

Breath knocked itself from Blue's lungs. She stumbled forward and grabbed for the phone, but her mother, startled, jerked away and laughed again with a higher pitch.

'No, tell them no!' Blue said. She must get the phone, cancel whatever reading her mother had booked. She would not go into that velvet-swagged room, would not shuffle those cards for anyone else, would not tamper in their fate, would not put herself in a position where she was alone on a stage or trapped in a corridor with an angry man or pushed with her spine against brickwork or punched full-on in the gut or made to feel so scared. It was vital, as vital as the need for her heart to pump blood.

She grabbed again for the phone and got it this time but too late; whoever it was had hung up.

'I won't,' she said, and her mother looked surprised and shook her head so her silver hair caught the light.

'I booked it myself,' she said, 'to help. You said we needed the money—'

'I said there's no money in it!'

'But there will be if I book more—'

'There's never been any money in it, never been *anything* in it; it's nothing, it's worthless!'

'But it's your whole life—'

'– it's your whole life!'

'– but you can do this, too—'

'I can't, I can't bloody do it, I can't—'

'But of course you can, my love, my sweet child, of course you can, you're a little go—'

'I won't! I bloody won't! Not anymore—' Blue ripped the notebook from Bridget and flung the book against the wall, where it hit the gilded mirror and cracked it.

Her mother cried out with surprise, fear, pain.

The crack was small, a spiderweb in the bottom right corner of the glass. Blue remembered how she had cried out when the man had hit her.

Blue looked at the crack and not the reflection of her mother.

'I'm sorry,' Blue said. She pressed the heels of her hands to her eyes and her fingertips gripped at her skull. The room was hot, the air close and filled with the sounds of Mother's disappointment. Blue hoped it was that, couldn't bear to think of her mother afraid.

'I'm sorry,' she said again, louder this time. The frustration and anger melted into self-loathing, self-doubt. She heard the cotton throw on the sofa shift with the movement of her mother's body, and she thought, any minute now she'll put her hand on my back. She'll tell me she understands, that it's OK, that I don't have to read anymore.

She heard Mother walk into the hallway and tread up the stairs to her bedroom.

The Moon

'I was happier once I was out of it,' said Blue and Sabina held up her hands in peace, said it was OK.

'I shouldn't have pushed you,' she said.

The corridor stretched long and quiet, the empty bedroom doors shut tight. No sounds rose from downstairs; Blue hoped Mr Park was still somewhere within. She had to get that password, get away.

'What's wrong? You keep looking over my—' Sabina looked behind her, searched for what distracted Blue.

'It's nothing, I was just hoping to talk to Mr Park.'

'What about?'

'I wanted to get the Wi-Fi code; figured I'd stand more of a chance getting it from him than his wife.'

'Missing Instagram?' Sabina said, and Blue shrugged but didn't correct her.

'Mrs Park wants us to paint this morning,' said Sabina, 'whilst we wait for the AA to call back. Says it will help lower our stress levels.' Sabina looked at her deadpan, and Blue laughed, couldn't help it. 'I'm no artist,' Sabina said. 'I haven't painted a picture since I was a child. So, if you get the code, for the love of all that is good, give it to me too.'

They took the stairs together; Sabina stifled a grin at the prospect of Wi-Fi, Blue's heart thrummed like the wings of a nervous bird. The hall was unoccupied, the fire was out. A loud spray of rain drummed the window and Sabina jumped.

'Jesus,' she said. 'This house really wasn't made to be empty.'

The passageway to the kitchen was clear. They took hushed, careful steps, heard movement from a therapy room; presumably Mrs Park with the easels. Blue felt suddenly foolish, putting herself and Sabina through an ordeal that was probably unnecessary. She could just ask Mrs Park for the code, could stand up straight and demand it with the same authority Sabina showed when she asked for her mobile phone.

But Blue didn't stop and ask her, and she held her breath as she walked past the door.

In the kitchen, their only witnesses were the dogs, their black eyes staring out from the frames on the sill.

Blue knocked on the green varnished door. There was no answer.

'Just go in and take it,' Sabina whispered. 'I saw the hub last time the door opened; it's right there, just inside. Take a photo of the password card and come out again.'

'What if someone sees?' Blue wondered why, if it was so simple, Sabina hadn't offered to go in.

'It'll take two seconds; no one will know. But, look, I'll go distract Molly, and if you see Joshua, just explain that you want the code. He'll be fine with that, just like he was fine with the wine last night.'

Blue nodded. She told herself it was OK, that the foreboding she felt from that door handle was her own, that her bird-heart hummed because of her own fear and nothing she'd picked up from the Parks.

Or Sabina.

'And then AirDrop the photo,' Sabina said. 'Here, give me your phone and I'll add you to my contacts.' Sabina exchanged their numbers, then handed Blue's mobile back. The mischievous grin still played on Sabina's lips, and Blue thought that their breach of rules gave Sabina as much of a thrill as the prospect of Wi-Fi.

'I'll go and make sure the hall is clear, then I'll talk to Molly. Meet me in the art room after, OK?' Sabina left and Blue gave the green door a final knock. No one answered. She turned the handle, ignored the bilious churn in her belly.

Blue stepped through. A radio was on in a closed-off room, the announcer's voice muffled.

'– *extreme weather after days of heavy rain and high winds*—'

The Parks' living room was more homely than the rest of Hope Marsh House and less well kept. A thick navy rug in need of a vacuum spread itself over the wooden floor, and the large leather sofas were worn. A crocheted blanket of bile green and yellow was folded over the armrest of the nearest.

On the mantle were half a dozen photos: Mr and Mrs Park arm in arm on the steps of a grey stone building; Mr Park in full ski get-up on top of a snow-covered mountain; a flush-cheeked, brandy-nosed Mrs Park in a Christmas hat. None of relatives or friends. No other people in the photos of the Parks. More pictures of the dogs that had died. A film of grime coated every frame, blocked shine or reflection.

'– *the Environment Agency has issued severe flood warnings for most of the south-west—*'

Blue spotted the slim black hub on the table behind the nearest sofa, tucked behind a frame that was faced away. She stepped closer, ears pricked for Mr Park's footsteps.

She pulled the card from the hub; her fingers slipped on the dust.

The air smelt damp. A lower corner of the wallpaper was tinged mildew grey.

With her spare hand, she reached for her phone.

A door handle turned.

Hinges creaked.

Blue spun round and knocked the frame from the table.

And she saw the face in the photograph.

Strength (Reversed)

Molly can't quite believe what she sees. She plainly stated that the apartment was out of bounds when she gave Blue the tour on Friday. Yet here she is in Molly's private living room, turquoise and orange eyes on her personal possessions, one hand on the back of Molly's particular settee as she bends down to pick up a photo frame.

Molly tells her to leave it alone, but it's too late; she stoops and collects it, holds it face-out towards Molly.

This is our home; it's not for guests, Molly says and reaches for the frame, hopes Blue hasn't scanned it with her peeping-Tom eyes. Is there to be no privacy? Molly snaps, and Blue apologises, says she wanted to speak to Molly's husband and thought he had come through here.

Molly can't remember the last time she snapped at a guest like this, but she can't seem to help it. She's exhausted, overwrought, fearful. Molly tells her that he may have done, but he's gone out again, through the rear door, back to the river, won't be back until lunch. She doesn't say how angry he still is after Molly told him what she'd seen in the therapy room last night, how he needs space to think, as though Molly doesn't need space, as though she can possibly think freely inside that house with guests everywhere, even where they shouldn't be, behaving how they should not behave, and how is she meant to keep it all running, the activities and the food and the dusting, the perpetual bloody dusting that demands her attention every second of every hour and doesn't he know that dust is mainly dead skin? How can she keep on top of all that when she doesn't have a second to think freely?

She does not say any of that.

Molly holds out her hand, takes the picture from Blue and holds it with the image of Eleanor's face pressed to her chest.

Blue apologises again, won't meet Molly's eye, and Molly can't bear to see her in this room, this one sacred place that's untainted by the retreat, the guests, that house. Even Eleanor didn't come in here; Joshua built it himself afterwards.

What do you want Joshua for? Molly asks and watches how Blue looks to the left as though rummaging her subconscious for an answer. Her hand is in her back pocket. Molly knows Blue will lie before the words leave her mouth. To see if he needs help with the flood, she says, and Molly snaps at her. No, he doesn't need her help; he's got everything under control. Have you something in your pocket? she says and Blue replies no and holds her hands up as though she's a hostage.

Heat rises up Molly's neck, and she has to get Blue out of that room before she loses her patience completely. She cannot let that happen, cannot let this girl think Molly is unhinged. Molly is calmness personified. She is collected, unflappable; it's unlike her to be so uptight.

The radio is on. An announcer drones, predicts more downpours, and Molly wants to go into the bedroom and hurl the machine out the window because how can she be unflappable when nothing is going to plan?

A smile plants its roots in Molly's cheeks and spreads across her face. She tells Blue in a calm, steady manner that everything is fine, that she's sorry for being cross, accidents happen, and really Blue shouldn't apologise at all, there is no harm done, and why don't they all go to the art room together and begin the lesson? The patience in her voice sounds forced, her smile false, but she is doing her best and Blue looks relieved.

Molly would feel relief too were it not for the quick change in Blue's gaze, the way it's drawn like a magnet to the photo in Molly's hands, the way her brow slightly creases, her mouth turns slightly down, and Molly feels her insides contract with panic. Had Blue seen the photo before handing it to Molly? Had she seen Eleanor on the sofa, Molly's arm round her, a half-built Jenga tower on the coffee table?

So what if she did, Molly thinks. It's just a photo – it won't bring Eleanor back; it won't force Molly to relive that bone-burning, heart-tearing agony. Still, there is panic. You shouldn't have come in here, she says senselessly.

Footsteps approach. Blue peers over Molly's shoulder; anxiety lingers in her strange eyes. Molly doesn't turn around; she knows who it is. There is no sound of a walking frame, no wheeziness, so it must be Sabina, and sure enough, Molly hears the German voice ask if everything is OK.

Blue says she was looking for Mr Park, but Molly cuts her off. Everything's fine, let's go, she says.

Milton's waiting for us, Sabina says, and Molly is sure that some silent thing passes between the two women. There is more to this, Molly knows, but she won't ponder it now.

She replaces Eleanor's picture on the console, ushers the two women into the kitchen, across the passage and into the room where the canvases wait. Milton, too frail to stand for the length of a lesson, sits in front of one easel. He's hung his hat on its corner, positioned his walking frame beside him. What took you so long, he says.

Blue looks sidelong into the open cupboard, where five more easels stand propped against the wall. Joshua went through it this morning to dig out the flood boards, a precautionary measure, he said, and they sit in a messy, dusty pile by the boxes of art materials. Molly closes the door.

Choose a workstation, Molly says; each has palettes, brushes, water and rags. Everything you need to get started.

She speaks too quickly. Milton frowns, has only caught half of what she says, and she has to repeat it all loud and slow. He already has a workstation, he tells her. Why does she think he's sitting like a lemon in front of it?

Do you know what you would like to paint? Molly says, and he shakes his head, puckers his mouth like a child, and Molly doubts he's painted a thing since he was one. Suspects he never painted even then. She waits for the joy of teaching to fill her, the satisfaction and delight that comes to her when she makes a difference in a guest's life, but it doesn't come.

Molly looks out on the flooded field, the dark woods, the river where her husband wades thigh-deep. You can paint whatever you like, she says and stands in front of an easel; Milton is to her left, Sabina and Blue to her right. She explains that some people like to make a faint pencil sketch first; others prefer going straight to the paint. There really is no right or wrong.

Milton says there's always a right and a wrong. How are they meant to do it if she doesn't give proper instruction?

Well, I'm going to go straight to paint, Molly says, and she picks up her brush and dips it in water before slicking it in pale violet. She sweeps a wide river across the diagonal. She smiles inwardly as the three other adults copy her like puppets.

The water's risen again, Sabina says.

She wishes Sabina would shut up about the bloody rain. Molly says that there are times when waters rise and times when waters retreat; no state is permanent.

Death, Milton says, and Molly says, excuse me?

True, says Sabina, death is irreversible.

Death? No need to worry about that, Molly says, and her voice is high like a badly stringed violin. No need to worry at all. We've everything we need to get us through, and Hope Marsh has never flooded, not even when the rest of the Levels were submerged. We've plenty of food, plenty of activities, the time will pass so we may as well make good use of it.

Classical plays from hidden speakers, the gentle strings of Arvo Pärt, and Molly lets her eyelids close, feels the sway of the music. She will paint her husband. She will paint away all her anger and fear from this morning, release it and replace it with forbearance.

Milton concentrates and stays silent. Occasionally he puts his palette down, takes a ragged breath; Molly offers him a drink of water. He tells her he's not a bloody cripple and if he wants water he'll get it himself.

Sabina makes progress on her river, adds the dark lines of trees, a sweep of the weeping willow.

Blue has hardly touched her canvas. She says again she can give Joshua a hand, and Molly tells her there's no need. Still, the girl looks out to the river. Her eyes are not on Joshua but on the bridge. Her skin has turned an unhealthy grey.

The girl needs a distraction. Molly tells them that she positioned the easels here to paint the scenery, but really, they can paint whatever takes their fancy. A memory, a place of importance, a person you love or miss. Molly lets the phrase hang in the air, dabs her brush in a darker purple and adds depth to the shape of her river. Art, she tells them, is an ideal therapy. When we focus on creativity, areas of our brain that are usually dormant come to life. If we allow ourselves to surrender to it, we often find the most surprising things. It can be very healing if you're able to give way completely.

Sabina stifles a yawn. Blue looks shaky. Molly suspects what is wrong and blames her husband for it. She gestures to a table on the far side of the room where a glass jug, several glasses and a plate of iced shortbread sit. She tells them it's lemon water, says citrates are good for a hangover. They are to help themselves.

The wind picks up outside and fights a mid-air battle with the branches. Blue squeezes her eyes shut, rubs her temples as if she's seen something unpleasant, and when she opens them and stares back out to the bridge, she looks like she might be sick. Molly thinks it serves Blue right, feels it's karma's revenge for Blue's prying. Outwardly, Molly tells her to go easy, to sit down if she needs to.

Try and relax, she tells Blue in her most maternal voice.

A heron stands in the willow's shadow, its beak angled towards the flood. Despite his grumpiness, Milton almost smiles, and dips his paintbrush in grey and makes a vague birdish shape on his canvas. He's far better than Molly thought he would be. She wonders why he had never joined the art sessions before.

Blue paints the water; she starts with the ripples then adds the curved shadows cast by trees. Sabina fills her pallet with blues, greens and browns, chooses a slim brush and also begins to paint, and Molly thinks there is hope for all of them yet.

Then Sabina says, look, the rain's stopped, and if the weather improves, maybe the mechanics can reach us.

It's best to concentrate on the task in hand, Molly says and tells Milton his heron is beautiful, even though the body is too wide, the legs too thick and short. She looks at Blue's river painting and tells the girl well done, despite it lacking any flair at all. She looks at Sabina's.

In the branches of the watercolour willow sits a figure. A girl. There is no face, no real solid shape, just a pale head, long strings of blonde hair on each shoulder. It's horrible.

Molly tells her it's good, interesting, and Sabina says that her niece loved trees, that the image of Lauren just came to her, and she felt the urge to include her. Molly is not listening. There is something uncanny about the figure in the willow; its featureless face paints itself with

Eleanor's eyes, nose, mouth, but she does not say this out loud. Molly would like to look away, but she can't.

She wonders why Sabina referred to the girl in the past tense.

Sabina washes her brush, dips it in red and gives the child a pair of scarlet shoes.

Why red shoes, Molly asks. She feels queasy. It's been a stressful weekend, she reminds herself. There are many girls with blonde hair, many with red shoes.

Blue has dropped her brush on the floor. She looks at Sabina's painting, says what—

The telephone rings in the hallway. Sabina says it must be the mechanic and Molly jolts, moves away from the painting that has disturbed her, away from Blue and her odd eyes and strange aura.

Molly hurries from the room, through the passage to the phone at the end. Sabina follows, eager to hear the news and escape the house that Molly has tried so hard to turn into a sanctuary.

Inner peace is restored when Molly lifts the phone and hears what's said. This is her house, after all. Her retreat. The guests are lucky to be here.

And, thanks to the weather, no one is coming to help.

No one can leave her.

The Star (Reversed)

Blue turned her back on the painting, but the image burned itself into her vision. She staggered to the table. Her mouth smacked of bitter medicine, so strong it was hard not to gag. She felt that same pressure against her nose and mouth, felt invisible feathers and dust fill her windpipe. Tension pressed at her temples, her brain throbbed, her stomach churned from the flavour in her mouth and the dryness in her throat.

'You all right?' Milton said. He had stood up and shuffled over to look at Sabina's canvas.

Blue poured a glass of lemon water, downed it in one go.

This was doing her no good. It wasn't healthy. Over the past few years she had gone through a rigorous re-education, had numerous explanations for the visions she saw, yet she couldn't get a handle on a single one. She wouldn't go back, wouldn't fool herself into believing that thing was real.

It was not real.

'I'm fine, just thirsty,' Blue said and refilled her glass. She had slipped the card with the Wi-Fi code into her back pocket and she could sense it there; an unpinned grenade if Mrs Park found it, a divining rod for freedom if she did not.

Minutes ago, the creature with long blonde hair and pale skin had balanced on the bridge above Mr Park's head. Now she sat, faceless, in the branches of Sabina's weeping willow. Blue had the feeling that, were she to turn around now, she would see it again in the room, hands reaching out, hair limp, dark eyes dead holes in her head.

Milton's wheeze turned into a cough, a deep-chested painful sound, and Blue turned, asked him if he was OK. She was expecting his usual eye-roll, but he shook his head, coughed again and again into his elbow. His eyes were fixed on Sabina's picture.

'What is it?' Blue ran to him, patted him on his back, but he shook her off and pointed instead to the water jug. Blue grabbed him a glass, and he sipped it in tentative swallows. His spare hand gripped the edge of his walking frame.

'Can I get you anything?' she said, and he shook his head, muttered something about his hat, a photo, but his voice was hoarse and low.

Blue couldn't look at Sabina's painting again but didn't want to leave Milton's side. Outdoors, the clouds thickened, and the view became grey, the shape of Joshua Park a blur of shadow and movement. The vice around Blue's temples tightened; the medicinal taste became stronger.

'Looks like Jessica,' Milton muttered. He was looking at the girl in the willow tree.

'Eleanor, Lauren, Jessica Pike.' She spoke without thought.

'What did you say?' Milton startled. His eyes bulged at her; his thick white eyebrows knitted together.

'Nothing, just—'

'What do you know about Jess?' His face was red, and Blue couldn't tell if he was angry, scared, worried, surprised. The only sensation she had was the pharmaceutical taste on her tongue, the tension in her head, the dryness in her throat.

The pain trebled. It burned at her temples, spread into her shoulders and brought with it the unbearable knowledge that she would die, that hands that should care for her would kill her.

She staggered to the drinks table, rested her weight in her hands, tried to catch her breath, but all she could smell was the sickness, and all she could taste was bitter pill.

Synaesthesia, it's all synaesthesia. It's not real.

Milton was at her side, talked to her as though she were the sick one. Was she all right, did she need a doctor and then, when Blue's breath steadied, he said, 'How do you know that name?'

The light brightened. Blue could sense it through her closed lids, could feel the pain lessen and she said, 'I heard it,' instead of *I felt it.*

Excitement and agitation filled Milton's face, made him younger for a moment, almost hopeful. 'Where did you hear it? Who said it?'

She heard the wind, the water, the birdsong faint in the trees, the wheeze of the old man. She saw something. Hidden beneath his old-man cardigan, beneath his frail health and his feigned indifference, were his fears, his secrets, his lies.

'Your name's not Milton,' she said. 'What is it? Who are you, really?'

The veins on his withered neck swelled. He grabbed her. 'What do you know about Jess?'

Blue cried out as his fingers dug into her flesh.

'I know nothing,' she said, and caught the fear in her voice, and her belly ached with the memory of being hit. 'I just heard it somewhere, I don't know where.'

His expression turned to horror. He dropped her arm, stepped back. 'I'm sorry,' he said, and he sounded it.

The door opened and Sabina came in.

'Molly's gone to start lunch; I didn't realise how late it had got. She asks if you'd like any tea?' Sabina stopped on the threshold. 'Are you OK?'

'The mechanic?' Blue said, though she knew the answer, could tell by Sabina's defeated posture.

'Tomorrow,' Sabina said. 'There's still too much water to reach us. Sit tight and wait it out, was the advice. Joshua is back; he couldn't clear the culvert. Something has wedged deep under the bridge again, so big that he can't pull it out. Another dead thing, he thinks.'

The drowned rabbit hopped through Blue's thoughts, chased by the black dogs, the twisted trees and that thing, that horrible, dead thing. No one was coming to help them.

'OK,' Blue said. 'I would like some tea, thank you. I'm just going to go upstairs, freshen up. I'll be down in fifteen minutes.'

'I'll tell Mrs Park you're meditating,' Sabina said with wry humour. Blue had an urge to reach out and hold her, explain everything, thank her for making these last few days bearable. To apologise for the fact she would soon run away.

'Thanks,' was all Blue said. Her tongue was still bitter, her head ached, her chest full of the horror that if she didn't escape now, right now, she never would.

'I'm sorry,' Milton said once Sabina had left. He looked at his hands, horrified. 'I forget myself, I'm sorry—'

'No, it's … I'm … I'm sorry,' Blue said and turned on her heel, couldn't bear it another moment, left the lying old man alone in the room with the painting and the echo of that name.

The Eighties

James and Marie had a council flat on Bath Row. He still worked in the factory office part-time. His lung had not got any better, but nor had it got much worse. Marie worked in the canteen, and when the canteen was closed and replaced with vending machines, she took a job in a local school kitchen. James thought he knew himself, knew his lot. He was an average man approaching happy middle age; life was life, and there was little else to it. Then there was Judith.

She waited for him at the hotel bar. She wore a bright pink blouse and a black-and-white checked suit, which nipped her waist and padded her shoulders. She was lithe and young, with big breasts and big eyes and big blonde hair that was permed and soft. Her lipstick was pink, so too her high heels, and it was the same outfit she had worn the last time. The first time.

Her martini glass was empty when James arrived, and he asked her if she wanted another and hoped it wouldn't be expensive.

'Are you having one?' she said. She was twenty-seven years old.

'Yes, OK, a small one,' James said. He had stopped at a pub on the way, had taken a whisky and water to level his nerves, then bought some mints at a corner shop. He didn't know what he was doing.

He ordered two drinks and sat on a high green stool beside Judith. She put her hand on his knee, and he looked around to see if anyone there might know him or know Marie. He didn't know what he was doing. But this young woman's hand was on his knee, and he could think of little else. He drank quickly.

He groped for conversation, remembered the newspaper headlines in the corner shop. 'Terrible about Chernobyl,' he said. His tongue felt useless in his mouth, his legs felt weak. 'All those people.'

'I have a room,' she said, 'shall we—'

'OK,' he said.

Afterwards, they lay beneath the polyester sheet, and she put her head on his chest, and her soft hair brushed his chin. He wanted to itch it, but one hand was pinned beneath her, and she held his other.

'I brought wine,' she said. 'Do you want a glass?'

He freed his arm and rested it across her shoulders, then moved it again, so it lay on the bed, its underside touching her body. Her skin was smooth and young, and he was middle-aged and married. He didn't understand what this young woman, this young career woman, saw in him. In the same way, he had never understood what Marie saw in him.

'I better not. That drink in the bar was strong.' He remembered how he used to not drink, play sports, go dancing, or know anything about music. Marie loved to dance. James loved to dance with Marie. He didn't know what he was doing.

'Go on. One won't do any harm. It'll help you relax.' She propped herself up on an elbow, and her soft blonde hair fell across her eye, and she kissed him on the mouth. 'Was it difficult getting away?' she said.

'No, not very,' he said.

'What excuse did you give?'

'I didn't give one,' he said.

'And she just let you go?'

'Yes,' he said.

'But won't she wonder where you are? Won't she ask you questions about it when you go home tomorrow?'

'Tomorrow?' he said.

She sat up, and the sheet fell away, and she pushed her hair back from her face.

'Yes, tomorrow. When you go home, tomorrow.'

James felt that same rush as he had done the first time she had looked at him like that, with want in her eyes, and no woman had looked at him like that before. And he didn't think, I can't stay, he only thought, I can't believe she wants me to stay.

Most people knew him too well; all the women in the factory had known him years, knew Marie too. They knew what James was, what was wrong with him, why he sometimes left his desk very suddenly to cough for minutes on end outside. Judith didn't know any of that.

They had sat beside each other in a meeting room, just them, and she had shown him samples of stationery from her sales bag, and he had told her he'd have to leave the decision-making with his boss who was away, would be back next week. She sat very near him at the table. She touched his hand. He asked her why she had gone into sales. She had said it was exciting, that she liked meeting people, that the money was good. She said she liked his voice, called it husky, and he didn't tell her that his vocal cords were damaged.

She said she lived near Warwick but was staying at a hotel and would he like to meet there for a drink that afternoon, and somehow he had gone. He didn't know why he had gone; he did not think about it. His shift finished at three, and he went to the hotel; he was home by nine, and Marie was out at a girlfriend's. He had sat in a chair by the window, five storeys up, and looked at the lights from the cars, and he couldn't believe it had happened. There had been no time to feel guilt or horror. He felt a dreamlike wonder. A beautiful young woman had looked at him that way, with no pity or humour, only that want in her eyes. No woman had ever treated him like he was a man to lust after. It had felt like a hallucination. He felt it had not been real, none of it, because something like that couldn't happen to him.

And yet, here he was with her, again.

'I can't stay the night,' he said. 'I have to go home.'

'I thought you would stay the whole night.'

'I'm sorry, I can't.'

'Will you have a glass of wine with me, at least?' she said, and he nodded, and she got up from the bed, naked, and poured them two glasses of wine, and she stood beside him at the bed, and his face was level with her chest.

'Do you have any children?' she asked as she put the glass in his hand.

He had been with Marie for four months before they had gone to bed together. They married a few months after that. Judith knew nothing about him. She stroked his hair and ran her fingers down the back of his head as if she knew everything.

'No, we don't,' he said. Judith's fingers were light and warm. His cock stiffened, and he thought, my God, you're beautiful, too beautiful, and then: what am I doing?

'Did you not try for any?'

'We did. It just didn't work out. I was unwell when I was younger; it rendered me, you know—' He gulped his wine, and his painful thoughts died, and he was aware of the closeness of her naked body. She finished her wine quickly, clambered across him and lay on her side of the bed.

'I'm sorry,' she said. 'You'd be a great dad.'

'I'm a great uncle, instead,' he said. He was a great uncle. There were seven nieces and nephews in all. He had painted a watercolour portrait of each one, remembered their birthdays, remembered which kids had Saturday football matches and when, which had dance recitals. They sat on his lap, and he felt the solid weight of them. They put their hands around his neck, and he felt their warmth. It was something. It was something, at least.

Judith put her hand beneath the sheet and felt for him.

Afterwards, he rose from the bed and went to the bathroom and sat on the loo. In the mirror, he saw a middle-aged man, the same man who had looked back at him this morning, and how was it he still looked the same? He had lost himself. He didn't understand it, didn't trust himself. How was it that a man can love his wife and yet forget her so completely? Forget himself so completely?

His watch showed the time. He'd have to get home soon. It was his father's watch. Had been his father's. A few months ago, it became James' watch. It had taken weeks before he was able to do up the strap himself. His fingers trembled; he was prone to tearfulness. Marie helped him with the strap, told him his father would be happy that he wore it. She reminded him of the Christmas when James' father took charge of the turkey and mixed up pounds and kilograms, and James laughed at the memory of an enormous bird that was big enough for twelve and that his mum couldn't fit in the oven. And Marie said, *There, you're laughing, much better than tears.* And she said, *He loved you so much.*

Towels sat folded on the shelf by the bathroom door, and he tied one around his waist.

'I'd better be getting on,' he said before he came back into the bedroom, doubting his nerve now, doubting himself.

Judith perched on the bed, knickers on but bare on top. She refastened her topaz earring. 'I wish you could stay,' she said.

James kept his eyes on the floor. 'I know, I'm sorry.'

'Next time, will you stay?'

'I don't know. It's difficult.'

'Try.' She stood and put her arms around his neck, and her hair brushed his cheek and his chin, and her bare breasts pressed against him. She took his hand and pushed it around her, so it rested on her lower back. 'Please,' she said, in the same voice she had said please in bed, *please, please, please.*

He held her, but looked over her shoulder for his clothes, saw them on the chair by the window. They were folded neatly, his shoes beneath the chair, his socks rolled inside them. She pressed her groin into his, shifted side to side, but there was nothing in him now but horror. She kissed his cheek, tried to kiss his mouth, but he turned away.

'I'm sorry,' James said. 'I can't. I can't do this. I better go.'

She held on. She moved her lips from his cheek to his ear.

'I have a son,' she said, as if it were an offer.

'A son?'

She nodded, and her hair brushed him again. 'He's called Sebastian,' she said.

'I've a nephew called Sebastian. He's seven,' James said and pictured the boy as he pulled socks on for Saturday football. Pictured him next to Marie at his birthday lunch, as Marie spooned jelly on to Sebastian's plate, the boy's face smeared with ice cream and full of glee. They had gone to all the children's birthday parties. Together.

'My mum's looking after him tonight. He's only two,' Judith said.

'Lovely age, two,' James said, and he unwound his hand from Judith's body. 'I really must—'

He got dressed in silence. Sebastian had been two when he started talking. James remembered Marie in the kitchen when the phone rang, and she answered, and her face looked confused then turned to joy, bright joy, and she laughed and called James over and held the receiver to his ear. In the background was James' brother, Milton, repeating the

191

words more clearly, but in the receiver, and in James' ear, was the full glorious sound of it.

'Murry, Murry, Aunty Murry,' the little boy said. Marie had her hands pressed in prayer to her lips, a smile caught behind them. All the children called her Murry from then on.

He would never have married Marie had he known what the sickness had done to him.

'He's just started talking,' Judith said now. She was dressed and rifled through her handbag, and pulled out her purse. Inside was a photograph of a little boy, black curls and black eyes and a sporadically toothed grin, and this was Judith's son, but James pictured the child hanging from Marie's neck, kissing Marie's plump cheek as she laughed, Marie's arms a safety net around him.

'A fine boy,' James said. Judith looked younger now she was dressed. Her make-up stained the hotel pillows. She started to pull on her tights, but one leg was laddered, so she took them off, put them in the bin. She squeezed her bare feet into her high heels, and the shoes dug into her skin.

'You'd like him, if you met him,' she said, and there it was again, that offering, that hope.

'I'm sorry,' James said. She shrugged and bent down, fiddled with her shoes, and her hair hid her face.

'Will I see you again?' she said.

James walked home. His legs ached, and he wanted them to ache because of the walk, nothing else. He sat in a pub for ten minutes, drank half an orange juice, waited for the smoke and cheap aftershave to permeate his clothes and skin. A reason to shower when he got home. He had to get home.

Marie was in the kitchen.

'I can smell you from here,' she said and turned to look at him. She batted the air as if the smell was a swarm of flies and laughed. 'You've been in the pub, you naughty wretch!'

She turned back to the kitchen counter, a pile of vegetables to her left, a stack of peeled, sliced veg on her right. 'Did you have a good day? I walked with Christa along the canal, with little Toby, all the way to Victoria Square; it's the longest walk his little legs have done yet. Two miles. And Bruno collected us afterwards in the nice car, not the work van, thank God, and took us all for cake at the tea room and we were there having the cake, and I suddenly realised which tea room it was – the same one we went to, do you remember? When we—'

He came up behind her, put his hands on her waist and buried his face in her hair, which was wiry and turning grey.

'– first met, and I walked you to the bus stop,' she said, still peeling potatoes. Enough potatoes for a family, but they hadn't a family, and so whatever they couldn't eat would be frozen for another day.

Perhaps he needed to give an excuse, but he couldn't. He thought that if he spoke, he would use the wrong words, say some wrong thing, or tell the truth, and so he kissed her neck and held her hips lightly and thought, I'm sorry, I'm sorry, I'm so sorry. And he thought, please, please, though he didn't know what it was he begged for.

He thought, please and sorry, and he held her lightly, and he felt her move backwards against him, felt the curve of her backside press into his groin, and she turned her head to the side and let him kiss her cheek. The potato and the peeler were still in her hands, but she moved her hips side to side against him.

He thought, I'm sorry, so sorry, and Marie gave a small moan of pleasure and laughed her dirty laugh when his palms moved up from her hip to her waist, and he thought, stay with me, I'm so sorry, and stay with me.

And his hands moved from her waist to her breasts; their heavy swell filled his palms, and she laughed again and pushed back against him, and she put the peeler down. She could not see his face, and he was glad of it; she could only see his hands on her breasts, and her hands reached behind and held his body to her.

He wanted to say, I love you, I love you, don't leave me; I love you, but could only think I'm sorry and said nothing. She hummed a giddy sound of pleasure, and he felt her more firmly.

He felt her more firmly.

Felt it, there, right there.

A chestnut lump beneath her left breast.

PART II

The Chariot

Blue packed quickly; most of her belongings remained in the suitcase, and she'd leave them as they were. She shoved a spare jumper into her rucksack, socks in case her feet got wet, and a bottle of water and the biscuits from the welcome pack. Her phone was connected to the Wi-Fi; the nearest house was a two-mile walk.

She slid the card with the password beneath Sabina's closed door.

The skylight above the stairs showed thick clouds, white rather than grey. Blue hoped it wouldn't rain again.

She stole into the boot room, put on her wellingtons and lifted a fresh set of waterproofs; she'd post them back to the Parks in time. She didn't worry about her car or suitcase. Small details.

The only need Blue had in the present was getting away from this house, these people, the endless questions, the doubt, the mistrust.

Giddiness muddled her thoughts as she stepped out into the watery field. Low blood sugar, perhaps. Remnants of the hangover. Stress. The collapse of her efforts to get over Mother's death and live a normal life.

The shallow water splashed at her toecaps; mud sucked at the wellingtons. She headed away from the bridge and towards the line of trees on the other side of the house. They reached their boughs for her, invited her to take their hands, twist her fingers through their many branches and let them ferry her away from Hope Marsh House.

She focused on her footsteps and the uneven, bogged ground. She had no plan beyond getting away from this place. Phone in hand, she followed the directions. Drowned catkins clung to her boots.

Those left behind would worry. She tried not to think about Mrs Park's crestfallen face, the panic she would feel that she had done something wrong, had upset Blue and driven her away. She didn't think of Milton's lies, or his horror at himself and the guilt he felt for his aggression. She couldn't think about Sabina. It was almost enough to turn Blue around.

Almost.

The further from the house she got, the more her thoughts took order. She was susceptible to other people's feelings, she knew this, and a grief retreat would harbour more people in turmoil than anywhere else. What had Blue expected? The thing she saw was a collective manifestation of everyone's pain and loss.

And what of the brunette girl in Mrs Park's photograph? The child who Mrs Park hugged like a daughter, who was photographed sitting on the small sofa in the hall, who was midway through the Jenga tower that Mrs Park could no longer bear to play, the girl who looked like a dark-haired version of the thing Blue kept seeing. Smelling. Sensing.

It was probably a niece, she thought, then remembered the Parks were both only children. Then it was a goddaughter, perhaps, the child of a close friend. It was a coincidence.

If she explained to Mrs Park the things she had experienced, how her brain played spirits before her eyes, made her question reality, made her fear for the fabric of her mind, what would happen? Would she counsel Blue, swaddle her in the warm therapy room and encourage Blue to talk through her problems? Hug her and tell her it would all be OK, brush her hair from her forehead and play mother? Would she be able to do the one thing that would save Blue and help keep her sane?

Too late. She feared her mind was lost already.

The water deepened the further she fled from the house.

She didn't look behind her for fear that she hadn't made as much ground as she wanted. The treeline seemed to move further away. The shapes of the shadows twisted and bulged.

A bird swooped over her head, large and black, and called Arlo's name.

It rang in her ear, made her wince.

She could smell the water, dank with leaf rot and animal musk.

The bird called again. Was it a raven, a crow?

Her mind folded in on itself, her head ached, her thoughts made no sense. The trees seemed close enough to talk to. They seemed to be far away.

'Blue!'

She stopped, turned; water splashed over the top of her boot.

Sabina leant out of a kitchen window, an ant stretching out of a doll's house. Her voice carried clearly through the damp afternoon.

'What are you doing? Come back!'

Blue raised a hand in goodbye, turned back to the trees. They were close after all. She had made it to the woods.

Through the woods, over a hill, across a bridge and along a road, and she would be there.

Woods, hill, bridge, road.

Don't think of Sabina, she told herself. Don't think about how unfair all this is on her.

A shadow darted into the trees on her right. She looked, expected to see a fox or large bird, but the animal had gone. Instead, she saw a small grey slab that rose from the ground. A gravestone for the two dead dogs.

Blue's phone vibrated, and a message appeared.

WHERE ARE YOU GOING? COME BACK. WE'RE WORRIED.

Her fingers were damp and smeared the screen. I'M GETTING HELP, Blue typed. She laughed at the message. The promise of help had drawn her to Hope Marsh House. Help is the last thing she had found. The disappointment made her head swim.

The clouds shifted and the shadows all shifted and Blue could see the grave to her right. She remembered the growls she had heard, the barks, the sound of dogs' claws that had infested her dreams. She kept her gaze forward, took a step to the left and walked on.

Her mobile rang: Sabina. She cancelled the call.

It rang again, the landline from Hope Marsh House. Cancelled.

Thin branches traced their spindles along her sleeve and dripped fat drops on her shoulders. They couldn't see her, now she was in the woods. They couldn't track her footsteps through water.

Mr Park would worry less, Blue thought. He would be the arm around Mrs Park's shoulder, the reassurance in her ear. He would comfort her and tell her it wasn't her fault, that Blue was an adult and could do as she wanted, and no one could stop her.

There was no one.

Blue wiped a hand across her face. There was rainwater on her cheeks. She thought it was rainwater.

There was no one.

A thought she had tried to push away surged forward and demanded her attention. The only ghosts Blue ever saw had been victims. Why would this one be any different?

What if the Parks killed the girl? Blue thought. What if I've left Sabina and Milton alone with the Parks?

What if Sabina killed the girl? What if I've left Milton and the Parks alone with Sabina?

What if it was Milton?

The trees were beech, alder, birch, oak. Thick branches, spindly twigs, dead leaves on the flood. She waded on. Moss covered the trunks, dense and soft and damp to the touch. Bridget had always loved pictures of trees.

On her wedding day to Devlin, she wore a crown of twisted willow, decorated with red rowan berries and leaves from a Crimson King maple. She knew the trees, their identifiers and their powers, the way they talked to each other with their network of roots. But it had been Devlin who had taken Blue to the forest. Devlin who had helped Blue climb into a yew tree's low branches, and had caught Blue when she slipped.

You don't belong in the woods.

Was that her thought or someone else's?

The desperation to leave Hope Marsh House withered in the dappled light. She had been in the woods twice in her life. Blue walked pavements, not footpaths.

Alone in the wild, trudging through floodwater towards a stranger's home, walking away from a house she thought was haunted. What was wrong with her?

Another message thrummed her phone.

PLEASE COME BACK. PLEASE.

She had tried to be good all her life, had listened to whoever needed it even when it terrified her. Every touch a thunderclap of self-doubt, uncertainty, pride, appreciation, love, disappointment, vengeance, fear, worry, humour, neglect, grief, aspiration, hope. She had never met another soul like her, not even when she was still part of that circle. If she were touched by someone similar, what would they feel?

Bridget had always loved trees. She had never taken Blue to the forest.

Blue had covered over a mile. So far away from any other person, she should feel free. She felt trapped.

She would make it to another building full of strangers, and what would she do then? Would they give her help? Would they help her return to her lonely house?

The cold pull of fate dragged her on.

The wind rolled through the canopy, sent down a shower of wet twigs and upset droplets. Her mobile went black.

Blue revived the screen, chest hollow as she waited for the map to reload.

Unknown road.

Unknown destination.

She shook it, rebooted it, held it above her head and down at her knees. She was well beyond the range of Wi-Fi. She thought the route had downloaded; it hadn't. There wasn't any signal for mobile data.

She pocketed her phone. Closed her eyes, pictured the map and the red dotted line she should take through the woods. She needed to go left and then pick up the path to the bridge.

Or was it right?

How would she tell if she was on a path at all?

The ground would feel different beneath her boots. There would be signposts. There would be something.

She opened her eyes and took a step forward. Her shin pushed a wave through the water.

Blonde hair disappeared behind a tree.

The heel of a trainer, stark red against silver birch.

No. This can't happen. What should she do?

If Blue turned, she would lose her sense of direction. She had to go on.

How could that thing be here? The victim stayed close to the person who killed her; Blue had always known that to be true. The child had only been near the Parks, Milton, Sabina.

And Blue.

But she was no murderer.

Blue could still see her dry red shoe. Could see her hair, unruffled by the wind.

Blue wiped her cheek. She needed to move; the muddy water sucked at her boots, threatened her balance, yet she couldn't take a step.

She's not real.

But what if she is?

The thing moved out, and it was the girl from the watercolour painting; it was the girl from Mrs Park's photograph. The gloom added purple to the shadows below her eyes. Her lips were colourless strips against colourless skin, her thin neck looked ready to snap.

Had it been snapped?

'What are you doing here?' Blue said.

They're coming for you.

'Who's coming?' And she thought of Sabina at the kitchen window. Thought of her name flash up on the mobile.

I need you to help me.

'Who's coming?'

I need you to take me to him. He's worried.

'For God's sake, who's—' Blue stopped, studied the thing before her. It wasn't a dead old man. It wasn't a beaten-up woman in fishnets and one boot. It wasn't a rotten-souled thug who sought revenge. It looked like a little girl.

Blue had never been good with children, but she tried.

'Who will be worried?' Blue said.

My brother.

'Mr Park? Is Joshua Park your brother?'

The girl shook her head. *I need you to take me to my brother.*

It fit no story that Blue knew.

'Are you Eleanor?' she asked.

The girl shook her head, kicked the birch with the toe of her trainer, made no sound, left no mark, caused no ripple.

'What's your name?'

The harsh lines of her face disappeared. She looked exactly like what she was: a child lost in the woods begging for help to get home.

I'm Jessica Pike.

The man who called himself Milton, but wasn't. He didn't look strong enough to kill someone, yet Blue's arm had throbbed where he had grabbed her. Fear had lurked in his eyes. He had lied about his true name. God knows when this girl died – a year ago, twenty years ago, thirty, or back when Milton was a young man?

'Hello, Jessica Pike.' Blue remembered being eleven. She remembered how the kids on the street ran from her, how she chased them and hoped it was a game, how the parents ushered their children away from the strange family with the wind chimes and pendants. She remembered what it was to be eleven.

'What happened to you?' Blue said.

22 to 23

Bridget lost so much weight that Blue could see the shape of her knee-caps through her skirt. She took her mother to the doctor. Then to the hospital. The consultant said the word cancer, and Bridget Ford stood up and left the room.

The consultant gave Blue leaflets, explained the tests that would be carried out to determine the type, the severity, how best to treat it. Bridget wouldn't be tested. Nature, she said, would run its course. She would carve some candles, lay runes at the altar, burn bundles of sage. Blue grew hoarse from trying to convince her otherwise.

Blue was on her third job in as many years: a packer in a warehouse, boxing items the pickers picked from vast shelves, eyes sore from the lack of daylight and the cardboard that spored dust. At lunch break, Blue stood outside with the smokers to get some sunshine, if not fresh air. One of the lads had an uncle with colon cancer, and she overheard him confess that his uncle took cannabis to help with the pain. When Bridget's own pain worsened, Blue bought her a bong.

She needed it. Within a few months, Bridget was bedridden.

'Do you see him?' she asked Blue every day, her leporine face above the quilt, eyes hopeful. Blue recalled the years they had lived in the Preston flat, when Bridget would ask Blue if she had seen Bodhi or Arlo, would ask what they were doing, whether they looked happy, would put amethyst crystals by Blue's bed so the spirits wouldn't disturb her sleep.

'No, he's at peace,' Blue said every day.

Routine was formed around Bridget's needs. Blue woke a little earlier to get a tray of breakfast things ready for her mother and then left for work. When she came home, before she changed her clothes or put on the kettle, she would go up and see Bridget, kiss her forehead, remove the tray of breakfast things and make a mental note of how much she ate. She'd make her mother some more food, prepare the bong, change sheets that had been soiled, clean the bedpan, brush her hair. Blue had bought a small TV that she fixed to the wall, so Bridget had something to do in the long hours Blue was at the warehouse. Sometimes they would watch soap operas together. Sometimes they would just lie side by side, quiet.

'Did you buy this with the money from your commercial job?' Bridget said one day, after her fifth lungful of smoke. There was pain in her voice, and a timidity Blue remembered from those days when she was four or five and Bridget would spend hours sitting in the kitchen with her head rested on the tabletop. 'Isn't it killing you? Isn't your soul being crushed by it? Aren't you stifled?'

'I like it,' Blue said. She sat on the end of Bridget's metal-framed bed. The room didn't have space for much else – two bedside tables, a single wardrobe in the far corner by the window. It overlooked the alley where Blue and Matthew had kissed. It overlooked the garden, where Devlin had put his soft brown arm around Blue when Matthew had run away laughing.

'It's a normal job with normal folk,' Blue said. Matthew's family had moved. The boys that had egged him on had left too. The old man who had taught Blue to drive was in a care home.

'I should have done more; you were so talented, had so much potential. Devlin would have done more. What would he say?'

'He'd not mind,' Blue said.

'Do you see him?' Bridget's hair was still in a plait, braided by Blue. It lay over her shoulder in a thin grey rope.

'No, Mum.'

Bridget turned her face on the pillow. Her hand relaxed around the bong, and Blue caught it before it fell to the floor. 'I should have taken better care of him. After the first heart attack, I should have taken better care of him.'

You could have made him take his heart medicine, Blue thought. You could have made him go to his hospital check-ups, helped him lose weight, encouraged him to have a bypass instead of feeding him wheatgrass and carving symbols in witching candles. But what good are should-haves?

'It wasn't your fault,' Blue said. 'You can't predict a heart attack.'

'You could have predicted it.'

'I never read for him.'

'You'd have saved him if you had.'

'I think you've had enough for today.' Blue sat the bong on the bedside table, next to the still-full plastic tray of yellow curry. Tomorrow she would buy a can of chicken soup. She could generally get Mother to eat chicken soup.

'What a terrible mother.' Bridget gripped Blue's hand; her fingers clawed around her and knocked the dish. Yellow sauce spilt on to the carpet. Bridget was stoned, and her pupils were large, but there was something else in her eyes. 'I should be looking after you; you're my baby, my last baby.'

Cars could be heard on the street; their neighbours coming home from work. A few had offered kindness after Devlin died – sympathy cards, the odd cake. She hadn't told any of them about Mother's health, nor had she told the people at work. She couldn't bring herself to explain. Whenever Bridget touched her, she felt her shame, her embarrassment, her awful sense of having let her daughter down. She could feel it now as Bridget held her wrist.

'You have an awful mother, if you even knew how—'

'Don't you talk that way about my mum.' She wagged a finger and mocked a frown.

'You're trying to make me laugh.'

'Then let me,' Blue said.

'I always tried to make you laugh, but I was no good. I'm sorry I was no good; you deserved better. You all deserved better.' She let go of Blue's arm and patted her hand. Blue felt the very insides of her mother's heart, and Blue wasn't ready for this.

'Devlin loved you,' Blue said. 'Almost as much as I love you. We wouldn't love you so much if you weren't deserving of it.'

'They should have left me to rot.' And Bridget's eyes rolled, briefly, in her skull.

'Never,' Blue said, and she pushed them away – the thoughts, the feelings, the thing Bridget was trying to silently confess, and Blue wouldn't hear it. 'How about some pudding? Some ice cream? Maybe you'll eat something sweet.'

It was dry outside, the autumnal sky clear and darkening by degrees. From her place on the bed, Blue could see the houses on the other side of the gulley and the orange leaves on their garden trees.

'Do you see him?' Bridget said, and the small terraced house felt big, too big to live in alone.

'Devlin? No, I—'

'Bodhi.'

Blue nodded her head, but Mother couldn't see, asked the same question again, and blue remorse filled Blue's heart, her mother's remorse.

'Turn your head, he's next to you,' Blue said.

The little boy stood by the splash of yellow sauce on the carpet. The scowl had dropped from his face; it had dropped the moment Bridget knew she was dying. Blue had thought that Bodhi knew better than to torment her with petulant looks and dark eyes, but now she wasn't so sure. He looked like he might cry, like he needed and wanted to be comforted as much as Blue needed and wanted to be. If Bridget reached out a hand, she would touch the cold air of him.

'I'm sorry, I was a terrible mother, I'm so sorry for all of it.' She reached up for Blue, and she thought her mother was talking to her, that her sorry was for Blue and their dirty flat in Preston, for the lack of toys and food, for making her stay home instead of going to school, but Bridget said, 'Tell Bodhi.'

The bedroom was dark now, but Blue didn't turn on the lamp.

Bodhi wiped his eyes, the sides of his small hands wet with tears. The child's shoulders heaved. Bridget's shoulders heaved.

'Aye, I will,' Blue said, and she kissed her mother's forehead. There was more Bridget wanted to say. Her mouth grimaced, her voice choked by tears, and she racked coughs into her quilt.

'It's OK, Mother,' Blue said when the fit was over and she'd sipped some water. Blue lay down beside her, hushed her and soothed her. She held her mother's hand and closed her eyes tight. She let Bridget's despair flood her, but she couldn't look at the boy. She couldn't look at Arlo, sat in the corner with a blank look in her eyes, damp ringlets framing her face.

Mother was frail in Blue's arms, each breath a rasp that stretched her ribcage and exhausted her lungs. Blue held her until she slept.

The Knight of Wands (Reversed)

Will you help me find my brother?

'I can try. You need to tell me what happened first.'

They took me.

'Who took you?'

Them what are coming.

The trees were close around them; their thin, sharp branches scratched each other in the wind. There came the odd damp rustle of a dead leaf that had failed to fall in the autumn.

'Who's coming?' Blue looked behind. The breeze rippled the flood. There was no sight nor sound of anyone else in the woodland.

They told me my brother was sick and he didn't want me no more but he'd never say that, he'd never.

The girl looked solid, real, alive. Her chest heaved, and Blue thought of Bodhi at their mother's bedside. Jessica tried to talk, but she was choked up, and Blue thought of Arlo, who had never spoken a word. Blue hunkered down on her haunches so she was eye level with the young girl. Water flooded into her boots, soaked through the seat of her trousers.

'Were you sick too?' The medicinal taste had returned to Blue's mouth.

Can you help me get back to my brother?

Blue knew what the girl wanted to hear, but to say it would be a lie. She couldn't take Jessica to her brother, even if she knew who and where that brother was. She couldn't do anything other than see her, hear her, feel her, and what good was that? What difference did that make? Blue was used to making people feel better, not visions, not ghosts.

That other voice returned, the one she had found hidden in research papers, sceptical articles, books disproving psychic ability. Jessica isn't real. She's a figment, a manifestation of feelings Blue absorbed from others, a phantom of her imagination.

'I don't know,' Blue said, and it was an answer to it all: questions about her life, her mother, her ability, Jessica Pike, Bodhi and Arlo.

She had seen her mother's desire to hold her children close to her breast and love them. Blue had known the reality of their neglect.

'What are you?' Blue asked, and Jessica's head hung. Her blonde hair fell either side of her face; she stared at the flood as if she didn't know the answer herself. When her lips moved to speak, Blue couldn't see them; she didn't need to. The child's response rippled the water, wound itself around Blue's heart.

I'm nothing.

She looked so like a little girl, a real child lost in the woods, ill-equipped both in clothes and in maturity. If Blue moved to touch her, her hand would feel cold air. If she hugged her, she would only hug herself.

A flurry of crows took flight, cawed above the bare treetops, and Jessica looked up, shaded her eyes, and she was so real, appeared so solid, and it was Arlo Blue remembered, sitting in the dry bathtub, arms raised to be lifted because all she needed was to be held. Blue never held her.

'How else can I help you? What can I do?'

If you can't find my brother?

'Aye.'

They weren't alone anymore. It started as a rustle in the distance, a slosh of boots through muddy water, the vacillating hum of heavy breath.

Set me free.

A horrible foreboding then, that Molly Park was coming towards them, that she was responsible for the girl's misery. Responsible, too, for her death. Blue didn't want it to be so. She thought of the warmth Mrs Park exuded, her desire to care and to love and heal. Blue remembered, too, her cold smile when she had discovered Blue in the Parks' apartment. The thunder that had lingered in her eyes.

The sound of their intruder grew closer. Blue knew that if she turned, she would see their shoulders barge through low branches, thighs caked in mud, boots calf-deep in woodland water.

She did not want it to be Mrs Park. She tried to think of her safe and warm in her house, not here in the cold, wet darkness, stalking Blue through the trees, someone who feigned a desire to heal but was capable of such harm.

'How can I set you free?' Blue said.

You know.

23 to 24

Bridget never spoke again. Blue convinced herself she was glad of it, fearful of what might be confessed. Yet she had always loved the lullaby music of Mother's American voice. If she'd known she would not speak again, Blue would have paid more attention to the sound.

She wanted to hold her mother, to stroke her forehead as Bridget had stroked Blue's when she was young. But to touch her would be to feel her despair, and it was more than Blue's body could take; her heart was too busy anticipating grief to deal with anything more.

She found the solution in a pair of white silk gloves they kept in the velvet-swagged room. When she first touched her with them on, Bridget frowned, aware of the difference.

'They're Devlin's,' Blue said. 'The ones he wore onstage.'

Bridget rested her cheek into Blue's hand. She felt the warmth of Mother's skin through the silk, the frailty of her sharp cheekbone and the hollow beneath it. Blue knew that Bridget wanted her to lie down and hold her, but she couldn't. Bodhi had taken that space, so close that Bridget's left arm was always goosefleshed. Arlo napped at her feet like the dog in the Arundel tomb. There was no room for Blue.

When the pain became visible, body-wracking torture that couldn't be lessened with the drugs they had at home, Blue called a hospice, and Bridget spent her last days there, wrapped in Devlin's black kaftan with Blue at her side and Arlo and Bodhi curled about her. The nurses brought Blue cups of soup and hot buttered toast, warned her when the end was near, but she knew.

Blue had brought the crystals from home, put amethyst under Bridget's pillow and a polished carnelian in her palm. Bridget's fingers curled around it, and Blue thought of those hands curling her tiny fingers around the handle of a wooden spoon and offering her a saucepan as a drum. She thought of her mother twirling beneath the light of the bare kitchen bulb. Bridget smiled, and Blue hoped she thought of that, too. She thanked Mother for those childhood games of Ford Family Band; she thanked her for teaching her to read, to count, how to watch the world. She thanked her for the kaftans she had sewed, the effort she had made, for the unwavering belief she had had in her. Blue thanked her for the love, the love, all that love and the millions of strange ways she showed it.

She felt her mother leave her as if it was Blue's own breath. Blue's chest stilled as Bridget's chest stilled, and she did not know what to do. She did not know what to do.

The nurses came, their voices low. One put an arm around her, handed her a tissue. Another gave her a cup of hot tea that she forgot to drink. It went cold. Perhaps it was the same nurse. She didn't notice. She didn't look. They didn't rush her, and she was grateful for that.

It was several hours before Blue realised how alone she was. No little boy. No baby girl. She knelt and looked under the bed, pulled back the curtains, checked the small cupboard, the corridor, the nightstand. She looked for them instead of looking at her mother, used the time to rally at their absence rather than hold Bridget's hand one last time, kiss her forehead, brush the hair that Blue'd once wrapped around her neck like a scarf, that Bridget had tickled Blue's nose with when she was a girl, that brushed her cheek whenever Mother kissed her goodnight.

They were not beneath the bed, behind the curtain, in the corridor. They were nowhere; they had left her. They had left her.

She was not yet ready to confront what that meant.

The Tower

'I can't do it.'

Please.

'I don't want it to be Mrs Park.' Blue thought of her earlier in the art room, her light touch, her encouragement, her kindness. She had been steely cold when she'd caught Blue in her apartment, then all warmth and heart as they painted. No one is all lightness, Blue thought. No one is all shadow. Don't let it be Mrs Park.

Wetness marred her cheeks again, raindrops or tears or both. She could see the sky, darker due to a setting sun rather than storm clouds.

Had so much time passed already?

She glanced at her phone, hoped to see the time, but the screen was black. Had it run out of battery? How long had she been in the woods?

'I can't do it,' Blue said again, and before the girl could object, she added, 'I've never fought anyone; I couldn't even defend myself.'

She was so close to getting away. Less than two miles. She could picture the map, could figure the way to go.

Jessica Pike didn't argue. She had gone.

Blue scanned every tree, looked into their tops to see if she'd climbed up like the child in Sabina's watercolour. There was no sign of her. Blue remembered how she had looked for Bodhi, for Arlo. How she sat in the kitchen till late in the night and waited for them to reappear.

Where had Jessica gone?

She had told Blue what she needed to do for her; the person she blamed was close, and if Blue could do this, Jessica would be free: a life for a life, a ghost for a ghost. Could the girl not bear to watch?

She was a child, Blue reminded herself.

And she was not real.

The trees felt closer, as though they had lifted roots and stepped forward, were huddled around. She could feel the currents change in the air, could feel the collective eyes of hundreds of insects, tiny and unseen, watch her. Wait for her to act.

Blue's bones ached from the damp, and her feet were numb and wet. The muscles in her neck complained as she craned to try and find Jessica. She was gone, but Blue wasn't alone.

She wanted to run, but the floodwater was a shackle at her ankles, and her phone was dead and wouldn't show her the way. She closed her eyes, pictured it again, but all she saw was Jessica; all she felt was the heavy, hot pressure inside her skull. She didn't want her to be real. She couldn't let her be real. She heard the girl's voice.

Kill them.

The wet crash of splashed water grew nearer.

Let it not be Mrs Park, she thought.

'Blue?'

It wasn't her voice.

Blue could have laughed with relief, but the relief was short-sighted, and she knew it. A girl had lived here, in that house and in these woods, but she was dead, and Blue knew why.

Blue was once eleven years old. She knew what it was to need a parent, to rely on them for their protection, guidance, love. Blue had grown up, could rely on herself. Jessica Pike had never had the chance.

'You need to come back,' called Jessica Pike's killer. 'It's not safe in this weather; we've all been worried.'

Jessica wanted Blue to set things right, would not be at peace until her killer was dead. Was she real, or had Blue's mind broken? Had it always been broken?

'Blue?' The voice was hesitant, a quiver to it as though Blue was not a woman but a wild thing. The dying light dappled shadows on her hands, the hands Jessica wanted her to wrap around the killer's neck. She didn't know if she should, didn't know if she was capable.

For Blue was young and fit, but slight.

And Mr Park was a bear of a man.

24

Blue went to work the day after Bridget died. She didn't know what else to do. She sat in the picking bay, stared at the list of orders and made a mistake on every one of them.

'Have you got a minute, Blue?' They sent Lucia from the office to talk to her. She was a small middle-aged woman, plump and pretty, with shiny black hair and shiny black eyes, who wore perfume sweet as bonbons. She took Blue into one of the ground-floor conference rooms and Blue thought she was about to get fired, but Lucia asked her, in a voice hushed and kind, if she was all right.

The warehouse gave her a week of compassionate leave.

There was a funeral to arrange and paperwork to do, and it was that that changed everything. It was to be a humanist ceremony in the crematorium on the north side of Blackpool. Bridget had few friends, but those she had would attend. Lucia said she would go as moral support, and Blue wondered if she knew that Blue hadn't anyone to turn to, wondered if the others at work thought Blue was as odd as she felt.

A eulogy should be given.

She put off writing it until the night before and sat in the kitchen to do it. The door to the velvet-swagged room remained closed, the space beyond it unchanged in years, but Devlin no longer sat at the table. Mother never pottered at the sink. Bodhi didn't stand by the window; Arlo didn't sit by the chair.

It was dark out, the evening autumn-cool, and Blue made tea as she waited for the laptop to fire up. She would add history to her mother's eulogy, find out the name of her school, the subjects she studied, find out about the place she grew up and how it had formed her ... There would be online records nowadays. It would be easier to talk about her past than her present.

Blue never knew her real father. She never knew her grandparents, presumed they were dead, knew only that they had lived in South Carolina but were originally from the UK. But she had her mother's birth certificate, her passport (expired the year after Blue's birth) and a laptop with internet access. A search engine would tell her a few basic facts.

There was no fresh food in the house, so she made toast with two frozen bread slices and smeared them thickly with honey. She turned on the radio, and a heavy baseline killed the silence.

Blue typed her mother's name into the search engine and pretended it was someone else's name, someone else's eulogy. Bridget's American hometown was added next, then the year of her birth. She held a piece of toast in her spare hand, pressed enter and licked a run of honey from the side of her thumb. She tried not to think that Bridget wouldn't walk in and pinch the crusts from the plate.

A notepad and pen lay ready.

The lamp flickered on the kitchen wall, and she made a mental note to buy spare bulbs.

The search retrieved a long list of results. The first showed a scanned-in copy of a forty-year-old newspaper.

Blue's toast was abandoned to the flies.

A young Bridget Ford, shot in monochrome, stared out from the front page. Her hair hung limp; her eyes had nothing behind them. The headline shouted something that could not be true because it shouted about Mother and Mother wasn't a— but at the same time, Blue was aware that it was true, of course it was true, and this is why, this is why, this is why.

Below Bridget's photo were two smaller ones. A young boy. A baby girl.

Blue snapped the laptop lid shut, pushed back her chair from the table. She wanted to stand, run away, run anywhere, but her legs were numb and wouldn't hold her.

The internet was a foolish invention, a fearmongering network of lies; isn't that what Bridget always believed? And what was Devlin's advice?

Only use computers for a specific purpose, otherwise, you'll waste hours lost in the spiral of clickbait.

There was a eulogy to write, Blue told herself. Now wasn't the time to get distracted by ... by what? By lies? By misinformation? She would pick up the pencil and handwrite a eulogy. Tomorrow she would go to the crematorium. She would say a few words. Her mother's body would disappear into the furnace, and 'May the Circle Be Open' would play.

She'd lost sensation in her limbs, was only aware of the fierce, solid hammer in her chest. Her hands moved against her will and lifted the laptop lid.

She would close the browser tab. She did not need to read it.

Her traitorous eyes scanned the page.

The article did not tell Blue how she killed them; she would find that out later from other articles. This one concentrated on Bridget's appearance at court, her blonde hair pulled back by a tortoiseshell clip, her figure slim in a thrift-store suit. It reported her tears as though she had no right to shed them.

Blue learnt that her grandparents, evangelical born-again Jehovahs, had disowned her when she bedded a Mexican Catholic and fell pregnant. Her lover had disowned her when she fell pregnant with their second child and claimed it wasn't his. Her psychiatrist disowned her when she could not renew her medical insurance and thereby pay for the antipsychotics she'd been taking since Bodhi's birth. Her mind disowned her sometime before all this, though the newspaper couldn't pinpoint when. They revelled in her beauty and in her evil, the two inexorably linked.

Possessed, Blue clicked link after link. She paused only to rub her sore eyes and turn the radio off so she could concentrate.

An unsettled mind will not keep focus for long, and Blue found that the stories she read online became tangled with her own memories of Bridget, her mother's life a spider's web weaved into the crevices of Blue's own, her past making sense of Blue's present.

Is this why she never sent me to school?

Is this why she didn't trust doctors?

Is this why I saw them?

Is this why they never let me be?

Is this why I was never like normal kids?

She read until she knew her again, until 'is' and 'this' swapped places and the question marks were removed.

This is why I could never be normal.

She read until morning blinded her through the kitchen window. The honey had crystallised on the stale toast, the cold tea had formed a film. She knew Mother better than she ever thought she would. The knowledge was not freeing but something to fear, added to the list of other things she never wanted people to know about her. About her mother.

Tiredness dragged at her eyelids, but she wouldn't sleep yet. She pulled her body through the shower, into clean clothes, into the car, into the crematorium. She did not count how scant few people were there. She didn't give the eulogy.

Beneath the new knowledge, the newspapers' facts and fabrications, lurked a thing that crouched inside her, waited to lunge. She felt it through the service, in her chest and in her guts, something that threatened to overwhelm.

Sandwiches on plates were served at the local afterwards, forty quid put behind the bar for those that turned up. Blue didn't eat, didn't drink, was aware of people telling her how sorry they were, and she mutely nodded. She didn't give out the crystals or sticks of Bridget's favourite incense as she'd intended.

It started as a slight tremor in her fingers. Nervous energy, she told herself as her house key shook in the lock. Overtiredness. Overstimulation. Low blood sugar.

The honey was still out on the kitchen counter. The laptop was still open. A dead fly in the cold mug of tea. No arms wrapped around Blue, no warm touch to her lower back, no hand to gently ruffle her hair or pull her in for a hug.

This is why, this is why.

She couldn't bear to be in the kitchen. The living room, sparse and cold, offered no comfort, no connection. She could go upstairs and lie in her mother's bed, fold herself inside the cotton sheets, breathe the last of Bridget in from her pillow and mourn her, cry for her, miss her, but she couldn't do that, couldn't bear it.

The velvet-swagged room called out, and she listened. She hadn't slept, hadn't eaten, yet felt the room fill her with unbidden energy. She grabbed at the velvet that hung from the walls, and her nose filled with its dust and mildew. She screwed it into her fist, felt the old, forgotten fabric in her hand and wanted to yank it, tear it free. She wanted to kick the chairs, rip away the pendants, hurl the crystals and the bowls and the rune stones.

A knock on the front door.

Lucia stood on the doorstep in a black dress and smart black coat. 'Sorry to call round, I know you might want to be on your own,' she said, 'but I wanted to make sure you're OK, see if there's anything I can do to help?'

Take me away, far away.

'No, it's OK. I'm fine, but thanks for offering.' She felt unkind for not inviting the woman in but thought of the messy kitchen, of the open door to the velvet-swagged room, of the laptop and what Lucia would see if she came in and lifted the lid.

The sky was overcast, and a gentle, chill wind swept the empty street, and the breeze caught the ends of Lucia's black waves. 'Have you eaten? I noticed you didn't eat at the pub.'

'I'll grab something before bed.'

'You need to eat. Promise me you will?'

'Aye, I will,' Blue said, but her tone was flat, and Lucia wasn't convinced.

She looked behind Blue, down the hall and into the kitchen. 'Are you sure you're going to be OK on your own?' She turned her big black eyes on Blue. 'I'm worried about you. I wish there was something I could do.'

'Thank you,' Blue said and wanted to say more, but Lucia's kindness was too much and Blue floundered.

'Oh, Blue,' Lucia said and stepped forward, arms open and Blue didn't pull away. Instead, she let Lucia fold herself around her, her hands on Blue's back, and she was so warm, so comforting, full of sympathy. Lucia's pity poured out, thick as clotted cream, and smothered Blue's heart with its unbearable compassion. *Poor thing is all alone, poor thing has nobody, poor thing is a sorry old state, there, there, poor thing.*

It made Blue feel worse, and she pulled away, made a mumbled, apologetic excuse and closed the door before the woman had time to argue. She heard Lucia call from the other side, caught the confusion and hurt in her voice, the slight undertone of having been wronged, and Blue did feel guilty, almost guilty enough to let her back in.

Instead, Blue stumbled down the empty hall, staggered past the kitchen table with the computer and cold tea. The velvet-swagged room patiently waited to be torn to pieces.

It would go on waiting.

Blue slumped into the chair she once sat in to read people's tarot. It was in here she had seen that woman's dead father. Devlin had hugged away her terror. Bridget had got overexcited by her burgeoning talents. And later, Bodhi had explained that victims will always walk in the footsteps of their killers.

He never told Blue what happened when the killer died.

Blue knew, now. When the killer died, the killed disappeared.

Blue didn't want to be alone. She wanted Devlin to help her through it, help her come to terms with it all; who her mother was, what she did, how it moulded Blue's young life. Her whole life. She wanted her mother to face her and tell her what she'd done and why and how could she do it? She wanted her to tell her, she wanted … she wanted her.

Like a child again, she wanted her mother. The arm round her, the hair against her cheek, the lullaby voice telling Blue it was all right, it was OK, and she could lean into her mother's body and rest her head on Bridget's shoulder and not have to face going to work. She wouldn't have to face going back to the crematorium to collect her mother's ashes. She wouldn't have to decide whether to scatter them, bury them, or keep them on the mantle.

She even wanted Bodhi and Arlo, alive and grown-up and there with her. They were older than Blue by years and would have looked out for her. They'd have been a family.

But they were dead. And now, at last, Blue knew why.

The Emperor (Reversed)

Joshua Park closed in, reached for Blue's shoulder. 'You all right? We need to go back, get you dry—'

Blue turned, and the man stopped talking. Blue could see herself in Mr Park's eyes, her bedraggled form caught in the man's wide pupils.

'You're paler than a— What's happened?' Mr Park said, and Blue turned away again and faced the tree where she'd conversed with a dead girl. Had she, though, had she?

She could not trust Mr Park's concern.

Nor could she kill him; the idea was so ridiculous she wanted to laugh, to say to this towering man that an invisible girl had asked her to wring his neck with her own weak hands. What was happening to her? She felt her soul had splintered somehow.

She had to get away. Blue felt water in her boots, rain down her collar, and an ache in her thighs and back. Felt exhaustion wrap its blanket-self around her, invite her to stop a moment, rest here, lie down in the water and forget about Jess and Arlo and Bodhi and Mother and the fact that no one waited at home. Exactly three years ago tomorrow.

'Will you just stop.' Mr Park grabbed Blue's arm and pulled her back. 'What the hell are you doing? Don't you know we've been worried? Molly's fret herself sick, Sabina has been trying to phone you, Milton's blaming himself – you can't just up and leave—'

Blue yanked her arm free, tried to say sorry, to tell Mr Park that she wanted to be left alone, but the only words on her tongue were, 'Jessica Pike.'

'What?' Mr Park lost the last of his colour, aged ten years in two seconds. Blue thought of Milton blaming himself, worried for her after his strange outburst.

Blue waited for Mr Park to question her. He didn't.

Blue knew, then, that what the ghost of a girl had told her was true.

She could no longer argue with herself over spirits or projections of grief, over what was real and what was not. She saw the truth of the past in the haggard man's face – the responsibility, the regret, the horror at that name.

'I don't want any of this, I didn't invite it in,' Blue said. She wouldn't look at Mr Park, focused instead on the trees and tried to see a path she could take through the flood. Her foot touched a root beneath the water, and she stumbled, steadied herself against a wet branch. 'I just need to get away, please, just go back.'

'I can't very well leave you out here. You'll catch your death. Why the hell do you want to stay out here, anyway? Where are you going?' Mr Park waited for an answer, but Blue couldn't speak. She had expected Mr Park to say he didn't know who Jessica Pike was, or at least express surprise, alarm, something other than this swift change of subject.

'I can't go back to the house without you,' Mr Park said. 'If I do, Sabina will call the police or an ambulance or— Look, will you just come back? We can sort out whatever problem this is back at the house.'

The thought of the house and Sabina and Milton and Mrs Park – of Jessica Pike everywhere, to see her beg again and again for Blue's help – she couldn't bear it. Hallucination or not, she knew that vision would come back to her, would give her no peace. The child wanted retribution. The child wished Mr Park dead.

Blue couldn't help her.

Nor could she turn and look at Mr Park because, when she did, all she saw was a murderer. A child-murderer. The knowledge made Blue waiver, but she had come too far, was too close to getting away to turn back now.

'Call whoever you like,' Blue said. 'I'm not coming with you.' She waded on, tried to move quickly but was slowed by the flood. The water had risen; it was up to the top of her boots. She just had to get far enough away from Hope Marsh House and its owners to not see that girl again. Then she could concentrate on finding some house, help, a way home.

Mr Park followed. Blue heard his breath, sensed his body behind her.

'Go back, Mr Park,' Blue said over her shoulder. Rooks called their crybaby sound, their black-feathered bodies hidden by trees and shadows.

'Not without you.' Mr Park raised his voice above the sound of the birds, and Blue could hear his panic and confusion. 'You'll kill yourself from exposure if nothing else.'

Why doesn't he just leave me? Blue thought. Why's he so bothered about bringing me back?

The ground was boggy and uneven from rocks and lost branches.

'Please, Blue, just come back. We can sort out whatever the problem is in the morning. Just come back, there's no reason to be out here—'

'I can't,' Blue said, teeth gritted and head sore.

'It's warm, dry, there's food, there's company … and look, if it's been a struggle, then Molly can help you. She's fully qualified, she can—'

'Just stop it, will you just stop!' Blue rested her shoulder against an oak tree, tilted her head back. Branches spread above her like cracks in broken glass. The sky was a dark, hazy grey, and Blue couldn't tell what was cloud and what wasn't, if the pinpricks of brightness were stars or raindrops. She didn't know what time it was, what direction she walked in. She turned to face Mr Park, knew she wouldn't be able to look that man in the face and so kept her gaze low.

There was Jessica Pike.

She stood behind the giant's shoulder.

Please, you have to.

'I can't, I just can't.'

'Can't what?' Mr Park said.

Why not?

'I just can't, I'm not that sort … How do I know, for sure? How do I know it's not just my mind playing tricks?'

You know.

'What the hell are you talking about? What's playing tricks?' Mr Park looked behind him, above him, back at Blue.

'I can't know,' Blue said to the girl Mr Park couldn't see. 'There's no proof, for God's sake, there's nothing.'

'Proof?' Mr Park was at a loss, and Blue saw that it was sympathy on his face, that the man felt profoundly sorry for her, wanted to help her but didn't know how.

I'll show you.

A flash of memory brought back Bodhi, curled up by her mother's side, brought about the memory of her pain and her sorrow and how it flooded Blue, and she didn't want that, didn't want Jess to show her anything of the kind. She didn't.

Jessica turned, instead, to Mr Park.

Whispered in his ear. Whispered and whispered.

Mr Park raised his hand, pressed his thumb and forefinger to the bridge of his nose. He squinted, looked pained, skin wan.

Blue saw Mother again. She saw Arlo. She remembered Bridget sitting at the kitchen table with her cheek pressed to its top, a look of incomprehensible loss on her face, the babe in tears at her feet. Blue thought of her mother in bed, a slim shape beneath the covers, unable to sleep or eat, and Bodhi staring daggers from the corner.

'You said—' Mr Park frowned, as though words were alien and his tongue unfamiliar. Gone was his jollying tone, his forthright manner. Gone was his sympathy. His skin looked yellow and sick. 'A name, you said—'

'Jessica Pike,' Blue said.

'How do you know that name?'

The girl was still at his ear, but she stilled her lips, lifted her eyes to Blue as if to say *I told you so.*

Blue saw, too, the girl Blue wished she'd been. The child with friends, education, experience that stretched beyond the narrow world of the mystic. She saw all she hoped she would one day be. It sank away from her as a stone sinks in water. There was nothing else but Mr Park and the girl he had killed.

Jessica Pike locked Blue with her dark, dead stare. There was the child she once was, running in red trainers to a brother she loved. Their mother had left them. The girl had friends: an Asian boy with black chin-length hair; a girl with a spherical afro and a cheek bleached by a birthmark. Blue saw them run through the concrete corridors of a residential tower block, heard the slap of their plimsoles, felt their out-of-breath laughs burn her throat. She saw a wide-hipped Polish woman who made bigos stew and bought Jess second-hand clothes. She saw how the girl would sit in her bedroom, still and quiet just like she was told, whilst her brother shot up in the living room, his pulsing vein blood-black. And she saw Milton take the girl by the hand and usher her into his flat next door. She saw him put cartoons on the television, comic books by her side, saw his Polish wife kiss the girl's forehead.

'Where did you hear that name?' Mr Park said, louder. The only colour in his face came from the brown-green mud that had splashed him.

The dead girl at his side was a girl in size alone. There was no innocence in her stare anymore, no youth, optimism, no life. She would never grow old, would not grow at all.

'You killed her,' she said.

'I what? I've never killed anything, not a fly.' Some of his strength returned; anger rose and marked his cheeks pale pink.

'She was only a girl,' Blue said. She could run, turn and wade through the water, fight her way to a safer place, but this knowledge would follow her. The image of this child, her lost youth, would follow and haunt her. 'How could you do that to a child?'

A thick black branch was in Blue's right hand.

'You're mad; you don't know what you're talking about. You need to come back to the house, the weather's addled you— Why are you shaking your head? What's wrong with you? What are you—' Mr Park backed away, his eyes on Blue as his arms felt behind him for trees that might block his path.

'You called her Eleanor, but her name was Jess.' Blue felt her mother's spirit flow through her, felt it more than she had these last three years. Her heart was inside her, breaking as Blue's heart broke.

'Get away from me!' Something jarred Mr Park's foot; he called out, stumbled, fell backwards into the water.

'What did you do to her?' Blue wasn't cold. The tiredness had gone. She lifted the branch higher and rested it on her shoulder like a baseball bat.

'Nothing, I haven't done anything, I—'

'She lived in Birmingham with her brother. It was just the two of them; their mum had left, and the boy was too scared to tell social services in case they got split up. He was a junky, couldn't look after himself but tried to look after her, tried his best, tried to get clean but couldn't. Then you found them. How did you do that?'

'How did you— No, no, you don't know what you're talking about.' In his panic, Mr Park scrabbled backwards through the water, his arms elbow-deep in the mire. He tried to push back with his feet but found no purchase. He called for help at the top of his voice, called again and again, but no one could hear, and now Blue was close.

Blue raised the branch.

Mr Park screamed for help one last time as Blue swung the bough at his temple.

He fell silent.

When Blue touched the hot, rough skin of Joshua Park's neck, she expected the man's soul to speak to her. She thought she would see all the man had done, all he had lost and all he had taken, that Blue would understand what had happened to Jess, but Blue didn't see a thing like it.

She saw Mother.

Blue's hands became Bridget's hands, holding and squeezing as Blue's hands held and squeezed.

Mr Park's face was under the water, his hair spread round him in a dank halo, but it was Arlo that Blue saw, her cotton-rompered body in the bathtub, her curls snaking through the bathwater, her eyes open beneath the surface, held there by Mother's hands.

She saw Bodhi struggle under the weight of a pillow. She saw Mother press the pillow against the face of the little boy she loved so much.

Blue held the man down.

Mr Park fought back, hit at Blue, scratched her, knocked her off balance, nearly had her, but Blue held firm. Certainty flowed through her that this was necessary, that this had to be, that there was no other choice, no other way. It was Mother's certainty, Mother's psychosis.

Mr Park fell still.

Blue let go.

Stood up.

Stood back.

What had she done?

Good God, what had she done?

PART III

The Sun (Reversed)

Joshua has been gone for over an hour, and it was Molly who had made him go, who said they couldn't leave Blue outside in the rain, think of her health, her well-being. Think of the publicity if a guest catches their death.

They'd already slipped up with Jago. Molly will have to smooth that crease at some point, but now is not the time. She cannot think of that boy, or the way his eyes bulged from their sockets when he realised his foolish misstep. How her husband carried the body to Jago's car, drove the pristine Range Rover away, returned alone and hid the car beneath a tarpaulin. She doesn't think about that. She only thinks of Joshua.

Water seeped beneath the boot room door within minutes of him leaving; Molly had to rescue all the boots and coats and hats and put them in the overhead cupboards to keep them dry, had to drag that infernal black suitcase through the house and into the attic. She had closed off the boot room and hoped it wouldn't get worse.

But now, a slither of water snakes under the living room door. The guests have yet to see it, and Molly knows she should do something – plug the space with a blanket, dry the floor, roll back the rug – but she cannot. She stands in front of the fire, her limbs lead-heavy, her head heavier still.

I shouldn't have let her go, Milton says from the armchair, and Molly closes her eyes and musters strength because this is the fifth time he's said it and not once has he mentioned Joshua. She smiles and pats his arm, tells him it wasn't his fault at all, that she's sure he didn't offend

Blue, that no one knows why she ran off like that, and the girl must be terribly troubled, but it will all be fine and could she get him cocoa, all the while thinking that if he says that phrase one more time, she's going to take that bloody hat he keeps fondling and shove it down his withered old throat.

Take the cocoa, she prays. Take the cocoa and sleep.

He shakes his head, says he doesn't want any damn cocoa, and Sabina says what she needs is a coffee.

Molly takes a breath. Smooths the front of her tunic. Linen was not made for such humidity, such stress. The creases are so sharp they could have been starched. She watches the rivulet of water as it thickens, lengthens, touches the front rug. A second finger of liquid joins it. How long before the guests notice?

Coffee it is, Molly says and asks Milton if he wants a cup too, but he taps his chest as he always does, says bottled water is better for his heart, and she says she'll get him one, and he reminds her that it has to be bottled and not that crap from the tap.

Molly tells him of course, smiles sweetly, wonders if it would be possible to break the seal, slip in a tramadol, and then reseal the lid without him noticing. She doubts she can do it tonight, but she'll keep it in mind for another day. A day when Joshua is with her, and there is no rain, and she has regained control of that house.

Molly makes to go to the kitchen, but before she even reaches the passageway, Sabina screams.

The woman points to the front door, says my God, my God, over there, look, as though it's not water invading the house but spiders. Sabina says they have to do something, Milton says where are the sandbags, and Molly says there are flood boards in the art cupboard.

Joshua had them made after the Levels flooded several years back. He measured the doorways, the windows, ordered them and collected them in his calm, practical manner, and he should be here to help Molly. Where is he? How much longer will he be?

It shouldn't take so long to walk into the woods, to find that girl, bring her back – and then another thought hits Molly, so bleak and cold and familiar that she stops dead on her way to the art room, one hand pressed to the wall to keep herself upright, one to her stomach to quiet its churn. A terrible thought.

What if he isn't planning on bringing the girl back?

What if she says something that makes him— Blue saw them arguing this morning, what if she overheard—

Molly tries to shake the thought but it lingers; she pictures Blue face down in the woods, imagines Joshua's excuses: he reached her too late, she must have stumbled and hit her head hard, and what did Blue think would happen if she ran off in a flood like that? The other guests would have to be lied to. Another hole would need to be dug once the rainwater dried up. Would anyone miss Blue? Would they come looking? Would Joshua be carted off to jail and leave Molly alone in that house, when she hadn't slept alone once in over a decade? Not since before they had Eleanor.

The stress must show on her face because Sabina has followed Molly to help with the flood boards and when she sees the look her host wears, she pulls Molly in for a hug, says it will all be OK, that she will help protect the house from water damage, that Joshua will find Blue and bring her back.

There is little comfort in a thin person's hug. Sabina's ribcage presses into Molly's cushioned body, her collarbones dig into Molly's chest, her bony arms pincers. Over Sabina's shoulder, Molly can see the water; it laps at the plate glass windows. How long before the whole of downstairs is flooded?

Sabina steps back and holds Molly's shoulders the same way Molly holds her guests. Held her guests. Sabina says they will get the flood boards and start with the front door, that next they will move the furniture from the living room upstairs, that they can clear the therapy rooms and the kitchen and Molly says yes, yes, yes, just to shut her up.

This is not your house, she thinks. This is *my* house. My husband is outside in that weather. My guest ran away. And there are things you don't know about that are threatening to overwhelm us all.

Aloud she says thank you, tells Sabina she's so kind to help, apologises that the retreat has fallen apart, and Sabina says it's OK, she's happy to help, and Molly feels a vice around her head.

In the living room, Milton has left his chair. Somehow, in his infirm state, he has managed to roll the rug up away from the water; it lies like a blood sausage at the foot of the stairs. He shuffles from the coffee table to the sideboard, using his right hand to guide his walking frame as his left lifts one spiral-bound journal at a time and stores them in the high drawers. He mutters to himself. Molly catches scant few words: shouldn't have said anything, what if she knew, kept my mouth shut, poor girl, poor girl, and it could be that he's talking about Blue. But Molly knows Milton: he could mean his wife, his daughter, his sister, his long-dead mother.

A clock hangs from the wall near the large dining table, the one they use when the retreat is fully booked. Joshua has been gone for nearly two hours.

The windows are dark, and Sabina moves to pull the curtains closed, but Molly stops her. I want to see when he gets back, she explains.

What about Blue, Sabina asks.

Her too, Molly says, but she doesn't give a fig about the girl who lured Joshua out into the cold, wet weather.

Milton still chastises himself, and Molly's thoughts echo the sentiment. She shouldn't have made her husband go out there, should've let the flood deal with Blue. Who does she think she is, this weird girl with the unnatural eyes and the horrible way of looking at you, really looking at you, as though she can see into your soul and make it better? There's nothing wrong with Molly's soul, no way to better it. Molly is the one to make it all better.

Water rushes beneath the front door and settles in a pool where the rug used to be. Sabina wrestles two flood boards through to the boot room, and Molly chases her, asks what she's doing, and Sabina tells her that she's boarding up the house.

That's not how it's done. The flood boards don't go on the inside but the outside, otherwise the door won't open, Joshua won't be able to get in, he'll be stuck outside. Molly pulls Sabina away, lifts the first board out, opens the door, and the wind blows in, pulls rain in with it, and Molly feels the cold, sees the dark ink sky and senses the menace out in those woods.

The dogs are buried in those woods.

Eleanor would have loved a dog, she thinks. Poor Eleanor.

Molly won't lose Joshua as well. She won't end her days alone in that house with no one about her who understands.

Milton asks her what she's doing, says she can't possibly go outside, but Molly pulls on a pair of wellies, drags her arms through a mac, stamps a hat on her head. The torches, she says, where did she put the torches?

You can't go out there, Milton says again, but his eyes are on Sabina, who follows Molly's lead and slides her feet into dark green boots and says that she can't let Molly go out alone. It's dark outside.

You can't leave me here, Milton says, and Molly hears the fear but doesn't care. She tells him she needs to find her husband; Sabina tells him they'll be back soon. She switches a torch on and off.

What am I meant to do? the old man asks.

Molly says whatever you usually do on your own, and Milton looks like he's been slapped. There are tears in his panicked eyes, and Molly wonders if that sadness is for his wife, daughter, mother, and sister, but suspects it's for Milton himself.

The Hanged Man

Blue left Mr Park semi-submerged. Water dripped from her hands as she waded away.

Her breath came in shallow gasps. Adrenaline turned her limbs grossly hollow. Pictures of Lucia ran through her mind, though Blue hadn't seen her in years. She remembered the face of a spotty-cheeked youth who served food at a local cafe. A memory of packing shampoo and a set of batteries into a cardboard box on the warehouse floor.

She laughed and didn't know why. Above, roosted birds cawed out complaints to the wind, rose from the treetops in a flurry and dislodged droplets of rain on to Blue. They landed on her cheeks and neck, and she thought that they must be cold though she didn't feel it. Her teeth chattered.

She walked and stumbled and fell and got up and walked on. If she didn't look back, then it didn't happen. If she didn't turn around, she'd not see it. If she could only get to a house, any house, then everything would be all right.

For the first time in years, Blue questioned her decision to stop reading. If she had stuck at it, maybe she would have found someone else like her, someone to explain this all, so she didn't feel crazy. She longed for proof that her mother had been right all along and that Blue was exceptional, was the little god Bridget heralded her to be, had gifts beyond anyone's understanding and therefore hadn't just murdered a man in cold blood.

Water had soaked through her socks, had breached the sealed seams on the waterproof trousers. Her sleeves were wet through to the shoulder, rain bled down her neck and back. She shivered and stepped, forced herself on and on towards warmth and safety and help.

The trees began to thin, the water started to drop; she was nearing the edge of the woods. She pictured the map in her head. Soon there would be a road. A flooded road, but a road all the same and she would follow it to salvation.

How long before Mr Park's body was found? Hours? Days? Should Blue tell anyone what she had done? Yes, yes, she would. She would confess it all and accept whatever condign punishment was thrown her way. The certainty offered comfort in the madness. If you kill a man, you are sent to prison.

How many other murderers would she meet there?

My God, she thought. How many other victims would she see?

The idea stalled her. She no longer knew what she wanted to be true – be mad and know she had killed an honest man in madness, or be sane and know that ghosts clung to their killers? That the man Blue killed had been a murderer too? And, if punished, Blue would spend years in a cell, living among ghosts and their killers?

It was dark, but some thin distant light filtered through the treeline. Something zipped through the air above, an owl or bat, she didn't know.

The breeze picked up as she neared the edge of the woods, and the skin on her face began to sting. She winced when she touched the scratches on her cheeks. They were made by tree branches, she told herself. They were made by the woods, not the nails of a drowning man. A man that I drowned.

In the distance was the shadow of a house, a large grand house. A farm or a hotel, Blue couldn't tell.

It was hemmed in by water, no sense where the paths were, the streams or the roads. Everything rose from the flood.

The farmer would surely come outside any minute now, maybe alerted by some sixth sense of their own. Did this farmer know the Parks? Would Blue tell them what she had done?

She was afraid.

A single light flashed here and there, and Blue thought of headlights, but there were no cars or motorbikes, no road for them to drive on. It flashed again; she heard a shout.

She saw the bridge.

Its whale's-back arch lifted from the water, curved and solid and impossible. The culvert that had trapped the dead rabbit had flooded again.

Hope Marsh House glowed like a beacon in the dark grey night.

The Six of Cups (Reversed)

The light was a torch.

The person shouting her name was Sabina.

Had Blue lost her way or been led here by some unearthly fate?

The wind blew cold on Blue's wet hair, rippled over the water and sent up its stink of leaf rot and dead animal.

Sabina waded towards her, called Blue and called, the water halfway up her shin. On this side of the stream, Blue was submerged to the knee. How was she here?

'Make your way to the bridge!' Sabina alternated her torchlight between Blue and the mire ahead of her. 'Don't try and walk through the stream; it's too deep. Go to the bridge!'

Blue's hands felt tender where they had scraped Joshua Park's stubbled neck. She hated the trees but wanted them too, the prison-bar closeness of their trunks, the certainty that in there no one would read on her face what she had done.

Wind moved the branches, creaked the boughs, made the trunks sway in the last of the light, and Blue couldn't see a break in their line.

Sabina came closer, called behind her to Mrs Park, and another flash of torchlight speared the darkness.

Blue's pulse throbs in her fingertips. How could she face Mrs Park?

How could she say I killed your husband, a ghost told me to do it, a dead girl who looked a little like the girl in your photograph, a little like Sabina's watercolour, a little like the imagined form of an eleven-year-old Arlo, a little like the generic blonde child on a thousand TV adverts?

How could she say she did it because she had, when she didn't have to? When the only immediate danger had been from her own strangled thoughts?

'She's OK, I'm nearly there, she— Jesus.' Sabina landed thigh-deep in the water on Blue's side of the bridge, lost her balance, dropped her torch. Blue heard the splash, heard Sabina swear, but she couldn't move to help, sure that if she did, Sabina would know what Blue had done. That if they touched, Sabina would feel Blue's sin as Blue had felt that of so many others.

Then something worse clawed its way to the surface of her thoughts.

Mr Park would come for her. His spirit would rise from his death pool and slouch through the trees to find her. Blue would never escape. She would never be free. How terrible had Bodhi been? How much worse would a grown man be?

As Sabina reached her, Blue's knees gave way. Sabina caught Blue, forced Blue's arm around her shoulder, held her up and held her tight.

'Molly! Molly, I've found her, come … come and help me!' She pulled and dragged Blue to the bridge, and Blue stumbled beside her, tried to right herself but had nothing left. Above the dank soupy smell of the river was the vanilla and honey of Sabina's skin. She could smell the clean laundry scent of her collar beneath the waxy waterproof coat. She felt Sabina's strong hands grip her torso and Sabina's shoulder dig into her armpit.

They crossed the bridge, step by lugging step and down the other side. The water was shallower here. Blue felt it drop from thigh to shin with a rush of ice-cold lightness. The wind beat her wet body. Clouds cracked open and more rain fell. Mrs Park met them and took the other half of Blue's weight, and together they stumbled to the house. The driveway was submerged. Water licked the doorstep, rushed into the flooded boot room when Mrs Park pushed open the door.

A pile of towels lay ready on the farmhouse table. Milton stood by the side, weight balanced on his walking frame. 'Thank God,' the old man said. 'Thank Christ.'

Blue undid her coat zip with cold-numbed fingers. Sabina eased Blue into a chair, and Mrs Park wrapped a towel around her so it covered her hair, back and shoulders.

The room was bright and swam before her. Eyes closed, she saw what she had done; eyes open, she felt at sea. Shivering and teeth chattering, she tried her best to undo the zips on the waterproof trousers, but Mrs Park stilled her hands and did it for her. She pulled off the boots, took off the socks.

'I'm sorry.' Blue felt waited on, felt useless.

'Hush now; we'll get you right as rain in a moment. Once these wet clothes are off, you'll feel much better. You need some dry things on, a cup of something hot inside you, and you'll soon feel better. Is Joshua coming behind you?'

Milton had turned away so as not to see Blue's body, muttered thank Gods under his breath. The old man trembled; if the walking frame moved, he would fall.

'I'm sorry,' Blue said again, and her jaws clashed so much she couldn't say more if she'd wanted to. She didn't want to. Didn't know what she would say if she could.

'I've put towels down on the sofa – we should let her lie down; she needs to rest.' Sabina peeled off Blue's hoody, and her shivers turned into body-wracking shakes as the fresh air rushed over her. 'Jesus, you're wet through, every bit of you. I'm sorry, we're going to have to take this off, too.' Sabina's hands were gentle, but the touch of the wet cotton T-shirt being pulled off her damp, tender flesh was agony.

Mrs Park rushed off; Sabina dabbed Blue's skin and hair with the towel. She lifted her arms to help but was weak and overwrought. Mrs Park returned and put a warm, dry sweater over Blue's head, eased her hands through its sleeves.

'It's Joshua's,' she said. 'He'll not mind you borrowing it. He was worried about you, went after you, but I don't suppose you saw him? Did you? You came from the bridge, and he went in the opposite direction, the way we saw you leave earlier. I tried his mobile, but it won't connect. I expect he'll come back soon, don't you think? Yes, he'll come back soon. He'll be pleased you're safe when he gets back. You didn't see him?'

Blue was cold as tombstone but felt herself sweat, felt the dead man's jumper stick to her skin. She tried to lift it, but her arms were so heavy, tried to wriggle free, but Sabina pushed her gently back on the sofa. She felt the soft towel touch her cheek, the blanket thrown over her body, the warm lick of heat from the fire, the events of the day ready to pounce on her dreams.

25

Blue convinced herself that she had the handle on living alone. She reheated supermarket meals, turned the radiator off in her mother's room, applied for the single-person discount on council tax. She pushed all thoughts of what her mother had done, of what she was, into a tight, locked box that hunkered in the alcoves of Blue's mind.

She read the magazines people at work left in the canteen and tried to understand how life should be lived when you had no one to care for or no one at home. On her lunch break, she would look up from her sandwiches whenever anyone mentioned weekend plans, tried to look interested, and felt her hands grow clammy with hope, anticipation, nerves, but she was never included. Once or twice the group had looked over at her strangely, the person speaking had lowered their voice, at least one of their companions had suppressed a laugh, and Blue had stared back at her cheese and pickle. At weekends she distracted herself with TV. She picked shows Bridget would never have watched: sports matches, medical dramas, the news, programmes filled with people who were nothing like Blue, even less like Bridget.

She watched every episode of Derren Brown and felt an unusual sense of connection. She watched the so-called psychics talk to ghosts on *Most Haunted* and laughed for the first time in weeks.

Time away from work dragged, and there was only so much distraction. The need to know more about Mother's crime was as insidious as dry rot; Blue's mind was bricked around that one oak beam – even the healthiest thoughts crumbled when poked. She would think, 'I will make breakfast,' and her thoughts would reply, 'What breakfasts did she give Bodhi and Arlo?' She would think, 'I need to put a wash on,' and her thoughts would say, 'Why did she do it? Why?' She would think, 'I can't cope with this, I need to get out of the house, need to go for a walk,' and her thoughts would say, 'Mum held Arlo under bathwater until the little girl was dead. How could she do that? How could she live with herself?'

She hadn't been able to.

Blue had known her mother almost by heart, and she wasn't all evil, wasn't all bad, because she had loved Blue, and Blue had felt it.

She used the Medical Records Act to apply for Bridget's file. Whilst she waited for its arrival, she read up on postnatal psychosis, long-term postnatal depression, on personality disorders. She pictured Bridget on the threadbare navy sofa, fingers picking at each other as she stared dead-eyed at the wall.

Bridget Ford had been dead precisely seven months when Blue received her medical information. The more recent records were emailed, the older sent in the post in a slim brown file, and Blue sat on that same threadbare navy sofa in the living room and went through them.

She was surprised by what could be read between the lines of the GP's notes. Devlin, it transpired, had helped Bridget in ways that Blue had known nothing of. He booked the GP appointments whenever Bridget spiralled, came with her to the doctor's office, took notes when Bridget wouldn't engage, collected prescriptions on her behalf, and Blue wondered how in God's name he convinced Bridget to take medication. Blue pictured the kaftan-wearing, mild-mannered man with dark brown skin, a bald head and round glasses sitting on the too small doctor's chair with a pad and pen. She pictured him crush bitter pills with the back of a spoon and mix them into Bridget's sweet tea. Blue remembered her stepfather stoop to kiss Bridget's cheek as she sat at the table with her cup. What would Bridget have been like, Blue wondered, if Devlin hadn't been there? Would she have done to Blue what she did to—

No. She wouldn't think about that.

Blue read it all through and then stopped for dinner. She poured boiled water into a Pot Noodle, ate three pieces of sliced cheese whilst the sauce thickened, wondered what it was in the records that had troubled her, couldn't shake the notion that she'd missed something.

She ate at the kitchen counter, looked out into the small patch of garden. She'd have to mow the grass that weekend. (Had it been a reference to her mother's time in prison?) She'd need to do an Aldi shop to boot. (Or a mention of her parents?)

It was a name that had raised the red flag. It was mentioned only once, when Bridget had taken newborn Blue for her six-week check-up at the GP and Bridget, in turn, had been checked up on. The doctor had recommended antidepressants. Bridget had refused, claimed not to trust modern medicine, had lost her faith in its power after Dr Bryant's antipsychotics. A note was written in the margin: *Her US doctor? Apply for access to US records?*

There was no other mention of it, the handwritten scrawl forgotten, or denied, or too difficult to carry out in the days before internet, email, tech. But it was the name that struck a chord. Blue had read it elsewhere; it was familiar … where did she know it from?

The court case.

A witness.

The newspapers hardly mentioned the doctor. There were references to Bridget being under a psychiatrist's care, that she had stopped treatment for psychosis before killing her children, but they didn't mention him by name. A broadsheet wrote in more detail about the trial itself, stating that the defendant's doctor was called as a witness for the prosecution.

Blue reread the line. There must be a mistake. Surely her mother's doctor would defend her, highlight the mitigating circumstances, explain that she hadn't been on her medication for weeks?

The State Law Library had all case files on record. There it was, cold and black on the laptop screen: Dr Magnus Bryant for the prosecution.

The prosecution.

The transcripts weren't kept online, but the librarian would scan and email them to Blue for a fee of twenty-five cents per sheet plus extra for time. She filled out the forms, paid the price, waited impatiently for them to be sent.

The week was a long one, made bearable because Blue's current job was relatively new, and the unfamiliarity pushed the minute hand round. She had left the last warehouse the week after her brief, uncomfortable relationship with Lucia ended, the same week she decided she would never again return to Blackpool Front.

Whilst on the pier, she and Lucia had been approached by a woman who peered at Blue from beneath a thick black fringe and pointed her red-nailed finger at Blue's throat. She knew her, she said, she'd recognise the eyes of Bluebell Devine anywhere. Did she still perform, give private readings, did she have a card? Shock knocked the voice out of Blue. She'd thought the simple acts of cutting her hair and wearing jeans instead of robes had rendered her unrecognisable. She took Lucia's elbow and marched away. Later, Blue fobbed it off as best she could, tried to make a joke about the weirdos you meet on the Front, but she had never been good at tricks or untruths and that night, after Blue dropped her home, Lucia googled Bluebell Devine.

If Blue thought the attention from the cheap rags was terrible, it was nothing compared to Lucia's interrogative spotlight. She could feel it in each of her touches, each kiss, how her feelings had altered. No more the dark, mysterious oddball … now she was something that piqued Lucia's interest, and Blue couldn't bear it.

Can you still do it? Is it true you claimed to see dead people? No one can see dead people, though, can they? Were you pulling their legs, was it a money-spinner, would you do it again, would you read my cards, why did you tell those people their son was dead, did you feel guilty, did you do it to anyone else, can you read my mind, are you doing it right now?

People at work whispered, looked her way, laughed behind their hands. Conversations hushed when she walked past. On Thursday, she found a pack of pornographic tarot cards on her packing table, and she walked out of the warehouse and didn't go back.

That same night, for the first time in months, she dreamt about Jean-Paul and his grieving parents. She woke with a stomach full of shame, her body slick with sweat, the memory of the father's fist fresh in her head.

No one at the new warehouse knew about Bluebell Devine. Blue would work hard to keep it that way.

After a week of agonised waiting, the court transcript arrived. There was no contents page or index; Blue had to trawl through the lot. The emotive language of the popular press was absent, and somehow this made it harder to read, the facts presented so clinically that all Blue could feel was revulsion. She had to skip past the testimony of the first paramedic on the scene, skipped the coroner and pathologist's testimonies. She'd asked that the photographs not be included, and she was glad.

Dr Magnus Bryant took the stand on the penultimate day of the trial. There was no description of him but, as Blue read, she could picture the man.

The courtroom would be all wood and green velvet. A male judge residing from his high plinth; a jury full of white, middle-class, church-going Republicans; a gallery of the journalists and nose-poking naysayers who had vilified Blue's mother. Dr Bryant, pillar of the community, would be tall with a chiselled jaw and cold grey eyes peering from behind rectangular glasses perched on a straight, long nose. His suit would be slim-fitted, expensive. His voice would be the slow, trustworthy drawl of the South.

DOCTOR: Miss Bridget Ford was under my care for a period of eight months during 1979, following her attempted suicide after the birth of her second child.

PROSECUTION: To clarify, Ms Ford had two young children, one just a baby, when she tried to kill herself?

DOCTOR: Yes.

Blue paused. She looked at the mirror on the living room wall, the bottom corner still cracked where she had thrown her mother's notebook. It was several minutes before she was able to go on. She hoped to read about the sympathy and understanding Bridget had received from her doctor.

PROSECUTION: Please go on.

DOCTOR: She attended weekly therapy sessions at my practice, and I prescribed her a mixture of antipsychotic and antidepressant medication. She responded surprisingly well to treatment.

PROSECUTION: Surprisingly well? What do you mean by that?

DOCTOR: Within a week, she claimed to feel better and no longer harbour thoughts of suicide. She repeatedly told me how thankful she was that I was helping her, that she was so glad to have someone to talk to. She was quite effusive. I even worried she may have formed an unhealthy attachment to me.

PROSECUTION: An unhealthy attachment?

DOCTOR: It's not uncommon for patients to attach themselves to the person they see as their saviour, even sometimes falling in love with them. I've had many patients fall in love with me.

PROSECUTION: Do you think Ms Ford fell in love with you?

DOCTOR: (LAUGHS) Not genuine love, no; I think she's incapable of that. I realised she was suffering from a want for attention; that once the medication had eased her out of her psychosis, she reverted to her natural state: a woman desperate for attention and prepared to go to extreme lengths to secure it.

PROSECUTION: Why do you think she tried to commit suicide in the first place, Dr Bryant?

DOCTOR: Well, she had left the hospital and was on her own with two young children; all the help she had received at the maternity ward had dried up, and she longed for that same level of care. Her need to be the centre of attention, compounded with a touch of the baby blues, led her to attempt to take her own life, knowing she wouldn't actually die but would instead get the attention she craved. It's a common cause of female suicide, this desire to be noticed.

Blue looked again to the mirror. Looked away from the mirror to the window. She remembered Bridget sitting on the sill with her cheek pressed to the glass, unmoving and immovable. She remembered her in Preston, crying herself to sleep on the worn-out futon whilst Blue sang her 'All the Pretty Little Horses' in the hope it would make her happy again. She thought of the phrase 'baby blues' and hoped attitudes had changed.

PROSECUTION: You saw Ms Ford for eight months in all. Do you think the treatment was a success?

DOCTOR: Yes.

DEFENSE: Objection.

JUDGE: Grounds?

DEFENSE: Ms Ford did not stop treatment because she was cured, but because her medical insurance expired and she couldn't afford to renew it. Had she done so, she would still have been under the care of Dr Bryant.

PROSECUTION: I'll rephrase the question, if I may.

JUDGE: Go ahead.

PROSECUTION: Ms Ford's treatment ended with you prematurely, is that right?

DOCTOR: Yes and no.

PROSECUTION: What do you mean by that?

DOCTOR: It's true that her insurance expired, and she had to stop treatment, but I was so pleased with her progress I was considering ending her treatment anyway.

PROSECUTION: You had cured her?

DOCTOR: I had cured her of any postnatal psychosis, yes.

DEFENSE: Objection.

JUDGE: Grounds?

DEFENSE: Ms Ford was still taking the drugs prescribed by Dr Bryant when her treatment was prematurely stopped. That would indicate that her treatment was ongoing. It's clear that she was in a state of psychosis the night she—

PROSECUTION: Objection, Your Honour, we have not yet confirmed that she was in a state of psychosis, hence the reason I have called Dr Bryant as a witness.

JUDGE: I agree with the prosecution. Go on.

Something else lit up in Blue; a puzzle piece turned clockwise and suddenly slotted into place. She dug out the name of the antipsychotic, found details of its description and use online, found out what happens if treatment is stopped cold turkey.

No doctor, Blue told herself, would let a patient drop from a near-maximum dose of this drug to nothing, overnight, with no support. No hospital, no community, no government would allow that to happen. Not today, anyway.

Blue put down the laptop. She went to the kitchen and made sweet milky tea. She stared out into the shadows of the garden until the tea had turned tepid and she dragged herself back to the computer.

PROSECUTION: Dr Bryant, I understand that you're the eminent authority on female psychiatry in the county, isn't that so?

DOCTOR: I have the highest success rate, yes.

PROSECUTION: And how much experience have you?

DOCTOR: I've been practising for twenty-five years.

PROSECUTION: And where did you train?

DOCTOR: Stanford.

PROSECUTION: Dr Bryant, you've told us that you're a graduate from one of this country's finest universities, that you have over two decades of experience working in this specialty; in fact, you are the most experienced psychiatrist in this county. Why do you think Ms Ford killed those children, Dr Bryant?

DOCTOR: I believe it was an escalation of her previous efforts for attention. This time, instead of trying to kill herself, she killed her children.

PROSECUTION: Do you think she was insane at the time of the murders?

DOCTOR: No, I do not.

PROSECUTION: Do you think her guilty of this crime?

DOCTOR: I'm afraid to say I do. Yes.

Blue looked for the cross-examination. There was none. The following day, an apology was made, stating that the doctor had fallen ill and could not attend court. A petition from the defence to delay the case until he was well. An argument against delay from the prosecution. The judge sided with the latter. Blue was willing to bet a week's wages that the doctor was fit again as soon as the trial was over.

Blue pictured Mother pleading on the lawn of a wealthy doctor's house, desperate not for attention but for treatment. A graduate from Stanford, twenty-five years of experience: he would have known what would happen if a patient was taken so suddenly off such strong medication. Did no one challenge him? Perhaps the defence team would have done had the judge not barred the motion to delay.

Blue ran the numbers through her head and guessed that the man would be in his late seventies, possibly mid eighties. Would he remember Bridget Ford? Would he remember Bodhi and Arlo?

She typed his name into Google, deciding there and then that she would find where he lived, confront him face to face, look in his eyes and tell him … what, exactly? That he had been callous forty years ago, that Bridget's mental health was his fault, the babies' blood was on his hands, that Blue's childhood was his fault, that he was the reason Blue had seen ghosts, had no friends, no life?

What good would that do?

And how true was it?

She looked at her hands resting on the keyboard, at her thin fingers, round palms, strong but undeniably small. What threat could she possibly pose?

The first link told Blue exactly where she could find Magnus Bryant: six feet under in a cemetery outside Richmond, Virginia. It came almost as a relief, because what would she have done to him anyway?

She'd never hurt a fly.

The Three of Pentacles (Reversed)

The room was lit by a torch beam. Blue awoke on the same sofa the Parks had sat on the day before when they pieced together the jigsaw. The coffee table was gone.

Wind threw raindrops against the window like gravel, sucked on the chimney like an old man on a pipe. Blue's head throbbed.

'Good, you're awake,' Sabina said, her torch angled on Blue's chest so as not to blind her.

Blue's mouth was so dry she had to prise her tongue from her palate. Her back, thighs, shoulders ached, and her arms were tender and sore. It took a moment to realise where she was, why she was lying on the sofa and not a bed, what she had done.

'Are you OK? Can you sit up?' Sabina said. 'No, don't stand; the floor's wet, the damn weather won't let up. I'll get your boots.' Her footsteps splashed.

The flood had risen whilst Blue slept; water had breached the house, and was now two inches deep. Sabina waded to the boot room for Blue's wellingtons, her torch reflected off the water. In the residual light, Blue could see that much of the furniture had been moved: the wooden chairs were all stacked on top of the dining table, the end tables were gone, the floor-length curtains looped over their pole to keep them dry.

'You should have woken me; I'd have helped.'

'We tried an hour ago. You were out cold. I was about to try again, but—' She shrugged and threw Blue a pair of clean, dry socks and placed the boots beside her on the sofa. She didn't meet Blue's eye.

A plastic flood board covered the air vent in the wall.

'We've turned off the electricity and gas,' Sabina said, 'and weighed down the plugs in all the sinks and bathtubs, moved most of the furniture.'

'Where's Mrs Park?'

'Fitting flood boards to the kitchen windows and the pantry doors, of all places. The cellar is flooded, I think maybe she's trying to save the pantry from the same fate.'

'And—'

'– Joshua?'

'Milton.'

'He's upstairs.'

'Upstairs?'

'I helped him up,' Sabina said, 'but he managed well. He's stronger than he looks, I think.'

Blue nodded dumbly, unsure of what to say. Her cheek stung, and she felt again the scratches Joshua had made in her skin. Blue's flesh would be underneath the dead man's nails. Defensive wounds, isn't that what they called them?

Sabina walked away, to the window or the door or the stairs Blue didn't know; she couldn't look at her. Blue's hands glowed red in the torch's light. She never thought she'd be able to—

'How are you feeling?' Mrs Park's voice startled Blue; she hadn't heard the door to the passageway open. The linen tunic had been replaced with practical attire: dark cotton trousers and a navy blue sweatshirt with a frayed hem and splashes of cream paint on one side. Her hair was roughly held back by a grey headband, and shadows darkened the space beneath her eyes, mascara smudged towards her right temple.

'I'm OK,' Blue said, and her throat felt constricted and sore, the way it did before a cold struck.

I killed a man. I killed your man.

'You're staring at your hands, do they hurt?' Mrs Park said. She sat on the edge of the sofa and took Blue's hands in hers. The edges of her sleeves were wet. Blue could smell the river on her. 'Looks like chilblains to me, from all that time in the rain. We need to clean those cuts on your cheek, too. Did a tree catch you?'

'No, I don't—' She had to shut her mouth. *I killed your husband.* Close up, Mrs Park looked exhausted. 'How long have I been asleep?' Blue asked and prayed it was nearly morning, that a new day would begin and Joshua Park would walk downstairs and make them all hot toast and fresh coffee.

'Not long, it's just gone eight o'clock. I think the rain woke you.'

Barely evening.

'We'll get you upstairs,' she said. 'The first aid kit's up there, I'll clean your cuts. We should have done it when you first came back, but you were dead to the world as soon as you lay on the sofa.'

'I'm OK, I can help; what more needs to be—'

'– there's nothing that needs to be done. You're better off getting some proper rest in bed, and maybe you'll be fit enough to help in the morning. Can you walk?'

She could. She slipped her feet into the boots, hauled herself upright. Blood left her head with dizzying speed; she swayed, righted herself, followed Mrs Park to the staircase on weak legs. The water splashed with each step, and she could smell the river again, the mulch of dead, rotted leaves, the earthiness of churned-up soil. She thought of the dead rabbit caught in the culvert, its small body. She thought of Mr Park.

The carpet on the stairs was spongy underfoot, the upstairs landing using it as a straw to drink up the water from below. All the bedroom doors were open except for Blue's and Sabina's; furniture had been carried up from downstairs and stored there, and Blue was alarmed that she'd slept through it. Wondered if the women had stared at Blue's sleeping form with disdain as they hauled the tables, chairs, easels up to the dry, safe rooms at the top of the house.

In weary silence, Mrs Park led the way to Blue's room. Her door was unlocked, and she tried to remember if she'd locked it before she left or not. It mattered little; the Parks would have spare keys to every room in the house.

The bedroom was largely untouched since Blue had fled it earlier. The suitcase was still on the floor, the duvet pulled back from the pillows, the half-drunk glass of water on the table. The curtains were open, and the windows behaved as a mirror; Mrs Park looked numb, her face drawn and eyes blank as she moved. A first aid bag was ready on the bedside table, and she unzipped it, tore off a small piece of cotton wool from a roll, doused it in antiseptic and bade Blue to sit on the bed.

'It might sting, but far better that than risk infection.' Her voice was robotic, but her touch was gentle. The smell of the yellow liquid reminded Blue of childhood, of being cleaned up by Devlin after having fallen from that tree, where the bark had scraped her elbows bright pink. She remembered her stepfather pouring a capful of the stuff into her bath that night. *It's all right, lass,* he'd said. *It's all right.*

Mrs Park cleaned Blue's wounds, and Blue didn't flinch. She wanted to rest her cheek in the woman's hand, to say sorry and sorry and sorry for it all. Silence shrouded them, and she knew she should break it, but she daren't. Couldn't think of anything to say other than what she had done to Mrs Park's husband.

She couldn't tell her. She didn't know if it was because it would be unbearable to cause such pain to this kind woman who so diligently cared for her, or because Blue wanted to save her own hide. She suspected the latter and hated herself. Kept her eyes closed as Mrs Park cleaned the last of her cuts, so she didn't have to meet her gaze.

'That'll do it,' Mrs Park said, and Blue heard her screw the bottle lid back on and close the first aid kit and in Blue's mind, there was Devlin again, putting away the plasters, fetching Blue a cup of sweet tea and a chocolate biscuit for the shock.

And in her half-dead voice, Mrs Park said, 'How about a nice choco-late biscuit, for the— Hey, hey, it's all right, no need to cry.' Her robotic voice melted, and the maternal one returned. She sat beside Blue on the bed, put her arm around Blue's trembling shoulders and her hand on Blue's head. Blue tried to sniff back the shame, but as Mrs Park held her, all the suppressed fear and panic oozed from her body into Blue's, and it was Blue's fear now, Blue's panic.

Please come back, Joshua, please come back to me, where are you, why aren't you home, please come back. Joshua, Joshua, please come back, please come back to me, please come back.

'I'm sorry,' Blue said, and her body tremored and teeth chattered. 'I'm so sorry,' and the urge to tell all bubbled up; she thought of those people she had read for, both the witting and unwitting killers, wondered how they kept such a thing locked inside. Marvelled, too, at how Mrs Park could hold Blue so calmly, wash her cuts and offer her food so calmly, when inside she burned with such fear.

Blue looked down at herself, shivering on the bed. She still wore the dead man's clothes.

She would tell Mrs Park. The poor woman had a right to know, and Blue had a right to be punished.

The floorboards creaked outside the bedroom door. Sabina. She, too, would discover what Blue had done.

'Mrs Park,' Blue began, and the wind rattled at the windows.

'I wish you'd call me Molly,' she said and hugged Blue's shoulders as though to stall the confession.

'Molly,' Blue said, but that was worse. It felt cruel to finally use Mrs Park's first name and tell her she'd murdered her—

'What is it?' She sounded so kind.

The corridor creaked again with the steady rhythm of footsteps, and in the reflection of the window, she saw Sabina poke her head around the door and ask Mrs Park if she could help.

Blue couldn't tell them.

Yet she couldn't live without telling someone.

When the flood eased and her car was running, she would drive herself to a police station. She would hand herself in. There was a small part, deep inside, that hoped that if she came forward and took the punishment on the chin, the spirit of Joshua Park might leave her be.

'I'll go and see if the Aga's still hot enough to heat some milk; we had to turn everything off, but that thing takes hours to cool down,' Mrs Park said and then, to Sabina, 'You could stay with Blue if you like?'

'I'll help you in the kitchen,' Sabina said and turned away before Mrs Park could say otherwise.

'She's exhausted, too,' Mrs Park said. 'You both need rest. I'll try and make some cocoa.'

She let go of Blue's shoulders, and Blue was left with the swell of her own fear. Blue didn't want to sleep again – she would see Joshua Park if she slept – so she rose from the bed and went to the window, tried to shake out the fawn-like weakness from her legs.

Outside, the sky was overcast, and the rain fell and fell. Her eyes grew accustomed to the night. She saw the wind ripple the water on the field. She saw the spindle-branched trees lean towards Hope Marsh House. What do you do in a flood, she thought. What happens to a body in a flood?

A white reflection marred the window, and Blue gasped and spun round, had the horrible sense that the girl was back, had followed her, that murdering Mr Park hadn't changed a thing, and Blue was still mad, still abnormal, still Blue.

The white shape was Milton. He leant against his walking frame in the doorway, his face drawn and as white as his hair, his eyes haggard.

'I'm glad you're OK,' he said and looked over his shoulder, 'but I wish you hadn't come back. I have a feeling ...' He shuffled closer, looked behind him again into the empty corridor. 'A terrible feeling.'

The old man had the same horror in his washed-out eyes that he'd had when he'd seen Sabina's painting, when Blue first muttered the name of the young dead girl.

'You knew Jessica Pike,' Blue said.

The Noughties

'It's quiet next door,' Marie said to James. She put down her book, cocked her ear to the living room wall. She frowned. 'A bit too quiet, no?'

James imagined the scene in their neighbours' flat – the good scenario, the bad.

'Very,' he said. 'I'll pop round and check.' He pushed himself up and passed Marie on his way to the door. She had removed the tropical-flowered silk headscarf (a Christmas gift from Milton). Hair dotted her pale scalp in grey, downy tufts. It had started to grow again, as the doctors said it would.

James' hair was white. Deep lines scored his brow; softer lines traced the contours of his mouth, eyes, neck. His left lung still ached, he still coughed, his voice had become grizzly as a bear. But his heart burned youthful bright when he looked at his wife, its core white-hot for her, its edges singed yellow by guilt, betrayal, horror at himself for a mistake he made decades before. Then, a year ago, something akin to fear had joined the mix when, after years in remission, they learnt it had returned.

James bent and kissed Marie's head, the spot on the crown where no hair yet grew. The skin was dry, smooth, soft as a baby's.

'I'll be back in a minute,' he said.

Marie reached for his hand. 'Bring him with you,' she said, 'if, you know—'

'Of course, love,' he said.

The corridor outside was cold, and rain leaked in through the window. Ten flats shared this floor, five storeys up. The concrete hallway gave each noise an echo, and the light was broken. James propped his front door open with a shoe from the rack, and the glow from his hallway lit the path.

He knocked lightly on his neighbours' door and pressed his ear to the wood to listen for footsteps. None came.

Holding the wall for balance, he got down on one knee, carefully lifted the letter box and whispered through the gap.

'Marcus? It's Jim. Are you OK?'

He peered through the letter box. A light was on in the living room, and feet hung over the end of the sofa.

'Marcus?' he said, a little louder this time, then looked through the gap again.

Shadows stirred on the living room wall. A stick of a boy sat very still, a comic book on his lap. He looked up at his name, then looked to the out-of-sight person laid out on the sofa. He tiptoed his way out of the room. His hair was dirty blond and in need of a wash and cut, his expression wary. James eased himself upright, and the boy opened the door.

'Fancy coming over for a bit of tea?' James said. 'I'll write your mum a note.'

The boy grinned, then bounded out his own front door and through James'. James heard the wall-muted joy of Marie's greeting.

James found an old receipt in his back pocket and looked for a pen, found a crayon in Marcus' school book bag and scribbled a quick note for Sasha, the boy's mum. He left it in the kitchen. Out of habit, he opened the fridge. A six-pack of special brew was on the bottom shelf. No food. He'd try and pop something round.

Back home, Marie had put on her headscarf, and Marcus had settled in her lap. He was eight years old and small for his age; he fit comfortably with his back against Marie's chest, their heads side by side. He had his hand palm up, and Marie traced the lines of it.

James made tea in the turquoise pot that Marcus liked best. He put four slices of wholemeal bread into the toaster. Later, they would have some of Marie's homemade bigos stew, but some inner wisdom told James that the boy hadn't eaten for a while and would need something before then.

'See here, your heart line is long and strong,' Marie said to the boy, 'and goes right the way to the other side of your hand, which is rare.'

266

'It is?' Marcus said, full of wonder.

James listened from the kitchen. He smiled. He fetched the peanut butter from the cupboard where they kept Marcus' favourite snacks. The bread began to turn to toast and wafted its scent through the flat.

'Oh, very rare,' Marie said. 'And see your lifeline? That's thick as a pencil lead but very short, it stops halfway to your wrist.'

'Is that rare, too?'

'Hmm, no, that not so much. The line of your head, however, goes right to your wrist, deep as a wound and strong as a tiger.'

'Did you know a tiger's roar can be heard a full mile away? Did you?'

'I didn't! You've taught me a new thing today. Did you learn that at school?'

'TV,' said the boy, and James laughed and spread the nut butter on the toast.

The living room was reflected in the microwave's dark door. The boy on the woman's lap, their heads side by side and cheeks pressed together, his small hand upturned, her fingers touching the lines on his palm. James tried to hold on to his smile. Tried not to think about what he had robbed Marie of by marrying her. Or what the first round of chemo, all those years ago, had done to her last stubborn hope.

Now we're bound in matrimony and infertility, Marie said when they had left the oncologist's office. She had nudged him with her elbow. Searched for some scant humour.

Till death us do part, he'd said, and he had wanted to put his arms around her, but she had put her fingers to his lips.

Let's not talk about that, she'd said, and she looked afraid, and he found he could not move, could only cling to the back of the hospital chair in the white, white corridor and could not step forward, or sit, or speak, or do anything other than reach out and hold on to his wife, who had lost all her hair, and was thin, so thin now.

He twisted the lid back on to that memory and stored it away, just as he twisted the peanut butter jar lid and put that away, too, besides the biscuits and raisins they kept for Marcus.

'So your line of the head and heart are both long, but that of your life is short,' Marie said. 'What does this tell us?'

'That I'm going to be a bullfighter?' said the boy.

'A bullfighter?' Marie said, incredulous. 'No, no, no. A bullfighter, indeed. Try again.'

James picked up the tray with the tea and toast and carried it through. 'He's going to study hard and become an engineer?' James said and winked at Marcus, whose eyes were fixed on the toast.

'Wrong again, old man,' said Marie.

'So what then?' said Marcus. He knew what came next and wriggled his bottom side to side in anticipation.

'It means—' She hovered her hands at the boy's waist, paused ... 'It's all nonsense, and you need to live your own life.' She tickled the boy on his ribs, under his arms, behind his knees, and he squirmed and giggled and cried stop, and Marie did.

Marcus looked worriedly at the wall, aware of his noise and his mother next door.

'It's all right, son,' James said. 'She'll not wake.'

'She might,' Marcus said. Wariness returned to his small face.

James thought about the cans of beer in her fridge, thought how drunk the woman must have already been to leave those few untouched. He hadn't looked in the bin, but guessed an empty bottle of vodka lurked in there. At least the flat hadn't smelt of marijuana. He had never understood where she got the money from. Marie said it didn't bear thinking about.

'Have some toast,' Marie said, and reminded Marcus to take a plate, to say thank you, to wipe the spill of tea on the coffee table with a napkin. 'We can get the little camp bed out for you later, if you like?' she said.

Marcus looked again to the wall, and James knew he wanted to say yes, but worried for his mother.

'I can ask her if you like?' James said. 'I'll pop by later, make sure she's OK, and let her know you're sleeping over.'

The boy's mouth was full of toast, but he nodded and smiled through the crumbs and peanut butter smudges.

In the cabinet by the TV was a drawer of clothes: underpants, pyjamas, tracksuit bottoms, jumpers, all in Marcus' size.

Marcus ate all four slices of toast and a banana that James cut up for him. Marie pulled out the new comic she had bought, and Marcus read aloud to them, and James told him how well he was reading.

After a while, Marie went to the kitchen and began to warm the stew on the stove. James sat with Marcus, who explained each of the characters from his comic book, their strengths and powers, their weaknesses. He asked if he could watch TV, and James looked at his watch. It was gone 6 p.m.

'It's just news and soap operas on now. I can read you a story, though, if you like?'

Their current library book was *The Firework-Maker's Daughter* and James turned to the page they were up to.

There was a knock at the door. A stone lodged itself in James' stomach.

'I'll answer it,' Marie said, and sighed as she walked to the hallway. James knew that a stone was in her stomach, too.

Marcus' mother stood on the step, shifted from foot to foot. She wore washed-out jeans and a grey vest top, and her right hand absentmindedly, constantly scratched her left forearm.

'Hi Sasha, come in—' said Marie.

'Marcus here?' Sasha said.

'Yes, just sitting with Jim on the—'

'I've come to get him.' Sasha's hair was long, the same dark blonde as Marcus', and her skin had the pallor of a hardened drinker. She followed Marie into the living room, and James was surprised to smell laundry detergent. He could smell shampoo. He could not smell alcohol.

'You didn't need to take him. I was just having a nap,' Sasha said. 'I weren't out of it or nothing.'

'That's OK,' Jim said, 'any excuse to have Marcus over.' And he laughed and nudged Marcus, who laughed too and nudged James back. Sasha looked at them blankly.

'It smells in here, what's that smell?' Sasha said.

'*Golabki*,' said Marie.

'Smells like cabbage,' Sasha said.

'It has cabbage in it. And sausage, and mushrooms. You're welcome to join us—'

'I don't need char—'

'It's not charity,' Marie said. 'Just one neighbour asking another over for dinner.'

'Nah, you're all right. Come on, Marky.'

'I want to stay, please can I?' Marcus said.

Sasha moved her right hand away from her arm and beckoned Marcus to follow her. Her left arm was covered in scratched scabs, but that wasn't what made Marie start.

'Oh, you're—'

'Four months gone,' Sasha said and covered her belly again as if she were afraid someone might reach in and snatch the unborn child. 'I'm keeping it this time.'

'That's—' Marie looked at Marcus on the sofa, then back to Sasha. Marie was very pale. 'That's so exciting. That's, well … Congratulations. Marcus, are you excited?'

'He is, yeah, aren't you, Marky? Dead excited. Come on now, let's go.'

'He can stay over, if you want to have a bit of a rest,' James said. 'It's no problem.'

Sasha sighed and said fine. She kissed Marcus, walked out of the flat, and down the unlit corridor, away from her own home. Marie followed into the hall, closed the door and stood for a minute with her back pressed against it, her hands over her face.

'A sibling for you. That's so exciting,' James said to the boy, and his heart reached for his wife. She uncovered her face, came back to the room and sat with them on the sofa. James wound his arm behind Marcus, held his wife's hand.

'Mum says she's not drinking until the baby comes,' Marcus said. 'She'll just drink on the weekend till then.'

Marie looked pained, and James could see she wanted to say something supportive but couldn't.

'Well, I hope you can still come and stay with us when the baby comes,' James said. 'You could bring the little one with you, too, if you liked.' And Marie squeezed his hand and took a deep breath and dried the corner of her eye.

'Oh yes, that's a good idea,' she said. 'Would you like that?'

Marcus nodded and settled into the sofa, his head leant on Marie.

'And which would you like? Brother or a sister?' Marie said.

'A sister,' Marcus said. 'I'd like a little sister. And then we can all look after her together, can't we? And it'll be OK, won't it? It'll be OK?'

'Yes, my love,' Marie said. 'We can look after her together, and it will all be OK.'

The Hierophant

Milton fiddled with the lining of his hat. There was a cut in its fabric, and he pulled out a small photograph, held it out to Blue to see but jerked his hand away when she tried to hold it. 'Just look,' he said. 'It's my only one.'

The photo looked old, its colour faded and edges frayed, but even in its sorry state with nothing but moonlight to go by, Blue saw it well enough. A blonde girl stared out, thin and alive, with colour in her cheeks. She wore a light grey tracksuit, mud on one knee, her pale hair long and loose. Beside her was a tall older boy with narrow shoulders who had the same eyes, cheekbones and chin. His arm was draped around her neck. Both were laughing.

Was this the same child Blue had seen? She wondered how long Milton had stored the picture in the lining of his hat, wondered if he was as desperate as Blue to find someone else who believed in her. She leant forward and focused on the print.

'That's Jessica,' Blue said; certainty and relief swam up her throat, stung her eyes, choked her voice and drowned her reservations. She wasn't the only one who thought the girl existed; she wasn't alone. 'Are you her brother?'

Milton shook his head. 'Keep your voice down,' he said. 'Are you looking for Jess too? Are you with the police?'

'No, I just—' How could she explain her sightings of Jess without Milton thinking she was unstable, without confessing what had happened in the woods? 'How do you know her?' Blue said.

'We were her neighbours,' Milton whispered, his old body tense and alert. 'My wife used to look after her when her brother was … well, not able to, if you catch my drift. Were you a friend of Jess or Marcus?'

'Marcus was her brother?' Blue asked, and Milton nodded, expectant.

Blue tried to piece a story together with the fragments he had given her, but she came up blank. 'I tried to help her,' Blue eventually said and wished she had been honest from the start, but the old man looked at her with such expectation, such hope in his pale blue eyes that to tell him now she knew nothing, had nothing, would be awful. 'Why are you looking for her?'

'I promised I would; I've been looking for her for years.' He looked behind him, alert for sound, but hearing nothing, he went on. 'Their mum had left them. It was just the two kids and they didn't want to be split up by the social, so we helped as best we could. But Marcus was drawn in by the wrong sort of people, got involved in the same sort of stuff his mother had been involved in and worse. He couldn't keep clean.' Milton stopped and wiped his eye and Blue thought again of Jean-Paul, of his father's desperate aggression, the punch in Blue's gut and the blood on her purple kaftan.

'I'm sorry,' Blue said. 'What happened to him?'

'He didn't make it. By the time I'd found out he had died, Jess had gone too. Vanished into thin air, couldn't find head nor tail of her. Social services claimed ignorance, police opened a case that went cold too quick. But you're looking into it now, aren't you? What have you found out?' Milton said.

'Not much yet, I—'

'– stop, don't say anything.'

The stairs creaked, and Milton drew back the photo and slipped it into the lining of his hat. Blue saw flashes of lined paper in there too.

Sabina walked in, a mug of hot chocolate in each hand and her torch clamped under her arm. 'Molly's cure for everything,' she said. 'I think it's a coping mechanism. When all else fails, make cocoa.' She attempted a smile and gave up halfway through. She stood at the foot of the bed, a distant look on her face, a cup still in each hand. Blue moved to take one from her, but she turned, put one down on the table beside the half-drunk water. 'Milton, you take this one, I can make another downstairs.'

He eyed the cups. 'Did you make it, or did she?'

'Molly did, I've just brought them—'

'I'll not take it,' Milton said. 'I'd advise you not to either.'

'Why?' Blue said.

'It's just a drink,' said Sabina.

'They put things in it, they—'

'What do they put in it?' Blue said and felt for her back pocket, though her anxiety pills were in the drowned pair of jeans downstairs.

'I think it's a mixture of diazepam and tramadol,' Milton said, eyes on the door, ear cocked for interruption. 'I found some last time I was here, in the kitchen cupboard.'

Blue tried to remember the advice on the leaflet that accompanied her meds, and if either drug was mentioned on the not-to-be-mixed-with list. She recalled the potential side effects, the warnings of paranoia and hallucinations. Doubt threatened her certainty. Her relief began to wither. *Let me not be mad*, she begged, *please don't let me be mad.*

'You're paranoid, it's just cocoa,' said Sabina, her tone dismissive and heavy with stress, and Blue hoped she was right. Sabina continued, 'I've had it every night, and I'm not dead yet. I'd have noticed if they'd tramed me up.'

'You've slept well, though,' Milton said.

'Just because you found a pack of diazepam doesn't mean Molly added it to the hot chocolate. It's quite a leap to make, don't you think? What were you nosing around for, anyway?' Sabina eyed the old man with suspicion.

Blue waited for Milton to connect the dots between Jessica and Mrs Park, to bring Sabina into the fold, but Milton jammed his hat on his head.

'Never you mind,' he said, and Sabina cursed, looked to the ceiling, and the air filled with Sabina's stress, with Milton's fear and concern, with Blue's discomfort. Blue wanted Milton to tell her everything he knew, wanted Sabina to hear it all so they were in it together, wanted this tension gone from the room so she could think clearly for one precious minute.

'Come in and rest for a bit,' Blue said, and Milton shot her a look of incredulity. Blue ignored it. She felt that soon the house would be divided, them and us, us and them, and she wanted Sabina on their side of the fence. 'You're wrecked, is there anything I can do—'

'You've done enough,' Sabina said, and Blue felt the sting in it. Sabina blew on the liquid in her mug, and steam dispersed into the air. Her torch shone straight at Blue, and she was blinded by it, couldn't make out the expression on her face. 'I'll go back downstairs.'

'Wait,' Blue said. 'Why don't you sit down for a minute?'

'I'll never get up if I do.' Sabina stared at the window and, with a rheumatic ache in her chest, Blue realised that Sabina couldn't look at her.

'I'm going to my room; I've been moved to the one at the end of the hall, on the left.' Milton said to Blue, 'You come find me when—'

'No, wait, please,' Blue said.

'He's been gone for hours,' Sabina whispered. For her, there was only one missing person. 'We have no idea where he could be; Molly called the police when you fell asleep, but they can't get anyone out, said that he'll probably return of his own accord. If he's not back by midnight, we should call again. Midnight. He'll have been gone nearly ten hours by then.

'Why did you go, Blue?'

Sabina's question stalled Milton's exit. They both looked to Blue but Blue did not want to talk about the woods. She wanted to talk about Jessica Pike, understand why she had seen her, to have Sabina learn, too, so the burden of knowledge would be lighter.

'I'm sorry,' she said and felt it was all she could say.

'That doesn't tell me why. We were worried sick. You just left in the middle of this shitstorm, and Joshua went out to help you. You just left.'

And she realised Sabina meant *you left me*. Left her alone with an old man maddened by loss, alone with a married couple who faced the destruction of their home and their business, alone without an ally.

'And then you just turn up again,' Sabina said, 'on your own, oblivious to the havoc you caused.'

Another sorry was futile; Blue saw that. She walked towards her, but Sabina sidestepped and stood with her back to the window, her torch still pointed at Blue's chest. Blue stopped, stayed at the foot of her bed, Milton just behind her, Sabina in front and the dividing line formed.

'Why did you go?' Sabina said again.

'It was my fault, I upset her,' Milton said, and Blue shook her head, said no.

'I had to get away,' she said. 'It was too much, I just – I can't explain it, it was an urge so strong I couldn't ignore it and, I don't know ...'

'What did you hope to find?'

Blue's answer caught in her throat; one word so simple but hard to say.

'Well?' Sabina said, Blue's silence unfathomable. A small, sad voice spoke up from the corners of Blue's mind. A voice she had believed on and off for three years, that kept her safe from everyone, that kept her alone. *They won't understand*, it said. *No one understands you, no one ever will.*

'Help,' Blue said and let the lie form on her tongue. 'I needed help.'

Sabina's shoulders softened. Action was something Sabina understood. 'That was the stupidest way to find help I've ever heard of. Were you trying to find neighbours or something?'

'Yes, that's right,' said Blue and heard Milton let out a small sigh of relief.

'Do you know how ridiculous that is?' Sabina said, exasperated, and shone her light at the floor as though trying to find something to look at that wasn't Blue.

With the glare gone from her eyes, Blue could see through the window behind her.

The alder trees were drenched by the rain. The field was a lake.

Sabina took a deep breath, tried again, asked Blue to tell her why she had come back, what had happened in the rain, and Milton told her not to fuss, said it didn't matter now; all that mattered was Blue was all right.

Blue did not answer.

Outside, she could just make out the bridge and the distant treeline. A shape. A movement.

A black far blacker than the rest.

It moved in time to the queasy lurch in Blue's stomach, waded up and over the bridge, and even though she knew that silhouette, recognised the lumped tread of the man, she wouldn't believe it.

Let it be Jessica Pike, let it be Bodhi or Arlo, let it be anyone else.

Across the bridge, coming this way, closer now, closer. Blue could see the outline of the man's wet hair and knew it would never dry, as Arlo's had never dried. The shoulders rose and fell with each rolling tread, the strong legs forged through the water.

Closer and closer, and Sabina talked on but Blue could not listen, could only watch as her fate closed in.

The past and future were inscribed in the man's shape, and Blue believed at last. How she wished that what Jessica Pike had told her was not true, wished she had been mad, that it was all a hallucination because hallucinations could be cured, and nothing, nothing was going to cure Blue Ford of this.

The hallway door opened.

Mrs Park came in, but Blue did not turn round; she could hear her voice but could not make sense of it.

Sabina left the window, exasperated, taking her torch with her, and Blue could see more clearly.

The rain fell heavily, and the shadow of a man was oblivious.

He looked up at Blue and raised his hand in greeting.

25 to 26

It has been six months since Blue read the transcript from Mother's court case and a little over a year since her death. She keeps her mind occupied. She has a new job at a different warehouse, packing boxes with trainers, hockey sticks, shin pads. The shift runs from 8 a.m. until 8 p.m., four days on and four days off, and there is so much to do – so many boxes to pack and orders to prep and labels to stick – that there is no time to talk to the other workers on the line, or her manager, or the good-looking guy with blond highlights who makes eyes at Blue from his forklift. Her toilet breaks are timed, her lunch breaks timed, she is searched as she enters and leaves the warehouse, and it is so busy, strict, inhumane that she has no time to think. The other days she works as a courier in Blackpool centre, rides her bike from one end of the town to the other all day and into the dusk, delivers pizzas, Chinese food, kebabs, bouquets of flowers, a pregnancy test.

Her mother fell pregnant within a month of leaving prison.

Don't think about that becomes Blue's mantra.

No one on the warehouse floor knows her full name. They will not find out who she is, what she has done; they will not know about Jean-Paul. They will not come across a mystic magazine in their grandmother's out-of-date stack; they will not find photos of Blue with long hair and crystal necklaces wearing a kaftan of purple, beaded linen. They will not read about the mistake she made. They will not tear out those photographs, make them into paper aeroplanes, throw them at her when the floor manager isn't looking. She will not be taunted by grown men and women singing snippets of 'Gypsies, Tramps and Thieves'. At the new warehouse, Blue is anonymous. On her bike, she is invisible.

She returns home tired. She sleeps and wakes and does it all again, and she grows thin, wiry, lonely.

The warehouses close on Easter Saturday and are not due to reopen until Monday. There is no courier work that weekend. Blue is alone at home in her clean, clean house, and she can hear the new neighbours' party next door. She watches TV but cannot concentrate, and the song coming through the wall is Cher's 'Dark Lady' and the crack on the living room mirror draws her eye. She hears laughter from beyond the party wall and the low rumble of conversation. She is alone.

A scene comes back to her from an old sitcom. A man knocks on his neighbour's door, complains about the music. The man is dragged into the party, a beer is pushed into his hand, a woman dances with him, and he no longer minds the loud music, the noise. Blue's trainers are white and clean, her shirt pressed, her jeans sharp. She checks the mirror, smooths her hair down. She has nothing to lose.

She has noth—

Don't think about that.

It is dark outside, and the sky is cloudless, and in the street the thump of music is clearer and mellow light leaks from behind her neighbours' curtains. Four cars that Blue doesn't recognise have parked on the street outside. One is an Audi. It has a steering-wheel lock and a sticker on each window advertising its alarm. Blue walks up the path to the house next door. She has only seen these new neighbours in passing. They look about her age or a little older, perhaps. She thinks that maybe they looked friendly. Maybe they nodded hello to her, but she didn't notice. Blue rings the bell.

'Hello.' The woman answers, her wavy brown hair loose. She wears bright pink lipstick, kohl rims her wide, blue eyes, blusher pulls out her cheekbones, and her long navy dress fits snugly. 'Can I help?' She looks over her shoulder and then back to Blue and wobbles slightly on leopard-print high heels.

'Sorry, I'm from next door, I—'

'Are we too noisy?' she asks with a laugh in her voice, and Blue straightens her back, feels her frown lines lift, and she thinks the woman is friendly; she is hospitable and welcoming.

'It's no bother, I'm on my own next door and can just hear your music through the wall is all—'

'Steve, turn it down!' The door opens wider as she shouts over her shoulder. Blue sees into the house, into the room that connects to her living room. A table of people, six or eight, sit with plates of hot food. 'We're bothering the neighbour!'

'You're not bothering me, not at all; I thought you were having a party—' Blue is aware of her smoothed-down hair, her pressed shirt, her try-hard too-white trainers.

'Sorry about the noise, we'll try and keep it down.' She smiles, and her front teeth are stained purple with wine.

'Sounds like you're having a good time.' Blue cranes her neck, tries to see what food is on the table, how many guests there are, but the door is closing.

'You have a good night, too,' the woman says, and now all Blue sees is the varnished wood and frosted glass, and the evening is cold, and she thinks how stupid she is, they weren't going to invite her in, why would they?

She walks to her own front door and sees it as her new neighbours must see it. Defunct wind chimes hang from rusty brackets, a peeling sign asks cold-callers not to call, Buddhas with sun-bleached skin and chipped thighs sit cross-legged on the wall. The monkey with the sticking-out tongue has lost an eye; his curved ear is cracked, his colour faded.

In the living room, she can still hear the music, but it's quieter now. The song is 'Gypsies, Tramps and Thieves'.

If she had alcohol, she would have got drunk. If she had any of her mum's weed left, she would have lit up a bong and buried her cares in a stupor. All she has is an empty house, a cupboard full of biscuits and a laptop. She doesn't want to think about her neighbours, about the folk at her last job, about Lucia or the other, even shorter-lived romances. Anything is better than staring at that cracked mirror, listening to that song.

The computer loads up with the last web page she had been on: rows and rows of high-school portraits in an online yearbook she'd found. Bridget Ford stares out from the bottom row, a fresh-faced seventeen-year-old with straight, pale brown hair and a wide smile. She wears a dark headband, strings of beads around her slim neck and a blouse with a pattern of flowers. Blue doesn't know if she liked school. She imagines not, seeing as she never sent Blue. She pictures this girl, young and bright, beside the photo that would be taken of her six years later, gaunt and hollow-souled on the courthouse steps.

And she imagines her on the lawn of Dr Magnus Bryant, desperate for the medication that would steady her mind, terrified of what she might do without it. She pictures that man saying no. She pictures that doctor tell a jury that he had done all he could, and Bridget was a cold-blooded, attention-seeking murderer.

Blue snaps shut the laptop. Her skin feels tight, and her pulse drums in her neck. It's late, she's tired, she shouldn't have looked online. Sleep will not come easy, and she vows not to search again; it's too distressing, too maddening.

On Sunday, she strips the front door of all the oddball ornaments until it looks like a regular front door. She sands down the rough sections, digs out a tin of wood varnish from the shed. She watches from the living room window as the young kids over the road tear about on an Easter egg hunt. She jumps on her bike and cycles the roads until her legs and lungs ache, and she's sure she's tired enough to sleep well. She doesn't.

She lies in bed and thinks of the only companions she had in her life apart from her mother: Arlo and Bodhi. Invisible to everyone else; confusing, upsetting, frightening to her. She thinks how she only saw them because of what her mother did.

Like a drug pull, like a smoker's habit, the lure of the internet is irrepressible. At eleven that night, when she should be asleep, she eats digestives in front of the screen, rereads a short paper the dead Dr Bryant had published in a small Republican-funded magazine years ago. She has read all of his papers and tried to understand why he was so callous and why he misunderstood Blue's mother so devastatingly.

The role of the mother is to mother, Dr Bryant writes, and some women struggle with the change from being the one who is mothered to the one who mothers, which leads to them seeking that care from other sources. That's why, he writes, Munchausen's and Munchausen by proxy is so much more common in women than men. It's all in the psychiatry of it. As one mother struggles, so she passes that struggle on to her child.

Her mental health fractures and so splinters the mental health of her child, Dr Bryant writes.

She is glad Dr Bryant is dead.

Blue goes to work tired, comes home tired, sleeps that night and dreams of the doctor. She tells herself she will not look again; it is pointless.

But she does. And again, and again. There is no one to stop her, no one to tell her this is unhealthy. She reads up on the hospitals Dr Bryant worked at, tries to find posthumous complaints against him online, searches forums and social media but finds nothing. The routine of work-home-clean-sleep becomes work-home-clean-search-sleep which soon becomes work-home-search-clean-search-sleep.

Summer comes, and life does not change. Eager for company and unsure what else to do, she joins Tinder. She goes on three dates with three different men and doesn't see any of them twice. The warehouse hours stay the same; she still has no time or inclination to talk to colleagues. Her courier schedule continues, and she gets fitter, stronger. She looks at her arms, at her hands on the bars of her bike; taut muscles hug her forearm, there's an elastic strength to her grip. She pictures her hands wrapped around the neck of the man who wouldn't help her mother.

What good would that do? she thinks. All I'd gain is my own bloody ghost.

Autumn comes.

Winter.

'Five returns last week, all with your stamp on.'

'Five?'

'Aye.' The floor manager stands with her arms folded, her iPad pressed screen-down to her chest. Blue hears someone snigger at a packing station behind them, and the floor manager shoots them a look, lowers her voice. 'Last month was your final warning.'

Blue's stomach hits the deck. Last month she had made an average of three mistakes a week. She had told herself to pull her socks up and concentrate, but her mind had taken to drifting into a numbness she couldn't escape. If she could just sleep, she would be better, but she couldn't sleep. Or she couldn't stay asleep. She would wake, wild-minded, two or three hours after going to bed, and sleep wouldn't come again. She would stare at the ceiling, shift on the mattress, reach for her phone and go online.

'Even now, I don't think you're listening.'

'I'm sorry, I will try harder, I promise, it's just—'

The woman closes her eyes and tells Blue to stop. 'I'm sorry,' she says, 'but with Christmas so near, we need to be running full pelt. We can't be risking mistakes.'

'No, you don't understand, I've—'

'Look, we've all got families to feed, all got presents to save for.'

Blue hasn't any family, has no presents to buy. *Don't think about that.*

'Don't think this comes easy to me,' she says, 'because it doesn't. It is what it is. You don't need to come in tomorrow.'

'No, please—'

It's the end of shift, and people file through the corridors between packing stations, ready to join the queue to be searched before they head home. They speak in Polish, Romanian, Czech. Nearly eighteen months Blue had worked here, and she doesn't know a single person's name, other than the manager's. She doesn't make small talk, has no friends; no one asks her who she is, where she comes from, what she's done with her life. No one cares. She likes it here.

Does she?

Does she like it here, is she happy, does she have anything to live for?

Don't think about—

Her manager says something, but Blue doesn't hear. She walks away, and Blue joins the queue to be searched, bathes her ears in the aural hubbub. It's the first time she's been fired. She should feel ashamed, she thinks. She should feel dreadful. She feels tired. Numb. She drives home.

Her neighbour stands in the front garden, with one hand on her hip and her hair pulled back into a high bun. She talks over the fence to the old lady who lives on the opposite side. Blue stands at her gate. Says hello. Waits to be invited into their conversation, but they just pause, smile at her and nod at her and pretend to be civil whilst they wait for her to go inside so they can talk together in peace.

The mirror in the living room is still cracked.

She looks at herself in the age-spotted glass.

Spring arrives, and Blue watches it turn the bleak branches to bud. She watches birds dart through the sky. She is slumped on the kitchen chair, her cheek rests on the Formica top. In a minute, she will clean the kitchen because it is the kitchen's turn to be cleaned. She will contemplate that if she fixed the puncture on her bike that has been there since December, she could get another courier job. She will think, I am alone and no one is coming. She will think, I need to clean the kitchen, and she will get up and clean the kitchen.

Later, after the kitchen has been cleaned and the stairs hoovered and the cushion covers on the settee ironed, Blue sits on the sofa and opens her laptop. An advert for the Samaritans appears and their phone number draws her eye, 116 123.

She closes her laptop.

She goes to bed and falls asleep straight away. She wakes two hours later and stares at the ceiling until morning. She remembers every strange thing Bodhi ever said and wonders what he would have said if he had been alive. She wonders how she can be so alone, so alone when she has a neighbour in the very next house. When a family live in the semi-detached house opposite. When an old man and his three terrier dogs walk past her front door every day. She is alone, she thinks, because she does not understand people. Because feeling what people think, reading what they feel, predicting what they want is not the same as understanding them. It's not the same as being understood in return.

That evening she opens her laptop and googles Dr Bryant, Alabama, North Carolina, Georgia, women's mental health. Again, the usual results come up, and Blue skips ahead to the page she has got to: 102. She clicks every article. Reads each one. The sidebar shows another banner for the Samaritans, and Blue closes the laptop lid again, goes to bed again, and wonders if the computer can read her mind the way Blue can read the tarot.

Next day she opens the laptop and types in *psychic computer*.

She reads articles about AI and clicks and reads and clicks and reads and finds another on neurolinguistic programming. She reads another on the myth of mysticism and mind-reading. Another.

Another.

Another.

She finds a blog written by a man who sees ghosts. He sees them behind every curtain, sitting on every chair, standing on every paving stone. They talk to him and tell him stories, mostly about life in the past, occasionally warnings about the future, and once a bizarre recipe for lentil Bolognese with red wine and sweet potatoes, and the author says he cannot tell anyone about this because they will think he is mad and he doesn't feel mad. He can see people that others cannot, that's all, he writes. That's all. Blue reads this and thinks of Bodhi. Misses Bodhi. She reads on until the final blog post. He writes that he is alone. He writes that the only people who understand him are the ghosts. There are no more blogs. A Google search for the author of the site brings up a coroner's report. Death by misadventure.

Blue picks up the phone and dials 116 123.

The sun is the late summer sun, high and sometimes hot, giving Blue back the colour to her forearms and nose. Blue has fixed the puncture and rides every day through the town. She winds her machine around bends, between cars, through parks and alleyways, and delivers hot food to hungry mouths. She delivers a pizza smelling of spice to a heavily pregnant woman who tips her and winks.

Mother fell pregnant the month she left prison, Blue thinks. She thinks, she tried her best, she loved me, we were so close I felt all she felt. I felt all she felt, and I saw it the way some people see colour. Everything will be OK, she thinks. I will get through this.

She has a date tonight.

When Blue had called the Samaritans, she spoke to a man whose soft-spoken voice and vague air of razzle-dazzle reminded her of being hugged in the garden by Devlin when Matthew ran away from her, of being helped to climb a tree and cleaned up when she fell out of it, of biscuits and sweet tea and the words 'I'm right proud'.

The online support group Blue joined soon after recommended social contact as a means of battling depression. She rejoined Tinder. She immediately got a date with a very blond man with fat pink lips, almost white hair, and black eyebrows. She will meet him at seven o'clock at Pizza Express in Preston town centre. He has a buy-one-get-one-free voucher.

She has two hours to kill.

The house is clean, her clothes are all laundered, all ironed. The habits she built up in the years since her mother's death are hard to break. Coping mechanisms, one of the guys online called them. One habit that's hard to break is the constant searching.

She searches for synaesthesia, grief, ways to cope with grief, psychic delusions, how to make friends, how to talk to people, NLP, reverse NLP, ways to stop feeling so lonely you fear your brain will melt and your heart will stop and your skin will never be touched again. She searches for ways to make herself feel better.

The online forum has been a lifeline. A lifesaver. She can chat to counsellors when she needs to or other women who struggle with similar issues. Every week she receives a piece of advice to help her on the road to recovery or, as she calls it, the road to normality. The path to living a life. This week: book something for six months' time, something to look forward to.

Blue has learnt to be careful with money. She has some savings she can tap into. The cost of booking something is not what frightens her.

In six months' time, her mother will have been dead for three years.

Don't think about that.

She will have been alone for three years.

Don't think about that.

There is still an hour and a half before her date at Pizza Express.

She gets out her phone. Searches online for synaesthesia hallucinations. Recognises the distraction and puts her phone away.

She opens her laptop. She will search for holidays or maybe stand-up comedy shows, but muscle memory gets there first. She searches for her mother. She sees the photographs of Bridget on the courthouse steps. Sees the mugshot. Sees the desperation and the fear held in the lines of her face, and the headlines that call her an evil child-killer.

There is an hour now until she has to leave for her date. Dry-mouthed and nauseated, Blue minimises the search and tries to focus. Tries to breathe. She thinks she smells incense leak from under the door of the velvet-swagged room, but that would be impossible. She hasn't been in there for months, possibly years; she must be imagining it.

From the front door comes the tinny sound of a wind chime.

It must be a neighbour's. Blue took down all the Buddhas and chimes last year.

Dizziness fills her head, her heart light and fast, and only the top part of her lungs suck in air. Focus, she tells herself, focus. Not on Bridget or Arlo or Bodhi or how different you are or how strange you seem, but on the task for the week. Breathe. Breathe. Book something for six months' time. She opens a new search page, but her fingers take over and the words INHERITED HALLUCINATIONS fill the bar. Freak, weirdo, other, oddball, alone, alone, alone fills her head.

Nothing needed to be done, a voice in her head pipes up. Nothing at all. In fact, why not just sit here awhile, sit with your head on the table, look out the window and let the world carry on. Just sit, just sit and do nothing, do nothing, be nothing.

Blue rubs her arm across her eyes. She will not do nothing. She will not fall back down that pit; she will try, keep trying. She will go on a date and talk to a man and find something to smile about. She will talk to the women on the forum. She will book something to look forward to.

Half an hour until she has to leave for the dinner date.

Another new tab and another search, less focused but with meaning. Breaks in the UK.

The list is vast, and an advert draws her eye, all the right words to attract her. Healing. Grief. Help. Companionship. Friends.

She books a place at Hope Marsh House.

A positive action, she tells herself. One step closer to a normal, healthy life.

The Queen of Swords

'I brought something to eat.' Mrs Park's voice was flat. 'Some Madeira cake I pulled out of the freezer; it's thinly sliced, so it'll be defrosted soon enough. You haven't drunk your cocoa, was it too cold?'

Blue did not answer, her eyes glued to the man outside. She felt hollow-boned, certain that if she dropped her hand from the glass, or dared turn her back on the window, then her body would shatter, her world would shatter, everything would irrevocably shatter.

'It's just fine, you worry too much, I wish you'd let me do more to help,' Sabina said. Her reflection played across the windowpane; her hand sliced through the image of the dead man as she reached for Mrs Park and touched her arm.

Mrs Park screamed.

'Oh my goodness, my God!' Mrs Park ran towards Blue; Blue braced herself for the motherly concern and thought that she must be bleeding from some unknown wound.

Mrs Park did not touch Blue. Her hands pressed against the window; her fingers framed the ghost outside.

'He's here, he's made it back!' The words spilt out of her as water had spilt into the house; they came as a rush and a wave then subsided, much as the truth came as a rush and a wave over Blue.

Mrs Park ran from the room, raced downstairs, outside, waded through the water until she reached the field, where the boggy grass slowed her.

Sabina ran to Blue's window, cupped her hands to the glass to see better. 'Thank God,' she said. 'He must have come the same route as you. Look at Molly; I'm going to take her a coat and help.'

'Don't.' Blue realised, with a noxious lurch, the one thing worse than having killed Joshua Park: not killing him. And have him live to tell everyone what she had done. 'We need to lock the doors.'

The Lovers

Molly shouts his name. The rain throws it back in her face. The weather has made short work of her clothes and hair; she is saturated, cold, wrung out. But she is a dry haven of health compared to her husband.

Her heart has fractured at the sight of him, the relief of his reappearance overshadowed by his state. She is still fifty paces away, but she sees how each step he takes is a battle.

She calls his name again and again, and he has not said a word, but she knows he has heard her, knows that he's aware that she's close because his speed has picked up; he lurches for her like an overboard sailor lurches for land. She is his land. She will save him.

The sky is dark, and the rain is fierce, but she sees his face in the storm. It is haggard, beaten, his eyes wild like a spooked horse. He only looks at that house. His hands reach out, feel for her as she closes in on him, grab her and hold her to him, and he is saying something, over and over again, and his eyes won't leave that house.

Her arms wrap around him, her hands press his body to her, she feels him tremble and shake and hears him speak that name over and over, and it freezes her heart in her chest.

Jessica, he says.

Jess-Jess-Jessica.

We named her Eleanor, Molly thinks. Stop it, she tells him. Talk to me.

She pulls him towards that house, step by painful wet step; he leans on her, and it's all she can do to keep upright, and the water is halfway up her shins, and the rain is in her eyes, and that name is in her ear.

We'll get you inside, she tells him, and pulls his body forward. Water splashes her thighs. He stops, immovable as a boulder in the middle of the flood, but his body shakes and his eyes are wild and Molly feels her strength sap because he is her strength and they are strong together but there is no strength in this place.

She follows his gaze to the window of that house. Sees Blue stare out at them, unmoving.

What happened? Molly says, why are you staring? What did she do? And Joshua looks at Molly, turns his wide-open horse eyes on her and Molly is frightened then. He grasps at her with drowning hands, gasps for air with drowning lungs, and his voice when it comes is broken and shallow and coarse and not his voice, not his voice at all. It is broken.

And he tells her what happened out there in the woods, what he fears Blue knows, what she tried to do to him, and Molly is not cold anymore. She raises her hand for him to stop, hugs his body to her body, drags him and helps him and cajoles him across the field and towards that house.

She is frightened.

Not of what happened to her husband, or what Blue knows, or did, or of what Molly saw in the therapy room last night, or her argument with Joshua that morning, or the state of the house, or business, or the water that won't stop rising, but of what she is prepared to do.

She thinks, fleetingly, of Jago.

She will not take Joshua through the front door and risk seeing that woman before these details have fully sunk in. The back door will take ten more minutes to reach in this weather, but she'd rather risk ten more minutes of wet and cold than one second unprepared in Blue's presence.

Joshua moves more easily now, feeds off Molly's vigour, and they walk together over the drowned field. She will share all her strength with this man. They will get through this together and deal with what has to be dealt with to survive.

Ahead the house looms, ethereal and bright despite the rain. The place Molly once loved, that they renovated so carefully, that they filled with beautiful furniture and art and, later, clothes and toys and bedding for a young girl. A girl who was born Jessica, but they called Eleanor. A child they made their own, whether she wanted to be theirs or not, in a house built for families.

It looks at Molly now – that house, unyielding and solid, offers no warm welcome, no hope or solace. Every promise that house ever made her has been broken. Its window eyes are glassy black and shine out from its cold, pale stone.

One draws her gaze more than any other, always has. It is the window in Sabina's room. The room Blue thought she saw someone stand in, the room with the door that won't stay locked, the room Molly saves for the guests she predicts will need mothering the most because it is a special room – she thinks that even now. A special room. Before the guests, years before, it was Eleanor's.

Blue stands at the next window, watches Molly drag her husband through the mire, does not move or call out or offer help. Molly can't see her face, can only guess what expression it holds as she watches the man she thought she killed stumble homeward.

How dare you come here and threaten everything, Molly thinks. How dare you lay a hand on my husband. How dare you come here and mutter the name Jessica Pike.

And Molly is not frightened anymore. Her blood is hot, and her house is close, and her mind is made up. She will not let that woman threaten her husband again. Let her try, and she will see what Molly is capable of.

The Seven of Swords (Reversed)

'She's already soaked, for God's sake, what's wrong with you?' Sabina was by the door, ready to go downstairs and out into the wild weather and pull that man back inside.

'We can't let them in.' Blue spoke firmly. Her uncertainty dissolved. There was nothing wrong with the house, she realised now. There was nothing wrong with the forest. It's who was inside them that scared her.

And fear was something she could believe in.

'Are you insane?' Sabina said.

Maybe I am, Blue thought, but that is no longer important.

Outside, Mrs Park stood as still as a panther before its pounce. Her eyes caught Blue's.

'Lock the door, please, now!' Blue didn't wait for Sabina to refuse. She leapt across the room, pushed Sabina aside, ran past Milton and down the corridor, down the stairs, splashed into the water and towards the front door, threw the bolts into place.

It would take mere minutes for the Parks to reach the house. Blue had to think fast.

'You can't lock them out of their own house in a flood! What the hell is going on?' Sabina stood on the last of the dry steps, incredulous but uncertain. The torchlight illuminated the fear in her face, and Blue thought, good, be afraid of that man, be afraid of them both; your fear will keep you away from them.

Until she realised Sabina was afraid of her.

'They'll come in through their own door,' Blue said. She remembered the layout of the house, and her chest tightened with the balloon-swell of panic. 'We have to block the kitchen, so they can't get to us.'

'No, what the hell?' Sabina jumped down into the water, went to unbolt the locks, shrugged Blue off when Blue tried to pull her back, and her vanilla scent was lost to the smell of the flood, to the dirt and the mulch and the rot.

'Stop – he's dangerous.' Blue's voice sounded crazed and Sabina looked at her with distaste.

'He went out there to help you,' said Sabina, and pulled the door open through the water, raised her hand, called Mrs Park's name.

Blue shrank back. She would go upstairs, shut herself in her room, climb out the window and down to the ground ... and leave Sabina and Milton alone with them? No, not again.

A muffled shout came from outside, and Blue feared that they shouted for her or yelled for Sabina to call the police, but Sabina shouted back, 'OK,' and heaved the door shut with her shoulder.

'She's taking him round to the back door,' she said, wary. 'It makes no sense; this way is far quicker and closer. Why stay out longer in the rain?' Her eyes scanned Blue's. 'Tell me what's going on.'

'She's right – he is dangerous and so's his wife. You need to lock the kitchen door so they can't get through, and then we need to call the police,' Milton called from the top of the stairs. He leant on the banister, his walking frame abandoned in Blue's room, his hat pulled firmly on. He looked feverish, excited, unstable.

Sabina said, 'This is ridiculous. Milton, you can't agree with her?'

'Do as Blue says,' Milton said.

'I'm not doing anything until you tell me what happened,' said Sabina. 'He found you, didn't he? In the woods?'

How long would it take them to reach the back door through the flood? Five minutes, ten? What was being said outside – could Mr Park remember what Blue had accused him of, had he told his wife what had happened? Did Mrs Park know about Jessica Pike, or was she just keeping her husband away from the woman who had tried to harm him?

'We argued,' Blue said. 'I lost my bearings in the woods; I was trying to get away from him but ended up back here instead—'

294

'Tell her about Jessica,' Milton said with something that bordered excitement.

'Who is Jessica? What did you fight about? For God's sake, just tell me! What do you think you know about— Oh my God.' Sabina's hold on the torch began to shake, and the beam of light trembled. 'You don't *know* anything about him, it's your ... your party trick. Is that it? You've conjured up something based on his ... his aura or some other bullshit, and he got upset and you fought him?' She backed away from the stairs and towards the passageway to the kitchen, as though Blue were the wild, crazy one, as though Sabina should hunker down with the Parks and hide from the deranged lunatic who believed in spirit guides and the power of crystals.

'Tell her!' Milton cried.

There was nothing left to lose.

'I think he killed a child,' Blue said.

Sabina flung up her hands; the torch beam lit the flooded floor, the sofa's arm, the solid oak beam on the ceiling. 'He tried to help you, and you accused him of killing a child? A *child*? Jesus, can you even hear yourself? Based on what evidence, exactly?'

'Tell her!' Milton called again, and he took a step down the stairs, both hands gripped on the banister.

The water was still rising.

Hot angry tears seared Blue's nose.

'I saw a girl. Her name was Jessica. I saw her in your room, and in the woods and ... I know it sounds insane, but I saw her. She made my food turn bad, my coffee go cold, she made the house smell—'

'You saw a ghost, and it accused Joshua Park of murder? A ghost? Are you for real? Can you hear yourself?' Sabina said, her brow furrowed, and Blue felt her pity like a scald.

'What the bloody hell are you talking about, seeing ghosts?' Milton said, two steps down on the stairs. 'Tell her what you found out, why you came here in the first place. About how you work undercover with the police—'

'I told you already, I'm not with the police,' Blue said. 'All I know is that a child lived here, and they killed her.'

'You saw ... a ghost?' Milton said, and Blue didn't know what to say or how she could explain it in any other way. She nodded.

'No!' Milton beat the rail with the side of his hand, and his knees looked ready to buckle. 'No! You're supposed to have evidence, I thought you had— I thought you were investigating her disappearance. I thought you'd come to find out what happened to Jessica.'

'What did happen to Jessica?' Sabina asked and Milton's face fell, his shoulders sank, his voice wavered.

'Her brother died of a heroin overdose,' he said, 'and I never saw Jess again. No one believed me when I said she had gone – they told me she was a runaway, that it happened, that she was a lost cause.' He looked at Blue, thumped his frail fist against the banister. 'I thought someone finally believed me! For years I've been telling the police it was *her*, that these … these monsters had something to do with Jess, but there was no evidence, nothing other than my gut feeling. That woman was Marcus' nurse. She left her job the day he died, left the city the day he died; I know in every one of my bones that she was involved. But the police don't believe gut feelings; you can't arrest people based on visions and ghosts, you need evidence, evidence!

'Twelve years I've been looking for Jessica, twelve years and I've tried and found nothing, and I thought you had something. Finally, I thought someone had something.' He turned and tried to take the steps up on his own, but weakness overtook him, and he stayed on the stair, spine hunched, his hands wrapped around the banister like it was a life raft. 'I've been coming here for three years, ever since I discovered they ran it – used every opportunity to search this place, looking for some sign of Jess. I've searched the empty bedrooms, the filing cabinets, anywhere I could get into for some scrap of evidence, everywhere save for their apartment … I've never stopped looking, but I've run out of time. I'm old and ill, and I've run out of time. I thought you had found what I couldn't, I thought you were good, but you're … you're—'

'Look what you've done.' Sabina shook her head at Blue and Blue wished she could prove it, wished she could lead Sabina through a cheap plywood door into a velvet-swagged room and sit her at a table surrounded by rune stones and incense, lay out her cards and justify her intuition.

She wished she could hold Milton and tell him his effort hadn't been in vain.

Instead, she reached out and grabbed Sabina by the wrist, held her, skin to skin, felt every ounce of her. Blue didn't flinch against it; there was no fear or elation or pride. Just Sabina. It wasn't all there, but it was enough.

'Get the hell away!' Sabina yanked her arm back, rubbed her wrist, her face full of disgust. 'You're crazy.'

'Your brother-in-law died two years ago; you told us your sister won't see you, but that's wrong. It's you who refuses to see her.'

'You have no idea what you're talking about. You look at me and make lucky guesses, but you can't just guess that a perfectly normal, friendly man killed a child and expect no one to argue against it. You can't lead an old man on and make him believe you know things that you don't. You need help, far more help than a fucking grief retreat.'

'And your parents didn't book this trip for you: your sister did. She wants to help you, and you can't bear it.'

'You've hacked into their computer, found out who paid. This is insane. I'm going to report you, I'm—'

'You were in love with your sister's husband. She doesn't know.'

'You've hacked my phone or ...'

'You can't bear to talk about your sister or see her or your niece or your parents. He would leave her for you, he talked about it as you drove to the airport on the day of the—'

'This is just your reverse NLP or whatever it is you—'

'That wasn't on Facebook, was it? Or on your phone, or in Mrs Park's client files.'

Even in the dimness, she could see Sabina's eyes burn. 'Get away from me.'

'Am I right?'

She didn't answer. Blue didn't need her to.

For years Blue had tried to fit in. She knew now she never would, that she didn't need to.

'It doesn't matter how I know these things, but I do know them,' Blue said. 'Mysticism, neurolinguistic programming, witchcraft, an AI brain – call it what you like, but isn't it just possible that if I know these things about you, I could also know things about him?'

'How do you do it? It can't be so simple as touching my wrist.'

'I don't know, I've never understood it,' Blue said and felt it was the truest thing she had said so far. 'Will you please help me? I need to block that door; I need to keep us away from them until the police can come.'

'This is insane,' Sabina said, but with less vehemence. 'You're saying Joshua killed someone, and we should lock ourselves in the main house until the police can arrest him? Because you have a feeling?'

'Because I know it. So does Milton.'

The old man had stopped. He listened to Blue, nodded at Sabina. 'Blue knew I was lying about my name, and she knew about Jess without me breathing a word.' He sounded defeated.

'Does Molly?'

'There's a photo of Jess with Mrs Park in their apartment,' said Blue, 'but she's not the one who killed her.'

'I can't picture her knowing that and staying with him,' Sabina said, crestfallen but resigned.

'Unless she was involved, too.'

'Molly doesn't have it in her. Besides, wouldn't you have picked up on it? Your knack, I mean.'

'It's not an exact science,' Blue said, and Sabina snorted a laugh. 'And I can do this alone.' The thought of that was a sickness in her bones, but she would do it if necessary, wouldn't guilt-trip Sabina for help. 'You can keep to your room with Milton and stay safe; if anyone asks, I'll tell them you weren't involved. Just promise me you'll stay clear of Mr Park – Mrs Park, too, if you can.'

'Don't throw a strop, I was joking.'

'I know you were,' Blue said. 'I wasn't, though. You don't have to get involved.'

They were silent, the rain a light percussion to their thoughts. Through the skylight, Blue could see nothing but darkness; the cloud cover was heavy, no moon or stars peered through. The raindrops were rendered visible by the torchlight, the beam bright on their silver edges.

'I either help you and believe that Joshua is some sort of madman, or decide that you're the mentalist and stay in close quarters with a potential child-killer?' Sabina exhaled a long blow of air. 'Not much of a choice,' she said.

'I know,' Blue said, 'but I don't have much time; they'll be in their side of the house by now, could be ready to come through at any—'

'This is Molly Park we're talking about,' Milton interrupted from his place on the stairs. 'Before she does anything, she'll nurse her husband to within an inch of his life; she'll dry him, dress him, wrap him in blankets, make him cocoa, probably spoon-feed him stew. There's time enough to come up with a better plan than locking ourselves in different parts of the house.'

'You'll help?' Blue said.

'I'd rather help you and be wrong,' Sabina said, 'than not help you and find out later that he killed that little girl.'

A simple plan formed: Milton would gather his scant findings and wait in Blue's room. Blue and Sabina would get some supplies then block the kitchen door and meet Milton upstairs, where they'd barricade themselves in the room and wait out the night. As soon as it was light, they would leave together, help Milton in whatever way they could, and head to the main road instead of the woods and wade along it until they found help. They wouldn't need to confront the Parks. There would be no need to try and play the detective and find out exactly what happened to Jessica Pike. Blue would tell her story to the police; they would look into it. And if the Parks pressed charges against Blue for her attack, so be it.

They were exhausted, overwrought, desperate. It may not work – the Parks may fight through, confront them – but it was something.

Sabina's help came with a caveat: Blue and Milton had to tell her everything once they were shut upstairs. They agreed.

'Grab a rucksack from the boot room, we'll fill it in the kitchen,' Sabina said once Milton was safely in his upstairs room. Blue obeyed, and set out three pairs of wellingtons, waterproof hats and coats on the benches, ready.

Sabina slipped her arms through the rucksack straps and together they paddled through the passageway. The corridor was windowless, the dark so absolute it seemed solid. They moved by the hazy light of Sabina's torch and could have been in a cave, a mine shaft, a flooded tunnel; it felt so far gone from the Hope Marsh of yesterday. At the kitchen, Sabina stopped. She pressed a finger to her lips.

They listened, heard nothing but the rain and the wind outside.

'I'll get food from the pantry,' Sabina whispered, mouth close to Blue's ear, 'you get the bottled water they keep for Milton.'

Blue nodded. Sabina eased the handle down, opened it part way, slipped inside.

Stopped dead.

Blue was right behind her, was about to step into the kitchen, too, but Sabina held the door in place.

'Molly,' Sabina cried, 'I was just coming to see how you are.'

She closed the door on Blue.

The Ten of Wands

'Are you alone?' Molly said, in that same dead tone she had used upstairs.

'The others are asleep, they're exhausted,' said Sabina.

Blue switched on her torch, pressed her ear to the slither between door and frame, felt the wash of relief that it was Molly Park and not her husband.

'I'm not surprised,' Mrs Park said and then added, after a pause that seemed too long to Blue's ear, 'poor things.' She heard no warmth in it, could only picture the look Mrs Park had shot her from outside when her hair was wet and eyes were fury.

'I think it was the shock of seeing Joshua; Blue just fell into her bed,' Sabina said, with impressive nonchalance. 'How's Joshua? Is he ok? I was going to make you both some food—'

'Sit down with me. I'll make us something,' Mrs Park said.

'But the water—'

'We've wellies on.'

'Really, there's no need, let me—'

'I insist,' Mrs Park said, and Blue told herself that the weather had turned her voice cold; it was worry for her husband and not suspicion. 'We can eat together, then you can go off and sleep well.'

'You're not going to bed?'

'No. I'll clear the therapy rooms, move some boxes into the attic above our apartment. I'll not sleep yet.' There was a catch in her voice. Doubt gnawed at Blue's certainty. Her house had flooded, her business was under threat, her possessions were at risk, her husband had disappeared and then turned up wet, cold, half-dead, and she was dealing with it alone. Above all that, she wanted to make sure Sabina was fed, would sleep well.

'I'll help you,' Sabina said. 'I can sort out the furniture, and you can make a start on your things.'

Blue thought of the cluttered, homely living room she had snuck into earlier that day, all those photos of the two of them, and the one picture of the girl who looked so much like a brunette Jessica Pike. She remembered Mrs Park's maternal contentment in the picture. Reread in her mind the dozens of testimonials from guests who had found solace at Hope Marsh House.

'No, you sleep; I can manage alone. Here you are, look, nothing exciting: just soup warmed up a bit on the Aga and the last bread roll from earlier,' said Mrs Park and Blue heard the bowl, plate and spoon land on the table, felt her own empty stomach clamp in response. Sabina said thank you, said she would save the bread and take it with her, in case she was hungry in the night, and Blue knew she was saving it for her and Milton, and loved her for it.

'Are you not eating?' Sabina said.

Mrs Park sighed. 'I haven't an appetite, not with so much—' There again was the catch in her voice, and Sabina said she was sorry, asked if there was anything she could do, any way at all she could help and Blue knew that Sabina's conviction was slipping away even faster than her own.

'Nothing, unless you can make this water dry up and stop Joshua from catching his death.'

'He's sick?'

'He's sleeping,' Mrs Park said. 'I don't know how he is, I don't know. He's been so … it doesn't matter. We'll find out when he wakes.'

He's been so … what? Blue thought, but she knew. Out of touch, distracted, upset. Guilty. Blue recalled the argument she'd seen that morning. Perhaps Mrs Park didn't know anything.

'Did he get lost in the woods?' Sabina said.

'He made no sense when I reached him; he was shivering and exhausted, and I couldn't make head nor tail out of him. He was asleep before his head touched the pillow, I had to peel his clothes from him lying down. He doesn't have a fever, thankfully. Maybe it's shock, maybe it's exhaustion.' She sighed again. 'I don't know.'

'Did he see Blue in the woods?' Sabina said, and Blue wondered what the hell she was doing. Hadn't they agreed not to act detective?

She's changed sides, thought Blue, she thinks I've lost my mind.

'Didn't Blue tell you?'

'She said she didn't see Joshua, but it's odd, no? Joshua must know the land so well, and he was gone for so long only to return from the same direction as Blue. It struck me as strange.'

'It'll all come out in the wash,' Mrs Park said. 'Best thing you can do is go to bed. We'll find out in the morning.'

'I'll help you first,' Sabina said.

'You're to do nothing but rest. How was your soup?'

'It was delicious, thank you,' Sabina said, and a change in her voice made Blue straighten up, a whimsical warmth that felt out of place. She heard Sabina slurp rather than sip from her glass.

'Eleanor loved homemade soup,' Mrs Park said, 'but her favourite was something called bigos.' That catch again; a glimmer of emotion, as though all the warmth of the house was sucked up and held there, to be heard but not felt in the air.

'Who's Eleanor?' Sabina said, and Blue thought, why, why, why would you ask that? But Sabina didn't know that name, had only heard Milton and Blue talk of Jessica Pike.

The chill crept along the damp lines of Blue's borrowed trousers, crawled like an ant up the sleeves of her knitted top. Mr Park's top. She shivered, clamped her jaw tight to stop chattering.

'We only ever had Eleanor.'

The torch handle turned cold.

The air was dry ice in Blue's lungs.

It's the bad weather, she told herself. It's the weather.

Her breath billowed in the torchlight.

'Was Eleanor like a daughter?' Sabina said, and Blue thought, no, don't dig, leave it be.

In the corridor beside her, she saw red shoes glimmer beneath the surface of the flood.

There is nothing like the cold that freezes from within.

'She was our everything,' Mrs Park said on the other side of the closed oak door.

'I've not heard you mention her before. Who is she?' said Sabina.

The red shoes moved closer; the torchlight first caught thin legs, then hands and arms that hung limply from shoulders. The currents carved like liquid arrows through the water, made fast work of reaching Blue's feet. Three, four, five small fluxes, each an accusatory point.

Blue's breath froze in mid-air like snared clouds, as though the promises she'd made were trapped in their billows and the girl had come to collect.

'She was our whole world,' Mrs Park said.

Blue lifted her eyes to meet the girl's face, and it was as no girl's face should be. Skin pulled mummy-thin across cheekbones, brown lips dry and stretched over yellowed teeth, sunken dark eyes that stared into Blue's.

You said you would help me.

I'll be trapped here if you don't help me.

Why won't you help me?

'I tried,' Blue said.

You lied to me.

The claw-fingered streams had reached her, crawled beneath her soles, dug their cold nails in her toes. Cramp seared up both calves, into both thighs. Blue clutched her torch, fell against the wall, tried to scream, but her throat was clamped tight.

'What happened to Eleanor?' Sabina said.

Blue's heart seized, wracked with ice and pain and fire, and she thought of Devlin clutching his chest, thought of her mother collapsed over the body.

'We'd have done anything for Eleanor,' Mrs Park said.

The torch fell from Blue's hand, landed with a dull splash.

'What was that?' said Mrs Park.

Temperance

It does not surprise Molly to find Blue collapsed in the passageway. The girl is pale and shaken, and Sabina tries to rush to her but is slowed by the water. Molly reaches Blue first, asks if she is all right, and follows her gaze along the torchlit corridor to see if she can spot what Blue is staring at.

It is empty. The door to Milton's bedroom is shut tight, so too those of the therapy and art rooms. There is nothing there, nothing but a sour, sharp smell that stings Molly's nose. Nothing but a cool feel to the air that makes her skin prickle in gooseflesh, makes the hairs on her neck and arms lift.

There is nothing there.

The same phrase had been her mantra last night when she had seen the spectral-pale Milton rifling through the filing cabinet, looking for God knows what. It is the same phrase she repeated to Joshua just that morning, when she told him what she had seen, and he had spooked and she had reassured him. There was nothing there, not one shred of proof that they had done anything other than run a retreat and run it well.

Still, Joshua had wanted to get rid of the last thing they had, the one thing that Molly could cradle to her chest at night when that house was quiet and she was awake, alone with her own grief, her own disappointment, and remind herself that once she had had it all. He wanted her to destroy Eleanor's photograph.

Molly would sooner burn every photo she had taken of her dearest guests, every picture of them sleeping and resting and proving that she was just as good a carer as they needed her to be. She would rather tear every page from the guestbook, delete every online review. She would not give up that photograph.

And she did not tell Joshua that Blue had seen it. Nor would she.

Muscle memory takes over now; habit takes over. Molly sees that Blue is upset, and she waves her into the kitchen. Her voice tells the girl to sit down, rest, not to push herself, whilst her feet carry her to the Aga, where there is still some warm soup in the pan. Molly's mind is on other things. As her body moves and mouth speaks, her thoughts remind her that Blue is the cause of all this. She pulls out a smaller pan. Fills it with milk and powdered cocoa.

The kitchen is lit by thick white candles. Molly strikes a match, starts to light those that went out when the door opened and the draught swept through. She says that she thought Blue was asleep, and Blue says yes, but she needed a drink and will just get one now quickly if that's OK and then go back to bed and Sabina says, in a voice that's too bright for the circumstances, that it's a good idea, that she'll go too because they're all so tired and need their sleep.

Molly knows she is being lied to. Did Sabina think she wouldn't notice the rucksack and boots? It is clear to her that Blue has said something, enough to put Sabina on edge, perhaps even enough to win over the old man.

A bubble of laughter is caught in her throat. I have seen you lying helpless in your bed, Molly thinks. I have stood over you whilst you slept; I could have hurt you, but I didn't. I cared for you, I tried to love you. Molly wonders if she has caught a fever, if the rain has made her body ill and her thoughts hot. If her racing mind and racing pulse are symptoms of malady or madness. She wonders if Sabina thinks her stupid.

Sabina tells her it's best if they all go to bed, that the worst of the flood has been dealt with, that some sleep will do them good and they can all pitch in to help in the morning when Joshua will be up and hopefully well enough to talk.

Molly is far from stupid. She catches the look Sabina throws to Blue, the silent communication that Molly's husband of twenty years is out of action, that somehow this makes them safe. Molly will not be bamboozled by another woman's quick tongue and sidelong looks. She tells Blue that Joshua is exhausted after his effort to find her, but he's all right, though so tired he could barely string a sentence together before he fell asleep, warm and safe, in his bed. Molly says she feels so much calmer now her husband is home. All the while her thoughts scream that this is all Blue's doing and how dare she look at Molly with those amber and turquoise eyes as though she's innocent.

Molly is calm, despite her strange fervour, despite her sick head. Joshua told her everything that happened out there in the woods. And Molly will deal with it.

She wants to laugh in Blue's face. She wants to slap her.

She does neither.

What was it Joshua always says? Take opportunity when it comes because hell only knows when it will come again. It's how he did so well in business, it's how they came to buy this fine house, it's how they found their sweet daughter. You see an opportunity, and you take it. You see a stock priced too low, and you buy it; you see a house that's been deserted, and you bid on it; you go back to work after your fourth round of failed IVF, and your first patient is a scrawny young man who can barely look after himself, let alone his young sister who needs a mother not a brother. So you give him enough methadone to end his struggle, forever. And you find that child in need of a mother not a brother, rescue her before word gets out that her brother is dead, before social services know she's in dire need or the police come knocking on her door, or her neighbours try to look after her themselves, and you mother her. You mother her. And in time, the girl will be grateful for it. She will learn to love you back.

Sit down, and I'll make you some food, too, Molly says, and Blue hides her shock very well. She doesn't want to impose, she replies, and there is all this water around, and Molly probably wants to get back to Joshua. Molly says it's no imposition, that Joshua is asleep, and Molly has already fed Sabina and would like to feed Blue, too. Have some soup with me, Molly says. Have some warm cocoa to help you sleep. Molly adds, with well-practised tears in her eyes and a voice that really does sound like she cares for them and doesn't know precisely what Blue did to her husband, that she feels lonely and could do with the company.

The candles flicker yellow light on the walls and the windows and the faces of the women. Outside there is light rain and strong wind. Joshua is safe, and Molly is calm, and the weather need not be feared. Water can reveal things, and it can hide things, and it can give you time. The flood is an opportunity.

Sit down and eat, Molly says, and then you can sleep for as long as you want.

The Seven of Cups

Shadows stretched in the low yellow light; the shade of the door handle reached for the floor, the chairs' silhouettes grew long-limbed and thin, Sabina's fingers made spider's legs on the table. The soup looked warm and soothing, but Blue hadn't the stomach to eat. She saw the girl's yellow teeth again and the dried lips, smelt the rank stench of her, and she thought of the taxidermy tents at the mystic fairs she'd gone to as a child, the dead ferrets with their wide black eyes, the reptiles with opaque hides.

'Have some cocoa and then head to bed.' Mrs Park poured the dark liquid into Sabina's cup. Milton's warning played in Blue's ear. She caught Sabina's gaze and gave an imperceptible shake of her head.

'It'll be easier to work in the daylight,' Mrs Park said. 'All this torch- and candlelight is bad for your eyes.'

'Your eyes, too,' said Sabina.

'I see well enough. Drink up.'

'I'm full from the lovely soup, I couldn't take a single sip.' Sabina spoke with charm, but there was a slur to her voice. She patted her flat belly with her palm, but her movement was clumsy. 'I'll get myself to bed, I'm practically falling asleep already.'

Blue sensed that Sabina had the same idea as her: forget the supplies, just get upstairs, lock the doors, wait for morning, and get the hell out. Even if she was tortured all night by Jessica Pike, even if she got no sleep and was weak with hunger, the simple prospect of leaving was enough to galvanise her to stand from the table and say goodnight.

'Everything will be settled by dawn,' Mrs Park said. 'No, Blue, you stay here and eat your soup. I'll see Sabina to bed.'

Sabina hid her panic well and Blue tried, tried hard to show she wasn't unnerved and that the sway in her friend's stance wasn't frightening, that the grip Mrs Park had on Sabina's arm was quite normal. Blue said, 'It's all right, I'm too tired after all, I'll come too.'

'No, you won't,' Mrs Park said. 'I insist. I can't let you sleep on an empty stomach; finish your soup.'

Sabina looked at the green varnished door: the entrance to the Parks' apartment, the living room with the photograph of Eleanor – the single proof Blue had of her existence. Sabina looked at it again and said, 'It's OK, Molly can help me up to bed. You stay, eat something.'

Mrs Park let Sabina's arm go. She didn't look at the door, or at Blue, or the uneaten soup, the rejected cocoa. Instead she scanned Sabina's face, her lips bowed in a tight smile. 'I'm fussing again, aren't I? Silly me. If Joshua were here he'd tell me off for mollycoddling you both.' She spoke as though the house had not flooded, the art session had been a success and that, at any moment, she would open the doors to a therapy room and business would resume as normal. She talked to them both as though her husband was not invalided next door, and Sabina and Blue were favourite, longed-for guests.

Mrs Park moved back from Sabina and blocked the apartment door.

'You both go on to bed,' she said. 'I'll see you soon. I best go check on my husband.'

They followed the torchlight back through the hall and into the main house. The sofa they hadn't been able to shift showed a tideline of soaked-up damp on its back. They shuffled through the water.

'We need to get the hell out of here as soon as we can,' Sabina whispered.

'You believe me?'

'I believe she's mentally unstable.' Sabina stumbled; Blue caught her, steadied her and Sabina said, 'I didn't drink her damn cocoa, so why do I feel like this?'

The carpet on the stairs had soaked up the flood, and the first four steps were boggy.

'It was the soup; we need to get you some water to flush it out of your system.'

'It's not too bad, I'm just a bit groggy. I'll cope,' Sabina said. They neared the top of the stairs.

They heard the creak before they saw the door open. Sabina, startled, grabbed Blue by the arm. 'Jesus!'

'It's the wind.' Blue reassured herself as much as Sabina.

'What wind?' Sabina said and swung her torch along the hallway to their rooms. Her bedroom door stood open but not still. It moved gently back and forth. Sabina buckled, righted herself and pushed her free hand across her shorn hair.

'Over here.' They turned and saw Milton at the other end of the corridor.

'We need to get our stuff,' Blue said.

'It's just stuff,' said the man.

It was just stuff, just clothes and shoes and underwear. It was roughly half of all Blue owned.

'We can get it in the morning.' Sabina rubbed her eyes, squeezed her temples, her movements sluggish.

'Let's try and get some sleep,' said Blue, 'tomorrow's going to be a long day.'

'You need to tell me what the hell's going on first,' Sabina said as they walked towards Milton and the door he had propped open with his walking frame. 'She saw me signal to the apartment door, she didn't want to leave you alone with the possibility you could go through it. Do you think that's because she's worried about Joshua or the photograph?'

'Both,' Blue said.

The room was as clean and white as the rest. The bed was made, the side table cluttered with ornaments rescued from the living room, a bottle of fresh water on the floor. Sabina stumbled as she stepped over the threshold. Blue caught her, and her body was dead weight.

'Blue, I don't—' Sabina began, an ethereal softness to her voice.

'Get her to the bed,' Milton said. 'I bet she drank the damn cocoa; I told her not to, I told you both!'

'It was in the soup,' Blue defended. 'Jesus, imagine if she'd had the cocoa too.' She hushed Sabina, ignored the panic in her chest, helped her over to the bed, pulled back the covers and had her lie down. As she held her, Sabina's confusion washed through Blue, her desire to sleep, sleep forever, to close her eyes and disappear, the jet-black want to never wake up unless she could wake up with the man she had loved, but he had died on the pavement beside Sabina's tree-wrecked car.

Dozens of TV shows reeled through Blue's head: medical dramas, A&E documentaries, old reruns of 999. What should she do?

Sabina's head lolled, but her eyes betrayed fear. Blue urged Sabina to stay upright, stay awake. She tried to get her to sip the bottled water, to help flush out her system, but Sabina was falling asleep.

'What do I do?' Blue said.

Sabina slouched, and again Blue righted her, only for her to slip to horizontal.

'Get her in the recovery position,' Milton said and talked through what Blue had to do. She pulled Sabina down so she was flat on the bed, rolled her on to her side, propped her with pillows, and moved her arms, leg, and head. A lump protruded from the pocket of her cardigan, something soft wrapped in kitchen paper: the bread roll she had saved for them. Blue's throat felt tight.

She didn't know whether to cover Sabina to keep her warm or leave her uncovered, and in the end Blue pulled the flat sheet clear from the duvet and draped it over her body.

Blue checked Sabina's phone for a signal, wanted to call an ambulance, have them send a helicopter to lift her to hospital, but her phone was dead, and Milton's was too.

In the funereal light, Sabina looked like a shrouded corpse. Blue had to fight the urge to rip the sheet off her again.

Why had Mrs Park drugged Sabina when Blue was the cause of their trouble? Blue had tried to kill Joshua Park, held his head below the water, and mistook his body's limpness for death. Sabina was a mere bystander, a witness.

Is that it? Had Molly Park simply ensured that Sabina didn't see or hear anything else tonight?

'You said there's a photo of Jess?' Milton said. He sat on the upholstered cream chair in the corner and contemplated Blue through his pale, weathered eyes. The navy hat was on his head, the one piece of colour among the browns and beiges of his clothes, and he looked old, very old.

Blue nodded. 'It's in their living room.'

'I've never made it into their rooms. I knew something would be hidden in there.'

'The police will find it,' said Blue but she knew that wasn't true.

Milton sighed, shook his head. 'She'll have destroyed it by then.' His voice sounded strong. Milton pressed himself up from the chair and his limbs shook with fervour not exhaustion. 'Stay with Sabina,' he said.

'Milton, you're not going anywhere,' Blue said, half laughing because it was ridiculous to think he would risk his own safety for a photograph, and because she knew that he wanted to, so badly.

'I've been trying to find proof for years and that's it. I can't leave without it.'

'It's not worth the risk,' Blue said.

'And who are you to tell me what's worth the risk? You, who ran into the bloody woods, who came back when you could have escaped? You don't know about any of this, you don't know about Jess or Marcus or Marie, or—' He stopped and held on to the dressing table and coughed and coughed and pressed his right hand to his chest. Blue stroked his back, hushed him and tried to soothe him as Devlin had so often soothed her. He was all at once the woman who had killed her old father, he was the victim of domestic abuse, he was the man who mourned his dead son; he was every soul who had passed through Blue's life and felt something she had never felt.

'I will do this,' he said when the coughing had stopped. Tears wet his cheeks and gathered in the creases at his mouth.

'It's all right,' she said, 'it's all right.'

He shook his head, grabbed both her hands in his and she felt she was holding him up, that if she moved he would fall, and she felt all of him, all of him, all of him.

'It's my fault,' he said, 'all this is my fault.'

'Tell me what happened,' said Blue.

The Tens

The door was open behind him and James did not want to close it. Doing so felt too official a statement, though he was unsure yet what that statement was. On the console in the hall was the mobile phone charger and a pad with a week-old note in Marie's handwriting: Elodie Cole, Birmingham Child Services, a phone number. James had watched his wife, mobile cradled between her ear and right shoulder, write down the details of the person to whom they would report Marcus and Jess. Her hand had trembled.

'We won't do it just yet,' she'd said to James when the conversation on the phone was over. Her voice was thick. She stared at the pad, the name and number, and her shoulders heaved. James hugged her.

'Not just yet,' he said. 'Give Marcus another week, let's see how he's doing then.'

'If he leaves her alone overnight one more time …'

'He knows, we've warned him already.'

'If he forgets to give her dinner or sells the food we've given him—'

'Then we'll call.'

'Jess won't want to go.'

'Kids don't always know what's best for them.'

'Maybe Marcus will stay clean. He seems to really want it this time.'

'Yes, maybe he will,' James had said.

He saw it play out before him again now, a second version of himself that hugged his wife and hoped a hope that was part dream part platitude. He would go back in time to that moment, he thought. He would melt into this memory and stay there. He would hug Marie and not let her go.

He stood in the doorway alone now and did not move. He did not turn on the light, did not close the door. His clothes were stale and sour, and stubble grew in white and pale grey patches on his jaw. He had arrived home enveloped in the same delicate numbness he had felt when his father had died.

The sound of fast feet tripping over each other carried down the concrete corridor. James knew he must move. He stood very still.

'Where've you been?' the girl said behind him, and James did move then. He picked up the pad and turned it over so Jess wouldn't read the note, wouldn't see that Marie had the details of the social worker, after promising Jess she wouldn't call.

'Hello, hello, hello.' His voice was hoarse and lacked genuine joy, but he turned and somehow formed his lips into a smile. Jess lolloped through the door, wrapped her thin arms around his waist, and rested her cheek against him. She was all long hair, wiry limbs, mucky face. He rested his hands on her warm back and felt the light beat of her heart through her ribs.

'Where've you been?' she said again and let him go, walked past him into the living room and sat down in Marie's particular chair, and he fought the urge to follow her, to pull her up and out of the chair before her scent could overwhelm the last trace of his wife on the fabric cushions. And he thought, that chair is my chair now. This flat is my flat. That kitchen is my kitchen.

And that bed. That bed, that bed, my God, that bed is mine. It's mine, alone, now.

'Where's Marie?' Jess said. She kicked her feet against the carpet, and if Marie had been there, she would have scolded Jess and told her to take off her shoes.

'Take off your shoes, love,' James said, and his voice was the frail, hoarse voice of a man whose soul had aged beyond his body. He still stood in the hallway. His bedroom door was ajar.

Jess took off her shoes and put them neatly by the chair.

'Good girl,' James said. He thought his knees might buckle. He wondered how he had made it on to the bus and off again, how he had made it up to the front door. He wondered how he had managed to

un-prise his arms from around Marie, and now James lifted his hands
to his face, tried to trace her scent on his palms, on his fingers, but all he
could smell was the hospital cleaning fluid and an undertone of petrol
fumes from outside.

'Why are you sniffing your hands?' Jess said. She folded her arm over
the back of the chair, rested her cheek against it. A vague yellow crust
clung to the edge of her eye. 'Where's Marie?'

'You not washed your face today, Jessica Pike?' said James. Dirt had
embedded itself in the creases of the young girl's neck and formed a
circle of grime at her throat.

'Marcus washed it wi' me this morning.' She looked at her arm instead
of at James.

'You had your dinner yet?' James said. He still stood by the console,
looked at the overturned notepad, thought of the phone number and the
tremble in his wife's fingers as she held the pen and tried to keep calm.

Jess kept her eyes on her arm and picked at an old scab on her elbow.
'Yeah, but earlier. Marcus made it me before he went out. Where's Marie?'

'What did you have?'

'Beans on toast,' Jess said, eyes wide. 'Marcus made it. He did!'

'OK, OK. Where'd he go?' James said.

'The clinic.' Jess still looked at the scab on her arm. Her feet were
bare, and her toes scrunched. James felt his numbness crack when he
watched her. He thought of the words he would like to take out of her
vocabulary, words no nine-year-old girl should understand: methadone
clinic, hepatitis, skag, cunch, baggies. Words James himself didn't know
until Marcus was dragged into a gulley after school and forced to chase
a dragon that was more vicious, more harmful than any of the creatures
in the fairy tales James used to read to the boy. And he was still a boy.
Just a boy.

'He'll come back,' she said.

James had known Jess from the day she was born, knew every line and
freckle, knew when she was telling the truth and when she was not. James
promised Marie he would look after Jess. He touched the notepad with
his fingertips and knew that before he called his brother, Marie's sisters,
or the funeral director, Marie would want him to phone Elodie Cole.

The last of the numbness was gone. James felt the breath move
through his lungs, felt the clothes on his skin, and smelt the faint trace of

his wife's perfume as he walked past their open bedroom door. His nose stung and his eyes began to fill and a pain lodged in his heart and belly at once, making him want to curl into a tight ball right there on the floor by the door.

'Hey, you've left your shoes on,' Jess said, and James looked at her and swallowed the smell of his wife and the pain in his chest and focused on the girl and nothing else.

'You're right, I'd better take them off. Thank you, Jess.'

'Marie would be cross wi' you. She'd say, *See that husband of mine traipsing corridor dirt through my nice clean home*, and she'd pretend to smack your bottom with a dish towel.' Jess giggled, and her face turned pink. James paused and had to put one hand on the wall to keep himself upright. He swallowed again and tried to find something to say but could not speak. His heart felt like a windowpane that had shattered but remained in the frame: one tap and the glass would fall into myriad broken pieces. He forced a smile for the child. He forced out a sound that resembled a laugh.

'Have you had your dinner yet?' Jess said in a small voice that had learnt not to hold on to hope.

'Haven't we always said that you can come here for some tea if you're hungry?' said James, but Jess never asked for dinner. She never asked for anything – too afraid, James supposed, of rejection. But he would never reject her. And he heard Marie's voice in his ear, a whisper whispered in the kitchen. *Children don't learn by being told; they learn by being shown – the more we show her she can lean on us, the more she will feel she can.* The memory bit chunks out of James' balance, and he was glad he still had his hand pressed to the wall.

'There's stew in the fridge, and I can't eat it all. Will you help me?' he said.

'Is it bigos?' Jess said, with the narrowed eyes of a connoisseur.

'*Kurczak*,' said James.

'OK, I'll share it with you. But you know bigos is my favourite.'

'There's some in the freezer, we can have that tomorrow,' James said and thought, the council is probably closed by now, I'll phone Elodie Cole in the morning.

'OK,' Jess said, and though her shrug was nonchalant, her eyes glinted with what James wanted to be pleasure but knew was relief.

'Why don't you read a bit, and I'll go and heat it up?' he suggested.

'Can I watch TV?'

'Do a bit of reading first, then you can watch TV.'

Jess huffed and went to the little cupboard beneath the window where Marie had collected children's books, games, toys, spare pieces of school uniform and pyjamas. She chose one and sat on the sofa and looked at James with a frown.

'How much do I have to read before I can watch TV?' she said.

'Ten pages.'

'Ten? What about five?'

'Ten.'

'What about six?'

'Would you rather it was eleven?' he said, and the words were his wife's words.

'Fine, ten pages.' She began to scan the book with grumpy, reluctant eyes, and for a moment, James was consumed with nothing more than his love for this girl. Her face was so expressive it was impossible to misinterpret. Her lower lip was puffed out, her chin so low in consternation that it was almost gulped up by her neck. Her entire forehead was pulled into a practised frown. The expression was one of such rehearsed dissatisfaction it was difficult not to laugh. Yet he knew how her face would light up once food was on the table. Her lips, so pouty now, would press a tight line of anticipation, and her eyes would grow big and gleam with delight. Her fingers would flex in and out of small fists as she waited to be served, and she would say 'oh, oh, oh' in excitement.

He was thinking about Jess and her quirks as he left the room, and did not prepare himself for the kitchen. He had not readied himself for the room where so much of life with his wife had played out.

On the wall was the telephone where he had learnt of his father's death. Here was the cupboard they kept stocked with snacks for the children next door. There was the cut-glass tumbler a nephew had bought him one Christmas. Here ... here it all melted into nothing because here was Marie's knife that she used every day. Here was Marie's particular mug. Here was Marie's apron. Here was Marie's notebook of handwritten recipes. Here was Marie's headscarf. Here was Marie's biro. Here was Marie's herbal tea. Here was Marie's favourite marmalade. Here was Marie's best spoon. Here, in the sink, was the smudge of Marie's mouth pressed to a glass.

319

And here is where James had stood and held his wife close to him and smelt her hair and felt her body and the beat of her heart big and strong. And this is where he had held her that day, that hideous day, and had felt that hideous lump.

He went to the sink and picked up the glass and pressed his own lips to the last traces of her lips in a hungry, hungry half kiss. He drank the last drops of water and tried to think of her falling inside him, filling him, never leaving him, because how could she leave him when she had been his whole world?

He did not know how he was going to go on. He did not want to go on.

The glass was empty.

The kitchen was empty.

He couldn't bear to take the glass from his lips, to take his lips from hers.

'I've read ten pages,' Jess called from the living room, and he heard her shuffle on the sofa, find the remote, turn on the TV, and the sounds of a kids' show filled the room. 'Can I watch TV now?'

James squeezed his eyes closed and felt grief fight with love in his chest. 'I believe you already are, cheeky thing,' he said, and Jess laughed and then stifled her laugh with a cushion.

He put the glass on the windowsill. Marie's lips were still marked there, as were his own. He was able to go to the fridge and remove the Tupperware of chicken stew, which he reheated in the microwave for Jess. He thought he would let Jess sleep on the camp bed tonight if Marcus didn't come home, and the shock of grief in his chest had tampered down a little. He cooked broccoli on the hob, laid the table, and filled a jug with water. After dinner, he would make sure Jess' uniform was clean for school. He'd make her take a proper shower.

'TV off and hop up to the table,' James said, and Jess did.

James carried the hot bowls of stew from the kitchen. He had promised Marie he would look after the girl, and wasn't he doing just that? If Marcus really fell off the rails or his own health worsened, he would call. And if looking after Jess helped James, then wasn't that a good thing too?

Carefully, so as not to spill the stew, James placed a bowl in front of Jess. Her fingers flexed in and out of small fists, and she said, 'Oh, oh, oh,' in excitement.

The Nine of Swords (Reversed)

'If I had called the social they would have taken Jess in, the Parks would never have got hold of her.' Milton's hands and shoulders shook and Blue held him firmly.

'You didn't do anything wrong; you loved her and looked after her,' Blue said and she could still feel it, all the love for the young girl locked inside him. But Milton shook his head.

'I did it for myself. I didn't want to let her go. I didn't want to lose her after losing Marie and I kept thinking that next week I'd call, then next week, and then one day it was too late. Marcus was dead, Jess was gone and no one knew a thing about her. Her school couldn't do anything and social services were oblivious. The police thought she was a runaway and kept a file on her, but never looked, not really.

'I promised my wife I'd look after her and I didn't. The last thing I can do is make sure she's found: I need the police to believe me. I'm going to make sure they get that photograph, even if it kills me.'

Blue let go of him then, unable to take any more. She was glad not to have her tarot cards, glad not to have the opportunity to read this old man's fortune. She had a fair idea what his cards would predict.

Sabina showed no sign of waking. The curtains were drawn back and showed a night's sky shrouded in cloud, a pale glow where the moon should hang. Milton wanted to go downstairs, into the apartment, take the photograph and hand it to the police, but if Mrs Park saw him Blue feared he wouldn't stand a chance; she could knock him down and blame his weak legs, weak heart and he would die feeling a failure.

'I can't let you go,' Blue said.

'I won't let you stop me,' Milton said.

Blue crouched in front of him, and her turquoise eyes met his washed-out blues. 'I'll go,' she said, though she didn't want to. He opened his mouth to say no, but Blue nodded firmly and said it again, 'I'll go,' and felt better about it this time.

A part of her wished Sabina could come with her. Another part of her knew she was always destined to do this alone. A notebook and pen were on the floor by Sabina's bed, part of the generic welcome package. Blue wrote a note, her script scrawly from her trembling hand, the ink an incongruous dark green. The colour of tranquillity, health, abundance, Blue remembered, but so too the colour of greed, envy, the colour of one never satisfied. The note was short and to the point: *Run away*, the message said, *don't wait for me, run away and find help.*

And don't come back.

'Give her this when she wakes up.'

Milton read it and concern washed over his face. 'But you'll come right back. You'll get the photo and come right back?'

'The Parks will probably be asleep by now,' said Blue, but the reassurance was all for Milton. 'I'll dash in, grab the photo and go. This is just in case.'

'In case they see you?' The first trace of doubt crossed Milton's face.

'They'll not see me. I'll be fine.'

'Thank you,' Milton said, and his hands gripped her hands fiercely.

'I'll be fine,' Blue said again, and wondered which of them needed that reassurance more.

The dead girl waited in the hallway outside. Blue knew she was there before she opened the door, before she made the decision to open the door, before she had even decided that she would leave the bedroom. Blue felt the certainty in her gut; the same certainty told her now that Jessica Pike would not leave her be until she had unearthed every truth from every corner.

The same certainty told Blue that it would not be so simple as dashing in and out of the apartment.

Jess blocked Blue's path, thin-faced and angry with her child-sized fists curled tight at her sides. Blue ignored her. She kept her eyes to the ground and walked around the dead child. Jessica's anger was inside her already; she didn't need to face it again, wouldn't let anything distract her from this path.

Fear burned at the corners of Blue's eyes; there she was again at the foot of the stairs.

Jessica's hands were still in fists.

And now, so were Blue's.

She forged on through the main house, waded through the water that flooded the passageway, into the kitchen. The solid oak door gave no resistance. She hoped that when she reached it, the green varnished door would be as easy.

It wouldn't be.

Molly Park stood in the kitchen, her back to the room, her face reflected in the window. The candles burned yellow.

'Is Sabina asleep?' The reflection of Molly Park spoke, and Blue felt that the reflection was the true woman, that everything she had hidden was revealed by the glass and Blue's need to be polite, quiet, good melted at the sound of her friend's name.

'She's unconscious, for Christ—'

'She'll rest well tonight. It's so important for guests to be well-rested.'

A second shape lurked but Blue ignored it, refused to pay Jessica Pike any heed. She focused only on Molly Park's broad back, her round hips, but not her face; her expression unnervingly pious.

'You will have some too; you need to sleep more than any of us.' She faced Blue, the mug of cool cocoa in her hand. It was the cup she had made for Blue, the one Blue hadn't touched. Her hair was held back in the same Alice band she had worn the first day; the red tartan clashed with her fever-pink cheeks. 'Sit down and drink,' she said. 'There's a good girl.'

'What did you give Sabina?' Anger focused her, pinned her attention to Molly Park.

'The same thing that I'm about to give you. Sit down.' She placed the mug on the table, unbearably calm, and beckoned Blue to the chair.

Blue raised her hand, intent on swiping at the cup, but the shadow in the background moved swiftly, jack-knifed Blue's arm behind her back.

'Sit down,' said Joshua Park.

The Eight of Swords (Reversed)

Joshua forced her into the chair. He stood behind Blue, held her arms in place, used his weight to keep her down.

Molly Park looked at the woman who had tried to kill her husband, at her arms pinned to her back. 'I'll get you a straw.'

Blue was never a fighter, not even as a girl when the kids pelted her with conkers and shouted *witch*, and so the urge to struggle, to tug and kick, was overridden by the impulse to talk her way out.

'And if I don't drink it?'

Molly Park put a candy-striped paper straw in the mug. 'Then I'll fetch the funnel,' she said, and in the window, Joshua Park's reflection winced.

She asked her husband for the strap, and Blue heard the susurration of fabric stroke leather as Joshua pulled his belt free. Blue's bowels clenched as Joshua raised the belt high, could almost feel the buckle hit her cheek, almost laughed when instead the belt was looped around her chest and pulled tight. It locked her to the backrest. It wasn't a perfect bind; she could still move her legs, could flex her hands, but Joshua was close, watchful.

'What did you give Sabina?' she asked again.

'The same thing you both had last night and the night before – a mixture of diazepam and tramadol, only this time with a touch of ramelteon as a treat. You saw the effect, how soundly she sleeps, how quickly and peacefully she'd have slipped under. Now it's your turn.'

'Why?' It made no sense. Blue had expected confrontation, a reckoning for her behaviour in the woods, not the promise of undisturbed rest.

325

'So you're nice and quiet.' Molly Park held the cup up; the straw touched Blue's lips. 'So you behave yourself.'

She flinched; the straw landed on her cheek. 'But why? Sabina hadn't done anything.'

'To keep her out of the way. She'll wake up in the morning right as rain, and when the water's clear, she can go back to London.'

'No, I'll tell her what you did.'

'No,' said Molly Park. 'You won't.'

Blue's heart hammered and her hands tingled, the belt cutting off circulation.

'Is this what you did to Jago?' Blue said.

'Never you mind about him,' said Mrs Park.

The window reflected the scene. Joshua Park looked away to the corner of the room, a look of anguish on his face that told Blue this wasn't his idea, that whatever was about to happen would be nightmarish and unwatchable.

'You're going to kill me,' Blue said. 'You're going to kill me because I know about Jessica Pike.'

Molly Park grimaced at the name. 'We're not going to kill you, Blue. We're not murderers.'

'Did you kill Jago?'

'We've never killed anybody.'

'You killed Jess,' Blue said.

The response was measured, as though Blue were a patient refusing their meds. Mrs Park sighed, lowered the cup from Blue's lips. 'We're not bad people; all we've ever wanted is to help. All of this was built to help folk in need; we've dedicated the last eight years to it. We didn't kill Jago, and we aren't going to kill you, Blue, but nor are we going to let either of you ruin our lives and everything we've built together or let you creep upon us in the woods. Did you really think your behaviour would go unpunished?'

Blue strained against the belt. She moved to kick the table, kick her, hoped to spill the damned cocoa, but Joshua lifted the back of Blue's chair and slammed it back into the ground. The force whiplashed Blue's head and neck. Bright spots blighted her vision.

'Is that what this is?' Her jaw ached, head throbbed. 'Punishment because I know what you did?'

'Drink up, Blue.' The straw was returned to her mouth, and Molly Park sighed again, deep and heavy, when Blue shook her head.

'I could have injected it, but all my needles are locked in the cellar, and the water got there first, so it'll have to be the funnel.' She opened a kitchen drawer and pulled out a plastic funnel, its tube long, thin and translucent.

'What are you going to do to me?' Blue's voice wavered; she felt like she did as a child when the black dog got hold of her mother: powerless, hopeless, worthless. Back then, she felt Mother would have been happier without her, that Blue caused her pain. It was no longer a haunting, unanswerable question. Now, she knew that Sabina would have been safe if Blue hadn't come here. If she had never existed.

A low, wretched part of her hoped that they'd kill her and it would be over. It would all be over – the pain, the guilt, the grief, the soul-eating loneliness, the knowledge that she would have to go home alone and live alone and deal with the bills, cooking, cleaning, life alone.

But fire overruled that darkness; she couldn't bring herself to drink. She wanted justice for Milton, for Jess. She wanted a life for herself. Joshua Park held Blue's head in his hands, tipped Blue's head back, squeezed Blue's cheeks to force her mouth open. Molly Park pushed the funnel through her lips, and Blue wretched, her eyes watered and throat constricted against the rigid tube. She gagged.

The cocoa, flesh-warm and sweet, filtered down her throat. Joshua Park squeezed her cheeks harder, forced her mouth open wider until the cup was empty.

Molly Park tore out the funnel, and Blue choked, gasped for air, howled with pain and frustration, tried to wrench herself free, but Joshua Park wouldn't let go. The man looked away, his rough hands strong on Blue's skull, his expression a grimace of self-loathing.

'He'll keep your head back until we're sure you can't spit it up.' Molly's voice was so soft, so maternal and calm, and she stroked Blue's throat. 'There, there. That wasn't so bad. And you'll sleep now, quiet as an angel.'

'And then?' The words leeched from Blue's raw throat.

'And then we'll call the doctors in and have you sectioned.' She was so calm, sounded so rational that Blue almost laughed at her, thought she'd misheard.

'You've had a mental breakdown,' Joshua Park said, and he let Blue's head go, walked around the table and stood with his wife. 'You're delusional, suffering from hallucinations. You're violent. They'll take you in and section you under the Mental Health Act. They'll look after you.'

They'll look after you. Blue thought of Mother, of her treatment at the hands of the system. It was different now, Blue knew this too, but how would they deal with a woman such as her? She would be pumped full of drugs, locked up, restrained and labelled insane for a second sight she had never wanted.

Blue strained against the belt, fought like a cat in a corner as she bashed and rattled the chair. She would break it to pieces, smash it and be free; she would run and run and run away.

She would find help, find the police before the Parks had a chance to condemn her.

'You've lost your mind,' she spat but Joshua Park laughed and said no.

'It's you whose mind is lost. It's all part of your delusion,' he said.

How much time did Blue have? It was roughly fifteen minutes before Sabina succumbed. But were their doses the same? Would she have as long?

'I'm not crazy,' she said. A part of her, the same that told her life would be easier if she were not there, told her to give up and sleep, that all was futile, that yes, she was crazy, delusional, out of her mind. She had been out of her mind all along.

Ghosts don't exist, dead girls don't talk to you, emotions don't flow out of one person and into another.

But another force reared its mighty head, told her to trust in her own hard grit. 'You killed that girl,' she said.

'We've never killed anyone,' said Mrs Park, so calmly it was terrifying. 'And if you carry on saying that, it'll just prove the diagnosis that you're paranoid and psychotic. The grief, the stress of the flood, the excess alcohol all wreaked their havoc on you, my lamb. I tried my best to heal you and make you better, but I couldn't; you need a hospital for that.'

'There's nothing wrong with me.' Blue tugged again, pulled but couldn't break free, felt her limbs heavy as lead.

'Rational people don't run off in a flood,' said Molly Park. 'Sane people don't try and kill those who offer help. Normal people don't create fantasies about dead children.'

'You may not have killed her,' Blue said, 'but your husband did. Who was Jessica Pike?'

Joshua Park's cheeks washed red, and Blue saw it. So, too, did Molly Park.

'You didn't know,' Blue said, surprised by the shock on the other woman's face. 'You know Jess Pike, but not that your husband killed her – that's it, isn't it?'

'He hasn't killed anybody,' Mrs Park said, her composure scalloped with impatience.

'She'll be asleep soon enough.' Joshua Park squeezed his wife's shoulder and then walked back to Blue and took out a roll of packing tape from his back pocket. He bent down and pulled Blue's feet together, ran the roll of tape around and around her ankles. His fingertips brushed her skin. Blue tried to kick out, but her legs were numb with fatigue.

'He used a pillow,' Blue said.

Joshua Park yanked Blue's bare hands together with his bare hands, wrapped the tape around her wrists. 'Ignore her, Moll, she'll soon be sleeping.'

Molly Park watched, still as a sculpture. Joshua unbuckled the belt. Blue bucked, tried to buck, felt her body respond too late and without vigour. An ox of a man, Joshua hauled Blue up and over his shoulder. Blue writhed, tried to writhe, would rather be dropped on the stone floor than dragged through the doorway to their apartment. Joshua Park didn't flinch.

'She wasn't well,' Blue cried to Molly Park, 'and she missed her brother, and instead of helping her, he held a cushion to her face.' Blue's head swam. She could see Jess Pike beside Molly Park, could see her standing in the woods, could see her in the hallway with her skin stretched thin, could see her peer through the window of Hope Marsh House.

The bright spots in front of Blue's eyes got brighter, and she blinked, shook them clear.

'He hasn't killed anyone,' Molly Park said again as she followed her husband through the house. Was that doubt in her voice, or were the drugs taking effect on Blue's hearing?

Joshua Park hauled Blue to the back of the house, where a small set of stairs led up to a dusty room full of old furniture, dust-cloth-covered frames and a black suitcase that was big enough to hold a man. The lid was open.

'I couldn't find the padlock,' said Molly Park.

'We'll not need it, she's well tied.'

Blue's eardrums were all cotton wool, her head a lead weight.

'I'll tell them … when they come,' said Blue, but her voice was slurred, her eyelids impossible to hold up, her mind flooded with memories that weren't hers. The hard surface hit her spine as she was dropped into the case. 'You said … sectioning me … what's going …'

'If we'd told you the truth, you'd have struggled more.' Molly Park bent over her, eyes squinted. 'I think she's nearly there,' she said, and Blue felt something soft land over her; a blanket. 'To keep you nice and warm,' said Molly Park in her honey-mama voice.

'I know what he …' Blue tried to say more, but her thoughts were as slurred as her speech. What were they doing to her?

She fought against the drug with thoughts of Sabina, of Jess Pike, even Dr Bryant. Blood oozed like a slug through her veins, her brain was slush, but she forced her eyes to stay open.

All was blurred; her vision gave in.

A pulsing, hazy shape of a man knelt next to her, reached for the lid.

Molly moved behind her husband, carried something. A smaller, matching suitcase, the smallest in what should have been a set of three. Where was the middle, child-sized one?

A final, valiant effort to speak, the words dropped from her mouth with streams of spit.

'You're going to kill me,' she said and was sure of it.

'We're not going to kill you,' said Molly Park. 'It'll be the lack of oxygen that eventually does it.'

The ghost of Jess Pike came close, not a desiccated corpse anymore but a child. She hunkered in the impossibly small space, her long hair thin and pale over her shoulders, her eyes not angry but sorry, very sorry.

I'm here with you.

Molly Park closed the lid. Joshua Park pulled the zip. Blue's eyelids fell.

I'm here.

Death (Reversed)

Something has been drawn out of Molly, drawn against her consent. She watches her husband of so long pull the zip around the nylon case, and she tells him they should leave now, go back downstairs, and he agrees, says they need to build their story, and those words make it worse.

There is only this minute, she tells herself; this is the only minute that counts. All minutes before this are done, unchangeable, all minutes ahead yet to come. And yet, from her mind spills images she does not want to see again, feelings she thought were long buried, deeds she did that she would do again in a heartbeat but prefers not ever to recall.

The suitcase – just that, a fabric suitcase, nothing more, nothing in it – squirms and writhes, and it was not like this last time. Then, the case had been still. Horribly still. Don't think about that.

Joshua looks at the suitcase, at the ripples that move over its surface. A strange, muffled moan comes from within, and he says it'll soon be quiet. It. Things would be quicker if it had been a hard-shell case, he says, less oxygen would get through, but what can you do? He tells her to go downstairs, to leave it a while, that they have things to do, and Molly looks at the state of herself – her dirty, flood-dampened jumper that she only ever wears for decorating, the ill-fitted jeans. Look at me, she says, I'm a mess. I'll get myself changed.

Joshua, standing on the opposite side of the suitcase, says she looks beautiful. I look a mess, Molly says, and Joshua says never, says she's always beautiful to him, and the case thumps again on the floor; it moans, then it's quiet.

The attic grows darker as Joshua turns away; he holds the torch, and the light turns with him. Molly follows him, follows the light down the stairs, and she feels it again, that sapping of energy, that pull of memories that she wants to keep locked up but cannot. Downstairs they close the door to the attic stairwell; Joshua smiles at her, kisses her forehead, and she tells him it will all be all right, and he says yes, it will all be all right, and then he says how about this for the story and he begins to talk, holding Molly softly by the shoulders, looking in her eyes.

Years and years ago, he held Molly just like this and said it would all be all right. They were in the sparse, Coke-can-, crisp-packet-littered woods on the edge of the city. At Molly's feet, curled in a little ball, was the corpse of a seventeen-year-old boy. He had been visiting the rehab clinic Molly worked at for seven months, had relapsed twice. Molly had known him well, heard all about his wasted, fucked-up junky life. Learnt all about his sweet little sister. He talked about her so much Molly felt she knew the girl, understood the girl, felt her heart tear open that this shitty excuse for a man was responsible for a child when nothing that nature or science could do would give Molly one of her own. She felt amazed that social services hadn't intervened, that they would allow him to take responsibility for another living thing unchallenged, and yet make judgements on Molly and Joshua, make them jump through hoops and take interviews and tests and still not give them a baby because even though they had money, they had no friends; even though they had a home, they had no family to support them; even though they had each other, it wasn't enough.

She doesn't want to remember the way the boy's eyes lit up when Molly took him to that place and showed him the needle. It's unhealthy to dwell on such things, yet the memory is sucked from her like blood to a leech.

And now, years later, Joshua holds her like he held her that day. She had called him, he came, and he held her.

And now he holds her again.

When the water recedes and help comes, we'll tell them our story, Joshua says. We'll say the flood was a terrible shock for Milton, his heart gave up in the middle of the night, and Blue, being that sort, went to get help. Unfortunately, she went back out in the flood. We'll look but won't find her. We can keep that story going long enough to satisfy Sabina – she can piss off back to London, and we need never see her again.

In the cellar, floating somewhere in the floodwater, is Molly's medical bag, even more comprehensive than the first aid kit. She didn't have time to fish for it earlier, but she does now. There are things in there that will stop Milton's heart. He is very old, Molly says, and he's miserable. And he's a bloody sneak.

Probably best if Sabina's kept doped up, at least until an ambulance can cart her off, Joshua says. Molly agrees, says there's plenty in her bag that will do that, too, and she waits to feel that calm feeling, that settled knowledge that their plan is coming together, that they will survive this, they will win, they will get what they need, but this time the feeling doesn't come.

Yesterday, they stood over Jago and had the same discussion. What should be done with the boy who, in the early hours of the morning, staggered downstairs and tried to get into their apartment? Molly had heard, taken him into the kitchen, listened calm-faced as he accused her of all sorts of things. Accused her of drugging him, that his body was his temple, and he knew it, knew something had been given to him and what was it? What had they poisoned him with? And Molly had said she'd done nothing wrong (well, she hadn't) and it must just be stress or exhaustion, and he had got angry. So angry that Molly had called Joshua and, when Jago turned his attention to her husband, raised his fist, raised his voice and threatened to wake the whole house, Molly had acted. She knew all about Jago – his medications, his allergies. She picked up the small glass mustard jar and blew the powder in his face. He struggled, reached out for help and knocked the jar out of Molly's hands and on to the hard stone floor.

It had been easy to deal with; the hour was so early and she was so calm. They waited until he stopped breathing. Molly gently wiped the powder off his swollen face, his bulging eyes, prised his hands away from his throat and wiped that clean too. Joshua had scooped the boy up and taken him to the Range Rover. Molly called an ambulance (he must have come down for a drink, knocked the mustard over, inhaled … oh help him, please help him, I feel so terrible) and arranged for them to meet Joshua on the road, to save time. Joshua played the part perfectly – he gave them his contact details, and those of Jago's next of kin, declined the request to accompany Jago to hospital on account of Molly, who was distraught and needed him at home. It had all been so straightforward, so simple. And yes, there would be questions to answer but by then their story would be so clear that they would never slip up, never betray each other.

They would never betray each other.

Molly tells her husband again that she feels a mess, wants to get clean, brush her hair. When she looks in the mirror, she sees her cheeks are spotted pink, that her eyes are bright, and when she closes them, she sees the dead heroin addict, curled on the floor among the leaves and the Coke cans and the crisp packets, with the needle in his arm. She had planned on using the boy's phone to call his little sister, would tell the girl that her brother was sick and she should come and meet Molly, who would take her to him. But the boy had no phone. When Joshua came, he told her it wasn't a problem. They would wait on the street where the tenement stood, a spot where they wouldn't be noticed, and wait for the girl, tell her in person her brother was sick, explain she was to come with them, and she would go with them. Molly looked at the boy on the floor by her feet. Her pulse slowed, and her lips smiled, and she told Joshua what a very calm and clever man he was. What a wonderful father he will be.

Now, the mirror shows a dishevelled, middle-aged woman with nervous eyes and feverish cheeks with floodwater up to her ankles, but even this woman can smile and think yes, what a calm and clever man Joshua is, what a good job it is that she married him. She picks up her brush and rakes her hair until it lies flat.

There, she thinks. Much better. She looks almost her normal unflustered self. Almost.

Above her head comes a thump, a thud, a creak of floorboards as the suitcase rocks back and forth, and how can Molly even begin to think with that damn noise in her ear? Joshua has lifted the dressing table up on to the bed, and Molly goes to it, opens the top drawer, takes out her lipstick and puts it on, but her hand trembles – the red is uneven and too thick and bleeds into the fine lines around her mouth. It will be a long time before anyone wakes and asks after Blue, but it will happen. Molly will have to deal with it. If she doesn't, if she lets it run its natural course, life will be over. All the guests who have booked for later in the year will have to find help elsewhere, from inferior therapists who won't care as Molly cares, who don't invest themselves so heavily in their clients' experience. Those poor, grieving people will be robbed of the help they need, and all because one idiot shoved her nose where it didn't belong.

The photo album is locked in her vanity table. Molly will box it up with Eleanor's photograph and put it in the attic – once the noise has died away – to keep it dry. Proof of all the people she has helped, the reason why it's essential she keeps on helping. It's all she's ever wanted.

Another memory. One that wipes out the nastiness of dead bodies and heroin addicts, one that is filled with glorious light. She remembers sitting with Joshua in their car near the block of flats. Their spirits were high, their nerves were on edge; Molly kept giggling and couldn't stop, and then Joshua put his hand on her knee and said, look, quick, look, there she is. Molly looked. The girl was nine years old, her hair pale blonde, her body pale and thin, and in a moment, Molly would get out of the car, go to her, show the girl her nurse's ID and slip the girl, without any fuss, into the backseat of the vehicle. But for a moment, Molly just watched her, and Joshua told her with a smile so broad that that was their new daughter, right there, walking their way, and Molly thought yes, there she is. Here is the girl who will love me, call me Mummy, hug me, tell all her little friends what a wonderful mother I am, who will make me breakfast on Mother's Day and give me handmade cards and will be so grateful and thankful and will feel lucky to have me. Oh, how she'll love me. That girl will be my daughter.

And she was. For a time, at least.

Molly wipes clean the lipstick.

Another thump from upstairs.

She reapplies the red.

There is a familiar smell in the air, cloying and rotten, a nasty stink that stings the back of Molly's throat. She tells herself it's the floodwater.

Her hand trembles. The lipstick smears.

Molly cries out an anguished cry, throws the lipstick at the wall, throws the hairbrush, throws the box of tissues, and they fall into the water where they float, bob, sink. The bedroom door sloshes open, and Joshua stands with the medical kit in his hands, tells Molly that he fished it out of the cellar for her. He asks if she is all right. She walks to her husband of so many years and rests her forehead on his chest and puts her arms around his waist and asks him to tell her what she needs to hear.

It's all going to be all right, he says and kisses the crown of her head. She trusts him.

Soon there will be no noise coming from the attic. It will be quiet. Milton will be dead, and Sabina will be docile. The ambulance will tell Molly what an excellent job she did looking after Sabina in the circumstances, how lucky Sabina was to have her, and Molly will thank them, and she will clean that house and make it new, ready for more guests.

The World (Reversed)

Blue opened her eyes and saw nothing that scared her.

She saw nothing at all.

The dark was absolute, and the air was close, and her eyes stung with the dust. Her nostrils filled with the smell of the earth: freshly dug potatoes, trainers caked in wet mud, a coat worn in the rain and allowed to go fusty with mildew. Her fingers touched the polyester lining of the suitcase; it was gritty with sand and flakes of dried mud.

Her hands were still bound at the wrists, her knees bent and legs curled beneath her. She was on her side, had enough space to move a few inches left and right, not much more, but she used that space. She would try and break the seam of the case, smash it from within. She writhed and butted, felt the case move across the floor, but her prison was stubborn and strong and little oxygen filtered through it.

How long until the air ran out? She didn't know, and that uncertainty was as vile as the certainty that it would. She was light-headed; was that due to the drugs or suffocation? Her hands and feet were numb; was the tape that tight, or was her body preserving oxygen for her organs?

She moved her arms until her fingers touched the lid of the case, inched along until she found the seam. She would tear at the edges with her nails. She would get out.

Fear, like a noose around her neck, drew tighter.

There was no gap in the edges, no weak spot, no out.

A bovine groan escaped her throat, and she stretched her mouth wide to scream but couldn't scream, couldn't yell, could feel nought but the fear in her chest, as tight-close as the walls around her. No light, no air, no out. No way out.

Just a voice.

I'm here with you.

And she screamed then, a roar that scraped out her mouth. She kicked out, jarred her knees, scraped the lining of the case with her nails.

I'm here.

Impossible.

Let me show you.

No.

This way.

There was no this way; there was no way out.

Then she felt it.

The floor softened, the charcoal darkness shimmered.

She sank. Her body melted through the soft base, through the hard floor beneath it, dropped into another world, another time, another locked case. The space widened, lengthened, filled with precious air and made room for her. There was someone else in there. Strands of long hair brushed Blue's cheek, hair that even in the colourless dark she knew would be yellow. Her feet touched shoes, and she knew they were trainers, red trainers.

Here I am.

Blue felt for her; touched her thin, dry arm, her thin, shrivelled leg. She wanted to hold her hand, reassure her that it was OK, that Blue would get them both out, that she would somehow break down these walls.

The girl didn't reach back for Blue.

'Where are we?' Blue said.

No answer.

'Who put you here?' said Blue, and she felt for the hand again. There was a softness to the floor: blankets, pillows, the hard, round eyes of a stuffed toy. Blue found the hand and held it, the fingers cool and brittle and dead, and Blue could see it all now.

Blue squeezed Jess' hand, but she didn't squeeze back. Blue felt the pure cold of her, and it was the same empty chill she'd felt whenever she'd tried to hug Arlo.

Far off, she could hear Mr and Mrs Park shout, could hear feet stomp and splash, fists bang tables, and she didn't know if it was real or imagined, if they were part of Jessica's past or Blue's present. She didn't know where she was.

The darkness was pure black, but the images played clear and bright in Blue's mind.

On a bed in a pure white room is a girl with long straight hair that has been dyed brown. For two years, she has been locked in the room at night, let out in the morning to have family time with the grown-ups. She is fed with cakes, fresh bread, chocolate bars, fruit crumbles and pies until her naturally thin frame is goose-plump. Her name is Jessica, but they call her Eleanor. Their names are Molly and Joshua, but she's to call them Mummy and Daddy. They hug her and kiss her. She misses her brother.

Sweat coats her forehead. Her stomach is sore, and the skin on her belly is dark red, mottled. A fever makes her shiver. Calpol does nothing to curtail it; the antibiotics the woman bought online don't help. They say she will get better. They say she has to get better.

She doesn't.

The couple talk in low voices, but she hears them. They say it's dangerous to call a doctor, they shouldn't risk outsiders inside their house. The woman is a nurse; she can look after her. The man is a strong, tall man with lots of money, but strength won't cure the girl, nor money.

It's appendicitis, or so the grown-ups whisper. Is there any way to cure it without a hospital? Is there anything that can make it better?

The woman has an idea. She is a nurse, after all, a good nurse. She will remove it. She will send the girl to sleep with strong drugs, lay her out on the table, cut her belly open, and prise out the diseased thing. Jess shouldn't be scared. Mummy will look after her. She will cure her and look after her, and they'll be a happy family.

Jess doesn't know when the morning will come; her brain has stopped tracking time, too occupied with the pain. She isn't scared at the thought of being cut open; she doesn't register the words or meaning.

The woman will wash the kitchen, disinfect every surface, every cloth, every blade.

A noble plan, says the man, but his eyes have glazed over. He hugs his wife, kisses her head, holds her face in his hands, and says again, a noble plan.

The woman cleans the kitchen.

The man says he will read a story to the child, calm her, take her mind off the pain, but there is no taking her mind off the pain. The man knows it. There is no getting better, and he knows that, too. If the woman plays surgeon, the girl will die on the table, and the woman will blame herself.

He reads Jess a story; he does that, at least. A story about a boy and his toy rabbit who wished to be real, a rabbit that watched over the boy when he fell sick and loved the boy so much that the toy became real after all. Jess thinks of her brother, thinks of home. She remembers sitting on Marie's lap, warm and held, remembers the home cooking, remembers the peanut butter on toast, remembers old Jim, who promised to always look after her. She had never been lonely at home.

The man finishes the story. Jess is too weak to open her eyes. He tells the girl he loves her, calls her Eleanor, and Jess thinks, my name is Jessica Pike. He says it has been a privilege to be her daddy, and she thinks, you're not my daddy. She wants him to say sorry, but he doesn't. He says it's time for her to sleep now, sleep now, sleep now, baby girl, with a pillow over her head instead of under it.

When the bleach-scented woman comes upstairs an hour later, the man pretends to be asleep. The book is on his knee. His chin rests on his chest. His eyes are squeezed shut. He waits until it's safe to cry, and when it is, when the woman has seen the girl and felt her pulse and checked her eyes and has shaken her and shaken her and shaken her to wake, the crying takes over. The man sobs and his shoulders shake, and the book falls to the floor.

In the numb hours that follow, they set on a plan. They will keep their daughter with them. No churchyard or crematorium for her. The woman dresses the girl in the clothes the woman liked best. She carries the girl into the kitchen, warms her cooling body with blankets, places a teddy bear by her side. She kisses Jess' dead cheeks and cries into Jess' dead hair. She rocks her, though Jess' dead body needs no comfort, and hushes her, though no noise comes from Jessica's lips. When the girl's body is settled in the small suitcase-tomb, the man lifts his wife in his arms and moves her into their bed, gives her zopiclone to make her sleep.

The man lifts the suitcase and carries it out to the treeline.

The Three of Wands

There was no mummified body when Blue opened her eyes; she felt no red trainers or brittle hand. But she knew where she was, and knew what her own fate would be unless she escaped. She would suffocate inside the suitcase and, once the earth absorbed the flood, Joshua Park would take her to the woods and bury her, as he had buried Jessica Pike.

Call it mysticism, call it intuition: she knew Jessica was there, beneath the small grey stone where the dead dogs lay, knew the buried pets legitimised the grave. Blue knew why she was there. She knew it would happen to her unless she acted.

Noise had guillotined the vision of Jess' death. Blue was groggy from the drugged cocoa, her back sore from being cramped; her head throbbed, but she heard the strange sounds from the rest of the house: voices at full volume, splashed water, thumped wood.

'Blue!'

Milton.

Blue cried out his name, but the sleeping draught muted and slurred her words. She kicked her feet against the bottom of the case, as hard as she could, but there was too little space and her movements were laboured, her breath shallow. She blinked and blinked, tried to clear the throb in her head; she was desperate to rub her temples, but her hands were firmly tied. When had she been trapped here, how much time had passed? She didn't know.

Milton called her again, but his voice was distant.

Galvanised, Blue tried harder. Her efforts to bang on the floor, to make noise, were feeble, but maybe she could shake the suitcase, even rock it to the stairs and push herself over the edge. It would be painful, dangerous even, but she would be heard.

She hugged her knees to her chest as best she could, tried to build enough momentum to shift the case, but progress was painful, and the narrow space gave no room. Milton called for her again, his voice nearer, as though he was pacing the whole house. Where were the Parks? How did Milton know to look for Blue?

She called out again, her voice louder now, but she couldn't maintain it. Her lungs burned, her head ached. How much oxygen was left? How much time?

Silence returned.

Where was Milton? Where was Sabina?

Blue screamed Milton's name, cried for help, knew she was wasting precious breath and screamed a noise that was terror itself. She beat at the case with the side of her fists. She hit her bent knees against the floor. She was trapped in the loft of a flooded apartment; did Milton even know there was an attic? How loud did she need to be, to be heard? She sucked in air and coughed on dust, coughed and hacked and tried to scream again.

'Blue!'

'Here, here, in here!'

She shifted and wriggled and made the case shake. She heard Milton come closer and felt the floor move with his shuffling steps. And then the mosquito-noise of the zip being pulled, and musty attic air hit her face. She thought she might be sick with the rush of it, might sob, was overwhelmed at the taste and the smell of dust and river and air.

The tape was bound thick and tight on her wrists, and Milton couldn't tear it with his arthritic hands. He searched around the attic for something to use, spotted a dust-cloth-covered painting and smashed the glass.

A new sound resonated – a heavy thump, a low groan that came from the other side of the attic wall; the place where the guest bedrooms must be.

'What was that?' Blue whispered. There was no window in the attic, but grey light filtered up from the staircase, and she guessed that dawn approached.

'Joshua,' Milton said. He chose a shard of glass and hacksawed at the tape until it snapped. 'Let's go.'

He helped Blue up and supported her as best he could against his shoulder until she was steady enough to stand on her own. He felt thin and hollow-boned. 'Quickly,' he said, and she followed him.

The stairs led to the drowned corridor by the Parks' bedroom. Milton steadied himself on the rails. The open door revealed a cluttered chamber decorated with more pictures of the Parks and a single framed photo of Jessica Pike. In her lap was the teddy Blue knew she was buried with. She grabbed the photo, removed it from its frame and handed it to Milton.

'Put it in your hat,' she said.

He held the picture in trembling hands and it was a few moments before he could speak. 'They dyed her hair,' he said and Blue wanted to say they did so much worse, but she didn't. 'You take it,' he said, 'look after it.'

The living room was a wreck: side tables overturned in the water, photos swept off the mantle, one tartan curtain ripped from its pole. Light washed in through the window, pale blue and ethereal, and Blue wondered if this was some strange afterlife, if her body was still trapped in that case, had suffocated, was dead.

'I looked for you everywhere,' Milton said.

'How's Sabina?'

'Awake.'

The living room led on to the kitchen. The pantry door was drunk on floodwater and lopsidedly hung on one hinge. The chair Blue had sat in was the only one still upright and unbroken, the belt thrown over the backrest. The funnel sat upside down on the table, and Blue thought, I'm not really here, how can I be here, how can that have happened to me?

'What happened?' Blue said. The sedative still dragged at the edges of her speech and her body was slow to move, mind slow to think, and hadn't she been given the same drugs as Sabina? 'How did you—'

'Molly's upstairs, locked in Sabina's bathroom,' Milton said, 'and Joshua—'

A loud thump came from above them. Another thump, and another.

Milton tried to pull Blue through the kitchen, but Blue was still weak and Milton was frail. They hobbled together, out of the kitchen and down the dark passage. The water was ankle-deep, ice cold. Another thump came from upstairs, the sound a shoulder makes when it smacks a wooden door.

'Sabina locked him in another bathroom,' Milton said. 'She knocked him out pretty good; he's come around faster than I expected. Come on.' Milton tried his best to help Blue again, down the passage and into the hall, but he needed just as much help himself. The sofa was several shades deeper, darkened by the wet. A jigsaw piece floated by its side, primrose yellow. Blue was flagging.

'Wait here,' Milton said. 'I'll go and get you some waterproofs. You'll need them.' Blue saw the concern in the old man's eyes, felt his fear that Blue wasn't fit enough to escape the house. Felt the fear in Milton that he wasn't fit enough either. The rain had stopped, but the land was flooded deep and cold, the ground uneven, the way unknown. Blue saw the early morning sun touch the trees through the window, the branches thin and black and beckoning. Jessica Pike is buried there, Blue thought, inside a suitcase with a small teddy bear and red trainers on her small feet. Molly Park had planned to cut her open. Joshua Park pressed a pillow to her face.

I should be dead. I should have suffocated. How am I still alive?

'Molly Park's in Sabina's room?' Blue said.

'Yes …'

'Then we'll go there.' Blue pressed herself up. She could make it. The cold water was nothing; Joshua slamming into a door was nothing; Jessica's small, murdered body was all there was.

'No, you need to go, before Joshua gets—'

'He's not out yet. I only need a minute with Molly.'

'I'm not going to let her out.'

'You don't need to. Look, I know what happened to Jessica, I know where they buried her – I just need one minute with Molly, just one, to make sure. Come on,' Blue said and waded to the staircase. The water was black round her legs. She could see herself in the reflection on the water, what she would look like to a child who looked up at her. What she would have looked like to Bodhi and Arlo, were they there.

What she would have looked like to Jess.

Blue looked to Milton. He rested his weight on the back of the sofa, her words difficult to digest. There was no walking frame in sight. Blue wondered where it was. She felt her head begin to clear. Milton's hair stuck up at all angles, his face grey. His breath came in rattles. 'I'll follow you up,' he said. 'I have to catch my breath.'

Another loud bang came from upstairs, and she knew Sabina would need help, but first Blue walked back to Milton, put her arms around the old man, said, thank you, thank you, thank you.

'You found out what happened to her?' Milton said, and his eyes were watery blue, his heart a struggling bird.

'I did.'

'And you know where she is?'

'I do.'

'And it was … them?'

'Yes.'

Milton wiped his eye, nodded and tried to speak, the words hard to find and painful.

'We would have looked after her,' he said. It was the truest thing Blue had heard in years.

'She knew you loved her,' she said, and Milton reached for her hand, clutched it, nodded his head, and there was nothing else he could say and he didn't need to. Blue wanted him to feel comforted by her words, but they didn't eclipse the fact Jess was dead, nor the blame Milton hung round his neck, nor his need to do something, any small thing, to avenge her and atone for his misjudgement.

She left Milton by the sofa, and though he said he would make his way up, she knew he didn't have the energy. He had used the last of it saving her.

Upstairs, the doors to the rooms all stood open but one.

'Thank God you're OK,' Sabina said when Blue stepped inside. 'Quick, help me.'

The bathroom door was blockaded with furniture; the dressing table, two bedside tables on top of it. They quivered every time Joshua thumped the door. Sabina wrestled with a chest of drawers and tried to shift it up against the dresser. Her left hand was bandaged in a torn strip of sheet that was damp and red with her blood.

'Take out the drawers first,' said Blue, and she helped pull them out. Blankets and spare towels fell to the floor, and the women kicked them aside and shoved the chest into place.

'What happened?' whispered Blue.

345

'Molly tried to fob me off with some story, and when I wouldn't believe her, she attacked me. Joshua was quick to follow,' Sabina said. 'We need to get the hell out of here before he gets free. Are you OK?'

'I will be.'

They would run, find help, never return.

But first, Blue had to find Molly.

Sabina went ahead and ran to her room. When Blue arrived, she was on her knees at her suitcase, dry socks and a hoody in her arms. She pressed a finger to her lips for quiet.

The room was a mess. Bedding lay thrown on the floor, one curtain was torn from the pole, the vanity table was smashed. A long dagger of broken glass was absent from the mirror. A strip of cotton ripped from the bed sheet. Blood splashed up the wall. Blue looked again at Sabina's bandaged hand.

In the bathroom, Molly Park cried, the soft sound made tinny by the bathroom tiles. Trapped within the windowless space, she had no easy way out. She would feel helpless, frightened, victimised, and it would have been a simple act to feel sympathy for her had she not done a similar thing to Blue. Had she not—

'Mrs Park?' Blue said.

The tears stopped.

'Sabina? Let me out, Sabina?' Molly thumped on the door, her voice loaded with her sense of injustice. Blue closed her eyes, tried to block it out but instead saw Jess ill in bed, heard Molly Park say she would cut the poison out on the washed and bleached kitchen table.

In the woods, she had presumed Joshua murdered the girl alone, and she'd wanted to strike the man down. But Blue knew now what it was to kill someone, to have thought you had killed someone. She would not harm Molly Park.

There were other ways to wield pain.

'I know,' Blue said, and she leant her head against the door, spoke her words through the gap in the frame.

'Blue?' Molly said, feverish, desperate. 'Help me, please, you must get me out. Sabina has—'

'We're not letting you out,' said Sabina as she pulled the jumper over her head. 'You've got one minute, Blue. I'm going to grab you some clothes, and we're going.'

She left them, and Molly cried more plaintive tears.

'You stole a child,' Blue said, and Molly Park gasped.

'No, I—'

'You thought she would forget her family, you expected she would be grateful to be lifted out of poverty and given a new home. You changed her name to Eleanor Park and locked her in your house and tried to make her think of you as her mother.'

'I don't know what you're talking about, you've lost your mind,' she said, but Blue could tell from her voice that she had backed away, distancing herself from Blue's words. 'You're trying to trick me,' she said.

'She fell ill.' Blue remembered all the people she had read for, the ghosts she had seen, the murderers and their various reasons for murdering, remembered the helplessness of their victims, the helplessness of some of the perpetrators. Yet she felt none of that seep through the locked bathroom door.

'Joshua told you that already,' Molly Park said, and still she defended herself, believed herself righteous, and Blue realised why it was Joshua that Jess was tethered to and not Molly. It was Joshua who felt the guilt.

Molly Park said, 'You're delusional, mixing up fact with fiction. Eleanor—'

'Jess!' Her fist hit the bathroom door, and Molly Park gave a porcine squeal, but her cry was one of fear for herself, for her safety, reputation and lifestyle. Blue saw in Molly Park what Jess had been unable to show her.

'You wanted to cut out her appendix,' she said.

'I don't know what you're talking about.'

'The kitchen had been cleaned; the knives had all been sterilised.'

'No, I looked after her,' Molly said. 'I loved her.' And in the raggedness of her breath, Blue heard it all: her plan, method and motive.

'But she never loved you back,' Blue said.

'She did!'

'No.'

'She would have done!' Molly said, and there it was.

'You were going to save her,' Blue said, 'and by saving her life, you would force her to love you; she would have to be grateful. And so instead of taking her to a hospital, you planned to cut her open yourself.'

The crying started again but was different in tone. The cry of a child caught out and afraid of punishment, and Blue thought of all the things she wanted to do to her, could do, and knew how to hurt her the most.

'Joshua knew you couldn't do it: you were a nurse, not a surgeon, not a doctor, not a hero.' Blue wondered how much time she had left, how soon it would be before the bear would break free from his cage and come find her. 'He didn't trust you. He waited until you'd left the room, and then he folded over the blue fleece pillow and suffocated Jessica to death.'

A gasp. Sabina stood at the bedroom door, a hoody folded over her arm and her hand over her mouth. Disgust burned in her eyes, and Blue had to look away to keep her nerve.

'Eleanor died in her sleep,' Molly Park said.

'*Jessica* was killed by your husband,' said Blue.

'We have to go,' said Sabina.

'She died in her sleep, naturally in her sleep!' Molly Park's tone was high and panicked.

'No, she did not. Your husband killed her, you helped cover it up, and now everyone will find out. I'm going to tell everyone. Everyone.'

She picked up the key and unsprung the lock but didn't turn the handle. A risk, a promise broken, but Blue knew it was the right thing to do, felt it as a hot certainty that burned behind her eyes and in her belly. Molly would come out, Blue knew that, but she wouldn't come after them.

'We need to go,' Sabina said again.

They ran down the hall and down the stairs. Milton had made it to the first step and moved to the side to let them pass. Blue turned back for him, held out her hand to help him down, but he shook his head, smiled at her and took another step up.

'What are you doing?' Blue said. Sabina had the boot room door open, but Milton had taken yet another slow step up.

'You go ahead,' he said. 'I'll not make it through that flood.'

'Of course you will,' Sabina said. 'For God's sake, Milton, we need to go!'

A sound of splintering wood; Joshua Park was close to escape. He shouted Molly's name, and his voice was clear now, and they knew he had split the door, knew it wouldn't be long before he shifted the block-ade of furniture and was out.

'Milton, come on,' Sabina said, but the old man shook his head and carried on up.

'I'll only slow you down; I haven't the energy for wading through this weather, I haven't the strength. We all know it. Best thing I can do is give you more time to get away.' He took another step up, and Blue heard his chest rattle from the effort.

'We're not leaving you behind,' Blue said.

Sabina said, 'I'll bloody carry you on my back, I will—'

'No,' he said, forcefully now, his eyes bright and fierce. 'You have to tell someone what happened here, the police have to find Jess, and when they do—' Blue ran up the stairs and stood with him. The old man gripped her arm, looked in her eyes. 'My hat, it has a gap in the lining, you remember? I wrote down the place her brother is buried, kept it with her picture; you make sure they put Jess there with him, OK?'

'We're not going without you.'

Milton let go of Blue's arm, took another painful step up. 'You make sure they're together, right? That's all I need. I'm going to put some more furniture across, give you more time.'

Upstairs, wood scraped against wood, the sound of Joshua louder and louder.

'If he catches you and stops you telling the police, then all of this will be for nothing. I need to make sure you get out.'

'You can't make us leave you behind, we can't do it.'

Sabina let go of the door, ran to the stairs, screamed at Milton to come with them to come with them, for God's sake, come with them, and they heard something crash to the floor.

'He'll not hurt me, I'm just an old man. But I can delay him, give you a head start. Now go!' Milton cried, and the effort sucked the breath from his lungs. He dragged his feet up another step, then another. At the top he began to push a sideboard from the edge to the middle of the corri-dor, invigorated by his own agency.

Sabina ran up the stairs, followed by Blue but unstoppable. Sabina wrapped her arms around the old man and lifted him into the air. 'I will literally carry you out of here,' she said and he struggled against her, kicked her and cried out, and a few rooms away Joshua hollered for his wife.

349

'Leave me be,' Milton said and he grabbed Blue, told her to make Sabina see sense. And Blue saw what Milton wanted to do, the atonement he wanted to make. And she saw what would happen if they dragged him through the water to safety, the havoc it would play on his lungs, the sad few weeks he would spend alone in a care home until he died, in pain. Sabina would be relieved she had saved him and Milton would die convinced he was a failure, filled with regret.

Blue felt she held them both, then. There was no right answer, no right move. The only difference was that one of these people had a lifetime to come to terms with their decision. The other did not.

'He'll be OK,' said Blue and she released Sabina's grip from Milton's arms. 'He's going to block the corridor with our suitcases and then he'll hide. We'll come back for him.'

'You promise you'll be OK?' Sabina said and Milton said nothing and hugged them both and Blue found it hard to let go.

Downstairs, Blue and Sabina pulled on wellingtons, rubbed tears from their eyes, and pulled on their coats, waded to the front door, tugged it open. Daylight seared their eyes and they stopped in the doorway to look back one last time at their friend.

Upstairs, Milton had pulled out Sabina's suitcase and lifted it on to the sideboard. He shuffled away to find more furniture but stopped mid stride.

A final, loud crack from the bedroom and Joshua was out. Rage robbed him of sense; he grunted the same two words, 'Where's Molly?' He stood on the other side of Milton's weak barricade. Blood dripped from his forehead; one eye was swollen shut.

'Molly?' He called again but there was no answer. Blue suspected the woman was still in shock, the information Blue had given her hard to digest.

Joshua saw Blue and Sabina at the open boot room door. 'What have you done to my wife?' he called and his face was twisted and his muscles taut.

Milton did not falter.

'Go, now!' he called to the women downstairs and then, to the man almost half his age and twice his size, 'You leave them be.'

'Get out of the way,' Joshua said and one sweep of his arm pushed Sabina's full suitcase off the sideboard, where it fell down the stairs with heavy thuds.

'We need to go,' said Blue and tugged on Sabina's arm. Blue's throat was still sore from the funnel. Her wrists still held the mark from the tape. If Joshua had done that before they had locked up his wife, God knows what he would do to them now.

'I won't,' Milton said and beside Blue, Sabina whimpered.

Blue dragged her arm and pulled her through the door and they heard a crack and smack as the sideboard was shoved away.

They fled into the bright daylight, their throats tight with fear and shame, their eyes squinting from the sun and from tears. They heard the bull-like heavy breath of the stronger, younger, bigger man as he tried to force Milton aside.

The water was cold and slowed their legs and Blue knew how much faster than them Joshua Park would be, knew they had to get as far away as quickly as they could.

They heard Joshua call for his wife.

They heard Milton shout.

And they heard another thud, another crack as something tumbled down the stairs.

Sabina stopped, turned.

'It was the sideboard, Mr Park shoved it down,' Blue said, but knew it wasn't true and knew by the look on Sabina's face that she didn't believe her.

'He wanted to give us a head start,' Blue said, 'don't let us waste it.'

Sabina nodded, swallowed her tears and her eyes turned steely as they focused on the gates up ahead. Blue and Sabina ran, and the water engulfed them, rose to their knees, sucked at their feet and penetrated their bodies with cold.

Joshua was at the door. His long legs made fast work of the flood.

They ran from him, fought the water, fought the cold, fought the exhaustion that hugged every muscle.

They didn't look back. But they could hear him. And he was fast, as fast as Blue feared he would be.

Closer, closer. The water rippled with his movement as well as their own, the air shot through with his hunter-dog grunts.

Blue pictured the grave at the edge of the woods, the strength it would have taken to dig it, to carry the dead dogs and stolen daughter towards it, what light work those hands would make of her life, or Sabina's. She thought of Jessica Pike.

'Joshua!'

The man stopped. Blue could hear it in the pause of breath, saw it in the water's changing movement. Sabina grabbed Blue's arm, told her to slow, to look.

They did so over their shoulders, heads turned but their bodies poised to run.

Molly Park stood in Sabina's room, the window wide open. The same window Blue had seen her through on that first day at Hope Marsh House. Now, she looked more harpy than host. Her hair was in wind-swept disarray; her fingers clutched the frame like talons, the wing-like arms of her tunic spattered with Sabina's blood.

'Joshua!'

The cry from Molly Park was barely human.

It was then that Blue saw Jess. Close as cotton to skin, she stuck to Joshua Park's side; small and thin and pale and sick, she whispered in his ear all the terrors he had done. She would never let him forget.

'Molly,' Joshua cried and there was relief in his voice and in the sudden softening of his shoulders – but when he turned back to face the two women, his expression had changed. An unparalleled viciousness gleamed in his eyes and pulled at the edges of his mouth.

'Don't worry, my love,' he called to her, 'it will all be all right.'

Blue and Sabina stepped backwards, but the gap between them was short now and the look on Joshua's face was brutal.

Molly called back. Her words froze the man's stride.

'You didn't let me save her,' she said and the wind swept her voice to them, the desolate, wretched sound of it. 'I could have saved her!'

Twenty feet below Molly's window, protruding from the water, were the sharp iron spears of the boot rack.

Joshua clenched his fists, and his limbs stayed taut and he looked from Molly to the spears below. 'Molly, no, don't, I didn't do anything, I didn't—'

She climbed on to the sill.

And Jess whispered home truths into Joshua's ear.

He ran then. Not towards Blue and Sabina, but back to the house, screamed at Molly to not move, to stay there, to wait for him. Blue and Sabina watched, shock-frozen. Molly Park's shoulders sagged, her knees softened, her body swayed on the sill, and her husband screamed again, called out so loud he woke the treetops. Starlings rose and sliced their dark bodies through the clouds.

'Wait for me!' Joshua Park screamed again, and his wife's body heaved with sobs. She lifted one toe over the ledge. It hovered, mid-air.

'Come on.' Sabina pulled on Blue's arm.

They were nearly at the gate.

Judgement

The road dipped beyond the boundary of Hope Marsh House, and the flood reached knee height. Water breached their boots and deposited silt beneath their toes as if they had become part of the river, part of the land. Sporadically Sabina looked back to the house, braced for Joshua to be hot at their heels. Blue looked ahead.

Their phones were unusable: Blue's was water-damaged from her time in the woods; Sabina's had smashed when she'd thrown it at Joshua Park in the early hours of the morning. It had hit his eye and dazed him long enough for Sabina to pick up a table lamp and swing it at his head.

'Tell me what happened?' asked Blue.

'I woke up in the bed you left me in, dazed and with a screaming headache, and Milton was there. He'd found an EpiPen, it did the trick.'

'Are you OK, is that—'

'I'll be fine,' Sabina said. 'I was angry when I read your letter, you know, that you felt you could do all this on your own, that you thought we could just leave you to it and run away. Imagine if we'd done as you'd asked, instead of helping you; you'd be—'

'Thank you,' Blue said.

The wind swept dead leaves from a roadside hedge and threw the confetti to the water. The brown fronds floated; a few stuck to Sabina's shin.

'Hey, do you think,' Blue said, 'that if I'd written telling you to stay and rescue me from certain death, you'd have run away instead?'

Sabina laughed, and Blue was glad of it. Sabina told her how she and Milton had feigned sleep, how they pretended to wake just as Molly checked on them.

'I asked where you were, and she said you'd left, disappeared into the woods again and hadn't come back. I knew she was lying.'

'How?' said Blue.

'Because it was her who came in, and not you; you would never have left me alone with them,' she said, and Blue thought, no one has ever been so certain about me before.

'I told her I didn't believe it, and she just smiled, said I must still be exhausted and should drink some warm milk and rest up. I pushed the glass out of her hand, and she changed, suddenly, into this ... thing I didn't recognise. The milk splashed all over her, the glass broke on the floor, but she kept dead calm, tried to force me back into the bed. She had a pill in her hand, and she tried to prise my teeth open like I was an animal.'

'What did you do?'

Sabina bowed her head. 'I fought back,' she said.

'How's your hand?' Blue said.

'It looks worse than it is.'

'We need to get it seen to.'

'We'll find a doctor in time.'

'And Joshua?'

'I thought if I could lock Joshua away like I had locked Molly, then I'd have time to search for you, but he was already in the kitchen, and he saw the blood. He asked where Molly was, I asked where you were. He lunged at me; I fought back. He chased; I ran; he followed. Finally, I ended up in a far bedroom – I threw my phone, hit his eye, then knocked him out with a lamp ... he landed by the bathroom door, and I managed to roll him through and lock him in ... and Milton looked for you. We figured you had to be somewhere in the house still.' She shrugged and began to shiver. The sun was low in the sky, the clouds breaking here and there to let the light bounce off the water.

'Thank you,' Blue said again.

Blood had turned Sabina's bandage black, and the light caught the wet spots, made them glisten. Blue hoped the cut wouldn't get infected. She hoped they would find a doctor.

'You'd have done the same for me,' Sabina said.

'Aye, I would.'

Rain fell lightly and washed over them in occasional bursts. It would take days, if not weeks, for the earth to drink up the flood.

'What happened to the little girl?'

As they navigated paths and ditches and sudden rises in the land, Blue told Sabina all she knew about Jess and all she had gleamed from Milton. Blue looked at the sun and thought of her cards: the Sun, the Moon, the World. She thought of Milton, his determination, self-belief, commitment. She thought of his courage. He was the Chariot.

'We should have taken him with us,' Sabina said when Blue was done and they stopped in the water and looked at each other. 'I could have carried him,' she said and she couldn't swallow the tears this time.

Blue held her, and felt Sabina rest her cheek on Blue's head as she hugged her back. 'If he came with us, he would have caught hypothermia and died, in a hospital or care home with no one around him. If we had carried him, against his will, he would have died thinking he was a failure, that he hadn't managed to do anything for Jess.'

'But that's not true – from what you just told me, he did everything he could for her.'

'Sometimes what we feel and what is true are different things. He felt he had failed her, and what he did back there, I think he needed to do something, to act and give meaning to the years he's spent searching.'

'Your party trick again?' Sabina said, and Blue smiled, said maybe.

'It's your turn,' said Sabina. 'It'll keep our minds off the cold.'

'I don't know where to start.'

'At the beginning,' she said.

The long road meandered, and the water slowed their headway. Potholes made them stumble, sunken branches and rocks caught their feet; there were no road signs and no signs of life. It would be a long while before they reached another house, so Blue did as she was bidden. She began with her mother and the small, dirty flat and the day they had played Ford Family Band with saucepan lids and wooden spoons. The day her young life took its turn.

The water soaked up their bodies as she spoke. By the time she reached Devlin's death, the water had breached the hem of her jumper and was

357

crawling its way to her chest. Sabina was quiet, save for the chatters of her teeth.

At the point where Mother died, when Blue had found out what she had done and to whom, she began to ramble. She talked about the logic she had found comfort in, all those scientific theories as to why Blue could do what she could do, and see what she could see: empathetic intelligence, synaesthesia, neurolinguistic programming, collective hallucination. They seemed ridiculous after the events of the last few days.

Sabina gave the occasional nod, the odd sigh of surprise or regret, did not laugh or refute her, did not stop dead in her tracks and tell Blue how terrible it was, how awful it must have been to find out what her mother was capable of. She didn't ask if it had changed how Blue felt about Bridget or any of the other trite empathy-signalling questions Blue had been asked in the past. Sabina listened. Blue spoke.

At last, they saw a distant house, and the lights upstairs were on; the modernised farmhouse seemed to float in deep water. The sun glinted off the ripples on the flood. Blue had reached the end of her story.

They were silent awhile. The house would take another five minutes to reach at least, and Blue thought they would walk in quiet, but Sabina asked if she could say something, and it must be something important, else why would she ask?

'Aye,' Blue said, 'go ahead.'

'You came here because your mother died. You felt you hadn't got over her death?'

'That's right,' Blue said and realised it was three years to the day, wondered what Bridget would make of her spending the anniversary knee-high in water, fleeing two murderers and their ghost. She'd be over the moon, Blue thought. She would cup Blue's face in her soft, dry palms, kiss her cheeks and fill Blue's senses with her smell, her laugh, her love and say she knew that she still had it in her. Blue's heart cracked and sank to her belly; the cavern of her chest ached and felt empty, alone.

'I don't think it's just her that you're grieving,' said Sabina.

Blue could have argued against that. She could even have said that Sabina was right and that she struggled with the loss of Arlo and Bodhi. But Blue saw the image of a fat, brown-skinned man with full-moon glasses and a bright, beaded kaftan and Blue's throat grew tight.

'I'm sorry you lost him, too,' Sabina said.

In the cold water, Blue felt a warm hand on the base of her back, the protective weight of an arm around her shoulder. She heard the razzle-dazzle voice saying, 'Well done, lass,' and was momentarily flooded by memory, not of a face or an action, but a memory of what it was like to know that if she needed him, her dad would be there. Always. A memory of what it was like not to have to deal with everything all on her own.

But that was a memory. There was no one there.

'I'm sorry, I didn't mean to upset you. I just ...' Sabina slowed her pace and spoke in a whisper. 'They found each other because of you. If it hadn't been for your ... whatever it is ... they'd have been alone.'

The farmhouse is close. The people inside see their approach, open their window and call to them – an old man with grey hair, a middle-aged red-haired woman.

'They'll help us,' Sabina says, and Blue knows it's true, that these people will do all they can to help them. 'They'll be able to see to my hand, they'll feed us and warm us and call the police.'

Sabina's hand is bleeding again. Blue can hear her teeth chatter. She can feel the water in her clothes and knows Sabina's are soaked too, and she knows they must reach that house, climb to safety, get help, but for a second, she cannot move. It's too much; it's all been too much.

'I just need a second,' Blue says, and there is a sign by the side of the flooded path bearing the name of the farm. She will lean against it for a moment, just a moment. It is all, suddenly, too much.

'You don't need a second.' Sabina pulls her hand from her pocket. Her fingers find Blue's. 'You need a friend.'

And she holds her hand fast in the rain.

THE END

ACKNOWLEDGEMENTS

The Grief House was a long time in the making, and I couldn't have done it without the support and belief of many people.

An enormous thank you to my fantastic agent, Emily Glenister, for taking a chance on my little ghost story; you understood Blue and the book from the very beginning, and I love you for it. Thank you to all at DHH Literary Agency, especially David Headley and Helen Edwards.

Thank you to Lisa Gallagher for your encouragement and support, and for taking Blue into your heart and over to NYC.

Thank you to all at Bloomsbury Raven, past and present, especially Sara-Helen Binney and Alison Hennessey, for your sensitive editing, enthusiasm and tireless support. It's been a delight to work with you both. So too Sharona Selby, who made the copy editing process enormously enjoyable. Thank you also to Faye Robinson, Emily Jones, Grace Nzita-Kiki and Beth Farrell; you make for an inspiring team. I feel privileged to work with you all.

I'm in awe of Mike Butcher, who designed the beautiful, sinister cover and perfectly captured the atmosphere of the novel.

It took an enormous amount of research to complete the book, and a special mention is due to Judy Dyson for her help in untangling the complex world of social services.

I wrote *The Grief House* in the hectic, stressful gaps between Covid lockdowns, and more than once I was tempted to give up – and I probably would have done had it not been for my friends, who encouraged me, spurred me on, advised me and sometimes just let me fall apart with them. So a huge thank you to Chris, Kevin, Tom and Simon, whose counsel and encouragement were vital, and to Douglas, Helen, Jessie and Gytha, who rallied round and pushed me on. I received tremendous support and encouragement from all those at The Quantock Villages Benefice, especially Reverend Eleanor and the wonderful Peter Higginson, who was one of the first readers of *The Grief House*. Thank you to Eve Hall and Emad Akhtar, who encouraged me to take my work in a new direction, Emily Kitchin for cheering me on from the sidelines, and Benjamin Dreyer for his kind advice.

Thank you to all my fellow authors who have offered kind words and quotes and to the early reviewers and book bloggers for their enthusiasm, recommendations and reviews.

And finally, my family, without whom I would be lost. Thank you to my mum, Hildy, for reading several early drafts. Thank you to my mum, Sarah, for always being there whenever things get tough and my dad, Martin, for your continuous pride.

Please spare a thought, kind reader, for my partner, Steve, who must cope with the reality of living with an artist and does so with patience, kindness and unwavering belief. And my children, Aoife and Ruadhan, all this, my loves, is for you.

A NOTE ON THE AUTHOR

REBECCA THORNE studied English Literature at university, and now works as a reader for Faber Academy. She lives in the West Country and divides her time between the Mendip Hills and Bristol. She is the author of two previous bestselling novels under the name Rebecca Tinnelly: *Never Go There* and *Don't Say A Word*.

A NOTE ON THE TYPE

The text of this book is set in Minion, a digital typeface designed by Robert Slimbach in 1990 for Adobe Systems. The name comes from the traditional naming system for type sizes, in which minion is between nonpareil and brevier. It is inspired by late Renaissance-era type.